IN THE SHADOW OF THE PAST

SHADOW SERIES BOOK 1

J. E. LEAK

CERTIFIABLY CREATIVE LLC

ISBN 978-1-955294-00-3 (eBook Edition)
ISBN 978-1-955294-01-0 (Paperback Edition)
Library of Congress Control Number: 2021911246
First Printing July 2021
Edited by Pam Greer

Published by Certifiably Creative LLC
Ocala, Florida
press@certifiablycreative.com

Printed and bound in the United States of America

To my wife.

SENSITIVE CONTENT

This novel contains mentions of suicide and instances of PTSD from war experiences. While neither is the central theme of the story, it is woven into the tapestry of the characters' lives, and I am mindful that for many, such forewarning is appreciated.

PROLOGUE

a gun can be your best friend. She never thought of a gun that way before—never thought about one at all, really—but war has a way of making the most abhorrent things possible and the unthinkable an answer to a prayer.

A gun can also be your worst enemy. Today, it represented both. Staring into the wrong end of the barrel brought equal parts relief and dread.

Twenty-four is too young to die by any measure, but life hadn't been particularly kind to her, so she didn't mind. The dead friend beside her, however, broke her heart. So much to live for, and a self-inflicted bullet through the head brought it all to an end.

Now it was her turn.

Chest? Mouth? Temple? Under the chin? She should have made that decision already, but fear and anxiety distorted time and muddled her thoughts. Her panicked breathing became drawn out whole notes echoing in her ears like a steam locomotive struggling to gain speed from a dead stop. Her movements were leaden and unnaturally slow. She knew she should hurry, but her body wouldn't cooperate.

The Browning semi-automatic's grip in her hand calmed her in a way she never expected. Her fate was her own. They would not make her a victim. She pressed the gun's cold slide against her perspiring forehead, in thanks for her impending release, and begged it to do its job quickly and painlessly.

She reached out and touched the body next to her: warm, but death already making the muscles under the skin rigid. Someone told her once that suicide was the coward's way out, but now, moments away from ending her own life, she realized the courage it took, especially if one was not yet ready to die.

She was taking her time. Time she didn't have. The German soldiers would arrive at any moment, and then it would be too late. Then she would pay.

The sound of rapidly approaching footsteps brought her back to reality with a jolt of adrenaline. The struggling locomotive in her head found purchase on the tracks and spun up to full speed, propelling her into action. She put the Browning High Power's muzzle to her temple and, without hesitation now, pulled the trigger.

CHAPTER ONE

March 1943: New York City

*J*enny Ryan exhaled a misty cloud of frustration into the cold night air and watched it evaporate like her big break. She should be halfway to Midtown by now, on the verge of cracking the biggest story of her nonexistent reporting career. Instead, she was stuck on the side of a Henry Hudson Parkway exit at the southern end of Riverdale with a flat tire, as precious minutes ticked away.

The damp evening covered everything in a moist film of misery, and her defeated huffs joined the distorted whoosh of the overpass traffic.

She was one nut away from removing the deflated tire, but it was stuck. She pulled on the lug wrench as hard as she could, but it slipped off the nut, and she lost her balance and stumbled over her flashlight, causing it to roll to the low curb of the paving stone street and into a puddle.

She threw down the wrench with a clank. "Terrific." Brushing a lock of dew-laden blonde hair from her cheek, she mentally cursed the war-induced dim-out for the lack of lighting on the street.

She just wanted something to go right for a change. When an off-duty soldier she'd met at the paper offered her a ride, she thought it was a good omen. But all the man's good deed gave her was a pulled shoulder muscle, a low-grade headache, and hands covered in cosmoline from the jack and wrench, thanks to the car's manufacturer covering everything metal and mobile in the thick preservative goo.

She retrieved her flashlight from the gutter and aimed it at the lug nut standing between her and victory. She tried freeing the wheel one more time and nearly wound up on her backside as she tugged with all her might, only to have her hands slide ineffectually off the end of the wrench.

"You mother," she said. She regained her balance and then kicked the tire for good measure. A string of wonderfully appropriate curse words gathered in her mouth, but she had a bet with her best friend, Bernie, that she could curtail her unrepentant cussing for a solid week, and she wasn't about to lose a fin over a stupid tire.

She heard someone approaching and directed the flashlight beam toward the hurried footsteps.

"I told you to stay in the vehicle," the young red-headed sergeant called out.

Anxiety had brought the maddeningly slow cadence of his usual southern drawl up to big city speed, and Jenny had to look twice to make sure it was the same soldier she had sent off.

They'd had a heated discussion about her staying alone with the car. Jenny insisted she would be fine and promised to stay in the car if he hurried to the nearest telephone to make sure her reserved table at The Grotto, an exclusive Midtown nightclub, wasn't given away when she failed to make the nine o'clock reservation.

Jenny feigned an uncomfortable pair of shoes as an excuse to get him to go on his own to the telephone, but she planned to have the tire changed before he returned so she would have a hope of getting to the club before it was too late.

The soldier had two speeds: slow and pardon me while I reinvent the wheel. If she waited for him to change the tire, they would be there all night. He was a swell fella, and caution had its charms, but she needed to get to that club on time. Her only chance was changing the tire herself, so she quickly sent him away and got to the task at hand. Her failure ensured she'd have to suffer his good-natured ribbing about the "weaker sex."

He looked at her filthy hands. "Aw, now, darlin', look what you gone and done."

His drawl had returned to its languid cadence, and he moved with all the urgency of a leaf on a river of molasses when he removed a folded handkerchief from his pocket and handed it to her.

She traded the slippery wrench for the handkerchief with a disgruntled smirk and snapped the white cotton square to its full size before wiping her hands with it.

The only thing she hated worse than losing was failing. She'd had more than her share of failures lately. Tonight, that would all change. She would get her interview with the despicable Marcus Forrester and show her uncle that she was more than just a fluff entertainment writer. As her boss, he would have to take her seriously, and she would finally silence the jealous whispers of nepotism at the paper forever.

It seemed ages ago now, but it had only been a few weeks since she'd burst into her uncle's office babbling excitedly about Forrester's alleged sins. Her uncle listened patiently before dismissing the proposed piece, saying, "Jenny, for every crank call about a scoop, there are twenty legitimate scoops out there. Go find one."

She initially thought her anonymous source was a crank call too. "I got a tip for you, girlie," the gravelly-voiced man said, trying and failing badly to hide a thick Brooklyn accent.

"Uh-huh," she said, as she dragged a notebook from her desk drawer and picked up a pencil just in case the call had merit.

Her tips were usually parents trying to draw attention to their child's stage debut (read grade school play) for her *About Town* column or submissions for her weekly *Victory in '43* column, which showcased the most patriotic rationing tips, stories, or events from the home front.

This caller accused well-known industrialist and philanthropist Marcus Forrester of everything from running an illegal gambling ring to Nazi collaboration.

"Marcus Forrester," Jenny said skeptically, having never heard a whisper of impropriety about the man.

Her mystery caller went on with a litany of offenses: war profiteering, blatant infidelity, labor manipulation via organized strikes on his own plants, and the list went on.

Jenny doodled on her notepad. "Where's your proof?"

"Do your job, honey," the man said, no longer hiding his Brooklyn accent. "Dig. It's all right there for the taking."

"Uh-huh," Jenny said, not above showing him who held the cards. "Bub, if I followed up on every joker who called in with the story of the century, I would—"

"He had your father killed."

Jenny's eyes snapped reflexively to her uncle, sitting behind his desk in the glass-enclosed office in front of her. A flash of panic and then a tidal wave of guilt crashed over her. For nearly a year, she had longed to blame someone other than herself for her father's death, and now a stranger at the end of a phone line offered her instant absolution.

"Just mention your father's name and watch him sweat."

The line went dead before she could organize a coherent thought, and she quickly double pressed the receiver button to contact Central Exchange and get the party back on the line. The operator merely chuckled over the background noise of chattering operators rapidly connecting and disconnecting calls from the switchboards. "Oh, honey, you can't be serious," she said before disconnecting the line.

That began weeks of frantic digging into everything she could find on Marcus Forrester. She had a contact on the inside at the police station who let slip that Forrester's lawyer had a full-time job putting out fires on his behalf. Nickel and dime stuff, nothing big enough to create a ruckus over, but hints of everything her anonymous caller had said were rising to the surface. She was slowly gathering evidence: photographs with the bimbo of the week, police logs, damning interviews with striking workers, and soon, she hoped, ties to the enemy would emerge. She would write the exposé of all exposés, and then the man would get what was coming to him. She would finally do something meaningful with her life, and no one would underestimate her again.

She found nothing connecting the industrialist to her father or his death, so she could only assume the man said that to get her to investigate Forrester further, but tonight she would know for sure. She would meet him face to face, lay the man's sins at his feet, bring up her father's untimely demise, and let the truth unfold in his beady grey eyes.

Flat tires and misogynistic soldiers were forgotten in the sweet anticipation of absolution.

CHAPTER TWO

They arrived at The Grotto forty minutes late. Forrester was still there, but the table Jenny requested in the exclusive third tier—the table catercorner to Forrester's usual banquette in the back—was gone. Instead, they gave her a table on the floor that required a minimum party of two, turning her driver into her escort for the evening.

Jenny had never been to The Grotto, but the club's exclusivity made her dub it The Den of Sins and Secrets. If you wanted to impress and be seen, you went to 21 or the Persian Room at The Plaza; if you wanted to impress and remain anonymous, you went to The Grotto. It was *the* place for high-powered businessmen, political figures, and mobsters looking for good entertainment, good food, and good times with someone other than their wives. You had to know someone to get in—her uncle was friends with the owner—and once you were in, it was an unspoken rule that on the way out, amnesia would rob you of anything seen or heard there. The place was tailor-made for the likes of Forrester, and it was no wonder he had a table on permanent reserve.

Jenny masked her disdain for the place with a polite smile for the checkroom girl as she and the soldier handed over their coats. The checkroom girl did not mask her disdain for Jenny's inappropriate evening attire, looking her two-piece gray suit up and down like a disapproving house matron.

Jenny raised her chin and straightened the red, white, and blue V for Victory rhinestone pin on her lapel. She'd given the club's dress code a passing thought when her uncle informed her that today was the big day, but she decided the sparkly bauble she always kept in her desk drawer for emergency dolling up was all The Grotto's cesspool of superficial grandeur was going to exact from her. This was her last chance to prove to her uncle that she could be a reporter. Her previous efforts, through no fault of her own, had been disasters. One more failure and she would be sentenced to the columnist's desk for life, with no chance for parole. Tonight, she was on the verge of exposing a dirty, rotten, murdering traitor. She couldn't care less about dress codes or the people who worshiped them. There was real work to be done. War work. She had bad guys to catch, and nothing was going to stand in her way.

Jenny took her soldier's arm in a show of patriotic indignation, and they headed through the black lacquered swinging double doors of the club proper. One of the doors nearly swatted her in the backside when she stopped in her tracks. She inhaled an audible gasp as the room unfolded before her.

The name of the club suited the place. She entered an unexpected hollow of earth tones, accented with warm bronzes and gilded golds. Crystal-laden columns of light hung from the high ceiling, casting soft patterns of twinkling lights throughout the room. Three tiered platforms created a gentle slope toward the large band shell at the front corner of the room, making the space look more like a theater than a nightclub.

The effect was stunning. The twelve-piece orchestra, clad in all white but bathed for the moment in amber gelled stage lights, accompanied a songbird on an upbeat swing tune sung over the din of its oblivious audience.

The hostess led them past the crowded bar on their right, and Jenny offered a lingering stare at the stylized glass tile mosaic above the mirrored backstop of the bottle-lined wall as they passed. It told the story of a nymph beckoning a young man to the water's edge.

Hylas, no doubt, Jenny was sure, and how apropos. Beyond the irony of the piece, she thought she recognized the work. "Say, is that a Meière?"

The hostess turned to look at the panel in question. "Why, yes, it is. There are several."

The young woman pointed to various panels around the room, all water themed: mermaids, naiads, and one Jenny swore was Circe poisoning the sea. She made a mental note to complement the owner on his taste in art and his sense of humor.

Jenny frowned when the hostess held out her hand to the worst seats in the house. "Enjoy your evening."

Two rows of small round tables arranged in a half circle around the edge of the dance floor offered nothing but dancing couples constantly bumping into their table and no clear view of the stage. Jenny looked over her shoulder toward the table she should have had, but the silhouette of a stout figure leaning on the third-tier handrail above the entrance to the club caught her eye and held it.

It was the owner, Dominic Vignelli, lording over his domain. He took a puff from his thick cigar and then disappeared into the office behind him. Jenny shook her head, wondering what kind of man would take pride in such a snake pit and how her uncle could possibly be his friend. She glanced at the far corner banquette on the same tier and found the rat bastard himself, Marcus Forrester, in all his slimy monkey-suited glory, surrounded by an entourage of what she was sure were equally slimy characters.

Jenny stared at the group for as long as she dared, struck by the dichotomy of the man in the center. Marcus Forrester had an irritating charm about him. If you didn't know he was a low-down snake in the grass, you might envy his elegant clothes, confident manner, and handsome good looks. His square jaw was anchored to a pear-shaped head, giving him a deceptively boyish face for a man in his mid-fifties, and it meant he was rarely without a beautiful woman on his arm.

He was stag tonight, but Jenny knew it was by choice and not for a lack of vacuous chippies willing to prostitute themselves for pretty clothes and a night on the town with one of the city's most powerful men.

Jenny turned and faced forward as her hatred of the man simmered. It was time to formulate a plan to get up there and confront him, and she certainly couldn't do it with the protective Boy Scout at her side.

As they settled into their seats, Jenny said, "Listen, soldier, you don't have to stay. I know you have to get back to post."

He smiled. "Not to worry, ma'am. I am all yours this evening."

Not exactly what Jenny wanted to hear, but she smiled anyway. "You're sweet."

"Cal," he said.

"What?"

"My name is Cal." The soldier paused. "Calvin Richards." He paused again. "Mailroom?"

Jenny snapped her fingers. "Of course!" She was glad the redhead finally supplied his name, because sergeant, buddy, brother, and mister were all wearing thin, and, as she feared, he soon realized that she didn't know what else to call him.

She thought she recognized him from her days in the mailroom at the paper, but that was years ago, when they were both still in high school, and as far as she could recall, she'd never actually spoken to him. That was the last she'd seen of the skinny copper-headed kid until he showed up at the paper a few weeks ago as a nicely filled out young man in uniform.

It wasn't unusual to see soldiers coming and going at the office building that housed her uncle's newspaper, the *Daily Chronicle*, but Cal stood out because of his red hair and the fact that he said hi with a broad grin every time they passed in the hallway, which seemed often. "Hey, Jenny," he would say, which always sounded like *Hay, Ginny*, and Jenny would smile and say, "Hey," in return, having no idea who the fella was.

He approached her desk in the newsroom earlier in the day while she was frantically gathering her things to rush out of the office, and his casual *golly, this is swell* appreciation of her rise to columnist got old quickly. She couldn't understand why he was being so familiar. She had several errands to run before her big night, and she was about to dismiss him as politely as her frazzled brain would allow when he offered to give her a lift to wherever she was going. She weighed juggling taxis, buses, and the subway, and found it an easy choice, but he'd now gone above and beyond, and whatever she was going to do this evening, his genteel southern sensibilities probably wouldn't approve, so he had to amscray, and now.

"Honestly, Cal, you can go. I—"

"Dinner or drinks?" a waiter asked, leaning into their space.

"Neither," Jenny said dismissively, focused on getting rid of her escort.

"Dinner or drinks?" the waiter repeated.

The waiter's tone made it clear that the cover charge merely bought you entrance to the club, not a lounging pass for the evening.

"Whiskey," Cal said.

Jenny rubbed her forehead as her low-grade headache put in for a promotion. "Scotch. Neat."

The waiter nodded and went on his way.

Cal leaned in. "Say, I think you're tryin' to get rid of me."

Jenny's patience was nearing its limit. She may never get this close to Forrester again, and she could not fail in this mission. Not this one.

"Listen, Cal, I've got a big story on the line—the biggest—and I'll do anything to get it, understand?"

He leaned back in his seat. "Naturally."

"I might do things that aren't very ladylike, or appropriate, or legal even, see? You may not like it, but sometimes that's what it takes. You're an innocent bystander, and I don't want you to get in trouble because of my actions, so if you want to sit at the bar while I put my plan in motion, I completely understand. In fact, I would prefer it."

Jenny noticed Cal's attention had drifted past her shoulder toward the stage. "Hey," she said, waving her hand to bring him back to her. "This is important."

"Yeah, ladylike," he said absently.

"What are you ..." She turned to face the stage, but expensive dinner jackets and shimmering gowns blocked her view as dancing couples crowded their table. The music was first rate, and the female singer's voice was pleasant enough, but Jenny couldn't imagine what was so interesting up there. When the dancing couples parted enough to allow fleeting glimpses of the woman on stage, Jenny's face took on the same bedazzled look as Cal's.

"Judas priest," she said under her breath. The singer's tall frame filled out a strapless red satin column dress that was magically suspended by her breasts. Her dark hair was parted at the side, rolled back off her angular face, and then gathered at the nape of her neck by the netting of a black snood. Her skin, bleached by the spotlight, glowed, creating a spectral aura that left Jenny momentarily transfixed. The dancing couples obscured her view again and the spell was broken, like a hypnotist snapping his fingers. She shook her head as if she'd just witnessed something otherworldly.

"Hubba, hubba," Cal said, propping up his chin on his hand. "I swear she's singin' right to me."

"She can't see two inches past that spotlight, Romeo," Jenny said, trying to make light of his infatuation to deflect her own. Her smirk evaporated when the singer's gaze landed on her. The intense stare pierced right through the dancing shadows between them, and Jenny stilled on a forced inhale until the singer looked away and released her hold.

When the song ended, the singer left the stage and wove a path right toward Jenny, through the dispersing couples. The rapidly diminishing space between them pushed Jenny back against her seat like an invisible hand to her chest.

It was her first personal encounter with such a creature, but Jenny knew the type. Her mere presence commanded attention. Heads would turn when she entered a room, and she would ignore them, either out of conceit or boredom, having had it happen so often that she no longer cared or noticed. She was untouchable. A *princesse loin-*

taine, confident and beautiful, leaving the mere mortals to swoon in her wake.

Jenny joined that wake as the singer lightly brushed her fingertips across the burgundy tablecloth as she passed. She never looked down, so she couldn't see the blush sweeping up Jenny's cheeks, or the furrowed brow, as a trace of recognition played across her face. Why did she look so familiar? Surely she'd never forget that face. She turned to see where the woman was going—not a bad view—and watched her casually place her hand on shoulders in greeting as she weaved her way up through the occupied tables in the tiered section of the club. Some patrons had the nerve to reciprocate her touch, and they earned an easy grin and a few words in return.

Jenny felt an irrational sense of disappointment that she wasn't the sole object of the singer's attention, but that disappointment soon turned to disbelief, and then outrage, as her path led straight up to Marcus Forrester.

He greeted her in a familiar manner, with a kiss on the lips and a gentle stroke on the backside, as she joined their table. Jenny sat open-mouthed for a beat until movement to her left, in front of Dominic Vignelli's office, caught her attention. The owner leaned on the railing and watched the meet and greet at Forrester's table like he had a vested interest in the outcome. Another man, still in his coat and hat, approached and held out his hand. The owner reached into his inner jacket pocket and produced a bulging envelope, which the newcomer took and put into his pocket before quickly departing.

Jenny turned back to Cal. "Did you see that? A mob payoff in broad daylight!" She threw up her hands. "Payoffs, prostitutes, and who knows what else. This place is giving me hives."

"Golly, she's swell," Cal said, still gazing blindly in the singer's direction.

Jenny stared at him in disbelief. "She's one of the bimbos!"

Cal slowly looked her way. "Your point?"

"You can't be serious, Sergeant."

He smiled unapologetically.

Jenny shook her head. "Honestly." Her disapproval didn't deter his adolescent mooning, though, and she had no intention of suffering *that* all evening, along with everything else.

"Cal, didn't anyone ever tell you it's impolite to ogle another woman while you're on a date?"

He snapped his eyes to her like she'd pinched him. "Are we on a date?"

She paused. "Are you offering?"

Cal's dumbstruck look made Jenny suspicious and she narrowed her eyes. "Did my uncle put you up to this?"

"Uh, who's your uncle again?"

Jenny moaned and buried her face in her hands. This was the third time in as many months that she had been set up by her uncle. She didn't know why he was suddenly playing cupid, but it would never stick, and because she could never tell him why, she feared a lifetime of setups in her future.

"How humiliating," she said, dropping her hands to the table.

"Aw, now, Jenny, it wasn't like that. He was worried about you bein' out all by your lonesome so late at night, and I happen to agree with him."

"Well, you would."

"Now, don't be prickly. Anyone would. You've got to focus, gal. We got the biggest story of the year on the line, right?"

Jenny took a breath. "Right."

Cal leaned in close. "So, what's your plan, and how can I help?"

Jenny attempted a passing glance at Forrester's table, but she couldn't get past the singer in the red dress cradling a coupe of champagne in one hand and Forrester's bicep in the other.

The woman said something funny to the bastard, who threw his head back in laughter, which brought his deep-set grey eyes out of the shadow of his brow. It earned the singer another kiss on the lips, and Jenny winced in disgust.

Forrester had a crooked smile, made even more obvious by the pencil-thin mustache above his cupid's bow-shaped upper lip. He looked like an idiot, beaming at the woman on his arm, and she kept stroking his ego as she nestled into his shoulder and fed him champagne from her glass.

A body suddenly blocked Jenny's view and made her look up. "Cigarettes?" the woman asked, holding up a pack of Chesterfields.

Jenny blinked at the shimmering figure before her. She looked like a tap dancer out of a Busby Berkeley musical, with her silver and gold lamé tails and short shorts, separated by a burgundy cummerbund. Jenny couldn't help but notice the woman's legs, as was the intent, and she silently reprimanded herself for falling into the club's web of sexual vice.

"No, thank you," she said.

Jenny watched her move on to the next table and had a stroke of genius. She scanned the room for an employee door but didn't see one. When a camera girl emerged from the door beneath the ladies' lounge sign adjusting her uniform, she snapped her fingers and said, "That's it!"

"What's the plan?" Cal asked, rubbing his hands together in anticipation.

"You stay here, and if anyone asks, you just picked me up outside, and you've never seen me before."

Cal sat back with a worried look on his face. "What are you going to do?"

She grabbed her clutch purse and stood. "I'm going to get that story."

CHAPTER THREE

*P*icking locks looked easy in the movies, but Jenny had no earthly idea what she was doing. She pulled the bent bobby pin from the lock and stood up. "Come on," she said, as she slapped the door below the Employees Only sign. She jiggled the doorknob again for good measure and glanced around for anything that would help her get into the changing room. The fire ax in the glass case down the hall looked inviting, but she settled on rummaging in her purse until she found a metal nail file. It was too wide for the lock, so she slipped the file between the door and the strike plate, hoping to catch just enough of an edge to release the latch. Once inside, she hoped to find an off-duty cigarette girl's uniform to fit her five-foot-three frame, and then she could get to Forrester unnoticed.

"Come on," she said again to herself when the file proved useless. "Throw me a bone tonight. Just one."

"Lose your key?" a woman's low voice rumbled into her ear.

Jenny sprang to attention. "Jiminy!"

She turned and hid the file behind her back. She found herself face to face with the singer and captured by the bluest eyes she'd ever seen. The spotlight on stage had drained the color from them, but in the light of the nearby hallway sconce, they were like pools of a never-ending blue ocean, and Jenny imagined drowning would never be so enjoyable.

"Are you new here?" the singer asked.

"New?"

The singer pointed at the sign on the door. "Employees only."

Jenny pretended she'd never seen it before. "Oh, my. So it is. Why, I was looking for—" She feigned confusion, then relief, when she spotted the entrance to the ladies' lounge. "There it is. Silly me. Can't see a thing without my glasses."

The singer held out her hand toward the proper door. "Let me help you."

"Thank you," Jenny said, as the woman held it open for her.

The singer parked herself in front of the mirrored wall at the end of the long multi-station vanity and fussed with a seam at her hip. Jenny retrieved a lipstick from her purse and leaned into the vanity mirror beside her.

"Nearsighted or far?" the singer asked with an arched brow, watching her reapply with no apparent visual handicap.

The lie about the glasses exposed, Jenny quickly made up a viable explanation for her supposed blind expertise. "They're lips," she said. "They're in the same place every day."

The singer laughed.

The woman's smile was dazzling, and her laughter caught Jenny off guard. She had a strange sense of pride for causing it and basked in the moment until the singer turned with her arms akimbo and said, "So, why were you trying to break into the employees' changing room, and why shouldn't I have you tossed out of here immediately?"

Caught red-handed and red-faced, Jenny gave up the charade and confessed. "I was going to pose as a cigarette girl so I could get to your table."

The woman put a hand to her chest. "My table? I'm flattered."

"Forrester's table."

"Ah," the singer drew out. "Gossip columnist or photographer? Do you have a tiny camera hidden in a pack of cigarettes?"

"No, but that's a great idea."

The woman smiled again, and Jenny hoped that wonderful laugh would follow. When it didn't, she said, "Listen, I'm harmless, I promise. I'm a columnist at the *Daily Chronicle*. I write the *About Town* and *Victory in '43* columns. I just want to interview Forrester about the wonderful work he's done for the underprivileged in the city."

"I see," the singer said. "He has an office and a secretary, you know. You could just make an appointment. I'm sure he'd be delighted to speak with you."

"Well," Jenny said, "he was here, I was here ..." She shrugged. "Why not?"

The singer responded with a withering glare that reminded Jenny of the first time she lied to her father and he scolded her with a somber *I'm so very disappointed in you, Jenny*.

The weight of her father's disappointment was so crushing that day that Jenny never lied to him again. Why she never wanted to lie to this woman again was a complete mystery.

The singer needlessly primped her hair in the mirror. "You're welcome to join the table this evening, but I'm afraid your quarry has flown the coop."

Jenny couldn't believe it. Forrester had left. She collapsed onto one of the vanity seats and exhaled an exasperated "No" to the ceiling. She rubbed her throbbing temples and mumbled, "What else?"

The singer pointed at Jenny's extended leg. "I'm afraid there's a run in your hose."

Jenny hiked her skirt to mid-thigh to look and then lifted her hand in utter defeat. "Terrific. My last pair." She looked up to see interested blue eyes staring at her leg through the torn hose and pulled down her skirt in an uncharacteristic display of modesty.

The singer turned back to the mirror and smiled with a hint of sympathetic amusement behind her eyes. "You've had a rough night."

"Story of my life," Jenny said, as she surveyed the torn hose.

After a beat, a heartfelt "Sorry" drifted down from the singer as if she'd witnessed, firsthand, every disappointment she'd ever had.

Her soothing voice warmed her from the inside out, like a high-octane drink. Jenny blamed the feeling on the scotch. "That's okay. I felt kind of bad about wearing them anyway."

"Why?" the singer asked.

Jenny shrugged. "So many people are without luxuries these days. I've been holding on to these as a reminder of how easy life used to be, what we're fighting for, how we all have to sacrifice. You know."

The singer raised her brow. "Goodness. All that wrapped up in a pair of hose. What does the 'Star Spangled Banner' do for you?"

Jenny looked up with pained reverence. "You have no idea."

The reply floated between them until the war sucked the life from the room. The singer looked away and cleared her throat. "Yes, well, shame about the hose." She looked in the mirror and traced the perfect arch of her eyebrow with her finger. Satisfied with her brow, she smoothed her skin-tight red satin dress down her hips and slid a long leg out the slit in the back.

Jenny couldn't help but notice the magnificently toned leg protruding from its red shroud as its owner peered over her shoulder to check her seams.

A slight twist interrupted the seam's perfect line just above the well-defined calf. "Seam's crooked," Jenny said, pleased that her voice sounded calm and did not betray the sudden fluttering in her stomach.

"So it is. Would you mind?" the singer asked. "The dress is a little ..." She paused and wiggled slightly. "Constricting."

Jenny swallowed. "Sure." She wiped her hands on her skirt, as if she'd soil perfection if she didn't, and knelt down beside her task. The singer leaned a little closer, and Jenny had the distinct impression she was flirting with her. That couldn't possibly be the case—not this woman, not toward her. She shook off her vivid imagination just in time for a foot to slip out of its red satin shoe and into her waiting hands.

Jenny cradled the foot in awe, deciding she had just developed a foot fetish. The singer wiggled her toes. "Don't be shy."

Jenny glanced up with a nervous chuckle. She hoped to see that

dazzling grin staring down at her, but the grin chose a fresh application of lipstick instead.

Shaking her head, Jenny placed her hands gently on each side of
the wayward seam and began slowly and methodically working her
way up the limb until she found the heat beneath her hands seeping
into her fingers, up her arm, and through her body, settling—*mmmph
... God ... hello*—somewhere just below her belly. She tried to remain
neutral, but the warm, firm leg in her hands, the smooth hose, and
the subtle hint of perfume dabbed behind the singer's knee made
indifference a struggle.

A warm blush filled her face as her hand passed the slightly bent
knee and moved up the thigh. Her hands disappeared beneath the
red column dress and came to an abrupt halt mid-thigh, when she
reached the end of the welt suspended by a garter belt and found her
hands wrapped around warm, bare skin. The urge to continue up the
leg respectfully contained, she ran both hands, one on each side,
slowly back down beside the seam, to make sure it was perfect. That
wasn't necessary, but goodness, that leg! She couldn't resist. As she
reached the foot, she thought she heard the woman exhale a low
moan. Jenny's body responded with a wave of arousal, and she
offered a shocked glance upwards, only to find the singer putting
away her lipstick.

"All done?" the woman asked nonchalantly.

"Yep," Jenny said, sure she was imagining things.

The other leg shot out of the curtain of red with a questioning
brow in the mirror from its owner.

"You're fine," Jenny said as she stood, her hands and body still
humming with pleasure from her little adventure.

"Thank you."

There was something behind the singer's smile when she said
"thank you," like a joke only she knew. Jenny panicked when she realized it must have sounded like a compliment rather than the state of
her seams.

"I mean, you're straight."

That brought an even wider amused grin in the mirror.

"I mean your other seam is straight," Jenny quickly clarified, a little flustered.

The singer turned from the mirror with a look of confusion, then recognition, followed by another amused grin. Jenny realized the woman understood her meaning the first time.

As if the singer could see self-recrimination written all over her face, the amused grin turned into an empathetic smile, and she mercifully ignored the whole thing.

"Thank you," she said, as she hiked up her dress at the bust line and settled her breasts gently into place.

Jenny swore the temperature in the room just went up ten degrees. She was staring but couldn't help herself. She looked at the amused face in the mirror and then quickly looked down and fumbled in her purse for she didn't know what.

"If you still want that interview with Forrester, come see me after the set," the singer said.

Jenny looked up from her purse. "Are you serious?"

"Sure. Stick around and I'll set it up for you."

"Wow, that would be terrific. Thank you so much. You have no idea how much this means to me, Miss—?" She stuck out her hand.

The singer returned the handshake. It was firm and confident but gentle at the same time. "Call me Kat."

"As in panther?" Jenny asked, and then regretted saying it out loud.

The singer smiled. "No, as in Kathryn. Miss—?"

The soft, warm hand in hers and the beautiful blue eyes boring expectantly into her made Jenny's knees weak and, for a moment, her voice deserted her. She was somewhere south of graceful when she finally said, "Uh ... Jenny, I mean Jen ... Ryan."

Kathryn paused. "Do you prefer Jenny or Jen?"

"Jenny," she said. Nobody called her Jen. Ever. She didn't know why she even said it, other than Jenny suddenly sounded juvenile for a twenty-three-year-old in the face of Kathryn's sophistication.

"Jenny it is," Kathryn said. "Pleased to meet you."

"Likewise, and thank you so much for the interview with Forrester."

"Don't mention it. It's my pleasure." After a few beats, Kathryn looked down at their still clasped hands and then up again. "Gotta get back," she said, squeezing Jenny's hand.

"Oh. Right," Jenny said, embarrassed for holding it so long. "Sorry."

Kathryn smiled as she turned and then prowled out the door. Jenny stood motionless for a moment, gathering her wits. She straightened her skirt to restore her dignity and then looked in the mirror, where she met her flushed, blotchy red face. "Good grief," she said. "That's attractive. Smooth, kiddo, real smooth."

She shook her head and laughed. Less than an hour spent in the den of sin and she'd already succumbed to the first shiny thing to cross her path. But, oh, what a shiny thing.

Jenny removed her damaged hose, trying not to remember Kathryn's eyes giving her legs the once over when she lifted her skirt. She had nice legs. Kathryn had nicer legs, and the memory of her bare thigh in her hands warmed her all over again.

Muffled tones of an upbeat song about a gold digger and the joys of having a sugar daddy drifted through the ladies' room walls as Kathryn continued her set, and Jenny looked at herself in the mirror with disdain for having lost her focus.

"Well, how appropriate," she said of the song, which reminded her just who, and apparently what, her new acquaintance was when she wasn't singing or disarming young women in bathrooms. She noted her rosy cheeks, remnants of her brief encounter with the sexiest woman she'd ever met, and pointed at herself in the mirror. "Don't even, Ryan. Just don't." She took a deep breath and raised her chin, snapping her purse shut on the whole experience. She headed back to her table with her priorities firmly in place.

CHAPTER FOUR

"There you are," Cal said, as he rose from his seat to pull her chair out. "Forrester's gone! I tried to warn you but, you know ... ladies only."

Jenny slid into her seat. "I know."

"Tough break. The bimbo went in there. Did you see her?"

"Yeah, I saw her."

He took his seat. "What took you so long?"

"Run in my stocking ... girl stuff. You know how it goes." She quickly drained the remainder of her drink, waited a beat, and then raised her hand to a passing waiter. "Could I have another scotch here?"

Cal raised his brow. "What happened in there?"

"I'm not sure."

"Did it have something to do with the bimbo?"

Jenny took offense to the characterization now that she'd met the woman, and she felt the need to defend her. "Turns out she's not such a bimbo."

"No," he said, as his eyes drifted past her shoulder and then slowly up. "I guess she's not."

Jenny turned her head to see the singer standing behind her chair.

Kathryn regarded the empty seat. "May I?"

"Yes, ma'am," Cal said, as he nearly stumbled trying to get to the empty seat to pull it out.

Kathryn's presence had Jenny mesmerized all over again. It was like meeting a movie star who was larger than life and twice as beautiful as she'd imagined.

"Cal, this is Kathryn," she said, but stopped when she realized she didn't know the woman's last name. "Um ..."

Kathryn extended her hand to Cal. "Hammond," she said. "Call me Kat."

Jenny smiled. "Don't bother, he'll just call you ma'am."

"Yes, ma'am," he said on cue. "I'm Sergeant Calvin Richards, U.S. Army. It's an honor to make your acquaintance. Can I just say you've got a beautiful voice, and I just think, well, gosh, you sure are pretty."

He continued to shake Kathryn's hand long after proper etiquette demanded, and recognizing the affliction, Jenny rubbed his arm and whispered, "Down boy."

"Yes, ma'am," he said, as he sat down.

Jenny kept her gaze firmly fixed on Kathryn's face, but she could feel Cal staring at her.

"Huh," escaped his lips as a statement.

Jenny broke her stare with effort and looked his way. "Huh what?"

He cut his eyes to Kathryn, who gave him a wink and a seductive grin.

"Uh," Cal drew out, "I'm gonna be over at the bar if ya need me."

Cal cleared his throat into the silence and thumbed over his shoulder. "Yeah, anyway, the bar." He stood and made his way across the club.

Jenny furrowed her brow. "What was that about?"

Kathryn claimed innocence with a shrug.

They sat in uncomfortable silence for a few moments until Kathryn asked, "How's your wrist?"

Jenny rubbed the recently healed injury, wondering how this perfect stranger knew anything about it. "What?"

"You sprained it pretty badly a few weeks ago, didn't you? Falling off the roof of that car in front of the courthouse? How did the camera fare?"

That explained why Kathryn looked familiar; she was the bimbo *du jour* on Forrester's arm for one of the photographic evidence missions. Jenny heard the man was attending the court date of one of his lackeys caught in a gambling sting, so she grabbed her friend Bernie, who also happened to be the paper's top photographer, and rushed downtown. She had no idea the lackey was a woman and no idea the place would be a madhouse after the case was dismissed on a technicality. Forrester's lawyer made like an offensive lineman and ushered the couple quickly through the crowd, toward the waiting limousine. Bernie couldn't position himself for a clear shot, so Jenny grabbed his bulky 4x5 Speed Graphic camera before the opportunity was lost and climbed atop the nearest vehicle, which happened to be a taxi that promptly took off, resulting in an undignified, legs in the air, plunge to the curb below. She protected her friend's camera like it was a newborn infant but sustained a sprained wrist and a concussion for her trouble, and no picture, to add insult to literal injury.

Jenny shook her head, embarrassed over the incident. "I'm surprised you recognize me from that," she said. "There was quite a crowd that day."

Kathryn smiled. "I'd recognize those legs anywhere."

Jenny blushed and braced herself for Occupational Flirting: Round Two. She vowed she would not succumb this time, despite Kathryn's obvious charms, which she wielded with deadly precision. Not only was she one of Forrester's many play things, she was part of his criminal ring too, and having anything to do with the woman, beyond getting the interview with Forrester, was off limits.

"Congratulations on your freedom," Jenny said, trying to remain neutral.

Kathryn smiled again, but there was nothing pleasant in her voice when she said of her arrest, "A misunderstanding."

"Of course."

Kathryn stared at her, and Jenny sensed it was a dare to say differently. Jenny had no intention of antagonizing her only path to Forrester, so she rubbed her wrist again and said, "Anyway, the camera survived, but I missed him that day, so when I heard he was back in town, I thought I'd try here."

Kathryn waited a beat and then said, "Office. Secretary. Appointment."

"Or singer with the right connections," Jenny said with a grin, to prove she could be charming too.

Kathryn did not grin. She leaned forward and crossed her arms on the table. "So, what are you really doing here? And don't hand me that line about Forrester's charitable contributions to society. I'm not buying it. Tell me the truth or your interview is in the wind."

Jenny weighed another lie against the truth and decided she couldn't risk losing her inside track. She chose the one thing she couldn't prove, hoping Kathryn might slip up and implicate Forrester.

"He killed my father."

Kathryn frowned. "What makes you think that?"

"I have my sources."

"And how was your father involved with Marcus Forrester?"

Jenny raised her chin, not willing to admit she hadn't a clue. "I don't think that's any of your concern."

Kathryn's lips twisted into a smirk. "Some sources."

"I know Forrester gave the order."

Kathryn raised her brow and leaned back in her seat. "So it's personal."

"So?"

"So that changes things."

"So now you're not going to help me?"

"When things are personal, people get careless, do things that are dangerous, maybe even deadly."

Jenny sensed her meeting with Forrester slipping away, and she wasn't about to let it go without a fight. "Don't presume to know anything about how I go about my business."

"Oh, I don't need to presume," Kathryn said. "You've done nothing but lie to me since the moment I met you. That makes you an untrustworthy person, and now you're an untrustworthy person with a vendetta. What could possibly give me pause?"

Jenny suppressed a flash of anger. She was the most trustworthy person in the world. She counted to ten in her head until the urge to lash out dissipated. "You said you would help me if I told you the truth," she said in a stern whisper. "You have no idea what I've been through or what it's like to lose a parent to murder, so, yes, I lied to you, and I'm sorry if you're offended, but I'll do anything to get to Forrester and the truth about my father's death."

"You're rather making my point, don't you think?"

"Are you going to help me or not?"

"If I bring you face to face with Forrester, how do I know you won't pull out a gun and shoot him dead on the spot?"

Jenny was shocked by the suggestion, but now that Kathryn mentioned it— "Would that be so awful?"

Kathryn smiled. "I would hate to see you go to the chair for it. He's not worth it."

Jenny raised her brow. "I'm flattered that you care."

"I'd give the same advice to anyone who was so woefully misguided."

"He killed my father."

"So you said."

Kathryn's dismissive attitude about something so serious was infuriating, and Jenny put a hand on her purse, ready to leave. "Look," she said, "if you're not going to help me, just tell me so I can quit wasting my time."

Kathryn leaned forward and put her hand over Jenny's, stilling her departure. "Desperation, determination—whatever you prefer to call it—is just human nature," she said. "I'm not insulting you. Whatever you're trying to do, you've got to be smart about it, and that's not easy when it's personal. That's all I'm saying."

Jenny relaxed. Kathryn's calm, reasonable advice made her feel like she'd just gained an ally. She hadn't told anyone what her mysterious caller had said about her father's death, not even Bernie. He would just say, "It was a horrible accident," and then he would comfort her and tell her she's too emotionally involved to see things clearly. Kathryn, on the other hand, wasn't shocked at all by the suggestion that Marcus Forrester had ordered a hit. She even offered advice on how to handle the situation. The den of sin was the last place Jenny expected to find a helping hand, but there it was, covering hers.

"Well, you know the man," Jenny said, some humor returning. "Just keep me from doing something careless, dangerous, or deadly."

Kathryn smiled and leaned back in her chair, pulling her hand away. "Something tells me that's no easy feat."

Jenny grinned, the statement probably true, but the grin faded as the absence of Kathryn's touch made her feel alone again. The loss made her uneasy. Kathryn Hammond was a means to an end, someone of questionable character, and either the smoothest operator she'd ever encountered or someone she had misjudged entirely.

The overwhelming urge to give Kathryn the benefit of the doubt made Jenny reevaluate the singer's relationship with Marcus Forrester. Maybe her boss, the mobster club owner, makes her play sex kitten to appease the degenerate clientele. That would be typical, and a reason to pity the woman, which, in turn, would make it perfectly acceptable to forgive her for the less than desirable company she keeps.

"Forrester comes here to see you, doesn't he?" Jenny asked.

"He's a fan, I guess."

"It looked like he was more than just a fan."

Kathryn tilted her head. "What are you implying, Miss Ryan?"

Jenny fidgeted, finding accusations a little harder to hurl with the target two feet away and staring at her like she'd just been called a murderer herself.

Jenny put on a sweet smile and thought better of her line of questioning. "Not a thing, Miss Hammond. I merely wondered if you have a following here at the club. You're very good."

"You're adding evasive to untrustworthy," Kathryn said, obviously not fooled by the compliment. "You'd garner a little more respect with a direct approach."

The rebuke straightened Jenny's spine. Who was this woman to talk about respect? "Fine," Jenny said. "You want direct? Forrester has a wife, so that makes you ... what?"

"His moll, mistress, prostitute, whore? Is that what you're after?"

Jenny had no retort. Bimbo would have sufficed, but having heard the others said out loud, she found even that distasteful and incongruent with the woman before her.

"I think you're judging me, Miss Ryan, and I don't think you've any right to."

Kathryn was right, but words were tumbling out of Jenny's mouth before she could stop them. "I just don't understand how you can be with him. You're talented and beautiful. Surely you could make a better living than—" She didn't finish her statement, not sure why she felt the need to express her opinion about this stranger's life choices.

Kathryn reached for her silver cigarette case. "Well, sweetheart, things are tough all over. We all do what we need to do." She removed a cigarette and began tapping it on the case to settle the tobacco.

Jenny watched the routine, mesmerized by Kathryn's precise but fluid movements, until she reached for the lighter. "You're not going to light that, are you?"

Kathryn held up the cigarette. "Does this bother you?"

"Just a bit of a headache tonight. It's been a long day, if you don't mind."

Jenny expected her to light it anyway, just out of spite, but she didn't. Kathryn carefully laid the cigarette on top of the case and folded her hands on the table in front of her. "So, you're a reporter or something?" she began pleasantly.

Jenny was surprised Kathryn seemed more amused than annoyed with her, but she wasn't going to question it. "Technically—"

"Martini, Bobby, please," Kathryn interrupted with a whisper to the waiter as he put down Jenny's second scotch.

He smiled and produced her usual drink. "Right here, Miss Hammond."

"You're a dear," she said and turned back to Jenny. "I'm sorry. You were saying?"

Jenny nodded thanks to the waiter. "I was saying, technically, I'm a columnist. I'd be a reporter if they'd give me a chance. I'm free-lancing right now, trying to prove my worth, as it were. As I mentioned, I write some columns down at the *Daily Chronicle*."

"*About Town* and *Victory in '43*."

"Yes."

Kathryn didn't comment further. She merely raised her brow slightly, as if to say, *And? So?*

Jenny cleared her throat into the uncomfortable silence and feared she had annoyed the woman after all. "Anyway, if I can get that interview—" She looked up in time to see Kathryn raise her brow even further. She noticed she didn't voice an outright refusal, so Jenny pushed on. "Why are you helping me?"

"Oh, I don't know," Kathryn said, "I just thought you might need a little help. It's obvious you're not very good at this ... flying in here on a wing and a prayer, hoping to topple the mighty Marc Forrester with your lethal pencil and notebook."

Jenny stared at her. The casual use of Forrester's name and Kathryn's condescending attitude stung. She felt like a teenager again, awkward and unsophisticated and wholly unprepared for her task. She supposed she deserved the attitude after insinuating that Kathryn was a whore, but it hurt nonetheless. "I don't need your pity, Miss Hammond."

Kathryn smiled. "You may not need my pity, Miss Ryan, but you obviously need my help, or you wouldn't be here. What do you think you're going to get from that interview? A confession?"

"If I'm lucky. At the very least, I'm going to prove he's in cahoots with Nazi sympathizers in this country."

Kathryn chuckled. "A Nazi sympathizer too? Good heavens. He's not stupid, Miss Ryan. You think he's just going to come out and incriminate himself?"

"I notice you're not denying that it's true."

"Now, why do you think I would know anything about that? And if I did, why would I care or tell you about it?"

"You're kidding, right?" Jenny could hardly contain her indignation. "That bastard is supporting the war machine that is killing our boys over there, or don't you care about that?"

"It'll take a lot more than one interview to prove that," Kathryn said, and then took a drink.

Jenny glared at her. "I think you know something."

Kathryn put down her glass and stared back blankly.

Jenny was dumbfounded. Making poor personal choices was one thing, but shirking your patriotic duty was inexcusable. "How can you just sit there and not even try to do something about this? Or at least help *me* do something about it?"

Kathryn leaned back in her chair and crossed her arms. "I do what I can. I did say I'd get you that interview."

The damn interview was losing ground fast to Jenny's temper. "You're despicable."

Kathryn chuckled. "Really?"

"Yes, *really*. The whole world is falling apart, and people like you try to skate through the debris like you're not part of it, like it doesn't affect you. Well, I've got news for you, sister, you enjoy the freedoms of this country, and when she's in trouble, it's up to every one of us to come to her aid and do anything and everything we can to preserve what so many have sacrificed and died for."

"Well, rah-rah," Kathryn said. "I bet you've got little American flags sewn into your panties."

"Fuck off."

"Ooh," Kathryn drew out, "a sailor at heart. Lovely." She reached out and picked up her cigarette with long, nimble fingers and then lit it with her slim silver lighter.

The motion was exquisitely feminine and equally seductive, as was the tilt of her head as the cigarette met the lighter, the pursing of her lips as she slowly inhaled, and the narrowing of her eyes as they reflexively protected themselves from the flame. Jenny hated her for it, for making her furious and aroused all at the same time. Her arousal was short-lived, however, as a veil of white smoke clouded her vision and assailed her nostrils on Kathryn's exhale.

The curtain of smoke slowly dissolved, and cold blue eyes stared back at her. Gone was the sparkle and warmth of the moments before. Jenny could hardly believe it was the same woman. It was disconcerting and instilled a strange sense of panic. The evening was spiraling down quickly, and Jenny was desperate to come away with something. People of Forrester's ilk understood threats, so she settled on that, determined to get her money's worth before some burly guard dog escorted her out.

"I've already got proof," she lied. "I'm just going to give him the opportunity to defend himself before I hang him with it."

Kathryn bowed her head, taking a doubting chuckle with her.

The laughter made Jenny's blood boil. This was her chance not only to move up at the paper but to impact world events, and this woman, who had no interest in anything but herself, was standing in her way, laughing at her. "Look," Jenny said, "I can't be a soldier on the front line, but at least—"

Kathryn snapped her head up, the icy stare back. "Dying on the front line is nothing to aspire to."

"But at least I'm trying to make a difference," Jenny continued, ignoring the interruption. "Unlike *you*. The only thing you're trying to make is room under your next meal ticket."

Kathryn smirked, unfazed by the insult. "Ouch."

Jenny had had enough. She pushed her chair from the table, grabbed her purse, and headed toward the exit.

"Hey, what about that interview?" Kathryn called after her. "I think we have some rope in the back."

An obscene hand gesture over the shoulder was Jenny's answer.

Jenny picked Cal up at the bar on the way out. She threw some bills on the counter and slapped him on the shoulder. "Come on. We're leaving."

He hastily finished his beer and wiped his mouth with the back of his hand as he slid off his stool. "Did she get you an interview?"

"Not worth the wait."

Cal pursed his lips in surprise and followed his charge to the checkroom for their coats. Once on the curb, Jenny looked up and down the block.

"Go home, soldier, I'll get a cab."

"No, ma'am," he said with a hand on her shoulder. "Stay here. I have my orders."

He retrieved the car and held the door open for her. Jenny slid in and crossed her arms as he shut the door and returned to the driver's seat.

Cal eyed her warily. "Say, you look mighty cheesed there."

Jenny worked her jaw, deciding whether she wanted to elaborate on her bad mood or just forget it. She rubbed her temples and let out a cleansing breath. "People like her—" She bit off a curse but realized she'd already lost her *no profanity* bet with Bernie. "Fucking chafe my ass."

Cal raised his brow and squirmed at her curse.

"Pardon my French," she said.

"Uh, well, nothin' I ain't heard before."

Jenny smiled as some of the tension drained away. "I'm sure."

"What the heck did she do?" he asked. "You wanted that interview awful bad to just walk out of there without it."

Jenny crossed her arms again. "She's one of *them*."

"Them?"

"Damn freeloaders."

Cal still had a questioning look on his face.

"Ignorant ostriches that stick their heads in the sand and deny that this war is about all of us," she clarified. "They'll keep on denying it until it's over. Then they'll pull their unpatriotic heads out of the sand and stand on the backs of those who sacrificed and say, 'Oh, what a pretty day.' Then they'll whistle a happy tune and pick up where they left off, none the worse for wear. It's disgusting, and it ticks me off."

Cal cleared his throat. "Well, you're preachin' to the choir here."

"I know, Cal, I apologize. Let's just get out of here."

"Are you sure? That interview seemed pretty important."

Jenny nodded.

Cal released the brake but eyed her before proceeding. "We meet people like her all the time. Why's this one stirrin' up the bees in your shorts?"

It was a good question and one Jenny was afraid to answer. She stared blindly through the windshield, knowing she wanted Kathryn to be better than that. "Long day, I guess," she said, as she rubbed her pounding forehead.

"Uh-huh."

"Uh-huh what?"

"Nothin'." He put the vehicle in gear and pulled away.

"Spill it."

Cal squirmed before he began. "I just didn't realize ..."

Jenny glared at him, waiting.

He squirmed a bit more before relenting. "I just didn't realize you leaned to the other side of the fence."

Jenny frowned and replied automatically to the dangerous accusation. "I don't know what you're talking about."

Cal started laughing. Evidently, he didn't find it dangerous at all.

"Sparks," he said with a grin, and then he waved his hand in a slow arc while wiggling his fingers. "Lighting up the night."

Jenny grinned and couldn't deny that she felt the sparks. She made a mental note to be more careful in public around beautiful women who sparked her interest. She eyed her driver. "You have a problem with that, Sergeant?"

Cal smiled. "No, ma'am!"

Jenny chuckled and shook her head. "I don't even want to know what you're thinking."

Cal blushed. "No, I don't think you do."

Jenny was glad for the distraction. She didn't want to acknowledge that she just lost her reporting career and her best chance to bring down Marcus Forrester.

CHAPTER FIVE

*K*athryn smiled as she recognized the uneven gait of a figure moving through the nightclub. The man broke into a broad grin when he reached her table.

"Hello, doll face."

"Hello, handsome," she said, welcoming John Smith, her friend and partner.

He was never far away. She would joke fondly that he was more constant than her own shadow, but his devotion had saved her skin more than once, so he was a welcome sight. Tonight, he wore a smart brown double-breasted suit with a two-toned tie that couldn't possibly match anything outside a clown's wardrobe trunk.

"Good heavens, Smitty," Kathryn said. "That tie is criminal."

"Hey—" He ran his hand reverently down the bright orange and yellow tie's short length. "My mother bought me this tie."

"I love your mother, but don't let her buy your clothes."

He chuckled as he sat down and scooted his chair in. "I had dinner with her tonight. She sends her love, by the way."

Kathryn smiled. "My love back."

"Already conveyed," he said, then tugged proudly at his sleeve. "Besides, the suit more than makes up for the tie."

"That's because *I* bought you that suit."

"Well, no wonder I look so damn handsome." He straightened his ugly tie. "I guess you'll just have to come over and dress me in the mornings."

"Ha." She took a drink. "In your dreams."

"Every night," he said.

Kathryn shook her head because she knew he wasn't kidding.

Smitty shifted his athletic form to a comfortable position in his chair and tilted his head toward Jenny's path out the door. "That went well. Quite the little firecracker, isn't she?" He motioned his usual drink order to the waiter across the room with a raised forefinger.

Kathryn exhaled her agreement and snuffed out her cigarette in the glass ashtray before her. "You didn't tell me she had a temper."

"Well, you were supposed to seduce her, not send her running from the building."

Kathryn laughed. "They said feel her out, Smitty, not feel her up."

"Oh. My mistake." He reached for her cigarette case, asking permission with a raised brow. "Think she has what we're looking for?"

"Should be easy to find out. If tonight's tirade is any indication, she's at least on the right side. She's also undisciplined, arrogant, judgmental, and naïve. In other words, perfect."

"She's also pretty sore. Are you sure you're playing this right?"

"Hey, she started with the insults."

He smoothed back his slick brown hair and rubbed the back of his neck, as was his habit when he sensed plans were going awry. "I'm not so sure she'll be back."

"Don't worry. She'll be back."

He lit his cigarette and then exhaled a plume of smoke upwards as he flipped his black Zippo lighter shut and dropped it into his jacket pocket. "You seem pretty sure of yourself."

A slow, seductive grin formed on Kathryn's lips, and she glared at him through half-lidded eyes.

Smitty grinned back and shook his head. "Oh, you're a wicked, wicked woman."

"That's why you love me, Smitty. That's why you love me."

And love her he did. He'd known Kathryn since childhood, and though he knew romance would never happen, it didn't stop his heart from beating, which is what it would take to change his feelings toward her.

The waiter brought him his drink, and he swirled the liquor in its glass before raising it in a confident toast. "She doesn't stand a chance, does she?"

Kathryn grinned. "Not a chance."

"Poor thing." He drank his shot of whiskey in one gulp, wishing that he were her victim. "What was that about a rope?"

"She thinks Forrester is behind her father's death, so the telephone call to her desk did its job. Claims she has proof and that she's going to hang him with it."

Smitty raised his brow and chuckled. "She's got nerve, I'll give her that."

"If she's not careful, that nerve is going to get her into trouble."

"We'll just have to make sure she stays out of trouble."

"From the reports I've read, trouble is her middle name. I'm not sure siccing her on Forrester was a good idea."

"In theory, it's a well-placed dead end. She runs around in circles, you reap the benefits. I have complete confidence in your ability to make it work for us."

"I'll deal with her Forrester obsession. You keep her uncle out of my way."

Smitty grunted. "An unfortunate complication."

"Not on my end. In and out, Smitty. We've got more important things to do."

Smitty shifted uncomfortably at the mention of *more important things*. It was Kathryn's euphemism for the war. He worried that in her blind determination to get back to the fight, she was looking past her assignment with Marcus Forrester and her little side adventure with Jenny Ryan. Such impatience could be catastrophic, and she knew it. That was the only thing stopping him from confronting her about it.

If he had his way, she would never see action again. Sure, she could do her bit for the cause: sing at the USO, sell war bonds, knit scarfs for the Red Cross, for Pete's sake. Just stay away from danger. For the love of God, be done with that.

He thought when she returned home from overseas and got the primo singing gig at The Grotto, she would be safe. Time would heal her psychological wounds, and she would live the life she was meant to live, free from danger at every turn. Then Forrester cast his roving eyes her way, and the government agents trying to get close to him saw the perfect way in. They drew Kathryn back into the fold, and she was more than happy to return. Damn her misguided, guilt-ridden heart.

Kathryn was looking at him expectantly, and unsure if he'd missed part of their conversation, he simply nodded. He never got in trouble when he agreed with a woman giving him that look.

"Good," she said. "This girl is just an edge piece, and I'll handle her accordingly. No one wants this over faster than I do."

"I know, honey," he said. Her frustration was understandable, given the glacial progress of their assignment to Forrester, but she was a professional, meticulous in her approach and flawless in her execution. Anyone can stumble and fall—a momentary lapse in vigilance, a misplaced trust—but he knew Kathryn would never make the same mistake twice. She was good at her job. Too good sometimes.

It made him sick to see her fawning over Marcus Forrester and even sicker to see Paul Ryan, and now his niece, treating her like a whore because of it.

He flicked his cigarette ash into the ashtray and scanned the club to make sure all was well. He glanced up to see Dominic Vignelli leaning on the third-tier rail outside his office door. He tipped an imaginary hat to him, and Dominic raised his customary glass of port in return. All was well.

"Okay, doll, guess I'd better blow," Smitty said. "Say hi to your *boyfriend* for me tonight." He nearly choked on the word.

Kathryn grimaced. "I think I need another drink."

"Come on, Kat," he said, as he stood to leave. "Love of country and all that, yeah?"

"Have I ever let her down, Smitty?"

It had let her down, but never the other way around. "Not-a-once," he said, and then he kissed her on the cheek.

She raised her glass. "God bless America."

CHAPTER SIX

"Morning, Frank," Jenny said, as she collected her mail from the elderly man with bright eyes and a quick smile.

She tapped her mail on the secretary's desk as she passed. "Morning, Bessie."

"Boss wants to see you."

Jenny waved her mail in the air as she continued walking. "Okay."

"Now," the secretary called after her.

Jenny stopped walking and turned around. "Uh-oh. Sounds serious. Any clue?"

The secretary shook her head. "He's been in a foul mood all morning."

Terrific. She deposited her mail on her desk and walked the few steps to her uncle's office. She paused at the door, straightened her skirt, and took a deep breath before entering.

"Morning, chief. You wanted to see me?"

Her uncle looked up from behind a mound of paperwork. "Sit down, young lady."

His tone told her she was in trouble. "Yes, sir."

He took off his reading glasses and, with a flick of his wrist, sent them skittering across the papers on his desk. "I hear you made quite a spectacle of yourself last night."

"Sir?"

"Foul language, obscene gestures." He crossed his arms and waited.

"Uncle Paul," she said in the most pitiful *I'm the only niece you have* voice she could muster.

"Don't you 'Uncle Paul' me, young lady! This is business."

"Yes, sir." Her uncle had made it clear that if they were discussing business, he was her boss, not her uncle. It made it easier for him to yell at her, she supposed, and she braced for the fallout from her brief visit to The Grotto.

He pointed his finger at her. "When I get you into a place like that, you are representing me and this paper, you understand?"

"Yes, sir. But—"

"No buts!" He stood and leaned forward on his desk to emphasize his displeasure. "Not only did you embarrass yourself, you embarrassed me, and you still didn't get your story, did you?"

"No, sir."

"The owner let you in there as a favor to me, and I'm sure he doesn't appreciate having his favorite songbird flipped off in front of the whole room."

"She deserved it."

"You need to show some restraint, young lady."

"I *did* show restraint. What I really wanted to do was take her out back and knock the stuffing out of her. You would have done the same, Uncle Paul. She's a disgrace." She crossed her arms, mirroring the man in front of her.

The parallel wasn't lost on her uncle, who reigned in his self-contained storm enough to crack a smile. He sat down in his large leather chair and then clasped his hands in front of him on the desk. "You get that temper from your father, you know."

Caught in his affectionate gaze, she couldn't help softening as well. "Yeah," she said with a smile, because the statement couldn't be further from the truth. "I hear it runs in the family."

"Well, I'm glad it skipped me," he said straight-faced.

Jenny barely resisted laughing out loud. His temper was legendary. He once threw a chair out his office window in lieu of an employee who had raised his ire.

"All right, kiddo," he said, leaning back in his creaky chair and folding his hands across his rounded belly. "Consider yourself reprimanded. Now, what would you like to do for your birthday?"

Jenny swallowed and wished she could just skip that day from now on. "I haven't really thought about it." Her gaze drifted out the window, focusing on the monotonous gray pattern of windows on the high-rise across the street as a distraction. Just the mention of her last birthday was enough to send her world into a tailspin. She clamped her jaw down tight and closed her eyes, fighting hard against the emotions threatening to overtake her. When she felt in control, she opened her eyes to find her uncle kneeling beside her.

He took her hand and held it tenderly. "Sorry, Jenny."

"I'm okay," she said, brushing a tear from her eye.

He handed her his handkerchief. "I know you are."

She pressed the soft cotton material to her eyes. "I'm sorry."

"Don't be silly. Your Aunt Betsy and I just don't want to see you sitting alone in that big house, drinking yourself into a stupor on your birthday."

Jenny smiled. "I promise you, I will not be doing that." *Again.*

Her uncle stood. "Well, see that you don't, because if you do, I will personally come over there and kick your pretty little behind. And you know I will."

"Yes, sir. I know you will." And he had.

Personal tragedy, on top of personal heartbreak, left her closer than she ever thought possible to utter despair, and she got lost in the bottom of a bottle until firm, but compassionate, intervention helped her back on her feet.

Her uncle moved back behind his desk and sat down before retrieving his glasses. "Call us if you change your mind."

"Thanks." She folded up his handkerchief and put it on the edge of his desk. She didn't know if she'd ever celebrate her birthday again, and she appreciated her aunt and uncle not pushing the matter. "Reprimand over?" she asked with an innocent smile.

Her uncle grinned and put his reading glasses back on. "Yes. Go. And stay out of trouble."

"Who, me?" Jenny smiled as she stood and walked toward the door.

"Yes, you," he called after her. "And that means no more chasing Forrester."

Jenny's grin disappeared. Her uncle was onto her. She closed the door and turned around. "What?"

"You heard me. Let it go. I know you went to The Grotto for Forrester, so don't even try to make me believe you're writing a story on home front excesses in a time of war and sacrifice. You're to drop it, and I mean this instant."

Her uncle looked down at the piece of paper in his hand, and Jenny glared at him until her death-ray stare burned a hole through his indignation. Finally looking up, he pointed at her with his pen. "You've sprained your wrist, conked your head, been tossed out of that club, and heaven knows what else you're going to get into on your wild goose chase."

"How was I to know that taxi driver was going to pull away with me standing on his roof?" Jenny said. "And I did not get *tossed* out of that club; I *walked* out of that club."

"And when you walked out of that club, you walked out on your story, whatever it was. If you want to make a go of this, you need to learn what's personal and what's business, and as for your behavior, I don't know how many times I've warned you about your foul mouth. It's undignified and unladylike. You're better than that, Jenny Ryan."

Undignified, unladylike, untrustworthy. Jenny was getting the works. "Okay!" She held up her hands in surrender. "I made a mistake, but I have a plan now and a way—"

"Jenny," her uncle interrupted sternly over his glasses, "this is not a discussion. You stay away from Forrester."

Jenny clamped down on her instinct to lash out in her own defense. Her uncle was not going to change his mind no matter what she said, but if she didn't put up a fight, he'd see right through to her plan to move full speed ahead. "Uncle Paul!"

"Jenny," he said sharply.

"This isn't fair," she said, stopping just short of stamping her foot, which she felt would be over the top, even for her.

Her uncle pointed again. "Not a discussion."

She did her best to look annoyed but defeated. "Yes, sir."

"I mean it, Jenny."

"I heard you, chief."

He gave her a wary glance. "And you apologize to Mr. Vignelli for your inexcusable behavior. You hear me?"

She held up one hand in a pledge. "I'm on it."

"All right. Get out of here."

"Later, boss." She slipped out the door and strode down the aisle, more determined than ever.

CHAPTER SEVEN

*J*enny stepped into her foyer and dropped her leather briefcase to the floor beside the coat rack. She told her uncle she had a plan and, as per usual, he dismissed it out of hand. There was only one thing to do. Ignore him.

Marcus Forrester was going to pay, and she would be the architect of his downfall. Kathryn was right. He would never confess. Confronting him would be cathartic, and maybe she'd find the answer she sought in his eyes, but Kathryn's evasive answers added fuel to the fire. It proved she was on the right track, not only about her father's murder but about everything else her anonymous caller insinuated.

She thought about Kathryn's suggestion: office, secretary, appointment. But, no, bringing down Forrester would take time and diligence and had to come from the inside out. She'd thought about it from all angles, and the only path into Forrester's secret world was the mistress who, from her reaction, knew a lot more than she was telling.

Jenny tossed her keys into the blue and white porcelain bowl on the cherry console table against the wall and then strode into her bedroom to peruse her closet. Step one was getting back into the good graces of Kathryn Hammond. That required lowering her standards to something a mobster's mistress would understand: sex appeal.

"This'll be a neat trick," Jenny said, knowing her rude exit from The Grotto the night before put her at a severe disadvantage.

She sifted through her closet three times before settling on a full-length gown of shimmering dual-weave silk taffeta in olive green and gold. The wide-peaked waistband of the fitted bodice gave way to a relaxed skirt as it passed the hips and continued to the floor, where it ended in a slight train. Dressing up for her return to the club reeked of hypocrisy, but solving her father's murder and exposing a traitor made stooping to Kathryn's level an easy decision. During a time of war, anything goes, hypocrisy included.

Jenny held the gown to herself in the mirror and smiled. Perfect.

She made up her face and hair, emulating the gorgeous blonde on the cover of the latest issue of *Harper's Bazaar*, then stepped into her dress. She tugged up the three-quarter-length sleeves and then settled her breasts into the scalloped arches of the princess neckline, which completed her transformation from ill-tempered reporter to sophisticated sweet talker.

"Two can play at this game, Miss Hammond," she said, pleased with the desired effect.

Jenny sat at a premium table on the exclusive third-tier level of The Grotto, feeling like an insect lured into a carnivorous plant, about to meet its doom.

The moment the doorman greeted her by name, a cold arm of unease wrapped itself around her shoulders. It tightened its grip when, in turn, the checkroom girl, the hostess, and even the waiter who delivered her unordered scotch, neat, did the same. Every instinct told her to back out of there slowly and reassess her plan. She countered the urge by welcoming the drink to the back of her throat.

She eyed the dim corners of the crowded club expectantly while trepidation pecked at her confidence like hungry crows devouring a stale piece of bread. They were buttering her up for something; she just didn't know what or by whom. Her uncle certainly didn't arrange her VIP treatment, so she looked around for—

As if on cue, the music swelled and the stage went dark until the spotlight revealed her benefactress, dressed in another skintight column dress, this time all black, with matching gloves extending just beyond her elbows. The side-swept wave of her dark hair flowed gracefully around her bare shoulders, framing her gorgeous angular face and the single strand of pearls clinging greedily to her neck.

"Holy smokes," Jenny said under her breath.

The energy in the room shifted to the woman on stage, but it quickly washed back into the ebb and flow of overlapping conversations and the tinkling of silverware and drinking glasses. Jenny's attention did not waver from the stage. Observing the singer from afar allowed her to think clearly and professionally. Why would Kathryn Hammond go out of her way to be nice to her? She must have a reason, but Jenny couldn't figure out her angle.

When Kathryn left the stage and headed toward her, Jenny straightened in her chair, bracing for the unknown.

"Miss Ryan," Kathryn said pleasantly as she arrived at the table.

"Miss Hammond," Jenny replied in kind, wondering if Kathryn's smile was genuine.

They both smirked in silence for a moment until Jenny gave in. "Won't you sit down?"

Kathryn complied, and, in no time, Bobby showed up again, this time with a martini. Kathryn gave him a wink of thanks, which sent him on his way.

"I guess I have you to thank for my treatment here tonight," Jenny said.

Kathryn smiled. "Well, I ruined your last visit here, so I thought I'd make it up to you."

Surprised by the apology, Jenny said, "No, I was rude, and I lost my temper. I have no excuses. I apologize."

The friendly twinkle in Kathryn's eyes disappeared. "Don't apologize for loving your country, Miss Ryan."

Jenny frowned. Kathryn made fun of her patriotic views the night before and certainly displayed none of her own. What game was she playing that she would make amends and then mock her all over again?

"I'm not apologizing for loving my country, Miss Hammond. I'm apologizing for being rude to you. How *you* feel about your country is none of my business."

Kathryn knitted her brow. "Miss Ryan, are you trying to be caustic, or is that just your general nature? I didn't come over here to have a repeat of last night, and I don't know why you're ensuring that we do."

Jenny realized she'd made a mistake and opened her mouth to apologize again, but Kathryn wasn't done. In a stern but not angry voice she said, "I know you came here tonight because you want an interview with Forrester, and I'm happy to help you with that. I even arranged this little peace offering to make it easier for you, so I can't, for the life of me, understand your attitude, but I *can* tell you that I'm not going to sit here and take it on the chin while you berate me again."

Jenny pressed her lips together, silently cursing her big mouth. "You're right, Miss Hammond. I'm behaving like an ass and, again, I have no excuse. I sincerely apologize. I—"

"Accepted," Kathryn said, before Jenny could continue.

Jenny paused, surprised forgiveness came so easily.

"You clean up well," Kathryn said, the friendly twinkle back. "Very *Harper's Bazaar*."

"Thank you," Jenny said, happy to leave her idiocy behind. "It's a delicious cover this month, isn't it?"

"Indeed," Kathryn said. She took a sip of her drink. "Your hair looks lovely, by the way, down like that."

"Thank you again. So does yours."

"And that dress is simply stunning," Kathryn went on. "The color matches your eyes perfectly."

"Thank you," Jenny said, blushing under Kathryn's attentive gaze. She fondled a shimmering fold of skirt material, trying to deflect the piercing blue eyes away from hers.

"Simply stunning," Kathryn repeated.

Jenny nodded dumbly as blue eyes continued to bore into hers with unwavering intensity. She found this mutual admiration business poisoning the well of good intentions. If she wasn't careful, she could get used to it, and growing fond of Marcus Forrester's mistress was most definitely not in the plan. Considering their previous encounter, Kathryn's friendly demeanor bordered on disingenuous, and she couldn't help feeling someone else was behind her about-face.

"Look, Miss Hammond," Jenny said, pushing her drink around, "you don't have to like me, and we don't have to be friends—"

"Oh, but I do like you, Miss Ryan," Kathryn said.

Jenny looked up to see if she was being sarcastic. She'd hardly seen anything to like.

"But, if you don't want to be my friend, I understand."

"Hey, I'm game if you are," Jenny said quickly, before Kathryn changed her mind. "I'm just saying, if it makes you uncomfortable, we don't have to."

Kathryn leaned back in her chair. "I'm not uncomfortable, are you?"

Jenny opened her mouth to say *No*, but the lie died on her lips and she said nothing. Everything about Kathryn made her uncomfortable. Her choice in men, her morals, her infectious smile, her smooth voice, and especially those piercing blue eyes accentuated by exaggerated stage makeup. Jenny cringed internally as her resolve took a left turn at the corner of You're Sinking Fast and Professionalism Is Overrated.

Kathryn's intense gaze had her on the verge of squirming, and if she hadn't produced another one of her amused grins, Jenny would have cried uncle on the spot.

"I'll tell you what," Kathryn said. "Why don't we start over?" She removed a long glove and extended her hand. "My name is Kat."

Jenny gladly took the warm, soft hand in hers. "Nice to meet you, Kat. My name is Jenny." As they disengaged, Jenny said, "I really am sorry about last night."

Kathryn pulled at the fingers on her other glove to remove it and looked genuinely puzzled. "I don't know what you're talking about, Jenny."

Jenny smiled, understanding the slate was clean. She picked up her glass and raised it in a toast. "To starting over."

That brought a dazzling grin from Kathryn, who reciprocated. "To new friends."

Jenny liked the sound of that. She smiled into her glass, peering curiously over the rim at her new friend as she took a sip and then swallowed. "Now what?"

"Well, Forrester should be at home by now, so before we go, I'm going to slip into something more comfortable." She folded up her gloves. "Would you like to come?"

Jenny froze for a beat, wondering if that was a trick question. Alone with a disrobing Kathryn Hammond after a glass of scotch on an empty stomach? That could be dangerous—wonderfully, wickedly dangerous.

Kathryn raised a questioning brow. "Jenny?"

"Yes, sorry. Of course. Lead on."

As they stood, Jenny reached into her purse to pay for the drinks. Kathryn encircled her hand with a squeeze and smiled. "Don't worry about that. It's on the house."

The casual, absentminded touch seeped deep into Jenny's core, igniting delightfully inappropriate thoughts of that black dress hitting the floor.

CHAPTER EIGHT

Kathryn led Jenny along the table-lined back wall of the third tier, in the direction of the stage, until she stopped and parted a luscious curtain of gold-fringed burgundy velvet, revealing a backstage door.

Once backstage, they weaved between columns of hanging curtains and dodged the tide of performers heading toward the stage from the dressing rooms located just beyond a wrought iron spiral staircase leading to the upper floor.

To Jenny's surprise, they took the staircase and left the backstage frenzy below. At the end of a short hallway overlooking the stage, they entered a small one-room studio, where Kathryn stepped out of her black heeled shoes with a moan of relief.

"Make yourself a drink if you'd like," she said, pointing at a hinged panel on the wall. "Bar's in there."

"No, thanks," Jenny said, distracted by the tidy bazaar of color and texture in the room. There were two chairs, a bed, a changing screen, and an oversized vanity, making Jenny wonder if it was a glorified dressing room or Kathryn's apartment.

"Suit yourself," Kathryn said while tying the ends of a hairband at the crown of her head to hold her hair away from her face. She plucked several tissues from their box, scooped some cold cream onto her fingertips from an open jar, then headed toward the bathroom, rubbing the cream onto her face. "I've just got to get rid of this clown face," she said. "Won't be a minute."

Jenny settled into the bergère chair at the end of the bed, and a slow grin split her lips. She was back in Kathryn Hammond's good graces and one step closer to Forrester—just like she planned. Soon, she would meet the evil bastard face-to-face, uncover his treachery, and bring him down.

Kathryn interrupted her maniacal revenge fantasy when she came out of the bathroom patting her face dry with a hand towel. All thoughts of Forrester faded as Jenny stared. *Makeup hides myriad sins*, her high school hygiene teacher used to say, but Kathryn Hammond apparently had no sins, because she was stunning without it.

Jenny had never seen a "glamor-puss," as her friend Bernie would call her, up close and personal before, and to see one shed the trappings so quickly, and with such disdain, was contrary to the narcissistic behavior she expected from such a person.

Kathryn stood at the open door to her small closet tapping a perfectly manicured red nail on the doorjamb. She passed up several finely tailored dresses in favor of a simple beige pantsuit and a maroon crewneck sweater, which she took with her behind the changing screen.

Wow, Jenny silently mouthed to the nouveau-styled water lilies on the back of the changing screen's dark panels.

Kathryn's stage persona had vanished before her eyes, but the subtle hint of her musky perfume remained. Jenny could almost feel the woman's long leg in her hands again. Her body basked in the memory and responded with a warm rush to all the appropriate places. She closed her eyes, as the original intent of the evening disappeared in a hedonistic blur of primal trickery. She laid her hands across her stomach, wishing the arousal away, but that made it worse, as her body's indiscriminate need for touch at that moment took what it could get.

She chastised herself for reducing Kathryn to a sex object, but, honestly, *Come up to my room while I slip into something more comfortable?* She shook her head and tried to find a modicum of professionalism, but that effort vanished when a pair of black hose, welts first, came floating over the top edge of the screen and settled there like an open invitation. Jenny all but bit her knuckle to stop from whimpering.

"Say, could you—" Kathryn said, as she appeared from behind the screen, struggling with the zipper behind her back.

"Sure," Jenny said, springing from the chair a little too eagerly.

"Thank you," Kathryn said with a frustrated exhale as she placed a hand on her chest to hold up the dress. "I swear, if a man designs a dress, you can bet he'll put the zipper in the most inconvenient place just so he can help you out of it later."

"The swine," Jenny said in mock indignation as she tried not to notice the lack of undergarments on the delicate valley of bare skin she'd just uncovered.

Kathryn thanked her again and began shrugging out of the dress before she stepped behind the screen. When the dress appeared over the top of the screen, Jenny purposely looked away, taking in the small room as a distraction from the naked body hidden from her sight.

She found the space a curious mix of eras and styles. She liked the comfortable looking club chair next to the vanity, with its deep rust colored velvet and exaggerated flared arms that tapered into gentle rolls at the ends. It reminded her of a queen's throne, and she imagined Kathryn looking quite regal indeed wearing the delicate flowered robe found neatly folded over the chair's back. She also imagined her with one leg carelessly flung over the arm while they discussed their burgeoning friendship, the move clearly a tease.

Jenny swallowed and moved on to something less likely to ignite her vivid imagination. The horseshoe-shaped Art Deco vanity in dark mahogany, with its oversized rounded mirror and mismatched white leather cushioned seat, seemed like a safe bet. Neatly organized makeup essentials dotted its surface, a stark contrast to the haphazard mess of her own vanity. It made her feel like an undisciplined high schooler, and she looked away. Her gaze fell on the bed beside her.

It was just a twin mattress and box spring pushed into the corner, but its damask coverlet and collection of decorative throw pillows piled high into the far corner made it look more like the setting for a Goya painting, with Kathryn filling in as *The Naked Maja*, a reclining nude with her arms flung over her head in entreaty. Jenny closed her eyes, begging her rusty libido to have mercy on her.

"This room is eclectic," she said.

Kathryn stuck her head above the screen and took stock of the room, as if she'd never noticed the contents. "Kind of a catchall for orphan furniture from the club and the hotel upstairs, I imagine."

"You don't live here?"

"No, but it'll do in a pinch."

"Find yourself in a pinch often?" Jenny asked, envisioning Forrester as a nightly supporting player in that Goya painting.

"More often than I'd like, I'm afraid," Kathryn said.

The solemn reply made Jenny regret the contempt behind her question. She was judging again, and as Kathryn had said, she hadn't any right to. Everyone has a story, and Kathryn's was still untold. Something Jenny intended to remedy.

"Thank you again for doing this," she said.

No reply came from behind the screen.

"Introducing me to Forrester, I mean."

Kathryn made a small noise of recognition as she pulled the sweater over her head.

"I was a real stinker," Jenny went on, "and you've been so graceful about it. I really don't deserve it after last night."

Kathryn stepped out from behind the screen and zipped up the side zipper of her slacks with a concerned look on her face. "Say, what gives? I thought we were starting over?"

"Well, since we're friends now, I feel it's only fair to let you know I'm headstrong and opinionated."

Kathryn raised her brow. "You don't say?"

Jenny smiled, glad Kathryn was so good natured, but a sudden surge of emotion had her on the verge of tears. Her father used to call her headstrong and opinionated and she, in turn, would quip *I wonder where I got that from?* He would feign consternation to save face, but it always gave way to laughter and a hug. What she wouldn't give for one more laugh and a hug. The memory caught her off guard, but it was hardly a rare occurrence. Swells of grief assailed her at the oddest moments, tightening her throat and blurring her vision with unshed tears. The feeling usually subsided before the first tear fell, but it never failed to leave a trail of guilt-laden breadcrumbs back to her father's death and her part in it.

She bowed her head to hide her red-rimmed eyes and found Kathryn's hand on her knee as she sat on the end of the bed.

"Oh, you're not so bad," Kathryn said with a gentle squeeze. "A few salty words and a belly full of attitude? Why, this country was founded on it."

Jenny wanted to take Kathryn's hand in hers for being so kind, but it was gone before she could act on the impulse.

"Frankly," Kathryn said, as she rose and moved to the vanity seat, "you've got to kick in some doors to get what you want sometimes."

"Are you always this accommodating to perfect strangers?"

Kathryn picked up a lipstick and smiled at Jenny from the mirror before turning to face her. "How many female reporters are there in this city?"

"Not enough."

"Right. So, if I can help a sister out and do something to even that score, I will. It's as simple as that, and to answer your question, no, I shun more strangers than I accommodate. So much so that some people have actually called me coldhearted. Can you imagine?"

Jenny was ready to take on anyone who thought that but merely smiled. "Jealousy, pure and simple."

"My thoughts exactly," Kathryn said and turned back to the mirror to apply her lipstick.

Jenny liked this side of Kathryn. She exuded confidence without arrogance and empathy without pity. She listened and respected her goals, unlike her uncle, who treated every suggestion like a hair-brained scheme just two moves shy of disaster.

She felt comfortable in Kathryn's presence now, and it allowed her to consider again her unlikely ascent to The Grotto's A-list.

"You were pretty sure I'd come back here tonight. Am I that transparent?"

Kathryn chuckled instead of answering, and Jenny slumped in disappointment at her own predictability.

"You seemed like the determined type," Kathryn clarified with a grin.

"Is that a compliment?"

Kathryn looked at her from the mirror as she capped her lipstick. "I dunno ... is that a compliment?"

Jenny smiled. "I've been told it is one of my greatest assets."

Kathryn pressed a smile between a folded tissue as she blotted her lipstick, but in doing so, Jenny swore she also glanced at her breasts, silently declaring them the clear victors in the greatest asset department.

Jenny blushed and then realized wishful thinking was clouding rational thought. Kathryn went on applying her makeup without looking her way again.

She dipped her mascara brush in a glass of water, dragged it across the dark cake, and stroked the color onto her lashes before fixing her lipstick with powder and then finishing with the slightest hint of rouge on her cheeks. Her movements were smooth but impatient, like the routine was keeping her from more important things.

Jenny should have seen her interview with Forrester as an important thing—as *the* important thing—but at that moment, she was perfectly happy to indulge in some Kathryn Hammond-induced navel-gazing.

Long after Forrester was put away and forgotten, would they still be friends? Or would this evening drift quietly onto the pile of lost opportunities bemoaned to friends after too many drinks?

Did I ever tell you about that woman? Jenny would begin.

Yes! all her friends would say in unison and then shake their heads as she went on with the story anyway.

Fortunately, Jenny caught sight of her stupid grin in the mirror and suppressed it when Kathryn stood and slipped into her suit jacket.

"Very handsome," Jenny said, admiring Kathryn's casual elegance. "I feel woefully overdressed."

"Oh, he'll love it," Kathryn said, as she pulled her dark hair back and corralled it with a large barrette at the nape of her neck. "I know I do." She picked up her purse. "Ready?"

Jenny nodded and beamed at the compliment as she followed Kathryn to the door.

Kathryn lifted her coat from the hook on the back of the door. "Do you have a coat up front?"

"I have a wrap."

"Good heavens, woman, it's March, and it's supposed to rain." Kathryn offered her coat. "Here."

"No, really. I'll be fine."

Kathryn rolled her eyes and settled the coat over Jenny's bare shoulders. "The things we do to look gorgeous."

Jenny smiled and basked in the glow of two compliments in the span of thirty seconds.

They wound their way down the spiral staircase, and when Jenny reached the bottom, she turned left, toward the club, only to find her trailing hand captured by Kathryn's as she tugged her in the opposite direction.

"This way, before Dominic sees me in slacks," Kathryn said. She let go of Jenny's hand to point toward the exit door leading to the alley.

"He doesn't approve?"

Kathryn chuckled. "Most definitely not."

"A bit chauvinistic, don't you think?"

"He's protecting the club's image. Heaven forbid I appear mortal to the paying clientele."

"Well, it is a crime against nature to cover up such lovely appendages."

Kathryn raised a brow as they strode side by side. "Et tu, Brute?"

Jenny lifted her hands in surrender. "Hey, if it's good enough for Kate Hepburn, it's good enough for me."

"Oh, don't you just love her? Mmph, redheads," Kathryn said, as she threw her shoulder into the heavy door and forced it open. A cold blast of damp night air met them as they stepped out of the club and into the alley. Jenny was happy to have the coat.

"Do you live in the city?" Kathryn asked, as they descended the stairs.

"No, Riverdale."

"Say, you've come a long way on the assumption I'd help you tonight."

Jenny smiled. She felt confident in Kathryn's mutual attraction, so she threw caution to the wind. "Actually, I was going to seduce you until I had you under my spell. And once that happens, well ... you'd have no choice but to obey my every command."

Kathryn stopped abruptly on the stairs and, with a steadying hand on the steel railing, looked over her shoulder. "When does *that* start?"

Jenny almost crashed into her. "I'm sorry. That was terribly forward of me."

Kathryn laughed. "Actually, I was just thinking that I capitulated too soon and I'm going to miss out on what would have been a very interesting evening."

"The night is still young."

Kathryn smirked dismissively and continued down the stairs. "Don't start something you won't finish, Jenny."

Jenny couldn't tell if it was a warning or a challenge, but she was up for either. She put a hand on her hip. "What makes you think I won't finish, Kat?"

Kathryn turned to face her with a predatory glare that shocked Jenny into questioning whether she could, indeed, finish what she'd started. Kathryn climbed the distance between them until she stood one step below and they were eye to eye. Jenny suddenly found it hard to breathe. She was drowning in a physical rush of sexual intensity meant to devour her mercilessly. She almost fell backwards, but Kathryn took hold of her bicep to steady her. Then something changed.

Kathryn's gaze softened, as did her grip on her arm. The predator vanished and Jenny saw something familiar—*someone* familiar, someone searching, and longing, and then, instantly aware that their search was over, someone confused by emotions they had no idea how to process.

The rest of the world fell away until all Jenny heard was her own labored breathing. Kathryn's lips parted, and Jenny swore she was leaning in to kiss her but, instead, she grimaced and blinked up to the heavens as raindrops started to fall.

Kathryn offered her hand. "Here, careful."

Jenny gathered up her dress and then took the offered hand, which led her beneath the awning over the kitchen back door and out of the weather.

"Stay here. I'll get the car," Kathryn said, before she disappeared into the darkness of the alley.

CHAPTER NINE

a conversational void between the two women made the ride out to Forrester's Long Island estate awkward. Jenny stared blindly through the rain-pelted windshield as a watery canvas of the evening's shimmering lights appeared and disappeared between every whoosh of the blue two-door coupe's wiper blades.

She played Kathryn's lean in to kiss her over and over in her mind, and for a change, Jenny didn't know what to say. She thought it was just more harmless flirting, but the longing in Kathryn's eyes denied it and startled her in its intensity. Judging from Kathryn's silence, it startled her too.

At any moment, Jenny expected an amused grin from her driver, signaling she'd been had, but it never came, and she couldn't stand the tension any longer.

"Wow," she began, "this weather is awful, isn't it?"

"Mm," Kathryn said, her eyes focused on the road ahead.

Jenny cringed internally. Some conversation starter. The silence grew heavier until the groan of the wiper blades became a metronome of cowardice, each swipe condemning her inaction. *Confront her*, she kept saying in her head, but she couldn't, for fear

Kathryn would deny anything happened, and then what could she say?

Deflated, Jenny put her hands into the pockets of Kathryn's borrowed coat. Her hand met with some small, cold cylindrical objects in the bottom of the pocket, and she frowned. She recognized the shape. A quick look at one confirmed it was a round of ammunition. She returned the object to the pocket and cast a furtive glance at her companion. Kathryn was concentrating on the slick road ahead, and for the first time, Jenny felt uneasy about her grand scheme.

She'd never considered the dangers of confronting Forrester. There was a wrong that needed righting, and she blindly threw herself headlong into the task.

If she had just taken the time to look at the big picture, she would have seen the obvious threat her accusations would pose to the likes of Marcus Forrester.

Suddenly, her special treatment at the club and Kathryn's flirting made sense; it was all an elaborate plan to facilitate her demise. Panic set in. They were on a dark and deserted road somewhere on Long Island, with no help to be found. Fear for her life gripped her and quickly replaced all other thoughts as she looked at her driver anew.

Jenny realized she didn't know anything about Kathryn Hammond except that she was easy on the eyes and irresistible when she wanted to be. She was a lethal honey pot for either gender—the perfect trap for Forrester's enemies.

After threatening to expose Forrester, Jenny knew she was one of those enemies now, and who better to neutralize that enemy than the man's disarmingly attractive girlfriend? Kathryn most assuredly had a gun to go with those rounds, and why not drive out to a deserted spot on Long Island and use that gun to get rid of the threat. Murdered by proxy, just like her father.

No one saw them leave out the back door of the club. The rain would cleanse the scene of the crime, and when the police stopped by to question her, Kathryn would feign shock, maybe even manufacture a tear or two as she put her hand over her heart. "Why, that's just *awful!* So pretty. So young. Who would do such a thing? Have you any clues?"

Jenny swallowed hard to calm her pounding heart. Her imagination was spinning out of control, and every scenario ended badly for her. How could she have been so stupid? Her uncle warned her to stay away from Forrester, but her juvenile attraction to his gun-toting moll led her straight into the lion's jaws.

She took a deep breath and steeled her nerves. She talked her way into this situation; she could talk her way out.

"Say, Kat," she began and then cleared her throat when anxiety strangled her voice into a childlike squeak. "The weather seems to be getting worse. Maybe we should forget all this and call it a night."

Kathryn strained to see the road. "We're almost there." She squinted harder. "I wish these blades went faster. Can't see—"

She didn't finish her sentence.

Jenny looked out the windshield. She saw shimmering lights, and then, with a swipe of the wiper blades, headlights. Headlights in their lane.

"Kat—"

"I see them."

Jenny braced herself. "Kathryn—"

Kathryn pumped the brakes to slow down as quickly as she could on the rain-slicked highway, but whichever way she swerved, the other car seemed determined to meet them head on. The car was on them fast, and in a flash, Jenny was pressed into her seat by Kathryn's protective arm across her body.

Kathryn yanked the wheel at the last moment, which avoided a direct impact, but a glancing blow sent the car into an uncontrollable spin. It hit the muddy sod of the shoulder with successive thuds and came to a violent halt on its side at the bottom of a watery ditch.

Kathryn was in complete darkness and momentarily disoriented. A sorrowful hiss emanated from her dead car, and the rain drummed a staccato rhythm on its corpse. Cold water pooled at her back and warm water dripped on her forehead. The driver's side door was now the floor, and she was nearly upside down on her back, with the armrest pressing into her spine and the window crank stabbing her in the ribs. Something heavy was on top of her, wedged between her hip and the back of the front seat. It pressed her forward and jammed her left shoulder between the steering wheel and the door. She fumbled along the dashboard and found the interior light knob. She hoped the battery was still connected. Nothing happened when she switched it on and off.

She reached out blindly to the pain in her thigh and found Jenny's knee digging into her. "Jenny? Are you okay?"

Jenny didn't respond.

Kathryn tried to move, but she was pinned down by Jenny's weight and the immobile steering wheel. Broken glass crunched beneath her shoulder blades when she tried to slide out from under the wheel, and she had a moment of claustrophobic panic when she couldn't free herself. Cold water from the bottom of the ditch caused an involuntary gasp when it reached the bare skin of her neck. More involuntary gasps followed, this time from panic, when the water continued to rise, enveloping her shoulders.

Fear of drowning in a rain-filled ditch drove her into a brief burst of frantic struggling, but it didn't help, and she knew from experience that panicking would not save her. She had to think, and quickly. Fighting every instinct to continue struggling, she took a deep, purposeful breath and stilled herself to take clear stock of her situation.

The water leveled off, sparing her a death by drowning, but she wasn't out of danger. Someone purposely ran them off the road, and whatever their intentions, they could be back at any moment to finish the job.

Kathryn remained calm, but the infernal dripping on her forehead was like Chinese water torture. She wiped her forehead with the back of her hand and could tell by the viscosity and the smell that it wasn't water. It was blood. Her heart raced. *Jenny*.

Intense light suddenly filled the interior when a pair of headlights appeared in front of the car. Kathryn could see Jenny now, suspended above her, arm tangled in the spokes of the steering wheel. Her cheek was pressed against the top of the wheel like someone napping on a very uncomfortable pillow. Blood dripped from her nose, and a glance just beyond her shoulder revealed a broken passenger side windshield. At first, Kathryn thought Jenny had hit her head there, but a single beam of light shining clearly through the center of the damage in the windshield told a different story. She focused hard on the hole in disbelief. It was a bullet hole.

Kathryn's senses immediately heightened. Was Jenny hit? Panic returned. "No, no, no, no," she pleaded, as she reached up and touched Jenny's face. "Hey ..."

Shadows moved before the headlights, and Kathryn made an adrenaline-induced lunge for the snub-nosed revolver she kept secured under the dashboard. She strained against the steering wheel, but it held her back, leaving the gun just out of the reach of her outstretched fingers. Ignoring the broken glass digging into her shoulder, she slid further under the dashboard and knocked the gun from its stiff metal clip with her knee. It tumbled down her body and landed with a splash next to her ear.

Someone climbed onto the car, and she managed to retrieve the gun just as the passenger door above her flew open. Cold rain poured in and then a flashlight blinded her.

"Christ," a man said.

"Jeez, lady. Are you all right?" a second man bellowed from beside her. Kathryn turned her head toward the face peering at her through her side of the split windshield and held up her hand to block the assault of rain, blood, and light from above. She could see a middle-aged face of a man who looked appropriately concerned, rather than malicious, but when the man above shouted, "She's not alone!" the man beside her was clearly shocked and then alarmed. He turned on a flashlight to illuminate Jenny, wrapped around the steering wheel.

The man cursed from above as another car approached from behind.

Kathryn looked up in time to see a gun hanging from a shoulder holster beneath the coat of the man above her. She tightened her grip on the gun concealed at her side, but the men shut off their flashlights and ran back to their car before she had a chance to use it.

Against the bright headlights from the rear car, Kathryn could see a lone figure in silhouette running toward her, a flashlight waving wildly with each stride. She felt helpless trapped on her back, and it infuriated her. She couldn't help Jenny, and she couldn't fend off trouble if she couldn't free herself. She struggled for a better position, but Jenny's body weight shifted, causing a shooting pain in her twisted back and down her leg.

The newcomer climbed onto her car, and in pain and frustration, Kathryn aimed the gun at the opening above her, prepared to shoot and ask questions later.

"Kathryn!" Smitty's voice boomed through the open door.

"Oh, thank God," Kathryn said, as she loosened her grip on the gun and slumped down into the water.

"Are you all right?" Smitty asked anxiously, as he leaned into the opening with his flashlight. "Kathryn, you're bleeding!"

"It's not mine," she said, wincing in pain. "Lift her off me, Smitty, will ya? Be careful, she's hurt."

Smitty eased a leg inside the passenger compartment, bracing one foot on the transmission mound under the dashboard and the other between the split front seat cushion. He slid his hands under Jenny's arms and gently lifted her up until he cradled her in his lap.

Kathryn moaned in relief as she slid back in her seat and relieved the pressure on her back. She wiggled out from under the steering wheel and untangled her long legs from the handbrake and gearshift.

She struggled to her feet and dropped her revolver in her jacket pocket. "Is she okay?"

"I don't know about okay, but she's still breathing."

Kathryn grabbed the flashlight from his pocket and anxiously swept it across Jenny's face and head. The nosebleed had stopped and there was no bullet wound. She quickly separated the dark coat covering Jenny's chest. She was met with clean, bare shoulders and an unspoiled green dress. Her knees nearly buckled in relief.

"Say, there'll be time for that later," Smitty joked.

Kathryn gently checked Jenny's head for any other signs of trauma. "Someone shot at us." She found a considerable lump on the side of her head and a small splatter of blood on her face. She felt nauseated.

Smitty eyed the hole in the windshield. "Son of a bitch!" He craned his head up out of the open door and stared daggers down the road toward the fleeing car. "Was it them?"

"They were packing heaters," Kathryn said, as another spatter of blood appeared on Jenny's cheek and then washed away in the rain.

"What the—" Smitty took his flashlight back. "Kathryn, your head!"

The moment he said it, Kathryn felt the throbbing pain over her left eye, followed by ringing in her ears and the immediate urge to throw up, or pass out, or both.

Smitty offered a steadying hand on her elbow. "Easy, gal."

She took a deep breath and grabbed his arm until the ringing in her ears subsided.

He reached into his pocket and handed her his handkerchief. "Here."

She wiped the blood from her eye just as Jenny stirred.

It was black. Then streaks of light were coming toward her. Jenny panicked, afraid she'd fallen asleep at the wheel. The lights stopped moving, and shadowy figures came into focus. They hovered above her with hushed voices. She slowly became aware of her surroundings. It was raining. Her head hurt. She smelled earthen dampness, sweetened by Kathryn's perfume, and something metallic. A soothing voice floated down to her, one she recognized as Kathryn's, but in a soft, gentle tone she'd never heard before.

"Hey ... there you are," Kathryn said. "Welcome back. I was about to do the look, listen, and feel on you."

"Ugh," Jenny groaned with a wince and wondered why Kathryn Hammond was spouting nursing jargon at her. "That sounds like fun.

Can I have a rain check on that?" She looked up and blinked as the rain dripped on her head. "No pun intended."

"Are you all right? Can you move?"

Jenny wiggled her fingers and toes and pronounced herself in one piece. Only then did she realize she was in the arms of a stranger. "Oh, hi," she said. "Handsome man, beautiful woman, this must be my lucky night."

Kathryn laughed. "You have no idea."

Jenny sniffed and tasted blood in the back of her throat. She wiped blood from her upper lip and looked to Kathryn to confirm the obvious.

"You had a bloody nose."

Jenny rubbed the side of her head. "Ow. What happened?"

"You don't remember?"

Jenny took in their absurd position in the upended car and it all came back to her. "Some drunken jackass ran us off the road!"

"There you go," Kathryn said with a grin. She straightened, rising above the shadow of the car's interior and into the beam of the rear car's headlights.

Jenny saw a blur of red and beige and nearly fell out of the man's arms when she grabbed Kathryn by the shoulders. She forgot all about the pounding in her head.

"Oh my God, Kathryn, you're hurt!" Blood streaked down the whole left side of her face and neck, soaking into her suit. Jenny turned to the stranger and said, "We need to get her to a hospital."

"I agree," he said.

Their evening was ending a lot like it began: with fireworks and then a car ride in contemplative silence. Jenny found it ridiculous that Kathryn made her lie down in the backseat of the car on the way to the hospital when Kathryn was the one bleeding all over herself. Not that she didn't enjoy using Kathryn's lap as a pillow, but not under these circumstances.

Jenny protested her prone position emphatically, and often, until Kathryn finally placed her hand on her forehead. "Please stop."

Jenny couldn't argue with the misery in her voice, so she conceded the argument, and her position, and remained silent.

Kathryn was soaked to the bone, and even wrapped in a blanket their Good Samaritan had supplied from his trunk, she was shivering. Her wound was still bleeding, and halfway to the hospital, she tossed the blood-soaked handkerchief to the floor in disgust and pressed her sleeve to her forehead. Jenny knew she was mad—who wouldn't be? Some jerk ran them off the road, wrecked her car, ruined her suit, and scarred her beautiful face for life. No good deed goes unpunished, and Kathryn was getting it in spades. Jenny felt terrible. Kathryn was doing her a favor, and the smelly end of the stick was her reward.

Jenny reached into her purse and produced a fresh handkerchief, which she tucked into Kathryn's hand. Kathryn accepted it in silence, passed it to her other hand, and pressed it above her eye as she leaned her head against the cold window glass and shut her eyes.

It looked like it was all she could do not to be sick, and Jenny didn't blame her for the silence. She did the only thing she could think of to comfort her: she held her hand. Kathryn didn't respond immediately, and Jenny felt awkward, wondering if she'd been presumptuous, but after a few minutes, Kathryn tightened her grip and didn't loosen it until they reached the hospital.

Jenny burst into the hospital barking orders like a field nurse. "We need a doctor and a warm blanket over here ... hurry!"

The busy emergency staff offered cursory glances, but three adults walking in under their own power would wait their turn. "Have a seat, be right with you," said a passing orderly holding out a fresh blanket to Kathryn from the pile in his arms.

That wasn't good enough for Jenny. She fine-tuned her attack and blasted the first target in her sight: a young woman in a pink volunteer's smock delivering cups of coffee on a tray. "You there!" She pointed at her. "What do I have to do to get a doctor around here?"

"Can I help you?" the woman standing behind the admitting desk called out, rescuing the startled volunteer.

"Yes. Finally." Jenny headed over. "This woman needs a doctor."

"Everyone here needs a doctor, honey," the woman said drolly. "Fill out these forms and take a seat." She slid two clipboards over the counter and placed a pencil on each.

Jenny raised her brow at the clerk's lack of urgency. "Do you know who this woman is? If anything happens to her, you're going to have to answer to—"

"Easy there, tiger," Kathryn interrupted, as she put her hands on Jenny's shoulders from behind. She didn't know what Jenny was about to say, but she didn't want it broadcast throughout the waiting room. "I think she's got a concussion," Kathryn said to the clerk by way of an apology.

"You don't look so red hot yourself," the woman said, looking her up and down.

"I'm fine."

Jenny turned to Kathryn in disbelief. "Clearly, you're not."

"Jenny," Kathryn said, as she put her hand on Jenny's cheek to calm her, "we need to fill out these forms and wait our turn. Okay?"

Jenny took a deep breath, blew it out, and then nodded. "Sorry," she said to Kathryn, and then she apologized to the admissions clerk and the volunteer who just arrived with a cup of coffee.

They sat in silence while they waited their turn, and after an orderly led Jenny to an examining room, Kathryn and Smitty just shook their heads.

"Wow," Smitty said, as he leaned forward, elbows on his knees and hat in hand. "She's a handful."

Kathryn exhaled and rested her head back against the wall. Now that the crisis was over and Jenny was out of sight, she felt lightheaded.

"Are you okay?" Smitty asked. "Do you feel sick?"

Kathryn leaned forward again, unable to get comfortable. "A little."

Smitty rubbed her back. "You did really well, tonight, honey. Really well. I didn't think you were going to keep it together on the ride in here."

"I nearly didn't." And then Jenny took her hand and everything went still.

Thoughts of Jenny led to thoughts of how much worse the outcome could have been. Someone was incompetent in their murder attempt, and they were just lucky to survive relatively unscathed. The logical question was who, and why, and she knew her partner started working on the solution the moment she said *Someone shot at us.*

"Forrester?" Smitty asked after a long silence. "Do you think he's onto you?"

"No. Not his style. If he wanted me gone, he'd tell me to my face just so he could see the look in my eyes."

"One of Forrester's enemies then, or maybe someone after the kid?"

Kathryn shook her head. "Enemies wouldn't dare, and those men seemed pretty upset that someone else was in the car."

Smitty thought a moment and then frowned. "Paul?"

Kathryn agreed. "Paul."

CHAPTER TEN

*J*enny sat on the edge of the hospital bed while her Aunt Betsy and Uncle Paul bickered in harsh whispers just outside her door. She didn't know what they had argued about on the way over, but the reprieve their concern brought when they first arrived quickly vanished when they saw she was all right.

She had a concussion, her second in as many months, which was news to her aunt. Her uncle was getting an earful from his wife for not telling her about the first one, sustained when she fell off the roof of the taxi at the courthouse. Jenny had insisted he not say anything, but it didn't save him.

When her aunt said, "I'm tired of the sneaking around and your lies, Paul!" Jenny knew their problems were deep-rooted and nothing she could say would help. She curled into a ball on the bed, wishing she were in a dark, quiet room, so she could sleep for a week.

While accusations flew in the doorway, the doctor slipped in to check on her.

"How we doing here?" he asked sympathetically.

"I'm feeling a little nauseated right now," she said, as she hugged herself.

The doctor nodded. "That's to be expected."

The hissing and pointing in the doorway stopped, and her Aunt Betsy came to the bedside wearing a sweet smile, as if the last ten minutes of arguing hadn't happened.

"She can go home, right, doctor?"

The doctor gave Jenny a hesitant look. When she nodded, he said, "Yes, she can. But she needs quiet, Mrs. Ryan." He glanced over at Paul, who stared back blankly with his hands on his hips.

"Oh, don't you worry, doctor, it will be absolutely quiet," Betsy said. She gave Paul a pointed look and then turned to Jenny. "I'm taking you to your house, honey, and I'm going to stay with you for as long as the good doctor advises."

"Now, wait just a damn minute—" Paul began as he walked toward his wife.

Jenny sat up with a groan and then got out of bed. She gathered her purse and Kathryn's coat and, on her doctor's arm, walked quietly past her arguing relatives.

"Don't hesitate to call if you have any problems," the doctor said. "Vision, headaches, disorientation ..." He paused and looked back to the relatives. "Irritability."

Jenny chuckled.

"I'm going to instruct your aunt to wake you every few hours this first night, so try and get as much rest as you can." The doctor's voice was soothing while, behind her, her aunt's shrill voice was about to deliver her finishing blow.

Paul leaned closer to his wife and issued his final command. "I want her to be with *us*, in *our* house tonight."

"Paul ..." Betsy leaned in and annunciated her words carefully. "*I* am calling a cab. I am taking her home to *her* house, and you ..." she stuck a finger in his puffed-out chest, "can take what *you* want and stick it right up your bottom!" She grabbed her handbag from the bed and walked triumphantly out the door toward the nurse's station to use the phone.

"Sorry you had to witness that," Jenny said to the doctor.

"You wouldn't believe what we see here," he said. "Crisis either brings out the best or the worst in people."

Jenny recognized her own lack of grace under pressure when they first arrived at the hospital. It resembled her uncle's display, and she made a mental note to add it to the list of character flaws she needed to correct.

The doctor patted her arm. "Call if you have any problems."

"I will," Jenny said. "Thank you."

No sooner had the doctor stepped away than she heard heavy, determined footsteps coming toward her from behind. It was her uncle, she knew, and she took a breath before turning to get it over with.

"Uncle Paul," she said, looking as pitiful as she could. She expected to see anger, but instead, her uncle had tears in his eyes and he enveloped her in a warm hug, rocking her slowly.

"I'm so glad you're okay," he said softly.

She hugged him back, thankful for the unexpected comfort. He was a tall man, like her father, but with a middle-aged paunch her father didn't live long enough to acquire. Her uncle was the exact opposite of her father in temperament, so the rare quiet moment of paternal love became an instant shrine to all the moments stolen from her upon her father's death. She lingered in her bittersweet memories until her uncle gave her a final squeeze and backed off slightly to look into her eyes.

"I'm okay," she said, rubbing his arm.

He put a hand under her chin. "I know you are."

He didn't ask where she'd been or what had happened; he just kissed her forehead and told her to take care of herself and he'd call her in the morning. She watched him walk down the hall, where he wiped his eyes and blew his nose into his handkerchief.

Her aunt arrived, took the coat from her hands, and draped it over her bare shoulders. "Are you ready, dear?"

"Almost," Jenny said. "I need to check on someone." She went to the nurse's station to inquire about Kathryn and was met with the standard "we can't give out that information unless you are a family member" speech. She leaned on the counter and propped her head on her hand. Her headache was getting worse, but she didn't want to leave without making sure Kathryn was all right. "Please, the woman saved my life. I just want to know if she's all right." She must have looked pretty pathetic, because the nurse gave a conspiratorial glance both ways down the hallway before she spoke. "What's her name, sweetie?"

"Kathryn Hammond."

"Hammond ... Hammond ..." The nurse riffled through the paperwork behind the counter. "Are you sure she came in here?"

"Yes."

"I don't see her here."

Jenny furrowed her brow.

"I'm sure she's fine," her aunt said, as she urged her away from the counter and toward the exit. "Cab's waiting. You can call your friend tomorrow."

Her head was throbbing, her aunt was trying to lead her away from the counter, and everything was getting a little fuzzy. They'd only taken a few steps when an orderly handed the nurse a folder.

"Oh, Hammond. Here we go." The nurse scanned the chart. "Treated and released. She's fine."

"See, honey," her aunt said, "your friend is fine." As they turned away from the counter and headed for the exit, she looked Jenny up and down. "You look very chic tonight, dear."

Jenny looked down at her wet, muddy dress.

Her aunt picked at a clean spot on the fabric. "I'm afraid that's ruined. Shame. One of my favorites."

Jenny agreed with a disappointed sigh. "Mine too."

Her aunt put her arm around her shoulder and gave her a squeeze. "Maybe I can make you a decent blouse out of it," she said, as she eyed the dress for yardage.

Jenny took stock of the ruined garment and snorted. "It's cut on the bias, Aunt B. You'll be lucky to get a scarf out of it."

"Oh ye of little faith," her aunt said. "I'm going to try. There's a war on, you know."

"Oh, is there?" Jenny joked through her aching head.

As they walked down the hallway, Jenny peeked into every

doorway they passed, looking for Kathryn. She should have known it wouldn't go unnoticed.

"Is she a friend? Or a *friend*?" Her aunt asked.

Jenny smiled. Her aunt was anything but subtle and not at all shy about interrogating her about her love life. As a teen, unable to hide the truth from the grand inquisitor forever, Jenny attempted to shock her aunt into minding her own business by revealing her sexual preference. Her aunt was not surprised, or shocked, and went on with her questions as if nothing had changed between them. Nothing *had* changed between them, and Jenny was grateful for the unconditional love, but she never got used to her aunt's shameless curiosity about her love interests.

"I'm not sure. I just met her."

"Well, I'm here if you need to talk about it."

Jenny smiled and put her arm around her aunt's waist. "I know."

As they left the hospital, Jenny swore she heard her uncle's booming voice coming from one of the many hallways. She turned to look, but her aunt urged her on and into the waiting cab.

CHAPTER ELEVEN

"There you go. Good as new," the doctor said, as he finished tying up the last stitch above Kathryn's left eyebrow. "Looks like some broken glass caught you right on the brow line. It's a clean cut, so you shouldn't see the scar."

"I don't have lines on my brow, doctor," Kathryn said in mock annoyance from her prone position on the examining table.

Smitty laughed. "You do now."

"I'll give you lines, Smitty," she said, poking him in the thigh. The doctor taped a small gauze patch over the wound and then smiled as he patted her on the shoulder. "I think it's safe to get up now."

"Thanks, doc."

She groaned as she raised herself up slowly. She was already queasy from all the blood, so to avoid the embarrassment of fainting to the floor, she received her stitches lying down.

"Okay," the doctor said, as he scribbled on her chart. "No concussion, just the cut above your eye and some abrasions on your shoulder blades."

Kathryn cut her eyes to the shredded back of her soggy suit jacket, lying beside her on the exam table.

"Here's your appointment to get those stitches out," the doctor went on. He handed her a card and capped his fountain pen. "Call the office if you have any problems or questions."

"Will do," she said, tucking the card into her pocket.

When the doctor left the room, Kathryn exhaled a breath and her perfect posture along with it. It was just her and Smitty now, and she didn't have to prove anything to him. She loved these moments when she could just be herself, and then she loathed these moments because she would just be herself.

Smitty looked toward the doorway as a sudden movement down the hallway caught his eye. "Uh-oh," he said, as a determined Paul Ryan headed their way. "Buck up, Kat. Here comes trouble."

Kathryn looked over her shoulder and sat up fully. She took a deep breath to gather her remaining energy and to mask the weariness she felt. The interesting shade of crimson on Paul's face told her he was furious, but he managed to civilly get out, "Are you all right?"

"Fine," Kathryn said. "How's your niece?"

"Fine, no thanks to you."

He looked like a teapot cover on the verge of a boil.

"Go ahead, Paul, before you rupture something."

"Just what in the *hell* were you doing? The only reason I let her go to that club was because you assured me Forrester wouldn't be there!"

"No, I said I would keep her away from him, and I did."

"And then you tried to bring her right to him! I told you to keep her away from Forrester!"

"You told us to keep her safe and get her off that story," Kathryn said, about to explain herself.

"*And*," Paul said at maximum volume, "how does bringing her right to him accomplish that?"

Kathryn rubbed her throbbing forehead. Once Paul's fuse was lit, there was no chance for rational discussion, but she would go through the motions anyway for the sake of her assignment.

"Look," she said, "you know her better than I do, Paul—"

"Damn right I do!" he interjected.

"But it seems to me," Kathryn continued, "she's a pretty determined young woman. She's not going to just give up because you or I say so. The best way to get her off that story is to show her there's nothing there to find. And if—"

"That was careless and stupid!" he said, cutting her off again.

"I'm neither careless nor stupid, Paul," she said, as her attempt at rational discussion evaporated. Enduring Paul Ryan's temper was the last straw in an evening that should have ended hours ago with a job well done.

"I don't want her anywhere near him!" he said.

"Oh, for crying out loud," Kathryn said, as she slid off the table, thankful that her legs held her up. "He doesn't know her from Eve. She's just some kid with a chip on her shoulder, scratching around in the dark, and if I had gotten to my destination tonight, this would all be over."

"As far as I'm concerned, it *is* over."

"You can't just bend her to your will, Paul!"

"Then bend her to yours! Just keep her out of this!"

"She wouldn't be *in* this if it weren't for you!"

Smitty lightly touched her back.

She ignored the warning. "None of this would be happening," she said, her patience at an end. "Her father would be alive, and she'd be a happy-go-lucky kid with no worry other than what color to paint her nails today. Instead she's—"

Paul suddenly had a death grip on her forearm, his face back to that lovely shade of crimson.

"Let go of my arm, Paul," she said through gritted teeth.

He didn't let go. The vise-like grip on her arm awakened an urge of self-protection, and it took considerable effort not to use her ample skills to free herself from the unwelcome grasp.

"Get your damn hand off me, or I swear—"

Smitty inserted an arm between them like a referee in a prize fight. "Okay, you two, ease up."

Paul relaxed his grip and Kathryn yanked her arm away as an orderly peeked his head in the door. "This is a hospital, folks, not a wrestling room. Keep it down or take it outside."

They all took that welcome break to collect themselves.

Smitty lifted an apologetic hand to the man. "Sorry."

Kathryn wasn't done. "For once, Paul," she said, "stay the hell out of our way."

Smitty glared at her, proffering another warning about her uncharacteristic outburst.

"Just ..." She paused and softened her voice to a more matter-of-fact tone. "Let us do what we need to do and trust our judgment. We know what we're doing."

Her softer tone did nothing to improve Paul's disposition. "Your judgment is for shit! You proved that tonight." He turned to Smitty. "Did you approve this?"

Smitty claimed innocence with raised hands.

Behind Paul's back, Kathryn responded with a disparaging eye roll.

"Dominic told me you people were top-notch," Paul said. "Now I'm not so sure." He turned back to Kathryn. "You just do what you do best, sweetheart; spread your legs for every Tom, Dick, and Harry that suits your purpose, but stop putting ideas into my niece's head."

"Stop putting—" She bit down hard to keep from saying something she'd regret.

"Honestly, John," Paul said, as he turned back to Smitty, "I recognize the perks of having this type of woman for an associate, but really, don't let her think for herself. Someone could get hurt."

Kathryn pursed her lips and narrowed her eyes, slowly cutting them to Smitty. She knew he would gladly sock the man in the jaw on her behalf, but they had a job to do, and, thankfully, he was behaving like the only adult in the room. She gritted her teeth and calmed her last raw nerve for just a little longer.

"Leave her to her silly songs and sexual favors," Paul went on. "From now on, I want you assigned to Jenny. Which is what I thought I was getting in the first place. And you," he said, offering a dismissive glance toward Kathryn, "well, I think I've made myself clear regarding any further participation by you in this matter."

"Yeah, crystal," Kathryn said, spoken like a true gangster's moll.

Paul's little pissing contest was so insignificant in the scheme of their larger assignment that Kathryn could barely contain a disparaging laugh. It was ridiculous, really. There was no protecting Jenny from Forrester if he had any interest in her, but he didn't, and he wouldn't, as long as Paul didn't do anything stupid.

Kathryn's goal of getting in and get out of Jenny Ryan's life without leaving a mark was evaporating quickly. Handling Jenny was one thing, but Paul on a rampage was beyond even Smitty's ability to contain. She had no doubt that the crash stemmed from Paul's meddling, but she knew Smitty wasn't so sure. With Paul's mindset and her mood, she knew that nothing productive would come from her presence there. She would leave the cleanup to Smitty.

"You boys work it out," she said, as she rubbed a kink out of her neck. "I'm going home." She tugged down her sleeve before sliding it into Smitty's coat. "Oh, and Paul, the next time you want to send me a message, try picking up the phone. Save the gunplay for the bad guys. You could have killed us both tonight."

Paul blinked at her. "Gunplay? I don't know what you're talking about."

"Well, there's a bullet hole in my windshield that says you probably do."

"A bullet hole? I don't know what you're talking about."

Kathryn was too tired to listen to his denial and too apathetic to wonder if it was genuine. She grabbed her bloody jacket from the table in disgust and issued a final statement as she headed toward the exit. "You owe me a new suit, and you're going to fix my car. The cut on my head and the bruise you just left on my arm, I'll treasure as reminders of just how dangerous you are."

"And don't you forget it!" he shouted at her back, oblivious to her insult.

"Meet you at the car, Smitty," she said over her shoulder without turning around.

"Be right there."

The two men watched her disappear down the hall, and then Paul pointed at Smitty. "You screwed this up, John," he said. "Guns?"

Smitty was on the short end of patience himself, but someone had to straighten this out. "Paul, I don't hire outside people to do my work, and I certainly don't send thugs without the brains God gave them to endanger people I'm trying to protect."

Paul seemed genuinely perplexed. "But I told you to keep Jenny from Forrester. I thought—"

"And I would have if your goons hadn't almost killed them!" Nothing made Smitty angrier than someone putting his partner in harm's way, but ever the diplomat, he remained levelheaded. "I appreciate your concern for your niece's safety, Paul, and I understand your apprehension with Kathryn's involvement, but she is right. We know what we're doing, and she's the right person to do it." He paused when he sensed a hint of doubt still lurking on the older man's face. "Besides, she saved your niece's life tonight. If someone is targeting Jenny, you couldn't have a more competent person watching her back." He paused for effect. "Honestly. She's good."

Paul rubbed his forehead, and Smitty could see his demeanor changing.

"She trusts Kathryn now," Smitty continued. "Just let us play this out. It'll be fine. I promise."

Paul exhaled and ran his hand through his thick salt-and-pepper hair. "I vehemently oppose Jenny coming into contact with Forrester."

"Noted."

"And as soon as I feel he's no longer a threat to her, we're finished. Right?"

"Right."

"Good." Paul paused. "I didn't have anything to do with those men tonight, John, I swear it."

"All right," Smitty said. "We'll keep our eyes open." He reached for his hat. "Please," he said, as he put a hand on Paul's shoulder. "Don't. Do. *Anything*. This is why you pay us."

A resigned nod was his reply.

As Smitty turned for the door, Paul reached for him. "Say, tell your partner I'm ... I'm sorry. I was upset." He paused. "And thank her, if you would, for doing her best to protect Jenny."

Smitty gave him a reassuring pat on the shoulder and allowed himself a proud smile. All quiet on the western front.

Kathryn went straight to the car and slumped down in the passenger seat. She closed her eyes and rested her head on the back of the seat. Her run-in with Paul didn't help her throbbing head, and she wanted nothing more than a warm bath and a good night's sleep. Unfortunately, the evening's events had turned a relatively simple information gathering assignment into a puzzling question of who done what and why.

She heard Smitty's uneven footsteps approaching the car, and she lamented the fact that they'd probably talk shop all the way home. Smitty slid into the driver's side and slammed the door.

Kathryn winced at the slamming door and then spoke before he could reprimand her. "Sorry about that in there," she said.

He had every right to be mad; she'd lost her temper all over an assignment, but instead of a reprimand, he put his hand on her shoulder. "Are you all right?"

He had a pitying look in his eyes that was all too familiar, and she sank further into the seat. "Oh, Smitty, don't look at me like that."

"I'm not looking at you like *that*," he said. "You're hurt, you're not yourself, and I'm concerned."

"Don't be."

"Kathryn, you don't make mistakes, and you don't get rattled, especially by a man like Paul Ryan. What gives?"

Smitty was right. She'd had a rough night, but she'd had worse. The man's insults were nothing new; in fact, convincing someone to the point of insults that she was someone she wasn't was a point of pride, like an actress validated with an Oscar for a brilliant performance.

"I'm sorry, Smitty. We're just so close to being done with him."

"Last mile home, honey?"

"Something like that. Won't happen again."

Smitty pressed his lips together in a grim smile and nodded.

"Any irreversible damage?" Kathryn asked.

Smitty started the car. "You're still on the kid."

Kathryn nodded.

"Oh, and Paul sends his apologies and his thanks."

Kathryn looked at him sideways. "I'm sure."

"No, he was quite sincere."

She raised her brow. "Wow, you're good."

He smiled his boyish grin and put the car in gear.

Smitty was always there for her, to clean up her messes, to save her life, to follow her on a dark road in the rain to make sure she reached her destination safely. To hear him tell it, it wasn't his job, it was his pleasure. She couldn't complain when he did things like show up out of nowhere to save her skin, but his devotion was a constant reminder of the dark past they suffered together, and she wanted more for him. Truth be told, she wanted more for herself. She exhaled and closed her eyes. She knew Smitty was thinking about the accident. She blamed Paul; he had his doubts.

"I smell sawdust," Kathryn said.

"I'm worried about Forrester."

She held up her pinkie. "Wrapped around my little finger."

"Beautiful women are a dime a dozen to men like Forrester, Kat. Don't be too sure he wouldn't rub you out in a second if it suited his purpose."

"Thanks, Smitty. You always know how to make a girl feel special."

"You know what I'm saying."

She did know, but she was sure of her place in Forrester's world. "I told you, won't happen. Trust me."

"Be careful," he said. "Arrogance has a way of making one careless."

"It's not arrogance if you know your subject matter." She lolled her head in his direction. "And I make it a point to know my subject matter."

Smitty shifted uncomfortably, and she knew he was thinking of her with Forrester.

"So," he drew out. "Just what *were* you thinking?"

"What?"

"Bringing the kid to Forrester."

She gave him a disbelieving glance. "You seriously think I'd do that?"

He responded with an unconvincing shake of his head. "Of course not."

"She's a bright girl," Kathryn said. "But she's got more nerve than sense. We know she's bluffing about having something on him, and without that, what could she possibly say to him? She was in over her head and she knew it. She wanted to turn around before we even got there."

"Don't you think you might have mentioned to Paul that you had no intentions of bringing his niece to Forrester?"

"Frankly, Smitty, I didn't hear anything after *careless and stupid*. Nuts to him. Let him stew."

Smitty smiled. "Forrester isn't even in town, is he?"

"Went upstate this afternoon. It's his wife's fiftieth birthday."

"Ah, the doting husband," Smitty said sarcastically. "So, what did you have planned at the estate?"

Kathryn grinned. "There's a note explaining Forrester's absence, I let the girl sniff around, she sees that I've tried to help her and that I'm on her side, and she sees that there's nothing to find at the estate. We have a few drinks, I press her about what she may have on him, she has to admit she's empty-handed, I impress upon her the dangerous game she's playing, and so on and so on ... and, well, before you know it, case closed."

"Just like that, hm?"

Kathryn smiled. "I can be very convincing."

Smitty shook his head at the understatement. "Why do I ever doubt you?"

Kathryn grinned. "I'm sure I don't know."

.   .   .

Smitty pulled alongside the curb in front of Kathryn's small Jane Street apartment in Greenwich Village and insisted on escorting her upstairs. He unlocked the outer door next to the heavy wooden garage door and told her to wait at the bottom of the stairs while he went up to her apartment. Once on the landing, he reached for the ever-present Colt 1911 in his shoulder holster and eased the door open.

Stealth was impossible due to the creaking floorboards of Kathryn's turn-of-the-century apartment, so he paused before stepping in. When he didn't hear anything, he pressed the light switch just inside the door and made a thorough sweep of the place.

"All clear," he called down, and heard her mumble, "Of course."

She entered her apartment and let her bloody suit jacket drop to the floor. Smitty handed her the key and she tossed it onto the low bookcase beside the door. She shed his overcoat and handed it to him, along with her thanks, and then she walked down the long hallway to the bathroom.

Smitty stepped over her discarded ruined shoes and leaned on the bathroom doorjamb as she sat on the edge of the tub with a groan.

"I'm going to stay on the couch tonight," he said. "Just to be sure."

"No one's going to try anything here, Smitty. This is Nicky's territory. There'd be hell to pay. Go home. I'll be fine."

The apartment belonged to Kathryn's boss, Dominic Vignelli, a powerful man with powerful friends, who felt he owed her a debt. He offered to let her live there for free, but she insisted on paying rent or she wouldn't take the apartment. He agreed to half the usual $35 a month and threw in a car she could use from the three vehicles stored end to end in the long garage below the apartment. That car was now in a ditch on Long Island.

"I don't like it, Kat."

"Why are you so sure it's Forrester?"

Smitty shrugged. "He's conveniently out of town at a very public event, so he has the perfect alibi, and using your reasoning about Dominic, you are Forrester's territory, so if something happened to you, by say, one of his enemies, he wouldn't hesitate to retaliate, which makes you pretty safe. The fact that someone did try to harm you points to him."

Kathryn opened her mouth to speak but was interrupted by the ringing telephone. She slipped past him and answered the call in the living room.

"Yes, darling, I'm fine," Smitty heard her say. She leaned into the hallway with her hand covering the mouthpiece and mouthed, *My executioner.*

Smitty smirked and crossed his arms. Kathryn went on in a soothing voice, assuring Marcus Forrester she was fine and it was just a silly accident. Listening to Kathryn talking to Forrester in such an intimate manner made his skin crawl.

"It wasn't him," she said after she hung up. "I think he started to cry when he heard my voice."

Smitty tried to protest, but Kathryn cut him off with a gentle touch to his arm.

"Honestly," she said. "I love you. Thank you for everything, but you need to go home. I need you to go home. I'll sleep with my gun close by. I promise."

Smitty reluctantly agreed and she hugged him, but someone tried to kill his girl, and he wasn't taking any chances. He spent the night in his car, strategically parked down the street for the best overall view of her apartment.

CHAPTER TWELVE

*J*enny stood at her kitchen window and watched her aunt and uncle argue on the dock beside the lake in her backyard. As per the doctor's instructions, her aunt stayed with her through the night and woke her every few hours.

Due to lack of sleep, neither woman was at her best in the morning, and pleasant breakfast conversation turned testy when her aunt touched every raw nerve available.

First came a well-meaning suggestion about her housekeeping skills. Her aunt was a notorious neat freak, and Jenny could never clean house to the woman's satisfaction, so, as usual, she accepted the suggestion gracefully through a fake smile and let her aunt ramble on about it. But when she casually said, "Why, your father's study had a year's worth of dust in it," a flash of panic ignited Jenny's short fuse.

She wanted to scream, "How dare you go into that room!" but instead she resorted to snark. "Dad's not here. I don't think he cares."

"Well, that's a fine thing to say, young lady."

Jenny rubbed her still aching head. She could feel her blood pressure rising behind her eyes and knew this was not going to go well.

"I know you don't like talking about your father, but that's no reason to be rude."

Jenny willed herself to keep silent before she said something else she'd regret. Her father was the last thing she wanted to discuss, but her aunt brought him up every time they were together.

Her aunt must have seen her distress because she exhaled a cleansing breath and relaxed her shoulders in defeat. "I'm being judgmental, aren't I?

Jenny bowed her head. "I'm doing the best I can."

Her aunt reached across the table and took her hand. "I know you are, honey. I'm sorry. You keep a beautiful house."

Jenny took what she could get, relieved that she'd dodged another conversation about her father.

"Now, this thing with your father ..."

Jenny pulled her hand away in exasperation. "I'm not doing this today."

"That accident was not your fault," her aunt persisted. "I don't know how many times we have to talk about it before—"

"*We're* not talking about it," Jenny said, as she pushed her chair back and stood. "*You* are, and I'm asking you, no, *begging* you, to please drop it! And I don't just mean today."

Her aunt slapped her palm on the table. "Don't give me that attitude, young lady. I can go home and get that."

They stared at each other in tense silence until Jenny put a hand over her mouth and burst into tears. She turned away, but her aunt got up immediately and enveloped her in a hug.

"I'm sorry," Jenny said into her aunt's shoulder. "It just hurts too much."

"I know you miss him, honey. I do too."

Jenny wiped her eyes with the sleeve of her robe and accepted the tissue her aunt offered from her pocket so she could blow her nose.

As they sat at the table, her aunt said, "I'm sorry, darling. I didn't mean to upset you. I just hate to see you in so much pain."

Jenny pressed the tissue to her teary eyes. "It's my pain to bear. You have to let me bear it in my own way."

Her aunt nodded. "I just need to learn to keep my mouth shut. No wonder Paul ..." She didn't finish her sentence.

Jenny sniffed and gave her a sympathetic tilt of the head, happy to change the subject. "What's going on?"

"Oh, honey, I don't want to bore you with my problems." She straightened in her chair and cleared her throat as she picked up her coffee cup. "Why don't you tell me about *your* love life?"

"You don't have to do that," Jenny said.

"Do what?"

"Play the long-suffering wife and change the subject."

Her aunt looked away. Jenny took her hand. "You've always been there for me when I needed someone. Especially this past year." She paused and then smiled, hoping to make light of that dreadful time in her life. "Granted, I was curled up in a corner, hugging a bottle of scotch, but ..."

Her aunt smiled. "I'm surprised you even remember. You were quite a mess."

"Obviously, I'm still a mess."

"Well, you walk upright and your head's not in the toilet, so I guess we've made progress," her aunt joked.

Jenny chuckled. "Okay, if that's the criteria, I guess I have." She waited for her aunt to come clean, but she could see that it would take a little coaxing. "Come on, Aunt B. You're not alone. It might make you feel better to talk about it."

"That's my speech, Jenny."

"Is it working?"

Her aunt smiled but remained silent on the subject. Jenny squeezed her hand and then sat back. "Well, I'm here if you need to talk."

Her aunt waited another few beats and then rapidly blurted out, "I think your uncle is having an affair. There. I said it."

"Uncle Paul?" Jenny said incredulously.

Her aunt responded with a hurt look.

"I'm sorry, but Uncle Paul?"

"He may just be a middle-aged dolt to you, dear, but he is my husband, and I do love him."

Jenny reached out and touched her aunt's hand. "I didn't mean it like that. I love him too. I just meant that you've been married for twenty-six years. I know he loves you. He just wouldn't cheat on you." Her aunt raised a doubtful brow and Jenny reiterated, "He wouldn't."

"Well, that's what I thought, but lately I just don't know. He's hiding something, and he won't talk to me about it. His temper is ... well, you've seen him lately, and ..." She paused and looked up, as if editing the next line.

"And?" Jenny pressed.

"And there's that woman."

"What woman?"

"A dark-haired sultry vixen sent directly from the devil himself."

Jenny wondered briefly if her sultry vixen was sent from heaven or hell. "Where does this woman come in?"

"I saw them."

"Saw them what?"

"Saw them talking at a party."

"That's it? You saw them talking at a party and suddenly he's having an affair?"

"You didn't see her, Jenny. She just oozes home-wrecker, and they were being very familiar."

"Aunt B, I hardly think—"

"You just know these things, dear," her aunt interrupted.

Jenny let out a humorless chuckle. "I didn't."

Thoughts of the infidelity that doomed her last relationship darkened her expression. Her aunt winced but didn't comment, and Jenny wordlessly got up to get another cup of coffee. The doorbell rang, breaking the uncomfortable silence.

"Ah, saved by the bell," her aunt said as she stood up. "I'll get it."

She came back into the kitchen carrying a long white box wrapped in a large yellow ribbon and bow and set it on the table. "It looks like someone got flowers."

Jenny set down her coffee cup. "Wow." She untied the ribbon and removed the lid to reveal a dozen perfect yellow roses. "Oh my, these are beautiful!"

"They must have cost a fortune!" her aunt said.

"And who knows that yellow are my favorite? Is there a card?" Jenny searched through the discarded ribbon and retrieved the card. She knew who she hoped they were from, and she was not disappointed. Written in beautiful sweeping strokes, the card read: *Sorry about the accident. Hope you are okay. Thinking of you.*

Jenny swooned.

Suddenly, her aunt was in her ear. "There's no signature. Very mysterious." She did a double take at Jenny's expression. "I guess from the look on your face, you know who they're from."

Jenny smiled.

"Your lady friend from last night?"

Jenny nodded.

"Very classy, dear. She's a keeper."

"I don't even know her, I told you."

"Well, she did save your life. You're bound forever now." She patted Jenny on the shoulder. "Just a friend," she mumbled, as she gathered up the fragrant flowers and took them to the sink.

Jenny just smiled and shook her head.

Her aunt reached under the sink for a large glass vase. "Ah, the days of flowers and romance," she said when she placed it on the counter.

"Please," Jenny said, as she began gathering the dirty dishes on the table. "You're a hopeless romantic." She set the handful of dishes in the sink and turned on the water.

"Please, nothing," her aunt said with a nudge. "You can't fool me. You're as hopeless as I am."

"True, but I'm afraid this woman's out of my league."

"That's utter nonsense, Jenny."

"Well, you've never met her ... trust me. I just needed something from her, and I—"

Her aunt raised her hand. "Okay, I don't think I need to hear about that."

"Information, Aunt B. I'm talking about information. Jeez."

Her aunt tugged on her chin. "Whatever you say."

Jenny rolled her eyes and let out a snort of laughter.

The slam of a car door interrupted their good-natured teasing. Her aunt went to the window in the living room and uttered a curse under her breath as she rushed back through the kitchen, heading to the back door. Jenny didn't need to ask who it was.

Her aunt pulled an old jacket from the rack on the boot room wall and headed out the back door. "Where are you going?" Jenny called after her.

"For a walk," came drifting back just before the back door slammed.

"Great. Talk about hopeless romance," Jenny said to herself as she dried her hands. She tossed the towel over her shoulder and headed toward the knock on the front door.

"Hi, Uncle Paul," she said with a warm grin.

Her uncle responded by raising two fingers in a V. "How many fingers am I holding up?"

"V for victory," Jenny said, tugging on his jacket. "Get in here."

He kissed her cheek and then hung his jacket on the hall tree. "How are you, kiddo?"

"I'll live," she said, as she headed back to the kitchen. He was hiding something behind his back, but she pretended not to notice. "Coffee?"

"Giving away your precious coffee? You must be feeling decadent this morning."

Jenny smiled. "Aunt B's already put a serious dent in that. No reason to stop now."

Her uncle stood awkwardly in the middle of the kitchen, trying to look nonchalant as he gazed around the room. Jenny leaned against the counter and put one hand on her hip. "She's not going to attack you from behind. She's outside taking a walk. You'll probably find her down by the lake."

"I don't give a hang where she is. I came to see you."

"Uh-huh." Jenny pointed. "What's behind your back?"

Her uncle looked like a shy schoolboy as he produced a small bouquet of assorted flowers. Jenny grinned. It was adorable.

He eyed the beautiful bouquet of yellow roses on the counter. "Well, these were for you, but I see someone beat me to it."

"You're an awful liar, Uncle Paul. Just go out there and make up already," Jenny said and turned around to wash the dishes.

"Is she really mad?"

"She didn't talk about it." She stopped and faced her uncle, who was now standing beside her. "Look, I don't know what's going on between you two, but I know she loves you, and I'm guessing you love her too, or you wouldn't be here with flowers."

Her uncle exhaled. "Time to kiss up, I guess."

"She's had a hundred cups of coffee, so she's pretty wound up. Be warned."

"Thanks for the heads-up." He put the flowers down and began drying the dishes. "Listen, Jenny ..." His tone became serious. "I don't have to ask what you were doing last night. I think I know."

Jenny faced him again and held up her hand, stopping him before he began his lecture. "I'm staying away from him. I swear it this time."

Her uncle's skeptical face said he didn't buy it.

"No. I mean it," she said sincerely. "That man is dangerous. The people he deals with are dangerous, and you were absolutely right in telling me to stay away from him. That wreck opened my eyes."

"Glad to hear it. Accidents will do that." Apparently satisfied that Jenny had learned her lesson, her uncle peered out the window and sighed. "I guess I'd better get this over with."

"Good luck," Jenny said with a pat on his back and then watched as he headed for the back door.

She'd meant what she'd said about trying to get close to Forrester. She didn't say she was giving up on her story, just that she wasn't going to go near him herself. That led her back to Kathryn Hammond, her only tangible link to Forrester.

She continued washing the dishes and periodically glanced out the kitchen window as she tried to decide her best approach with Kathryn.

It wouldn't be hard to see her again; she had several reasons now

—checking on her after the accident, returning her coat, retrieving her wrap from the club. The trick would be using her to get the goods on Forrester without getting her hands dirty.

Kathryn was willing to introduce her to Forrester, but would she go a step further and help her bring him down? No one was in a better position to surreptitiously collect damning information.

Jenny stopped assessing her options when a mental vision of Kathryn caught her off guard. A disgusting short film played in her head of Kathryn positioned under Forrester's sweaty body as he took what he wanted from her. His hands pawed at her flesh like a greedy master, and his mouth drank from hers like a starved man feeding for the first time in weeks. He grunted like an animal as he pounded into her with no regard for her pleasure or pain, and through it all, Kathryn was indifferent to his performance, for Jenny refused to give her a speaking part in the vile drama. Jenny shuddered and felt nauseated.

"Fucking Forrester," she said aloud, unsure if the curse was an adjective or a verb. Both, she decided. How could Kathryn do it? How could she stand to have that pig touch her? Why would she do it? For nice things? For money? For the attention?

Jenny closed her eyes briefly and exhaled. Her aunt wasn't the only judgmental one. Kathryn's personal life was none of her business. Why she was with the man was irrelevant. Only finding the truth and breaking the story mattered. The dominoes of justice would fall on their own after that, and to that end, she would ignore Kathryn's moral failings. She was a source, after all, not a girlfriend. Jenny glanced at the bouquet of roses. If only she could remember that. If only it didn't seem like more.

As Jenny watched her aunt and uncle finally make up, she folded her dishtowel onto the counter and had a sudden pang of loneliness. Her thoughts drifted back to Kathryn Hammond, and she couldn't help that those thoughts had nothing to do with her mission to bring down Forrester.

She told herself Kathryn was just a source. Anything else was just asking for trouble. She wiped the countertop and tried to ignore the beautiful bouquet of yellow roses warming the room—and her heart. She would never ask for trouble. Never.

CHAPTER THIRTEEN

*K*athryn rolled onto her back and was met with a rude reminder of the previous evening, as pain radiated from her shoulder blades and lower back.

"Ow," she said aloud to the thin crack in the uneven plaster ceiling.

She exhaled wearily as she remembered her run-in with Paul and then smirked at Smitty's ridiculous notion that Forrester was through with her. It was absurd. Forrester was hers, hook, line, and sinker.

She knew men. She knew their strengths and weaknesses and was able to exploit either at will. Forrester was a dangerous man, which raised the stakes considerably, but it was precisely that life and death challenge that made her feel alive and placated until she could get back overseas to the real work of winning the war.

Forrester was a distraction, a test, for all she knew, set in motion by her superiors to evaluate her mental health. The test was as good as passed. For all of Forrester's complexities, his motives and emotions were transparent. She'd struck a delicate balance between subjugation and independence; it gave him the illusion of control while keeping him off-guard and intrigued. She'd worked hard to get him right where she wanted him, and every indignation suffered at his hands was worth it to keep him there. Smitty didn't know the half of it, and she decided it was better that way. Murdering Forrester mid-assignment would look bad on his resume.

Kathryn slid out from under the sheets and was met with a grapefruit sized purple bruise on the side of her right thigh where Jenny Ryan's knee introduced itself during the crash. "Lovely," she said and then winced when she flexed her leg and it ached.

The bruise was just one of many Kathryn would soon discover when she shed her robe before the bathroom mirror and took inventory of her nude body. There was an oblong shaped bruise running from the base of her neck down across her collarbone, thanks to the steering wheel, bruises on her back from the window crank and armrest, and a few abrasions on her shoulder blades from grinding into the broken glass of the driver's side window.

"You're a train wreck, Hammond," she said to herself, and then she mentally sifted through her wardrobe at the club to find a dress that would cover up the damage. She gently pried off the gauze patch taped over the wound on her forehead and peered closely at the five neat stitches just above her eyebrow. "Nice job, doc."

She'd never considered herself a vain woman; in fact, she took her beauty for granted, regarding it as just another tool in her arsenal. That particular tool was going to take some work this morning. A dark bruise surrounded the wound. She frowned and lamented the fact that covering it would require the use of heavy foundation, which she generally disliked. She used it when she had to, like at the club, or when Forrester wanted to show her off, but, usually, a quick application of powder, mascara, and lipstick sufficed. The extra effort her appearance would require today annoyed her, and then she realized it didn't matter. Smitty was filling in for her at headquarters, and she had a rehearsal but no performance at the club.

The thought of The Grotto's brass section blaring in her ears all afternoon during rehearsal made her realize how lousy she felt. Her body ached all over, and she shivered as she pulled her bathrobe up around her shoulders. She didn't like taking a day off. A day off meant time to think, and time to think meant her demons would rear their ugly heads and drag her down into hell, where she belonged. It took mere seconds to self-fulfill the prophecy.

Kathryn lifted her eyes to the mirror, where her sight blurred, and she gazed beyond her reflection into the dark pit of her past. "No, no, no, no," she said on an anguished exhale, trying to gain control of her floundering mind. She knew she shouldn't fight it if she wanted to avoid a full-blown panic attack, but it was her first instinct, and the fear she'd lose her mind and never recover made suggestions by therapists to "just let it pass through you" sound like bunk spouted by someone who had never experienced such a terrifying loss of self-control.

As the first wave of adrenaline swept over her, horrific memories coursed under her skin like poison pushed from a syringe. Sweat seeped through her pores, and panic constricted her chest muscles until each breath was shorter and more painful than the last. She felt sick and grasped the sides of the cold porcelain sink to stop herself from falling into the hole opening up beneath her. *Breathe*, she urged herself, but she couldn't catch her breath.

"Breathe," she said aloud but did the opposite. She held her breath to stop gasping for air and then forced herself to comply to the mantra in her head: *Breathe in slowly ... hold ... then out even slower. In slowly ... hold ... out even slower.*

She felt lightheaded and sat on the closed lid of the toilet seat beside the sink. With a flick of her wrist, she turned on the cold water tap and held her hand under the icy stream to find a tangible focus before she lost all reason. The frigid water enveloped her hand, pulling her mind away from the demons clawing at her soul. She made a fist, balling it as tightly as she could. She squeezed until her nails dug into her palm and her breathing came under control. Her mind cleared and she relaxed her hand while the cold water washed the episode down the drain.

Tears filled her eyes with equal parts relief and anger. What hope did she have to get back to the war if just the thought of a day off sent her spiraling out of control? She thought this was over. The nights of waking up in a cold sweat, screaming, had passed—she hadn't had an attack like this in over a year—and when last night's accident didn't set her off, she thought she might be in the clear for good.

She splashed her face with cold water and then glared at herself in the mirror. "This is ridiculous. It's a day off." Nothing but determination stared back at her, and she dared the blackness to come after her again. Equilibrium restored, she called the club and took the day off.

The receiver was barely out of her hand when the small bell at the baseboard rang out with an incoming call. It was Marcus Forrester, full of concern for her well-being and apologies for the brevity of their conversation the night before. There was no need for either, Kathryn assured him, and niceties out of the way, he quickly got to the point of his call.

"You were very close to the estate with your friend," he said. "Were you going to have sex in my house?"

"She's not that kind of friend, Marc."

"Could she be?"

The implication made Kathryn pause. "We have an agreement."

He laughed. "I know, I know. Your personal life is your personal life."

"Yes."

"Except when it happens under my roof." All humor was gone from his voice.

This was one of those moments when she had to tread carefully. Remaining in Forrester's inner circle required an uncanny ability to sense the man's moods and react accordingly. Her instincts hadn't failed her yet.

"You can't blame a girl for wanting to make an impression, can you?"

She could hear the grin in his reply. "Anyone who isn't impressed by you at first sight needs their head examined," he said.

"What can I say? I'm insecure."

Roaring laughter came through the line and Kathryn smiled. Played perfectly. Then came the price for her well-played hand.

"Revision to our agreement," he said.

"I'm listening."

"No sex under my roof unless I'm there to watch. Agreed?"

There was no hesitation. "Agreed."

CHAPTER FOURTEEN

*J*enny sat on the end of her dock with her arms wrapped around her knees while she stared peacefully out over the shimmering lake. It was an unusually warm day, and she took the opportunity to enjoy her favorite spot before the last few days of winter resumed its bitter chill. She'd spent many hours here as a child with her grandparents and her father. Every milestone in her life happened right on this dock: her first step, her first kiss, her first breakup, even the news of her father's death.

She worried that the last memory would mar the magic of the place, but it hadn't, and she was thankful for that. She'd allowed her father's death to consume so much of her life—neglecting friends, family, and work—but now she felt as though her strength and spirit were returning. She couldn't deny that her campaign against Marcus Forrester had a lot to do with her renewed vigor, but she had learned her lesson about vendettas, and she'd be smarter about it going forward. Her uncle had given her the rest of the week off, and she had a course to plot, but today she would just enjoy a lazy day.

She cast her eyes to the sky as she lay back on the dock and put her hands behind her head to watch the ever-changing canvas of clouds shift into this form and that. Her father used to cloud watch with her when she was young, and he would come with up with outrageous description after outrageous description of the cloud shapes until she was reduced to giggles and finally begged him to go back to work in his study and leave her in peace.

She smiled at the memory and then realized it was another first. It was the first time since his death that a memory of her father made her smile instead of cry.

"You're okay," she whispered. It was her father's magic cure-all. From skinned knees to a broken heart, if you believed you were okay, then nothing else mattered. She felt close to him again. "I know I am," she said to the sky. She closed her eyes, content to drift off on that happy thought.

She awoke to the hollow thud of a tripped camera shutter coming from her left. She lifted a hand to block out the bright sun and opened one eye to find the paper's chief photographer, and her best friend, Bernie, sitting next to her, grinning as he peeked up from his camera's frame finder.

"Hey, cutie." He slipped the dark slide into the exposed side of his film holder. "You don't look too damaged."

She grinned. "Hey, Bernie. You snuck up on me. What are you doing here?"

"Don't move." He quickly flipped his two-sided film holder and then pulled the dark slide to ready the film for the next shot.

Jenny put a hand in front of the lens and giggled. "Stop."

He cocked the shutter. "Come on. You're adorable when you sleep. And you looked so peaceful."

"Mm," she said, as she rolled onto her side. "I am peaceful right now." She propped her head on one hand. "Aren't you supposed to be working?"

"I am working." He triggered the shutter with the cable release. "I'm taking pictures. That's what I do."

"Well, I'm pretty sure your assignment didn't include pictures of me."

He chuckled as he replaced the dark slide, protecting his exposure. "I was over to Johnson and Sons this morning. Rumblings about a strike again. Scuttlebutt says tomorrow."

"Oh, for crying out loud. Now what?"

He shrugged. "Some guy got a hangnail on the line and is claiming unsafe working conditions or something."

Jenny rolled onto her back in exasperation. "And before that, some popular guy got fired, and before that, they thought the women were making too much money. When does it end? There's a war on, dammit!"

"Hey," Bernie said, "was that a curse?"

Jenny stopped her tirade. "Oh, yeah. I owe you a fin. Tell you about *that* in a minute."

Bernie clapped his hands in glee. "Ha! I knew you couldn't clean up your act!"

"And do you know who owns that plant?" Jenny said. "Marcus Forrester. He doesn't want production to run smoothly because he's working for the Nazis. When he took over that plant last year, trouble came with him."

"Jenny—"

"No, Bernie," she interrupted. "I mean it. Work stoppages, strike threats ... it's deliberate sabotage, and he's behind it. I'm sure of it, and I'm going to prove it." She paused, and then, with a mischievous glint in her eyes, she snapped her fingers. "Say—"

Bernie held up his hand. "No. Absolutely not. I know that look. Whatever it is, it was not my idea and I want no part of it. When you break your behind, or get yourself arrested again ..."

"I was not arrested. I was escorted off the premises."

He threw up a dismissive hand. "Whatever. I'm not going to explain to your uncle how you got into trouble this time."

She put a hand on his knee. "It is not your job to explain my actions to my uncle."

"Says you. I almost got fired when you fell off that cab."

"Your indecision required immediate action on my part."

"Hey, my cat-like reflexes almost caught you."

"*Almost* is the operative word there," she said. "I saved your fancy camera, so the least you could have done was save me."

He shrugged. "I tried."

Jenny shot him a doubting glance.

"You're heavier than you look."

"I can't believe you said that!" She tried to slap him on the leg but he scrambled away. When she got up to pursue, she stumbled, as a wave of dizziness hit her. "Whoa," she said, as she reached out to steady herself.

"Jenny!" Bernie caught her before she fell. "You okay?"

She put a hand to her forehead. "Yeah. Watch that first step, it's a doozy."

"Come on, sit down."

"No, I'm all right. Honest. I just got up too quickly."

"You're sure?"

"Yeah, yeah." She looked into his serious round face and punched him in the arm. "Heavier than I look."

Bernie hugged her and kissed her cheek. "You're perfect."

"And you're blind, mister." She put her arm around his waist as they walked up the gently sloping hill to the house.

"I don't need to see color to see you look fantastic."

Jenny smiled and shook her head. Thank goodness for Bernie. He'd stuck by her even after she'd alienated her other friends. He recognized her brashness for the pain that it was, and he refused to let her push him away. She would love him forever for that.

He put his arm around her shoulders. "You okay?"

Jenny nodded as tears of appreciation welled up.

Bernie reached in his pocket and handed her his handkerchief. "I mean it, Bug, you're looking swell. We were all worried about you there for a while."

"I know," she said softly. She pressed the folded handkerchief to one eye and then the other. "Thanks for weathering the storm. There weren't many left on board when the ship finally got to shore."

He hugged her tighter as they continued walking. "You're my best friend, Jenny. I can be myself with you, and I know you'll always be there for me, no matter what. That's what best friends do, right?"

Jenny smiled. "Right."

They walked in silence for a few paces, and Jenny made a mental list of all the things she was thankful for. She looked at the beautiful house and grounds that were now hers, left to her by her father. And she was thankful for the trust fund that enabled her to keep it. She tightened her grip on her friend's waist.

"What's that for?" he asked.

"Just for being you. For being here."

He smiled and tightened his own grip.

"I know after Dad, I was a real stinker," Jenny said quietly. "And before that, I was ... well ..."

"Occupied with Satan herself."

"Yeah, Marcella."

"Oh, God!" He put a hand to his ear. "Don't say its name." He looked around frantically, as if mentioning her name would bring forth the embodiment of pure evil itself.

Jenny laughed and shook her head. "What was I thinking?"

"Ugh. Next subject," Bernie said, as they reached the back door of the house and entered.

"Gladly," Jenny said. "How about your love life? I've noticed a little extra twinkle in your eye lately. Anything momma needs to know about?"

"Well," he drew out, "as a matter-of-fact, there's a handsome young man who may be courting me."

"You're not sure?"

"It's hard to tell. He seems kinda shy."

"Do tell."

Bernie wrinkled his nose. "Um, I don't want to jinx it. I'll tell you when I'm sure."

"Fair enough," she said.

CHAPTER FIFTEEN

With a frustrated exhale, Kathryn snapped shut the book she was reading like someone interrupted once too often. The offender was her own anxiety. She couldn't concentrate. It felt like the walls had eyes—a ghoulish audience awaiting her next breakdown.

Her sudden loss of control was a crippling blow to someone who prided herself on control and precision. At times, her life depended on it, which was why she was stateside and not overseas. Her exile was maddening. Couldn't her handlers see she would be fine over there? The past lost all power there; only the present mattered. Save your life. Save your friends. Evade capture. Plan. Plot. Execute. Move, move, move. It was hell, and she missed it.

The electric hum of the Bakelite clock on her bookshelf drew her attention to the time. Smitty's meeting with brass at HQ would be over by now, and with that realization came a sudden sense of dread. She should have been there. Her absence showed weakness, and there were enough people doubting her durability.

"Stupid," she muttered, tossing the book on the end table beside the sofa.

The telephone rang.

"Hi, doll face," Smitty said, chirping his usual greeting.

She couldn't help but smile. "Hi, handsome. How'd it go?"

"Fine. How are you?"

"Fine. How'd it go?"

"It went fine," he said. "Just fine."

She knew it was a lie. "Branson had nothing to say?"

"Branson always has something to say."

"Smitty ..."

"Kathryn, relax. Branson started his usual nonsense, and Walter told him to shut his pie-hole. You were in a car wreck, for crying out loud. Everyone understands why you weren't there. Best wishes from all, by the way."

"I can't afford to lose ground, Smitty."

She could hear her partner scrubbing his face in exasperation. *You have an unwarranted inferiority complex about them*, he would say, if he hadn't said it a hundred times before to no avail. She appreciated his unwavering support, but he was biased, and if being a woman in the male-dominated world of espionage wasn't tough enough, she had a bloodstained past hanging around her neck like a sign that said *Screw loose!* She would fight for every inch of real estate to prove her worth and fight even harder to hold the line.

"They think you're the tops, doll. A swell cookie, the cat's meow, a goddess on a half-shell—"

"All right, all right," Kathryn said, cutting him off. She couldn't help but smile. "I get it."

Smitty chuckled. "You didn't miss a thing, honey, I swear. I'll swing by around three to take you to the club."

"I'm not going in."

He paused. "Are you okay?"

"I'm just not up to it today."

"I'll bring lunch over." His pause and cheerful about-face betrayed his concern. He knew what idle hours meant.

"I'm okay, Smitty."

"First sign of trouble, Kathryn, you call me."

"I know."

"First sign. I mean it."

"I will."

He exhaled like someone going against his better judgment. "Okay. Call me later."

"I'm fine, Smitty."

"Call me later or I'll show up at your doorstep. Your choice."

Kathryn knew he would do just that. "I'll call you later."

She wouldn't tell him about her episode. In the end, it came to nothing. Smitty was always there to pull her back, but this time she brought herself under control—significant progress. She couldn't rely on someone else for her mental stability. She needed to be one hundred percent self-sufficient, sooner rather than later. She had a war to get back to, a debt to pay.

CHAPTER SIXTEEN

*B*ernie insisted that Jenny take it easy while he prepared lunch. He draped a towel over his forearm and presented her sandwich. "*Pour vous, mademoiselle*," he said in his best French.

"Ah, merci," she said. "Fancy."

Bernie sat down and laid his napkin across his lap. "Say, speaking of fancy, I hear you got into The Grotto again. Is it as gorgeous as everyone says?"

"Well, yeah, but it was kind of dark, and I was kind of ... distracted."

"Aha! Now we finally get to hear about the hot tomato!"

Jenny lifted her hands. "Is my life somehow connected directly to the office bulletin board or something?"

Bernie chuckled. "The *Daily Chronicle*," he said in a low voice, mimicking the company motto. "When news happens, you can count on us to bring it to you first."

"I am *not* news."

He leaned into the table. "Come on, spill it, girl." He paused and rubbed his hands together. "So, you were on your way to her place for some hot sex. Then what?"

She threw her napkin at him. "You're awful!"

"That's what the bulletin board said." He shrugged nonchalantly as he took a bite of his sandwich.

She shook her head with a smile and retrieved her napkin.

"And?" he drew out with a mouthful of sandwich.

"She was taking me to Forrester."

"Gosh," he said, almost choking. "That was kinda stupid, Jenny."

For a split second, she was annoyed, but he was right.

He saw her look. "I'm sorry, honey, but that man is nothing but trouble." He wiped his mouth with his napkin. "Taking pictures from a distance and yelling questions at him in a crowd is one thing, but to crawl into his den with a complete stranger as your only means of escape? Stupid."

"I've already given myself that lecture, thank you."

"Well, good. What does she have to do with Forrester anyway?"

"I think she's his mistress."

Bernie scrunched up his face. "Ew."

"Yeah."

He waved his hand in the air. "Okay, forget about the hot sex thing. That woman's got no taste. I'll go change the bulletin board memo immediately."

Jenny blushed. "She *is* really hot."

He raised an eyebrow and lowered his chin. "How hot?"

Jenny leaned into the table. "So hot that even after I cursed her out—hence the fin—she flirted with me, sent me flowers, and I'd consider sleeping with her even if she is Forrester's mistress."

"Jenny!" Bernie exhaled in shock, placing a hand over his gaping mouth.

"I know!"

He fanned himself with his napkin. "My, my. That's pretty hot."

"You have no idea. There's just something about her."

"Yeah, it's been too long; that's what it is about her. You're desperate."

"No, more than that. Something familiar ... something ... I'm not sure. Weird."

"A weird hot mistress of a known criminal who works at a mobster's club. Good choice, Jenny."

She had changed her opinion about Kathryn's workplace. "The Grotto is not a mobster's club. The owner is a friend of my uncle's, for crying out loud."

Bernie gave her a doubting glance.

"They were college chums."

He rolled his eyes. "Oh. Okay then. It must be legitimate."

She threw her napkin at him again.

"Hey ..." He threw it back. "That's my job from now on, get me? If I had told you what a psychotic witch I thought Marcy was, maybe I could have saved you some heartache."

Jenny moved some crumbs around on the table. "No. I would've just told you to kiss my ass. Besides, she was not *that* bad."

Bernie held his head. "Oh my God, Jenny."

Jenny stared back blankly.

"Jenny," he said again. "Oh. My. God."

She grinned. "Stop."

"Listen, I'm all for the concept of time heals all wounds, but ..." He raised his fist in the air and mimicked the war poster remembering Pearl Harbor. "Never forget!"

"Well, if she was *that* bad, why didn't you say something?"

"What, and have you tell me to kiss your ass?"

"You could have made an effort. I never stay mad at you for long. You know that."

"Honey, you were so gone. There was no point. Believe me, I've been there."

"Good grief, yeah. What was that guy's name? Everett?"

He put his hand over his heart in mock agony. "Ugh, stop! The memories!"

The two friends laughed over relationship disasters with a humor only found with the passage of time. Neither had been particularly lucky in love, but they hadn't lost hope in the idea that somewhere out there, someone was waiting just for them.

Their stories left them grinning from ear to ear, and Bernie said, "It's good to see you laugh again, Miss Jenny Bug."

She folded her napkin. "Yeah, it feels good. I guess time is finally doing its thing."

"Speaking of time ..." He looked at his wristwatch. "I guess I'd better get back. These pics need to get in." He began to clear his place at the table.

"Leave that," Jenny said as she got up. She wrapped the rest of his sandwich in his napkin and handed it to him. "Take this with you. Come on, I'll walk you out." They walked down the long hallway from the kitchen toward the front door. "Will I see you at the armory to decorate for the dance?"

He smacked himself in the head. "Oh, jeepers, I almost forgot! Beth wanted me to tell you that the Banyan Trio canceled for Monday night."

"Oh for—" She put her hands on her hips in irritation, "Those boys are shipping out Tuesday. Who's going to play for them?"

"You could set up the phonograph again."

"That's a fine send-off. Their last night at home and they get a phonograph for entertainment. I don't think so." She paused. "Wait, why does Beth want you to tell *me*?"

He scratched his head sheepishly. "I think she wants you to take over planning again."

"What do you mean, you *think*?"

"Okay. She quit. The job's yours, and we don't have any entertainment for Monday."

"Thank you." She paused and stared at him pensively. "You can just spit it out, Bernie. You don't have to sugarcoat everything."

He looked down. "Sorry, Bug." He paused before looking up again. "I'm glad you're getting back to your old self."

"I don't know about my old self, but hopefully a better self, and thank you." They shared an affectionate glance, and then she noticed something was missing. "Hey, boy genius ..."

"Yeah?"

"Camera."

"Jeez, what a lughead." He made his way back into the kitchen and retrieved his bread and butter.

"You've given me a great idea," Jenny called out as he came back. "I think I'm going to go down there and interview the strikers. Maybe I can weaken their resolve from the inside out."

He pointed a finger at her. "Look, no running off without your uncle's permission. It's gotten pretty dicey down there."

"It's that damn mob mentality. Get some of those strikers alone, and maybe someone will listen to reason."

"This is a rough crowd, Jenny, and tempers are pretty high. Promise me, when you get ready to go down there, you won't go alone. And," he said sternly, "you run it by the boss first."

"I promise."

"Jenny," he said, his tone skeptical.

"What?"

Bernie shook his head.

Jenny laughed and held up her penance for cursing—a five-dollar bill she'd retrieved from her purse. "Here's your fin."

"Thank you," he said smugly, plucking it from her fingers with a flourish.

Jenny smirked and shoved him out the door. "Go back to work. I'll see you Monday night, with live entertainment."

"Great! Thanks for the eats." He kissed her on the forehead. "Take care of your noggin." And with a wink he was down the steps. "Love ya, hon," he said over his shoulder as he headed down the walk.

"Love you too. Do you want a ride down?" A dismissive wave was her reply as he started the ten-minute downhill trek through the winding roads of Jenny's neighborhood to the elevated 242nd Street Station.

Jenny smiled as she closed the door and then caught sight of Kathryn Hammond's coat hanging on the hall tree. That gave her an idea. She picked up the telephone and asked for The Grotto's exchange. While she waited for someone to pick up at the other end, she said, "You wouldn't work for a mobster, would you, Miss Hammond?"

CHAPTER SEVENTEEN

fraid. Kathryn mindlessly traced the word with a pencil on the notepad balanced on her knee. *Guilty* it read beneath that. Across the top of the page, she'd written Forrester, Daniel Ryan, Paul Ryan, and Jenny Ryan, separating each name with a vertical line. She'd spent more time pondering Paul Ryan's column than she should have. He wasn't her assignment, Jenny Ryan was, but Jenny wasn't the one hiding something. Or was she?

Kathryn exhaled and massaged her stiff neck. Working for the Office of Strategic Services did little to bring comfort to someone accustomed to meticulous preparation. Information was always compartmentalized on a need-to-know basis, and she felt like an actor given a script containing only her lines, leaving the rest of the plot and players a mystery.

It started months ago with Marcus Forrester. "Keep your eyes open for any unusual activity," her superiors instructed after she'd grown accustomed to his routine and the people surrounding him. There were important files missing from a War Department research facility, thanks to a traitorous scientist, Daniel Ryan, and Marcus Forrester was suspected of brokering deals to pass this information into the wrong hands—enemy hands.

Kathryn had found nothing to connect Forrester to such a plot, much to her agency's frustration, so they leaned on the scientist's brother, Paul Ryan. He was wholly uncooperative and claimed he didn't know a thing, which wasn't surprising, since the brothers were infamously estranged. The investigation went nowhere. Jenny Ryan was a long shot in their efforts to uncover her father's missing work, and Kathryn couldn't help but feel she was purposefully given a dead-end assignment, because there would be no harm done if she fell apart in the middle of it.

The agency's lack of faith in her made her more determined than ever to find what they were looking for, and, to that end, she would turn over every stone in her path if it helped her piece things together. Paul Ryan was irrelevant, they'd told her. "Focus on the girl." But Paul kept stepping on their toes, which made him relevant to her.

Thanks to the drunken rambling of Forrester's accountant, she found the only thing linking the Ryans to Forrester was that Paul Ryan owed Marcus Forrester money—lots of it. It wasn't hard to imagine that an out-of-control gambling debt led to Forrester's thugs going after Paul's family, and that resulted in his brother's death, which may or may not have been a scare tactic gone tragically wrong. That was her best guess, anyway, and definitely something Forrester's bookies would order, and from Paul's reaction at the hospital, her guess didn't seem that far off the mark.

She shouldn't have thrown his brother's death in his face during their confrontation—that was cruel—but he'd meddled in their plans once too often, and this time it almost got her, and his niece, killed.

Kathryn didn't know whose idea it was to send Jenny Ryan after Marcus Forrester, but it showed that the agency didn't trust her to set up her own introduction. To make matters worse, it inadvertently set Paul Ryan into action, and now she had to work the father angle, appease Paul, and convince Jenny Ryan to stay away from Forrester.

Smitty believed Paul when he said he didn't have anything to do with the men with guns, but she had her doubts. Paul had a penchant for taking matters into his own hands, usually with catastrophic results.

The man's outburst in the hospital was more than concern; it was desperation. Kathryn knew all too well that anger had its roots in guilt, insecurity, and fear. Paul Ryan had a reason to fear for his niece's life, a reason to believe their crash was no accident. His brother was dead. Was his niece next?

Why? She wrote beneath *guilty* and circled it. She had no answers. She exhaled and rubbed her stiff neck again. It was time to focus on her assignment. The corners of her mouth curled up into an involuntary grin when she moved on to Jenny Ryan's column.

She remembered the first time she saw Jenny as she tumbled from the roof of a taxi outside the courthouse. She smiled at her temper, displayed at their first meeting, and her promised seduction at their second meeting. Her recollection turned serious as she remembered the accident and how she'd held her hand in the car on the way to the hospital. She shook off the useless recollections, ignored the tendril of warmth they evoked, and got back to business.

She'd written *file access* under Jenny's name, and *innocent,* followed by *determined, arrogant,* and *hot-tempered.* She tapped her pencil point over *file access* and could only imagine what the traitorous Dr. Ryan was selling to the enemy. Unfortunately, due to the secretive nature of her work, she would never know.

She stared at her list and frowned. She scratched out *arrogant* and wrote *naïve.* She shook her head. The child of a traitor. It would kill her if she knew. "Poor kid," she muttered, hoping the girl would never find out.

She traced the word *innocent* and started to get that wistful feeling again. She caught herself and frowned. She didn't know that for sure yet. She crossed the word out.

She returned to Paul's column again and tapped on the circled *Why?* What had Paul done now? Was Jenny in danger? Her instincts said no. Those men last night were after her, not the girl. She wrote another *Why?* on the page. It wasn't Forrester, she was positive. *Who?* she wrote and circled it. More questions than answers. A typical day.

Kathryn dropped her pencil and rubbed her eyes. The closest she'd come to connecting Marcus Forrester to Nazis was Jenny Ryan's accusation, which was based on OSS propaganda. She stared at Jenny's column again. The woman was dogged and determined and had followed Forrester's every move for weeks before they met. Did she find something? Kathryn's ego told her no one was closer to Forrester than she was. If she hadn't found anything, there's no way some amateur snooping at a distance would. Finding her professional objectivity, she picked up the pencil and wrote *Is she hiding something?* and underlined it twice.

Out of habit, she tore the page from her notepad and the two beneath it that retained an imprint of her writing and tossed them into a metal garbage can. She opened a window, placed the garbage can on the wide ledge, and then set the papers a blaze with a well-tossed match.

CHAPTER EIGHTEEN

"Come on in. It's open," Kathryn called down the hallway from the bathroom, in response to Smitty's typical double rap on the cellar door.

"Are you decent?" he asked, sticking his head in her apartment.

"Does it matter?" Kathryn said, leaning out of the bathroom, fully dressed and putting on her makeup.

"Could be the difference between a good day and a fantastic day," he said with a mischievous grin.

She capped the jar of heavy foundation. "You're early."

"Yeah, just couldn't wait to see your funny face this morning." He gave her a peck on the cheek and pointed to her stitches. "Hardly noticeable."

"Mm, you should have seen it ten minutes ago." She held up the jar.

"Ew. You hate that stuff."

She nodded and made a face.

"Bad?"

"Which color do you want? Blue, black, or yellow?"

Smitty grimaced. "Ow."

He leaned against the doorjamb and watched intently as she put on her mascara. "You ever poke yourself in the eye with that stuff?"

She gave him a side-eyed glance. "Only when I'm distracted."

He smiled and leaned back.

Kathryn rinsed her mascara brush and then put it away. "Any news on our friends from last night?"

"Nada. Without a plate number or a better description than *the guy looked like a middle-aged boxer with a scar on his chin*, it's a dead-end."

His reply sounded like a dig, but she chalked it up to residual crankiness on her part. "Best I could do under the circumstances," she said of her description of the man who peered at her through the windshield.

"Thought anymore about who's behind it?" he asked.

"You mean have I changed my mind? No. Paul is my one and only suspect. It's not Forrester."

"And that's that," Smitty said.

Kathryn stared at him for a beat. She'd made her pronouncement a little sharper than intended, but Smitty's attitude annoyed her. If Forrester wanted her gone, it meant she wasn't doing her job, and that certainly wasn't the case. She'd gone above and beyond with the man, and the fact that her partner doubted her effectiveness irritated her to no end. She just barely resisted an accidentally on-purpose shove with her shoulder as she passed him on the way to the kitchen.

Smitty followed her. "Did you talk to the Ryan kid?"

"I thought about her."

Smitty's footsteps ceased, and she could feel the stare at her back.

She looked over her shoulder. "About calling her."

Smitty nodded warily.

"What?"

Smitty drew down his mouth and shrugged with a shake of his head. "Nothing."

Kathryn continued on into the small kitchen. "I feel sorry for her, that's all. Don't you?"

"Hadn't given it a thought." He paused. "Is that all?"

Kathryn felt a past mistake flung at her back like a dagger. She stopped and turned to face him. "What's that supposed to mean?"

Smitty frowned. "What is wrong with you, Kat? Why are you so agitated this morning? And why are you agitated with me? What did I do? I want to know if you have any thoughts about the case and you give me *the look*." He planted his hands on his hips and threw one out in a feminine pose, a mirror image of her stance. "What gives?"

Kathryn briefly closed her eyes and exhaled a frustrated breath that ended with a chuckle. Smitty always found a way to deflect her ire, and it always made her realize that she was probably out of line.

"I'm sorry. This whole situation is getting to me."

"Clarify."

"They're just yanking us around, sending us on a wild goose chase. We're never going to bring Forrester down any more than that kid is going to prove he killed her father."

"The agency wouldn't have us—"

"We should be overseas, Smitty!" Kathryn said in frustration. "Really fighting the enemy."

"Ah," Smitty said. "That."

"Yes, that."

"Well ..." Smitty cleared his throat and pulled a chair out from the kitchen table. "You may want to sit down for this one."

Kathryn warily followed his lead and sat across from him.

"There's something I didn't tell you about yesterday's meeting."

Kathryn resisted shouting *I knew it!* "Go on," she said calmly instead.

"The British have come aboard."

"As in SOE?"

"They're calling themselves Inter-Services Research Bureau down at HQ, but we both know that's SOE."

Kathryn sat back in her chair, stunned. The British Special Operations Executive wouldn't stick its nose into this assignment if it weren't important and didn't have international implications. In fact, the OSS wouldn't involve itself either. If she had been thinking clearly, she would have wondered why this wasn't a case for the FBI, who had domestic jurisdiction, but she was so absorbed in her selfish delusions of persecution that she'd lost her objectivity.

"And that's not all," Smitty said. "They sent Archibald Holmes to head the contingent."

"Colonel Holmes?"

"The same."

Kathryn rubbed her jaw. "What are the odds?" Her brief career with the SOE left the man with a well-deserved hatred for her. "Any clue what's going on?"

Smitty shrugged. "I don't know, doll, but they're certainly not yanking us around for their own amusement."

She released the pent-up tension in her shoulders and fell back in line like a good little agent. "No, of course not." She stared at the kitchen tabletop. When did she start doubting the OSS? She mentally shook her head. Probably when she started doubting herself. Maybe they were right to keep her stateside.

"Hey ..." Smitty took her hand. "Are you okay? You've been out of sorts since the accident."

She covered his hand with hers. "I know. I'm okay. I just lost sight of the horizon for a minute. This assignment has gone on for so long, with no progress, and now this kid is dragged into it. It just seems so pointless."

The futility of Jenny Ryan's mission to bring down Forrester exposed the same flaw hindering her mission: Forrester was too careful. It would take a colossal misstep to expose his sins, and he didn't make colossal missteps.

"I know it's not exactly dodging bullets in the dark alleys of Paris," he said, "but I'm not ashamed to admit I'd rather have you here than there."

The sooner he gave up the hope that she'd never make it back to the fight, the better. "You know my goal, Smitty."

He dropped his gaze to his shoes and nodded.

. . .

Smitty dropped Kathryn off at the club with an unsettling feeling that something was wrong. Kathryn never questioned what the OSS asked of them. Never. She followed obediently, just as they were trained. They were small cogs in a big wheel, and each cog had to play its part if the scheme had any hope for success. Blind trust. It was essential. She knew that, but something had upset the delicate balance between personal will and professional obligation.

Smitty thought it was the accident. Perhaps the life and death drama had awakened a battle lust he prayed had left her. But he feared it was the girl. Kathryn felt something for her. Part of him was glad. She was feeling *something* at least; even if it was pity, it was a start. Her time overseas in the cursed fight she was so eager to rejoin had left her dead inside. She came alive on stage, lost in a song or, maddeningly, in Forrester's presence, because she had to, and now playacting with the girl, but she was a pale imitation of the woman she was before. She slogged through one melancholic day after the other, with the singular goal of returning to the war that stole her life.

He didn't know if she wanted to go back to reclaim her life or to let the battle put her out of her misery. She felt she deserved that fate, and it broke his heart. He loved her, and he couldn't save her.

There was a spark in her eyes today that he hadn't seen in years, and though it came out as anger, he saw it as a sign of life. He began asking if she felt more than pity for the girl—a professional disaster in the making—but the look on her face when she turned to him showed the question had hurt her deeply. In her eyes it was an accusation, and given her history, that was understandable. He quickly lied to deflect the perceived slight with an attempt to make her laugh.

She had a wonderful laugh that came from deep in her throat and rolled past her lips in an infectious wave of modulated warmth. That too was gone, replaced by the half-hearted efforts of a woman robbed of every last ounce of joy.

He blamed himself for the chain of events that ruined her, and he would fight for the rest of his life to see her happy and whole again.

CHAPTER NINETEEN

enny sat on the floor in front of the coffee table in her living room and set the six .38 caliber rounds she'd retrieved from Kathryn's coat pocket on their ends, like little toy soldiers at review. She drummed her fingers on the polished oak surface of the table and wondered what kind of woman keeps such things in her coat pocket?

Jenny smiled. "My kind of woman."

She leaned back against the couch and gave each a name: Strong. Confident. Talented. Smart. Beautiful. Connected.

She paused. Connected. To Forrester. The traitorous, murdering, philandering mobster.

Her heart sank as soaring expectations fell back to Earth. She had to stop thinking of Kathryn as a potential girlfriend. She wasn't even sure Kathryn had an interest in women, let alone her.

Strong. Confident. Talented. Smart. Beautiful. Mistress.

"Ugh." Jenny threw her head back into the couch cushion and stared at the ceiling. "Why, Kat?" she whispered, as if Forrester was the only thing keeping them apart. She was losing focus again, and she scrubbed her face with her hands. "Why, Jenny?"

Why couldn't she stick to her plan? She knew what she *should* do; she should focus on her exposé, get Kathryn to help her, and then sit back and watch Forrester go down. But what she *wanted* to do kept convincing rational thought that she was crazy for not going for the girl *and* the story. She and Kathryn could be a team. Bring Forrester down together. Why not? What obstacles? Her imagination grabbed her by the hand and led her astray like a giddy teenager defying curfew. She rode the momentary surge of excitement until reality deposited her back in the middle of her living room, where she stared at six deadly projectiles on her coffee table.

Jenny exhaled. Kathryn wasn't her kind of woman. She was a mobster's woman. How many times did she need to remind herself that she was Forrester's mistress? The people around her were dangerous. Dangerous enough that Kathryn kept ammunition at the ready.

Jenny turned her head to the right and looked past the arched entrance to the living room, to the foyer sideboard where she'd placed the beautiful bouquet of yellow roses. She smiled involuntarily and then chastised herself for confusing *considerate* with *interested*.

It was only natural she was attracted to the woman; who wouldn't be? But she was supposed to be a professional journalist chasing the story of her life, not behaving like an undisciplined juvenile chasing the unattainable. She imagined her uncle's smug look as her actions affirmed every criticism he ever had about her.

Jenny checked the time on her small gold wristwatch. She'd called the club yesterday to speak with Kathryn and was concerned that she wasn't there, but the gentleman assured her that she was okay and would be in for rehearsal this afternoon. Perfect.

She gathered the cartridges and Kathryn's coat and then paused to look at herself in the foyer mirror before heading out the door. "Professional," she said. "Friendly but professional."

She would use the train ride into Midtown to embrace her inner hard-nosed journalist and convince herself that Kathryn Hammond was nothing more than the gateway to Forrester's demise.

She steeled herself to that thought and then plucked a yellow rose from the vase before her—because she was considerate too.

"Good afternoon, Miss Ryan," the club's doorman said as he swung the door open.

Jenny smiled her thanks as she passed, still not used to The Grotto's employees addressing her by name, as if she were a club regular.

Visiting The Grotto in the daytime was like catching a glamorous star without her makeup the night after a bender. Chairs were resting upside down on the tables, and the stale smell of cigarettes and alcohol hung in the air. The public wasn't supposed to see the club like this, but Jenny was welcomed without hesitation.

Bobby approached her with a grin. "Can I get you anything, miss?"

"No, Bobby, thanks. Don't you ever leave here?"

He smiled. "Whatever for?" He reached for a chair leg. "Have a seat?"

"No, thank you." She motioned toward the stage with a tilt of her head. "I'm just going to make my way up there."

Bobby nodded. "Yes, miss. Nice seeing you again."

"And you."

She made her way toward the stage area, where the musicians were playing in street clothes. It made the rehearsal feel like a casual jam session, and she moved slowly along the back aisle so as not to attract attention to herself. Kathryn was in the middle of a slow, melodic song Jenny had never heard before, singing to whichever section of the band played the lead at the moment. The clarinets took over the musical bridge, and Kathryn closed her eyes. She let the music sway her into a leisurely, solitary dance, and Jenny had the urge to volunteer herself as her partner.

Kathryn had one hand behind her back, tucked into the waistband of her dark slacks, and the other hand resting across her abdomen. She looked fantastic, even in casual clothes. She had the sleeves on her pressed white cotton blouse rolled up to mid-forearm and her dark hair pulled into a loose ponytail, with several long loose strands framing her beautiful face.

Jenny stopped momentarily to watch, and her body warmed to the idea of those arms wrapped around her as they swayed across the stage to the rise and fall of the music. She could almost feel Kathryn's strong arms around her and smell her subtle perfume as she rested her head on the taller woman's shoulder. Jenny's fantasy was interrupted when she did smell a strong fragrance, but it wasn't a woman's perfume.

"She's good, isn't she?" a man's low voice said over her shoulder.

"Oh." Jenny said with a start. "I'm sorry, I didn't see you there." A slightly overweight Italian man smelling of cigars and too much cologne stood grinning back at her.

"She's good, no?" he asked in his thick accent, motioning toward the stage.

"Yes, very," Jenny said.

"I'm Dominic Vignelli. This is my club."

"Oh," Jenny said in a delightful tone as she put a face to the silhouette she saw on her first night there. "Oh," she said again when she remembered that she'd upset him that night by flipping off his songbird. "I'm sorry about the other night, Mr. Vignelli."

He held up a hand, dismissing her apology. "Ah. Call me Nicky." He put out his hand and Jenny shook it. He lifted his chin toward the stage. "Miss Kathryn, she says you're a good egg. So that is enough for me."

Jenny liked the sound of that. "That's mighty big of you, sir. Thank you. You have a beautiful club."

"And beautiful talent, no?"

They both turned their eyes to Kathryn.

Heat rose to Jenny's face. "Yes, she is." Story, story, story. Friendly but professional.

The orchestra began tuning for a new song, and Dominic patted her on the shoulder. "Say hello to your Uncle Paulie for me." He walked away but stopped and turned. He shook his finger toward the stage. "You be nice to her. She's good people."

"Yes, sir," Jenny said. She held up the single yellow rose. "Peace offering."

The club owner smiled and clasped his hands together. "Ah, wonderful."

Jenny turned her attention back to the stage, where Kathryn pointed something out to the piano player on his sheet music. He nodded, as did the rest of the musicians. Jenny was ready to settle in and enjoy the performance when she remembered her mission at the club was two-fold. She turned on her heel and followed Dominic's path to his office.

When she emerged a few minutes later, a flamenco guitar was just introducing the next song. The percussionist joined in, gently adding a Caribbean beat on his bongos. Kathryn moved her hips to the beat and broke into a full rumba as the clarinet added its voice and floated effortlessly above the soft percussion. She worked the stage as she sang, relaxed in a way that didn't come across in the pretentious atmosphere of the evening performances.

It was a song about love, longing, and hope, despite the uncertainty of the outcome. Jenny found it ironic, and a little cruel, considering her struggle to maintain a strictly professional relationship with the woman.

The idle band members watched with stupid grins on their faces as Kathryn let the music take her, and Jenny couldn't blame them. Nice work if you could get it, watching that on stage every night.

Jenny let her mind drift along with the melody until she found herself the newest member of The Cult of Kathryn Hammond, her stupid grin proof she'd paid in full. She couldn't help it. The woman was mesmerizing without even trying.

Kathryn made her way through the seated musicians as she sang, placing a hand on a shoulder here, a lean on a chair there, and a playful tug of the chin for the smiling rhythm guitarist to accentuate a tantalizing line in the song.

For a brief moment, Jenny resented Kathryn's coquettish behavior. It was the same misplaced emotion she'd experienced the first night they met at the club, when Kathryn felt her way through the crowd on her way to Forrester's table.

The more attention Kathryn paid to others, the less significant the attention she'd paid to her seemed. Jenny frowned and wondered when she'd decided she had exclusive rights to Kathryn's attention. She looked at the yellow rose in her hand and knew it was the minute she'd laid eyes on her. It was wrong, and it was irrational, and it was like nothing she'd ever experienced.

She repeated her *friendly but professional* mantra in her head. Kathryn showed no more interest in her than anyone else she encountered during her day. She had yet to see her interact with anyone without flirting.

Flirting, to the disarmingly beautiful, came as easily as a kind word, or a smile, or a casual touch. It inspired hope and adoration in the willing victim and jealousy and resentment in everyone else. Jenny closed her eyes and fought against emotions that had no place in the pursuit of her father's murderer. She could flirt with the best of them if that's what it would take to cajole Kathryn Hammond into gathering information on Forrester, but she couldn't, under any circumstances, fall for the woman. She just couldn't. Kathryn was Forrester's mistress, who had no romantic interest in her whatsoever. Heartbreak was not on the agenda, only the complete ruination of Marcus Forrester, and the woman on stage was her instrument of destruction.

Jenny lifted her eyes to the stage to find Kathryn staring at her from the edge of the footlights, her hands behind her back.

This was the perfect time to try on her new thick skin. Her heart was racing, but she grinned with a slight lift of her chin, hoping she appeared calm.

Kathryn delivered the final verse directly to her, and a cheery song about love, longing, and hope became less about uncertainty and more about the involuntary fluttering in Jenny's stomach.

The music stopped, and Kathryn waved her to the side of the stage.

Jenny bolstered her resolve with a deep breath. "Here we go," she whispered, as she made her way forward.

"Perfect timing," Kathryn called out with a broad smile when she got closer to the stage. "We're done here."

Kathryn's smile struck Jenny in all the wrong places if she was supposed to embrace friendly but professional. It warmed her heart and made the rest of the world fade into irrelevance. Kathryn belonged to her again.

"Thanks, fellas," Kathryn said, as she hopped off the stage. The trombone player produced a wolf whistle with his instrument as Jenny arrived. Kathryn shook her finger over her head without turning around. "Nope," she said, just before enveloping Jenny in a hug.

One of the band members called out, "Who's your friend, Kat?"

Jenny had barely recovered from Kathryn's enthusiastic greeting when she was presented at court with an arm casually draped over her shoulders.

"Boys, this is Jenny Ryan," Kathryn said. "Jenny Ryan ..." She extended her hand to the group of men on stage. "The boys."

The band members simultaneously picked up their instruments and blared the musical equivalent of *ta-da*.

"Time to go," Kathryn whispered into her ear as she led her into the wings.

"Bye, boys," Jenny called over her shoulder. "You play beautifully."

"Thank you, Jenny," they said in singsong unity.

As Jenny followed Kathryn up the spiral staircase to her dressing room, the drummer began a striptease rhythm on his hi-hat cymbal, and then the brass section filled in their part. By the time Jenny stepped foot on the landing and looked down, the band had succumbed to adolescent giggles.

"Good grief! Are they always like that?"

Kathryn laughed. "Only with fresh meat."

Jenny raised a shocked brow, but Kathryn assured her she was kidding with a squeeze to her shoulder. "Sorry," she said, opening the door to her dressing room. "That wasn't meant to be as predatory as it sounded. They're a swell gang, really. Can I get you anything?"

"No, thanks." Jenny stopped in the middle of the small room and stared in disbelief at three ridiculously large colorful bouquets of flowers obscuring the entire surface of the vanity. She felt like an idiot with her measly rose, and she wished she had left it behind. She tried to cover it with the coat draped over her clasped hands but was interrupted by Kathryn's hand cupping her cheek.

"I'm so glad to see you," she said. "How's your head?"

"F ... fine," Jenny said, undone by Kathryn's gentle caress. Her hand didn't stay there long. It was just a passing touch as she brushed by on her way to get a glass of water, but all thought left Jenny's head, and just like that, she was under the woman's spell again.

Kathryn filled a glass with water from a pitcher. "Why were you frowning out there? Were we out of tune?"

"Oh, gosh, no," Jenny said. "You were beautiful. Uh, I mean your voice ... er ... the music, I mean the song was ... beautiful."

Kathryn put the pitcher down and a widening smile disappeared behind a sip of water.

Jenny wanted to melt into the floor in embarrassment. She couldn't even manage friendly without a humiliating demotion to lovesick schoolgirl; professional was, without a doubt, beyond her grasp in Kathryn's presence, and, God, if she touched her one more time—

Jenny couldn't ignore her hopelessly romantic nature, or the electricity coursing beneath her skin, and for the moment, instead of fighting against it, she allowed herself the dizzying high of attraction, with no fear of the inevitable tumble to the ground. Nothing could stop her ear-to-ear grin. "And you were beautiful. *Are* beautiful, and this ..." she produced the rose, "is for you. A thank-you."

Kathryn accepted the flower. "Beautiful. A thank-you for what? Putting us in a ditch?"

"I'm pretty sure you saved our lives. That guy was—"

"Drunk or something," Kathryn quickly interrupted.

"Yeah. Or something."

"Well, thank you for this," Kathryn said. She held up the rose and then glanced around the room for something to put it in, settling on the pitcher of water.

"And thank you for this," Jenny said, handing Kathryn back her coat.

Kathryn set the glass down on the small table beside the bed and took the coat with a smile before tossing it dismissively behind her on the bed. She retrieved a white box with a red ribbon around it from her vanity seat and held it out. "For you."

Jenny's heart swelled. "A gift for me?"

"Your wrap."

"Oh, right. Thanks," Jenny said, as her heart sank.

Kathryn sat down on the bed and patted the cushion of the bergère chair beside it. "Take a load off," she said, as she leaned back on the bed and supported herself on her elbows.

Jenny had a moment of indecision. The bed looked more inviting than the chair, but she removed her coat and played it safe in the chair. She looked at Kathryn's wound. "How's *your* head?"

"Just a scratch."

"Uh-huh," Jenny said. "Just a scratch that required ..." she got up and leaned in close to count, "one, two, three, four, five stitches."

"It looks worse than it is. I promise."

Jenny settled back into the chair. "I'm really sorry, Kathryn. I feel awful about that."

"Why? It's not your fault."

"Well, you were doing me a favor, after all. If you hadn't been driving me out there ..."

"Then I may have wound up in that ditch all by myself. Where's the fun in that?"

Jenny shook her head and chuckled.

"Maybe it was just my time for an accident," Kathryn said with a shrug. "Maybe I should apologize to you for dragging you into my bad karma."

"Do you have bad karma, Kat?"

Kathryn paused, and Jenny noticed a subtle change in her expression. It went from amused to serious and then back to amused. "You're here, I'm here, we're both okay, so maybe it's not as bad as I think it is."

Bad karma seemed incongruent with the beautiful creature stretched out before her, and Jenny had the urge to throttle anyone who dared harm a hair on her beautiful head.

"I can't help but feel guilty that you got hurt, that's all," Jenny said.

Kathryn acknowledged the sentiment with a tight-lipped smile, but then looked pensive. She sat up and clasped her hands around one knee. "I've found guilt to be a very unproductive emotion. You either let it swallow you up or you kick its behind around the block and carry on."

Jenny could appreciate that. Having let guilt swallow her up for most of the last year, she would love to learn how to "kick its behind around the block." Kathryn's confidence made it seem possible, but the shadow of her father's death cast a pall over any glimmer of hope.

"Sometimes the consequences of your actions are so horrific that you deserve to be swallowed up by guilt," Jenny said.

Kathryn reached out and placed her hand on her knee. "That's a tough spot."

Jenny saw pained comprehension in the blue eyes staring back at her, and she sensed the woman shared the same anguish. "How do you get out of that spot, Kat?"

Kathryn pursed her lips and let out a humorless chuckle. "One stinking day at a time."

Jenny looked down and nodded her head. That was about it, in a nutshell.

Kathryn removed her hand. "Sorry. That wasn't very helpful."

"No, you're exactly right. No one can lead you out of that darkness. That's a path you have to find by yourself." She paused. "For yourself."

"Have you found your path, Jenny?"

Jenny smiled. "I'm getting there. And you?"

Kathryn leaned back on one arm and smirked. "Guilt and I ... we have an understanding. It stays out of my head, and I don't kick its behind around the block."

Jenny laughed, but Kathryn's smile faded and her face became serious.

"Does your path include getting back at Forrester for what you think he did to your father? Is that what this is about?"

Jenny's first instinct was anger. "Not what I *think*," she said. "What I *know* he did to my father."

Kathryn nodded in what Jenny perceived as an unspoken apology for her choice of words, but she continued.

"What do you expect to find? Proof that he killed your father? Because you're not going to find it."

Jenny wanted to lash out, because that was the last thing she wanted to hear, but there was only kindness and concern in Kathryn's voice. Deep in her heart, Jenny had the sickening feeling Kathryn was right, but letting go of Forrester meant letting him get away with murder, and her father deserved justice.

"Are you saying you know he did it but I'll never find proof?" Jenny asked. "Or are you saying he didn't do it, so don't bother looking?"

"I'm saying if that's the only reason you're here, I suggest you move on."

Jenny paused for a moment while she processed what she was hearing. Kathryn was taking Forrester out of the equation, effectively removing him from their relationship. The romantic schoolgirl in her made her momentarily lose her mind.

"If I were here for something else," Jenny said hesitantly, "would you stop seeing Forrester?"

Kathryn laughed out loud. "No. Why?"

"Because he's a pig?"

"Oh, it's not so bad," Kathryn said. "He comes in a few times a week, grabs my ass, shows me off." She shrugged as if it was nothing.

"It's disgusting."

"It's part of the job."

"To have your boss pimp you out?"

Kathryn smiled and took Jenny's hand. "Let's not talk about Forrester."

"I can bring him down, Kathryn. *We* can bring him down."

"Jenny ..." Kathryn sat up and took her hands in earnest. "He's dangerous. You, of all people, should know this."

To Jenny, it was an admission of the man's guilt, and she couldn't believe Kathryn cast it out so casually. "So, he did kill my father! He killed my father and you know it!"

"Jenny ..."

Jenny yanked her hands away. "*No!* You know he did! Why won't you help me?"

"He's dangerous," Kathryn repeated.

"And he was dangerous yesterday, and the day before that, and the day before that! You were willing to help me then."

"That was before."

"Before what? Before you changed your mind, or Forrester changed it for you?"

Kathryn pursed her lips and shook her head.

The stitches above Kathryn's brow caught Jenny's eye, and a horrific thought seized her. "What happened to us wasn't an accident, was it?"

Kathryn cast her eyes downward.

"Kathryn," Jenny said, grabbing her hand and forcing her to look up, "did someone try to kill us?"

Kathryn paused before she answered. "I don't know. Maybe."

"Why?" Jenny's eyes widened, as the likely reason took root. "Is it because I'm going after Forrester? Did I do this? Are you in danger? Would he hurt you? Of course he'd hurt you. He sent someone to run you off the road!"

Kathryn rubbed her hand. "Jenny, I said I don't know. It could just be an accident."

"Bullshit," Jenny said. "You know it wasn't. God." She tried to stand and pull away, as if her mere presence put Kathryn in danger, but Kathryn held fast to her hands.

"Jenny, it's my fault. I shouldn't have taken you out there. It was reckless and selfish."

Jenny relaxed back into her seat, her panic held in check by Kathryn's strong hold.

"I thought I could help you," Kathryn said. "I wanted to help you. I just wasn't thinking."

"No," Jenny said. "I wasn't thinking." She only wanted justice for her father. She didn't consider the consequences of her blind obsession. "I'm in over my head. As usual. I'm sorry I put you in that position."

Kathryn smiled and tugged on her hand. "No one makes me do anything I don't want to do."

"Forrester does."

Kathryn's smile disappeared, and Jenny regretted her words. "I'm sorry, Kat. That was uncalled for."

Kathryn withdrew her hands and sat up straight. "Would you like to have dinner with me?"

Jenny blinked. "What?"

"Dinner."

She was caught off guard by Kathryn's open gaze, and an invitation to dinner became an invitation to so much more.

Kathryn smiled innocently at her assignment. The scene had gone exactly as planned. She'd cured Jenny Ryan of her Marcus Forrester obsession, and now it was time for phase two: setting the hook. Jenny would accept her dinner invitation, naturally. She would stay for the show, maybe drinks afterward, and a variation of this pattern would repeat until Kathryn found out what, if anything, Jenny knew about her father's work.

To Kathryn's utter shock, Jenny stood up and said, "No, thank you. I've got to go."

"Oh," Kathryn said, and she rose to her feet as well. "Rain check?"

Jenny slid her arms into the sleeves of her camel hair coat and settled it onto her shoulders. "No, I don't think so."

Kathryn paused, not sure if Jenny was serious. "Something I said?"

Jenny tucked the box containing her wrap under her arm and smiled. "No. It's a lot of things, but I do want to thank you." She extended her hand, which Kathryn warily accepted. "For everything. You've really put things into perspective for me, and I'll never forget you for that."

Jenny turned Kathryn's hand over and placed six .38 caliber cartridges into her palm and closed her fingers around them.

"These belong to you, I think," she said. "Please be careful, and take care of yourself."

Jenny gave her a final squeeze on her closed fist and was out the door before Kathryn could blink herself into action.

"What the hell just happened?" Kathryn muttered aloud into the silence and then opened her hand. She frowned in confusion at the rounds cupped in her hand and then cast an accusatory stare over her shoulder at the coat on the bed. "Stupid, Hammond! Stupid!"

She hurried out the door, down the stairs, through the club, and burst through the front doors and onto the sidewalk. Jenny was gone, lost in the bustling flow of the city.

CHAPTER TWENTY

The tears came suddenly and unexpectedly. Jenny couldn't get out of the club fast enough. She scolded herself as she clambered down the steel stairway leading into the alley behind the club. It was just a story, no need for tears. The lie was ineffective. Tears blurred the gateway of sun bathing Seventh Avenue at the end of the alley. She headed toward it like a sinner seeking absolution in the cleansing brilliance of Heaven's open door.

What she wouldn't give to be the strong, confident woman she was before her father was torn mercilessly from her life. For a year, she blamed herself and barely survived the crushing guilt of his death. When Forrester was offered as the true villain, she found life again, strength again. Her confidence returned, and hope and purpose began to heal her shattered world. How quickly it all came crashing down again, and like insult to injury, it only fed the maelstrom of uncontrollable emotions. She had three blocks to pull herself together before reaching 50th Street Station. Three blocks to wrangle frustration, grief, and disappointment in herself into a mask of public indifference.

Jenny was still crying when the 1 train rumbled into the station.

She found a seat on the narrow, crowded car, and the woman beside her passed her a tissue.

"Blasted war," the woman said of the tears.

Jenny nodded as she dabbed at her eyes and then wiped her nose with the tissue. The war would suffice as a scapegoat while the truth crushed her into the ground with its well-traveled heel. The familiar ache of failure settled into the void that hope abandoned. Jenny didn't know what hurt more: her inability to accomplish anything of importance ever or the realization that she failed this time because she'd fallen for a mobster's mistress.

One look into Kathryn's eyes and she was lost. She told herself she was imagining it, that it was just Kathryn's natural charisma combined with the trauma of the accident that led to a false sense of intimacy, but there was nothing false about the physical and emotional longing she felt in Kathryn's presence.

When she realized she'd put the woman in danger because of her pursuit of Forrester, it was like the night her father was killed all over again. The unbearable guilt of causing harm to someone she cared about was suppressed only by Kathryn's steadying grasp. When she let go, Jenny knew Kathryn's invitation would cost her more than she could give.

She had no intention of being the mistress of a mistress and no intention of letting Marcus Forrester get away with killing her father. Giving in to Kathryn would mean both. She couldn't involve Kathryn in her plan any longer—it was too dangerous for her—but without Kathryn Hammond to help her, she was back to square one. Worse than square one. She lacked the discipline required of any good investigative reporter, and she'd burned her one good lead because of it. Alternative career options turned over in her mind, but she lamented that she'd probably fail at those too.

Anger finally made her stop crying. This wasn't her. She'd always looked at failure as an opportunity to learn and grow, but instead of building on her recent failures, she was letting them drown her in self-pity.

She examined the failure, traced it back to its root, and soon, disappointment in herself turned into disappointment in Kathryn Hammond. So beautiful, talented, and kind. Jenny tried hard not to blame Kathryn for Forrester's interest in her, but the woman showed no aversion to the pig's advances, even privately, where she should relish the chance to express her disgust with her situation.

Jenny shook her head. She didn't understand it, but, in the end, it didn't matter. She couldn't deflect blame for this one. As much as she'd like to lay her failure at Kathryn's feet, she couldn't. She had to lift her chin, accept responsibility for her failure, and adjust her sights—sights well above Kathryn Hammond.

Her brush with the most attractive woman she'd ever met did teach her one thing: If she wanted to bring down a man like Forrester, she'd need a bigger weapon.

Smitty strode around the corner to see Kathryn staring down the busy Midtown block with her hands on her hips. "Hey, doll face," he said, as he came to her side. He mimicked her stance and the scowl on her face and followed her gaze into the distance. "Yeah?" he said, having no idea what he was looking for. "Problem?"

"Jenny Ryan has given up on Forrester."

"Oh." Smitty relaxed, glad he'd misread Kathryn's tense disposition. "Good. You can get in there now and see what she knows."

"She's given up on me too."

"What?" It was impossible. Inconceivable. No one walks away from Kathryn Hammond.

Kathryn covertly gave him a peek at the shiny cartridges in her hand and then deposited them in her pocket.

"Gee, Kat, for a gal who's not real fond of guns, you're racking up time here lately. Who're we shooting today?"

She turned around and started walking back to the club. "Myself in the foot, I think."

He rushed before her and held the door open. "This is going to be an interesting story."

"Jenny Ryan found the rounds in my coat pocket."

"Ah," he said. "The range last week."

Kathryn nodded. "That, combined with the wreck, got her off Forrester, but then she said 'thanks but no thanks' to getting closer and wished me a great life."

From what he'd seen of Jenny Ryan, that seemed thin-skinned. "Over the ammo?"

"I don't think so. She had them when she walked in here today, and things were going fine until ... well, until they weren't."

That was still inconceivable to him. "Maybe you're losing your touch, Kat."

Kathryn threw a seductive glance over her shoulder and didn't need to say another word.

Smitty wiped a sudden flush of perspiration from his brow and followed her silently through the club and up the stairs to her dressing room.

Kathryn deposited the troublesome rounds on her vanity and sat down in the chair previously occupied by Jenny. Her scent still hung in the stillness of the small room, and Kathryn couldn't resist filling her lungs with the pleasant fragrance. It wasn't strong, like perfume. It was soft and delicate. She didn't know if it was her shampoo, her soap, or her laundry detergent. Whatever it was, she wished for its owner to appear again.

Smitty threw his coat and hat on the bed, and himself after them, replacing Kathryn's olfactory reverie with the stale odor of cigarette smoke clinging to his clothes.

"So, what did she say?"

"About?"

"About the cartridges."

"Nothing."

"She didn't want an explanation?"

"No."

"Hmph," he said. "Some reporter."

Kathryn swallowed her irritation at his criticism and the loss of her pleasant memory. She tried to find a positive to mitigate her darkening mood. "At least she's smart enough to get out of Dodge before the showdown."

"Do you think she knows something's in the works?"

"I don't know, Smitty. She gave me no indication, one way or the other."

"If she's wise to you, you know sweet-talking isn't going to work. We'll be out and the big guns will take over."

"I know," she said quietly.

"The kid's life as she knows it will be over. There's no turning back after that."

"I know, John."

She said his name gently, not harshly, like she usually did when she had occasion to use it, but she knew she'd tipped her guarded hand.

"Kat," he said softly, and then he paused. "What is it?"

She shook her head, unwilling to admit to herself, or her partner, her burgeoning affection for Jenny Ryan. "Just a blow to my ego, I guess," she said. "I was sure I had her."

Smitty's face brightened and he leaned back with a satisfied grin. "She's really in for it now, isn't she?"

Kathryn brightened too. The game was on. "Yes, she is."

CHAPTER TWENTY-ONE

*J*enny got to work at her usual time, refreshed after her four-day weekend. Frank was there to greet her with her mail, as usual, and after a gauntlet of well wishes and jokes about her hard head from the other employees, she entered the elevator feeling pretty good about herself. With her ill-conceived assault on Forrester behind her, she felt relieved that she'd come to her senses before someone really got hurt. She would find a realistic, reasonable approach to his downfall as part of a larger offensive— safely, without dramatics—and as soon as she found that path, she would set upon it, but for now, she was content to keep her head down and her eyes and ears open.

She couldn't, however, think about Forrester now without also thinking of Kathryn Hammond. Over the weekend, she'd spent an entire day and night lamenting her loss and fantasizing about a relationship until she could envision a future for years to come. It seemed so possible, she had to stop before her heart broke from the quixotic love.

She expelled a heavy sigh, a habit now forever linked with Kathryn's memory, and raised her chin as the elevator came to a halt and the doors opened. She stepped out to see a huge banner stretched over the entrance to the office. Happy Birthday Jenny! it read in towering letters.

"*Surprise!*" everyone yelled.

Jenny's jaw dropped. *Oh my God*, she mouthed, as she quietly stepped backwards into the elevator.

"Oh, no!" Bernie said, as he wiggled his way out of the crowd and took her hand before she could escape.

"You ..." She pointed an accusing finger at him as he led her to the waiting swarm of colleagues. "Are a dead man."

He raised his hands. "Not me."

Her uncle made his way out of the group and engulfed her in a big bear hug. "That honor is mine," he said, grinning, and then he kissed her on the top of the head. "You're not mad, are you, kiddo?"

She smiled and shook her head as she looked around, overwhelmed by the sudden attention. "Thank you, everyone."

She smacked her uncle playfully in the gut. "I can't believe you did this." Bernie was within striking distance, too, so she pinched him on the arm. "And I can't believe you didn't tell me!"

Everyone laughed and offered their congratulations and then slowly moved the makeshift party into the office space. In short order, the commotion died down and everyone got back to work.

At lunchtime, Bernie came strolling down the aisle. "Come on, birthday girl, I'm taking you to lunch."

Jenny tossed her pencil over her shoulder. "Yippee!"

As they walked out of the office and under the birthday banner, Bernie thumbed over his shoulder. "You okay with all this birthday stuff?"

"Honestly, I forgot until I got here and saw that banner."

"And you're okay?" he asked again as they got into the elevator and turned to face the closing doors.

"I'm okay. Honest."

The elevator got to the ground floor and Jenny turned to head out of the building, but Bernie grabbed her arm and led her in the opposite direction. "This way."

"I thought you were taking me to lunch?"

He grinned. "I am."

She stopped. "The cafeteria? You're taking me to the cafeteria for my birthday lunch?"

He reached out and dragged her along. "I'll have them all sing "Happy Birthday" to you if it'll make you feel better."

"No thanks," she said in mock disappointment. "Deadline, huh?"

"You know how it goes."

They weaved their way through the crowded cafeteria lunchroom and grabbed their trays.

"Bernie, you don't have to do this. We'll go out tonight, after the shindig."

"Hey, gotta eat, right? I may as well eat with you. Besides, I want the dirt."

"What dirt?"

"The chick, the dame, the hot tomato. You know." He nudged her. "What happened?"

Jenny picked out a sandwich. "Nothing happened. Let me hear about your weekend. How was the wedding upstate?"

"Typical," he said, as he accepted a bowl of soup. "My sister looked beautiful, Mom cried a lot, and Dad drank too much and avoided me."

Jenny wrinkled up her nose. "Sorry."

Bernie shrugged as they sat at a table. "What do you mean, nothing?"

"I mean nothing," she said. Vintage Bernie. Disappointment was written all over her face, and he wouldn't let her get away with not talking about it. "I'm not going to see her again."

"Jeepers." He paused. "Again, I ask, what happened?"

"Who are you, Hedda Hopper?"

Bernie sat up and pretended to straighten a woman's hat on his head. He wet the tips of his fingers to smooth out the hat's long, protruding feather and cleared his throat. "Dish, dahling, dish. We have a deadline. The gossip must flow!" he said, in his best imitation of the Hollywood gossip queen.

Jenny laughed and gave in. "You were right. She would be a bad personal decision, and I've made enough of those."

"Cripes, Jenny Bug, since when did you start listening to me?"

"You just happened to be right this time."

Bernie picked up his spoon and shook it at her. "I am not going to ask you again."

"Promise?"

He poked the spoon into her shoulder, accenting each word. "What. Happened?"

Jenny relented. He wouldn't quit until he had the whole story. "Things were going great. I went to the club to see her rehearse—"

"And?" he interrupted before she could gloss over any of the juicy details.

"*And*," she said back, grinning, "she was fabulous, incredible, beautiful, funny ..."

"Yeah," Bernie drew out. "So far, so good."

Jenny leaned back in her chair. "She's also Forrester's mistress." She paused and waved her sandwich in the air as if to clear the area of a dark cloud. "Oh, and I spoke with Mr. Vignelli and got the band to play tonight."

"That's great," Bernie said dismissively. "Back to the girl. She was Forrester's mistress last week, too, and it didn't bother you then."

Sometimes talking to Bernie was like talking to herself in a mirror, except reflected in his eyes, all that is irrational, far-fetched, and downright stupid is not rationalized into a brilliant plan of action.

"It does bother me," she said. "It always has. She's better than that. Just the thought of her sleeping with that pig ..." She shuddered. "It makes my skin crawl."

Bernie dipped his spoon into his soup. "How do you know she's sleeping with him?"

Jenny thought about it for a moment. Kathryn never denied it, and, surely, she would have if it weren't true. "Believe me." She crossed her fingers. "Like this."

"Why does she upset you so much? What do you care who she's sleeping with?"

Jenny glared at him. He knew why she cared. He just wanted her to admit it out loud so that he could tell her how insane she was for falling for a mobster's mistress.

She couldn't hide anything from him. "Yes, I've fallen for her. Yes, I know that's crazy, especially with my track record, and, no, I've not convinced myself that this time is going to be different. And *that* is why I'm not going to see her again." She picked up her sandwich and took a bite with pride of purpose.

Bernie raised his brow slightly and went back to his soup. "That's the saddest thing I've heard all day."

Jenny's heartbeat quickened as hope lifted its head like a napping dog hearing its master's key in the lock. "You think I'm wrong?"

"I don't know her, sweetie."

Part of her wanted him to convince her to go for broke; the other part wanted him to applaud her decision to stay away. "She's a train wreck waiting to happen, and I don't want to be on board for the tragic ending."

Bernie shrugged. "You know best."

It wasn't what he was saying, it was the way he said it. He had a knack for getting his point across without actually saying anything.

"I'm not strong enough, Bernie," she said. "I don't want to go through that again."

"No guarantees, Jenny, you know that. You can't just turn your back on love because you're afraid you might get hurt."

"It's more than that. The odds are just not in my favor." She wouldn't tell him that the accident was probably anything but, or about the rounds in Kathryn's jacket. That was all over now.

Bernie didn't say anything; he just continued eating.

Jenny inwardly rolled her eyes at the dreaded silent treatment. He knew she couldn't stand it. "Look," she said, "it's one thing to go into a relationship with anticipation, everything hearts and flowers. But to go into one knowing all the pitfalls and you do it anyway? That's just asking for trouble."

"It seems to me, you're one up on the rest of us. At least you know where the pitfalls are. Half the battle is in knowing where trouble is and avoiding it."

"Exactly. That's what I'm doing."

Bernie smirked. "That's not quite what I was getting at, but, as I said, you know best."

She stared at him. "I hate it when you say that."

He blinked innocently. "What?"

She shook her head and pointed a warning at him with her sandwich.

"So," she said, and looked around the cafeteria. "Let's dissect *your* love life. Where's your stalker?"

"Umm ..." He looked around. "Don't see him."

"Figures. You get to stick your fingers in my love life, but you don't have one for me to return the favor."

"What fingers?" he said in mock bewilderment. "I didn't do anything."

Jenny smirked. "Right."

Jenny walked Bernie back to his basement office on the lower floor, which they affectionately called the dungeon.

"What's your deadline?" she asked, as she rummaged through some photos on his desk. She spotted one of the photos he'd taken of her on the dock a few days before. "Ha. Nice. I want the negatives."

"No chance."

"These will not wind up on the bulletin board, Bernie."

He held up his hand in solemn oath. "I swear. My eyes only."

She smiled and looked at the series. "I kind of like this one, actually." She held up the one of her sleeping.

"This one's my favorite." He held up the one of her squinting into the sun while using her hand as a visor to shade her eyes. "The shadow play across your face ... your expression ... it's so you."

She took the picture and had to agree with him.

"Take 'em if you want 'em," he said, twirling an imaginary mustache over his evil grin. "I can always make more."

Jenny chuckled at her own vanity. "Thanks. I think I will."

Bernie opened a file and spread some photos across his desk. "Anyway, the local family section runs today. This is Carl Robinson's funeral."

Jenny ran a reverent hand across his high school photo. "Gosh, yes."

"Lost at sea," Bernie said.

Jenny picked up a photo of the boy's mother clutching the customary folded American flag triangle as she placed a flower beside the grave marker over her son's empty grave. "This is so powerful, Bernie."

Bernie tapped the photo. "She picked that photo to run with the article. I was going to use his yearbook photo, but now that the powers that be have decided we can show the hard truth about this war, she said she wanted that one." He shook his head. "She lost Bill at Pearl."

"I know." Jenny swallowed the lump in her throat at the woman's unimaginable loss. "Two sons lost, and I'm crying over some stupid woman I barely know. Ridiculous."

Bernie looked at her with surprise. "You cried over her?"

She blushed and nudged him. "Quit."

"I didn't say anything."

Jenny put the photo down. She took two other photos, flipped them, so that their white backs were showing, and laid them on top of the graveside photo, cropping the image of the distraught woman.

He watched her try different positions. "You can't help yourself, can you?"

She smiled and continued cropping until she found a composition she liked. "Reprint?"

"Wow," Bernie said. The crop removed all the extraneous information of the original image and forced the viewer's eye to flow seamlessly from the mother's face, in the upper left-hand corner, to the clutched flag, residing on the right-hand side center, to her hand placing the flower on the ground, focused just left of center on the bottom.

"Reprint," he said. "Nice job, Jenny. You should be working in the dungeon with us. You've got a great eye."

She smiled. "Light meters, f-stops, and shutter speeds ... oh my," she said. "I don't have the head for it."

"Bullpucky."

Jenny laughed and gathered the photos he'd taken of her. "I've got a job, thanks." She pointed at the cropped photo. "*That* is an incredible use of depth of field. Nice job, yourself."

"Come on down here. You know you want to."

"Nuh-uh. I've gotta run, or I may be looking for another job." She kissed him on the cheek. "See you tonight."

"That's the plan."

"Thanks for these," she said, as she waved the photos over her head and disappeared around the corner.

Jenny took the stairs back to her office, glad for the physical activity in a workday that usually found her trapped behind a desk. She smiled as she passed under her birthday banner, but the smile soon turned to a frown as she saw Calvin Richards sitting on her desk. His head was held high, buoyed by an ear-to-ear grin that made him look like he'd just won first prize at something. Jenny swore that if this was another of her uncle's setups, she was going to scream. She was a twenty-four-year-old grown woman, for crying out loud, perfectly capable of getting her own dates.

She braced herself and bravely marched down the aisle toward her desk. "Sergeant," she said.

"Hi ya, Jenny."

She threw her photos on the desk and he followed them with his gaze. "Cute," he said, about the sleeping one. She turned them over against further comment.

"What can I do for you, Cal?"

"Did you get 'em?"

She paused. "Get what?"

"The flowers!"

Flowers? With furrowed brow, she cast her mind back. *Not the ...* "What flowers?"

"The yellow roses. Didn't you get them?"

Jenny's eyes widened and she put her hand over her mouth to contain a curse. "Good grief."

"You didn't get them?"

"No," Jenny said, still trying to comprehend that they were not sent by Kathryn. "I mean, yes, thank you, they were beautiful."

He sat back proudly. "Yeah."

Jenny rubbed her head and cringed, remembering the flower that she gave Kathryn and how forward the gesture must have seemed. "Cripes," slipped out against her will, and she put a hand to her forehead.

Cal put his hand on her shoulder in concern. "Is your head all right?"

She nodded and then looked around for a secluded place to talk. Impromptu dates set up by her uncle were one thing, but hanging around and sending her expensive flowers? There was a misunderstanding somewhere.

"Come on." She grabbed his hand and led him out of the office. She found a quiet corner and pushed him gently against the wall. "Cal, I'm sure you're a really great guy. But, and I thought you understood this ... I'm not ... I don't ..." She didn't know how to come out and say it, if he didn't get it already.

"Jeepers crow," Cal said, as the tips of his ears turned red. "You thought ... oh, jeez." He shook his head.

Now Jenny was confused. "You want to ask me out, right?"

He laughed. "Nothin' personal, Jenny. I think you're a swell gal and all, but, uh ... no."

"Then what the ...?"

Cal looked around and leaned in close so no one but Jenny could hear. "You're friends with that photographer downstairs, right?"

"Yeah."

The soldier leered at her.

"Oh my God!" Jenny covered her mouth. "You're the stalker."

He drew back. "What?"

Jenny laughed and put her hand on his chest. "I'm sorry, you sure didn't seem ..." She looked around before she said anything more.

He laughed before she could finish her sentence. "I'm in the U.S. military, darlin'. If you don't want your ass ... er ... behind beat up and/or thrown out and into jail, you put up a pretty good front."

She patted him on the chest again. "Well, nicely done, soldier. I hadn't a clue." She relaxed and had a good chuckle now that she didn't have to worry about explaining things to him. "Hey." She frowned. "If you're interested in Bernie, what are you doing hanging around me? And where did you get the money for those flowers?"

Cal grinned. "The flowers were your uncle's idea."

Jenny rolled her eyes.

"He thinks I want to date you."

Jenny shook her head. "Of course he does."

"So, he gave me a few bucks, said yellow roses were your favorite, and sent me on my way."

"Too rich," she said, still amazed at the whole sequence of events. "Next time, sign the card."

"I had the shop gal do it. My handwritin's no better than chicken scratch."

"Well, she didn't sign your name. It led to some interesting conclusions on my part."

"Anyway," Cal said with a shrug, "I wasn't sure about your friend." He paused. "You know."

Jenny laughed. "You weren't sure about Bernie?"

"You never know, Jenny," he said. "Sometimes they're just ... artistic."

She laughed again and agreed.

"And that's just downright embarrassin', if not dangerous."

"And how," she said. She grabbed his sleeve and led him down the hall to the elevator.

"Where're we goin'?"

"You'll see."

They got on the elevator and Jenny told the attendant they wanted the basement. When they reached the dungeon, she dragged Cal to Bernie's office, but he wasn't there. "Where's Bernie, Joe?" she asked his coworker.

"Darkroom."

She headed back down the hall with her soldier in tow. "Happy birthday!" she heard Joe yell.

"Thank you!"

"Oh, yeah, happy birthday."

"Thanks," she said. The darkroom entrance was a huge black cylinder with one opening that turned like a revolving door. "Coming through," she said, as they stepped inside and then turned the cylinder until the opening was facing the darkroom

"Wow," Cal said. "It's dark in here."

"That's why they call it a *darkroom,* Cal."

He laughed. "Mm. Kinky."

She slapped him on the chest. "Save it, boy. Come on."

She led him into the darkroom and moved slowly until her eyes adjusted to the low red lighting and she spotted Bernie hanging up some prints.

"Aw, jeepers," she heard Cal say.

Jenny went around behind him and rubbed his back. "It's okay, sweetie. He's very friendly."

She gently pushed him toward an oblivious Bernie. "Hey, you," she said over his shoulder.

"Hey, you," Bernie said, still engrossed in his work. "Come to take me up on my offer?"

"Nope. I brought you a present."

"Oh," he said cheerfully as he turned around. "Oh," he said again, this time disconcerted when he saw his mysterious stalker.

"Bernie Roth, this is Calvin Richards." She put herself between them. "Cal ... Bernie." She joined their hands in a handshake. "My job is done here." She slapped both men on their shoulders and walked away.

"Wuh ... wait!" Bernie said.

Jenny kept walking, held up both hands, and wiggled her fingers. "I've got fingers too!" she said, then disappeared into the revolving black door.

Cal scratched his head. "Fingers?"

CHAPTER TWENTY-TWO

*K*athryn arrived home in the late afternoon from the training center on Long Island dragging the day behind her like a sack of bricks. The club was dark on Mondays, and once a month, she made an appearance at the sprawling Long Island estate, whose lands and structures were on loan to the OSS for the duration of the war.

She was exhausted, both physically and mentally. Field training recruits was hard enough, but Branson was assigned as her training partner, and he had made the session hell. They'd had a disagreement in procedure during a joint exercise with the new trainees. Branson claimed that Kathryn's way didn't work in the actual field of battle because it was too structured to allow for the unexpected. Kathryn, aware of the trainee's expectant eyes on her, calmly explained that it was a by-the-book exercise in discipline that leads one to make the right decisions automatically when under fire. She was right, and Branson knew better, but it didn't stop him from committing the cardinal sin of undermining her authority in front of their fresh-faced charges.

Kathryn was furious. The lives of those trainees depended on their unwavering confidence in the methods taught to them. In the field, doubt leads to hesitation, and hesitation to death. Branson was a selfish, spiteful ass. Whatever their history, compromising the training of those recruits was not the way to exact his revenge.

Word got back to brass about his behavior and he was reprimanded. Naturally, he blamed Kathryn and whined to anyone who would listen about her preferential treatment because, as he put it, "She was a dame and clearly slept her way to the top," and so the day went. Welcome to Monday. She was glad it was over.

She dropped her gear bag just inside her door and tossed her keys on the bookcase as she scanned her mail for anything interesting. "Garbage," she said, throwing it to her keys for company.

She opened her bar cabinet and sloshed some vodka in a shot glass. It was that kind of day. She collapsed into her favorite chair and threw one leg over the arm as she settled her head into the crook of its winged back. She closed her eyes and blew out a tired breath, happy to leave the day behind.

Branson was right about the preferential treatment. She wanted to be in on every field training Monday, but brass assigned her only one day a month, something she was sure had more to do with her mental history than her field capabilities. She had more hours in the field than anyone there besides Smitty. And Branson.

She swallowed her drink in one gulp, hoping to drown the unpleasant memories that were trying to crawl out of the pit of her soul. She opened her eyes before ghosts of her past appeared in the dark void, and she turned to the piano that occupied the bulk of her narrow living room. Setting on it was a reminder of something else. Someone else.

The late afternoon sun illuminated the bright, fully opened yellow rose that now resided on the piano in a proper bud vase. The simple gesture of giving one flower had always meant more to her than the overkill of a whole dozen, and it brought a bittersweet smile to her lips. How long had it been since someone she cared about had given her flowers? She let out a humorless chuckle. How long had it been since she cared about anyone?

She focused on the rose, a subconscious act to drag her mind away from its dour train of thought, and wound up sitting at the piano, where she studied the light and shadow patterns on the delicate petals. The incredible color momentarily drew her attention to the closed door down the hallway. It was her painting studio, and she thought about capturing the image on canvas. It was a distraction that was quickly discarded.

Her thoughts turned to Jenny and her shy smile as she presented the flower. Kathryn instinctively found her fingers resting on the piano keys, and she played a few quiet notes until the opening lines from "I've Got a Crush on You" passed her lips. She quit playing and laughed at herself. *Jenny Ryan.* Just the thought of her made her smile. Her smile soon disappeared as the business end of that thought overruled any pleasantries associated with it. She played a few chord progressions that turned into the chorus of "But Not for Me." She purposely hit a sour chord and stood up, almost knocking the piano bench over. She stalked the few steps to the vodka bottle and sloshed another shot into her glass. "Remember that, Hammond," she said, before swallowing it down on the way toward the bathroom to draw a bath.

The long day and the bad mood floated away as she slid deeper into the bath. Her tense body gave in to the weightless cradle of the warm water's womb-like sanctity, and with her demons at bay and her mind mercifully set adrift, she allowed herself the luxury of a rare evening to herself.

Jenny leaned against the wall at the back of the cavernous armory and watched Bernie weave his way toward her through sweaty, exuberant, jitterbugging soldiers and their volunteer army of female dance partners.

"Wow!" Bernie yelled into her ear over the noise of the band and the crowd as he arrived at her side. "This joint is jumpin'! I can't believe you got this band in here."

She polished her nails on her shirt with pride. "It's all who you know," she shouted back.

So far, the night had been a great success. The soldiers were dancing and having a great time, thanks to the gals, who were doing their best to dance with as many guys as they could. The boys always outnumbered the girls at these things, and Jenny was taking a well-deserved break from the jitterbug brigade, as she liked to call the enthusiastic young men.

She looked across the room at Cal, who was getting something to drink at the refreshment table. She leaned into Bernie's shoulder. "So, are you enjoying your stalker?"

"Yes, ma'am!" he said with a grin.

Jenny backhanded him on the chest. "Do not start talking like him, Bernie."

Bernie giggled and gazed at Cal as he made his way through the crowd with two bottles of Coca-Cola. "Speak of the devil."

Cal held out one of the bottles. "Hey, Jenny, want one of these?"

"No thanks."

Cal passed the bottle to Bernie and then turned to Jenny as he thumbed over his shoulder toward the stage. "Say, where's the singer?"

"What, the band isn't enough?"

"I thought you had an in," Cal said, winking and giving Jenny a nudge. "What's a band without the singer?"

Bernie elbowed him in the side. "Ix-nay on the inger-say, buddy," he said in Pig Latin.

"Whoops. Sorry, Jenny."

Jenny shrugged. "She was busy."

In truth, she hadn't asked her. She'd asked Dominic about borrowing The Grotto's band for the event on their day off, and the club owner left it up to the players, who were happy to oblige.

She had no intention of ever seeing Kathryn Hammond again, let alone asking her for a favor. Her pursuit of Marcus Forrester had put Kathryn, and her, in danger, and she knew her decision to walk away was the right one. If only her resolve could extinguish the regret weighing her down. She feared this particular road not taken would haunt her for the rest of her days.

She hid a wave of melancholy with a forced smile and excused herself. "Hold down the fort, boys, I'm going to get some air."

Bernie watched Jenny weave her way through the crowd toward the door and put his hand on Cal's shoulder. "Hold this for me, buddy," he said, as he handed over his soda. "I'll be right back."

"Wilco," Cal said.

Bernie popped his head out the front door as the first mellow strains of "For You" came from the clarinets on stage. He spotted Jenny leaning up against the building, her arms crossed against the chill of the night.

"Hey," Bernie said as he approached. "You okay?"

Jenny smiled. "Yep. Just getting some air."

He scooted up behind her and wrapped his arms around her to keep her warm. "You'll catch your death," he said.

She leaned into his warmth. "Mmmm. I've never been sick a day in my life. A little cold air isn't going to kill me. Feels good out here. Helps me think."

"I always said you were part Eskimo. Keep me warm then." He snuggled in closer. "Thinking about that singer?"

"Trying not to, actually."

"Sure you want to give her up?"

Jenny's hesitation betrayed her faltering resolve, and Bernie took the opportunity to probe further. "Maybe you two just have a big ol' failure to communicate. Ever think of that?"

"It's not that. It just wouldn't work out." She patted his arm, a gesture he knew signaled the end of that topic of conversation.

He squeezed her a little tighter. "Sorry Cal brought her up. He was just joking around."

Jenny leaned her head back onto his shoulder. "I know. He seems like a sweetie. I like him."

"Me too. He's quite an interesting fella."

Jenny laughed. "Yeah, if you think chicken sexing is interesting."

"He is not a farmer, Jenny!" He paused and then added, "He just sounds like one."

That made Jenny laugh, so he tried to keep it going. "I would like to hear more about this chicken sexing, though," he said.

Catcalls and whistles drew their attention to the gathering inside the building. Bernie released Jenny. "Maybe Cal's showing them how to sex a chicken."

Muffled music drifted through the entry doors as they approached, and Jenny's stride faltered when she heard a familiar voice added to the band.

Bernie opened the door and looked to the stage. "Holy smokes, is that her?"

Jenny couldn't contain her ear-to-ear grin. "Yes, it is."

"I have got to get a closer look-see at this," Bernie said, heading toward the front of the room.

Jenny reached out for him. "No ... Bernie!" But he was already lost in the howling crowd.

Jenny knew she couldn't avoid Kathryn all night. The place was big, but it wasn't that big. She would just stick to her guns, cordially thank her for coming out, and everything would be fine. She lingered near the back of the armory while she shored up her defenses, then waded into the sea of dancing soldiers, where she was passed from one man to another, like Tarzan swinging from a vine every time the song changed.

Kathryn's performance was nothing like her nightly shows at The Grotto. Her hair was down, and she wore a sleeveless blue dress that showed lots of leg, which the boys appreciated. She was relaxed and talkative, mixing swing songs and slow songs and even a dirty blues number that, in all its double entendre glory, had Jenny looking to the dark corners of the auditorium for the decency police.

During one raucous number, Kathryn brought soldiers up on the stage to join her, and Jenny thought a riot might ensue. She sent Cal and Bernie to the edge of the stage in case they had to intervene, but

Kathryn handled it all like a professional, and order was quickly restored when the song ended.

Cal made his way back to Jenny's side. "She's somethin' else," he said.

"I'll say. Where's Bernie?" Cal didn't answer, and Jenny looked up at the stage to find Bernie whispering something in Kathryn's ear. Kathryn smiled while searching the crowd with her eyes, and Bernie backed off with an evil grin as he pointed her out from the stage.

"I am going to kill him," Jenny said.

Cal laughed. "Please don't."

Kathryn gave instructions to the band and then returned to the microphone. "We've had a request. It seems your activities director is having a birthday today."

Jenny buried her head in her hands.

"Folks, how 'bout a big hand for the lovely lady, and while you're at it, you can thank her for the entertainment tonight."

The crowd showered Jenny with whistles and applause. She smiled and waved and then slapped Bernie in the chest as he arrived and engulfed her in a hug.

Kathryn leaned into the microphone. "Happy birthday, Jenny, from Bernie."

The band began to play "Too Marvelous for Words," and Jenny's eyes glistened with appreciation as Bernie swept her into the dancing crowd.

"You're not crying, are you, Bug?" he asked.

Jenny was on the verge of it but denied it with a shake of her head. "I love you," she whispered into his shirt.

He kissed the top of her head. "I love you too. No more crummy birthdays, huh?"

Jenny answered with another shake of the head and a tighter hold on his back.

They danced the rest of the song in silence, and Jenny reflected on how lucky she was to have such a good friend. A year ago this night, her world almost came crashing to an end. She didn't know how she survived it, but she did know that a big part of it was the love and patience of the man in her arms.

The song ended with a heartfelt, "Happy birthday, Jenny."

Jenny looked up at the stage expecting to get lost in those blue eyes, but Kathryn had already turned her back and was leaving the stage to an appreciative crowd that called for more. She politely declined and blew them all a collective kiss.

The band began an upbeat version of Cole Porter's "Begin the Beguine," and Jenny got swept into the arms of one of the enthusiastic jitterbug brigade. He was good, so she didn't have to worry about crushed toes or bruised shins, which was both unusual and a relief. Toward the end of the song, she saw a crowd gathering in front of the refreshment table. The crowd parted briefly to show Kathryn greeting the troops. There was a crowd of soldiers waiting to dance with her, much to the chagrin of several of the girls. She picked one soldier and dismissed the others, which pacified the annoyed girls.

And so it went. Kathryn spread herself around and danced with as many men as she could without causing a riot or a pissing contest. It was obvious that she was a veteran of this sort of thing. It was so contrary to Kathryn's unpatriotic stance at The Grotto the night they met that Jenny hadn't the faintest idea of the woman's motivation. Perhaps her appearance was purely selfish, the actions of an attention whore. For every positive thought, she entertained its equally possible negative thought. She wanted to believe Kathryn was good, and kind, and patriotic, and all the things that would allow her to follow her heart, but then there was Forrester. Forrester the traitor. Forrester the murderer. How could Kathryn be involved with him?

Jenny caught herself drifting back into Kathryn's irresistible orbit. She shook her head and watched the singer gracefully excuse herself from the group of men and head toward the front doors. A soldier at the entrance put his jacket around her shoulders, another one held the door, and yet another offered her a lit cigarette, which she took with a smile and then disappeared into the cold night air.

Almost against her will, Jenny had the urge to follow her. She should thank her, at least, for the terrific show she put on for the boys. Jenny was the activities director, after all. It was her duty.

Kathryn smiled pleasantly as she took long strides past the mingling soldiers outside the armory. They couldn't see her holding her breath, couldn't know she was seconds away from losing control. She shouldn't have come. She thought she could do it, but there were too many soldiers inside. They were joyous and laughing, but they reminded her of the dead. Her dead.

The warm air in the crowded hall was choked with cigarette smoke and the smell of heated bodies. The cavernous walls felt heavy and suffocating. She had to get out of there.

She turned the corner of the hulking brick building and ducked behind one of its supporting ramparts, where she placed both hands on the wall like a criminal awaiting a frisk. She breathed in the cold night air in a desperate gasp and wished for something, anything, to keep her present.

Breathe. She just had to breathe. She tried to clear her mind. Tried to focus on her purposeful breaths, but images of laughing soldiers mingled with dead soldiers. The sounds of laughter turned to taunts and then screams of terror. God, not now. Not now!

Her heart hammered in her chest like it was trying to escape. Focus on something. One focus. She imagined the cold air circulating through her lungs until she expelled the darkness poisoning her reason. One simple thought. One focus. Intellect would not save her now. Thinking it through was the very thing that perpetuated the vicious cycle of anxiety once it started. If she couldn't stop thinking about what set her off, anxiety would turn to panic, and it would pull her away from reality like a riptide carrying her out to sea, where she would drown in the ocean of her sins. Breathe. Hold. Exhale.

When her racing heart calmed and the brick beneath her hands came into focus, she pushed off the wall and brought a trembling hand to her lips, taking a long drag on the cigarette crushed between her fingers. She exhaled and then quickly took another drag, hoping the soothing rush of nicotine would save her. Footsteps from behind forced her to outwardly compose herself and pray she could bluff her way through the encounter.

"Hey there," a woman's voice said.

Kathryn recognized Jenny immediately and exhaled the smoke into the night sky. She flicked the cigarette to the ground and turned with the broadest grin she could manage. "Well ... hey there yourself, birthday girl. I knew we'd catch up to one another sometime tonight in this zoo."

Jenny followed the glowing ember to the ground. "You didn't have to do that."

Kathryn looked briefly at the discarded cigarette as she traded one life preserver for another. "It slipped," she lied, rubbing it out with her foot. She focused intently on Jenny, the perfect distraction, and someone who had no connection to her horrific past.

"I just wanted to thank you for your performance tonight," Jenny said. "You did a fabulous job, and I really appreciate you coming up here."

Kathryn felt the ground beneath her feet solidify now that she had a role to play and another shot at completing her assignment to Jenny Ryan. "Honestly, I wasn't sure I was welcome. You invited the band, but you didn't invite me, and after your abrupt departure from the club, well, I wasn't sure where we stood."

Jenny hesitated. "I wasn't sure you'd accept."

"May I ask why?"

"Well, as you said, I made an abrupt departure, and it seemed wrong of me to ask a favor of you after that."

Kathryn knew it was a lie. She stepped closer. "I'm sorry if I did something or said something to upset you."

Jenny shook her head. "No. It's not you. I just ... I have some things going on."

Kathryn saw her opportunity and put a hand on Jenny's shoulder. "Anything I can do?"

Jenny looked at her with the same momentary surrender she had on the stairs outside the club, and Kathryn smiled internally because she knew she was only a few subtle moves away from luring Jenny back in.

Her plan was interrupted when Jenny removed her hand from her shoulder and began rubbing it brusquely.

"Kat, you're shivering, and your hand is like ice. Come on, let's go back inside." She started pulling her along.

A cascading wave of dread seized Kathryn at the thought of reentering the soldier-filled hall and she yanked her hand back. She pulled the soldier's jacket tighter around her shoulders. "I'm all right. I just need some air. You go ahead. I'll be in soon."

"Okay." Jenny lingered a beat. "Thank you again. You really gave the boys a night to remember."

Kathryn smiled, despite the renewed tightening in her chest, and she tilted her head in the armory's direction. "It's my pleasure. They deserve it."

Jenny nodded in agreement and walked away.

Kathryn looked at her trembling hand and balled it into a tight fist before she shook it out with a silent curse.

Jenny looked over the thinning crowd and smiled. It was the end of a successful night. She'd survived an encounter with Kathryn Hammond without giving in to her charismatic pull and managed to keep her distance when Kathryn made her way back into the swarming crowds, dancing and talking to soldiers until the band packed it up and the troops headed for their buses.

No one else resisted Kathryn's easy smile and friendly banter, and Jenny certainly couldn't blame them. Outside, when Kathryn put her hand on her shoulder, Jenny was thankful she had the cold as an excuse to remove it before she gave in, confessed her attraction, and fell into her arms. Oh, how she wanted to fall into those arms.

It was maddening. Kathryn's intense gaze disarmed her every time. It promised something more, wanted something more, and Jenny swore she wasn't imagining it. Something was happening between them, and every encounter reaffirmed it. She wanted to ask Kathryn if she felt it too. She had to feel it.

There was definite longing and desire in each look and touch, but not tonight, when she pulled her hand away as if she'd touched a hot poker. Jenny shook her head. Maybe she was imagining the whole thing. After all, what would a woman like Kathryn Hammond possibly see in her? Would Kathryn even feel such things toward a woman? Jenny would drive herself crazy trying to figure it out. After one step forward and three steps back, she was left wondering, does she or doesn't she feel the same? How was she supposed to move on with such questions niggling at her? Avoidance was her only hope, and that would do just fine, because Kathryn was nowhere to be found now.

Cal and Bernie wanted to take her out for her birthday, but she didn't feel much like celebrating. Bernie wouldn't take no for an answer.

He put his arm around her shoulders. "Jenny Bug, we are going to O'Malley's. We are going to drink beer. We are going to play darts, eat stale pretzels, and celebrate your twenty-fourth birthday. Okay?"

She put a hand to her chest. "Be still my heart. Who can resist stale pretzels?"

"After last year? Certainly not you."

"I cannot argue with that."

"You said it, sister." He handed her a bottle of Coca-Cola, and he and Cal raised theirs. "Here's to a successful evening."

Jenny took a swig and nearly spit it out all over the grinning men. "Good Christmas, Bernie!" she said, wiping her mouth.

Cal lifted a shiny silver flask halfway out of his back pocket and grinned. "Rum and Coke?"

"Put that thing away," Jenny said. "And warn me next time."

Bernie laughed. "What, and miss that face?"

Jenny winced. "Have a little rum with that Coke, why don't you. That's a big boy drink."

The two men simultaneously struck a bodybuilder's pose and laughed at each other. Bernie pointed at Cal. "Jinx! You owe me a

Coke." They both laughed again and raised their bottles. "Cheers," they said, then knocked them back.

Jenny shook her head. "Bernie, don't show Cal your ass so soon."

Cal must have decided that wasn't such a bad idea. He reached for the flask. "Drink, darling?"

Bernie held up his bottle. "Hit me."

Jenny put herself between the soda bottle and the flask. "All right, bad choice of words." She situated herself between the men and put her arms around their waists. "Let's see if we can at least walk out of the building tonight."

"Don't worry," Bernie whispered, "Cal said he'd carry me." He leaned across Jenny's body toward Cal. "Didn't you?"

"As a matter of fact, I did."

Jenny eyed the room for fear the two would go too far in public. Bernie knew better, and, as a soldier, Cal definitely knew better, but alcohol was involved, and that always threw good sense out the window.

"Break it up, boys," she said. "Not in front of the children." She untangled herself from Bernie's slightly intoxicated arm. "Can I trust you two to behave while I go get our coats?"

Bernie nodded earnestly.

Cal stiffened and saluted. "Yes, ma'am!"

As Jenny walked away shaking her head, she heard Bernie say, "Carry me, baby?"

It was already a birthday to remember. After last year, any birthday but that one would be one to remember. Jenny shook off her melancholy, exhaled her ridiculous attraction to Forrester's mistress, and headed toward Bernie and Cal, waiting at the front door. Cal must have said something brilliant because Bernie snapped his fingers in agreement and scanned the dispersing crowd.

Jenny assumed he was looking for her and waved as she approached. He acknowledged her wave with a lift of his chin but went on searching.

"Who are you looking for?" she asked, as she passed out their coats and followed his eyes over the thinning crowd.

"Nobody," he said, opening the door. "You ready for stale pretzels and warm beer?"

Jenny grinned. "I am."

When they entered the parking lot, they passed a car with steamed windows. Bernie nudged Cal in the side with a wink and a smile, which brought a fit of giggles from both men. Jenny wedged herself between them again.

Thankfully, Bernie realized what she was doing and kissed the side of her head. He leaned back to Cal. "Behave now, son," he said in an exaggerated southern drawl.

Cal chuckled and thumbed over his shoulder to where Kathryn was just about to get into her car.

"Ah," Bernie said. "There you are." Before Jenny could stop him, he was trotting the few yards to Kathryn's car.

"Bernie ... no!" Jenny stage whispered to his back to no avail. Cal took her hand and followed after him.

"So, we were taking Jenny here to O'Malley's for her birthday," Bernie was saying as they arrived, "and we were wondering if you'd like to join us?"

Please say no, Jenny screamed in her head, not sure she could resist the woman in a one-on-one situation twice in one night.

Kathryn smiled. "I appreciate the offer, but it's been a long day."

"Of course it has," Jenny said. She grabbed Bernie's sleeve and pulled him away. "Thank you again for coming, Miss Hammond. Have a lovely evening."

"You're welcome. You too, and happy birthday."

"You don't know what you're missing," Bernie said as he was dragged away.

Jenny flagged a taxi when they reached the curb. "What the hell were you thinking, Bernie?"

"What? This could have been the start of a beautiful friendship. Say, Cal, did you see *Casablanca*?"

"Yeah."

Jenny exhaled in exasperation. "Don't start that again."

Bernie envisioned a gay character or relationship in every movie he saw. His dissertation on *Casablanca* was legendary, and Cal would get an earful as soon as they exited the taxi.

"You're wasting your breath on Cal; he's already a member."

Bernie crossed his arms and lowered his voice. "Only the board shall judge his application." He nudged Cal and whispered, "You're a shoo-in!"

Jenny shook her head and snorted as a taxi pulled alongside.

CHAPTER TWENTY-THREE

*K*athryn smiled briefly as she folded herself into her car. She could see Jenny gesturing excitedly at Bernie and knew he was getting an earful for inviting her to the birthday party. She put her hands on the steering wheel and watched the trio pile into a taxi.

This was the life she wanted for Jenny. Good times with friends, far from the intrigue and horror of the war.

She should have taken Bernie's invitation. Brass was anxious for answers. It wasn't up to her to decide what kind of life Jenny Ryan should or shouldn't have. Only sentiment, brought on by exhaustion, explained her refusal. She reasoned it was Jenny's birthday, and after her last birthday, she deserved one full of fun and free of drama.

Kathryn bowed her head and exhaled the uncharacteristic shirking of her duty. Sentimentality wasn't in her job description. She wanted this assignment over too. She had a war to get back to, a debt to pay. This lapse in her mission would be the last, she decided. Tomorrow, Jenny Ryan would feel the full force of her charm offensive, and no one *ever* resisted that.

A smile split her lips just thinking about it until, out of the corner of her eye, she saw headlights illuminate the curbside. A dark sedan pulled out after the taxi. Was it a coincidence, or was Jenny being followed? To be on the safe side, she joined the procession.

The taxi dropped off the trio at O'Malley's bar, and the dark sedan pulled off the side of the road and parked. Kathryn followed a respectable distance behind and waited for the driver to make his move.

When no one got out of the sedan, she reached for the binoculars under her seat and focused on the tag number. "Keep those lights on ... that's it," she said, as she memorized the tag, illuminated by the parking lights. She tossed the binoculars on the passenger seat and removed a pencil from the sun visor. She looked around for something to write on and settled on the ration book in her purse.

After she wrote the tag number on the ration book's outer envelope, she stared at the car. Her heart rate quickened, anticipating some action. No one got out, and the lights continued to burn.

"Any day now, buddy," she said.

As if the driver sensed her criticism, the lights went out, but no one got out of the car. Kathryn relaxed back into her seat and tried to figure out the dope's game. A shuttered newspaper kiosk blocked his view of the bar's entrance, so he couldn't see anyone coming or going. It defeated the purpose of a tail if he couldn't keep eyes on the subject. How wonderfully irresponsible of him.

She drove around the block and parked on a side street, which enabled her to enter the bar unseen. Just inside the entrance, she slipped inside a telephone cabinet and dialed Smitty.

"Yeah?" he said, his voice heavy with sleep.

"Smitty."

"Kat? What the ..."

She could hear him dragging his wristwatch across the surface of his nightstand. "Sorry I woke you. Listen—"

"Are you all right?" he said before she could finish.

"Who's the tail on Jenny Ryan?"

"We don't have a tail. She's your gig, doll."

"You're sure?"

"Yes, I'm sure. What's going on? Where are you?"

"I was singing at the armory tonight and—"

"I'm sorry," he interrupted. "I thought you said you were singing at the armory."

"I did."

The line was silent.

"Smitty?"

He cleared his throat. "Are you all right?"

She knew what he was asking. "Yes, fine."

He waited another beat and then got back to the original question. "Listen," he said, "if there's a tail, do not engage them by yourself. Do you hear me?"

"Relax, Smitty, I'm not engaging anyone unless they engage me first."

"Okay, that's not very comforting. Where are you? I'll meet you."

"Write down this tag and see if we can get anything tonight."

"Not likely, but shoot."

She gave him the number, and then he asked again where she was.

"I'll be fine, Smitty. I'm just going to stick by the kid here and make sure she gets home safely."

"Where are you?"

She could hear an edge to his voice, which made her uncomfortable. "I'll call you in a bit. Don't worry."

"Kat! Where—" she heard him yell as she hung up the receiver. Smitty was worried, which could just be his overprotective nature, or he knew more than he was telling her. Either way, it didn't look good for Jenny. How long had this been going on? She thought back to their accident, and for the first time, she seriously considered it may not have been about her. What if they were after Jenny? But why?

She glanced out the door toward the dark sedan. Convinced the tail was content to wait for Jenny to leave the bar to make his move, she stepped out of the phone cabinet and straightened her jacket. She would worry about the tail later. She had a charm offensive to implement. It was time to get this assignment over with.

· · ·

Much to Jenny's chagrin, she couldn't get Bernie to stop talking about Kathryn Hammond. "I'm not interested," she said over and over again, but he scoffed at that.

"Since when? You were a goner at first sight, and why not?"

She couldn't tell him why not, so she dug herself a deeper hole by claiming Kathryn wasn't on their "team." Bernie took that as a challenge. No answer satisfied him, not even the fact that Kathryn Hammond was Marcus Forrester's mistress.

There was no reasoning with a drunk, hopeless romantic, so their conversation devolved into a stalemate.

"So, what makes you think she's not?" Bernie asked again.

"What makes you think she *is*?" Jenny said, putting the onus on him, since nothing she said made any difference.

He took a drink of his beer. "You started that."

"Yes, but I was mistaken." She reached across the small table and put her hand on his forearm. "Please drop it, Bernie."

He smiled sympathetically but ignored her plea. "Next time you see her, you can give her the *Casablanca* test."

Jenny shook her head. "You and your ..." She gave up with a dismissive wave of her hand. "It doesn't matter. I don't anticipate seeing her again." She paused and glared. "So drop it. Please."

The glare worked until he got to the bottom of his beer.

"So, what makes you think she's not?" he asked again, as if he'd never uttered it before.

Jenny buried her face in her hands. Bernie was getting drunker, and she was losing her patience. She couldn't be angry with him—he just wanted her to be happy—but it was going to be a long night if she couldn't get him to move on.

"What makes you think she *is*?" she repeated.

He smiled. "I asked you first."

"Look, Bernie ..." Her voice took on a quiet sternness. "Even if she is, which I'm not conceding, I'm not interested. Get me? And neither is she."

"Liar."

Jenny put a hand to her heart. "You wound me, sir."

Bernie chuckled.

Jenny leaned back in her chair. "Besides, she refused your invitation to my party; that should tell you something."

Bernie looked toward the door and casually popped a few pretzels in his mouth. "And if she *had* accepted my invitation?"

"Then I would have to adjust my theory accordingly."

Bernie dusted off his hands and stood up. "Well, get adjusting."

Jenny froze and then relaxed. "Ha ha, very funny."

"Hilarious," Bernie said as Kathryn arrived at the table.

"Is this a private party or can anyone crash it?"

Bernie quickly offered his seat, opposite Jenny. "It's not crashing when you're invited. Beer, Kathryn?"

"That would be grand, thanks."

"Coming right up," he said, then bounded toward the bar.

Jenny suppressed a sudden urge to panic when she heard Kathryn's voice, but seeing her face to face again, the familiar dulling of anything she deemed important only moments before overtook her, and she smiled stupidly as Kathryn settled into the seat before her.

"You came," Jenny said.

"Do you mind?"

"Of course not. Why would I?"

"You didn't seem thrilled with the idea in the parking lot."

Jenny pursed her lips in regret. Her protest to Bernie seemed a lifetime ago. Looking into Kathryn's eyes now, she couldn't imagine purposely avoiding her; in fact, she wouldn't mind staring into those blue eyes forever.

"It wasn't Bernie's place to ask you. It was mine."

Kathryn lifted her brow. "But you didn't."

"I should have."

"But you didn't."

"Well, after your generous performance this evening, I didn't want to impose further."

Kathryn's slow smile bloomed into a full-faced grin. "Celebrating your birthday is not an imposition."

Jenny matched the full-faced grin and got lost in Kathryn's kind eyes.

Kathryn's smile faded, but her eyes were still kind when she asked, "Is that really the reason?"

Caught in another lie, Jenny couldn't hide the flush of embarrassment. "What do you mean?"

Kathryn leaned in and clasped her hands together on the table. "We were getting closer. Friends, I thought. And then we weren't. I um ..." She stared at her hands and then cleared her throat. "Maybe I'm just a little insecure."

Jenny laughed out loud, then covered her mouth against the outburst. "I'm sorry, but I find that unlikely."

"You'd be surprised."

"Yes, I would."

Kathryn paused. "Are you avoiding me, Jenny?"

Jenny reflexively began to say no, but Kathryn's use of her name felt like a syringe of truth serum plunged directly into her heart. "Is it that obvious?" she said instead.

Kathryn grinned. "It's unusual."

"Bruised ego?"

"Yes, actually."

Jenny deflected the accusation while the truth serum wore off. "You're the one who pulled away from me earlier this evening. Who's avoiding whom?"

Kathryn acknowledged the scene outside the armory with a nod. "The dance floor was a little tight. I just needed some air."

Jenny softened, noting a vulnerability in Kathryn's voice she'd never heard before. "Claustrophobic?"

"Occasionally. I just wasn't ready to go back in yet."

"I'm sorry."

Kathryn shrugged. "Don't be. It was a great night. I didn't mean to offend you."

"I'm not offended."

"You seem offended."

Jenny waited a beat before answering. She was offended. Forrester stood between them like a physical wall. Kathryn moved through the wall at will, but Jenny was trapped on the outside looking in, and what she saw, she didn't like.

"I can't figure you out, Kathryn Hammond."

Kathryn's kind smile returned. "I'm sure I can help you with that." Her voice was low and unmistakably seductive.

Jenny smiled and leaned in to play along just as four large glasses of beer filled her vision.

"Here we go!" Bernie said. He set down a tray of beers in the center of the table.

Jenny took a glass and leaned back, silently cursing Bernie's timing.

"So ... Kat," Bernie said, settling into his seat, "did you see *Casablanca*?"

Jenny leaned an elbow on the table and momentarily covered her eyes with her hand.

Kathryn picked up her beer. "Yes, I saw it." Her eyes darted back and forth between Jenny's obvious discomfort and Bernie's triumphant smirk. "Hm, I get the feeling I've stepped in the middle of something."

Jenny turned to Bernie. "Trust me, there is only one person who's stepped in anything here, and he is up to his neck in it right now."

Kathryn raised her brow and looked at Bernie. "Sounds like you're in trouble, brother."

He shook his head. "Jenny's the one in trouble. She still isn't convinced you belong to our club."

Jenny's eyes went round and she kicked him under the table.

"Ow!" he said, rubbing his shin with more vigor than her light tap deserved. "Whadja do that for? You wanted to know."

Jenny glared at him. Dead. He is a dead man. Tomorrow, in all his hangover glory, he will pay. "Drink another beer, Bernie," she said, pushing his beer closer.

He grinned. "Don't mind if I do."

"What club is this?" Kathryn asked.

"The *Casablanca* Appreciation Society," Bernie said.

"Ah," Kathryn drew out, as if she knew it well. "I have no idea what you're talking about."

"Nor should you," Jenny said. "Ignore him."

Kathryn dropped her gaze to the fourth beer on the table. "Did you lose your friend?"

Bernie looked around. "Um, yeah, he's here somewhere, securing us a dartboard, I think." He continued to scan the bar but failed to spot Cal. "Lemme go find him."

While Bernie headed toward the back of the bar, Jenny exhaled in relief. "Oh, thank you," she said. "I'm sorry about that."

Kathryn smiled. "No apology needed. He seems like fun."

"He's a great guy. I love him to death, but some days ..." She gently shook her fist in his direction.

Kathryn chuckled and then sipped her beer.

Jenny stared at her. Here they were again. Despite all her intentions to stay away from Kathryn, something seemed determined to throw them together. Kathryn followed her this time, and while accepting a birthday party invitation was a logical reason, it had to be something more. Jenny hoped it was something more.

"You look tired," she said.

Kathryn's shoulders relaxed, as if a director had just yelled 'cut,' but she smiled. "It's been a long day."

"Why did you come out here, Kathryn?" Jenny asked, hoping the use of her name would have the same truth-inducing effect.

"I can't stop thinking about you," Kathryn said.

It definitely had that effect. Jenny's heart rate picked up.

"I've been thinking about you since you left the club so abruptly."

Jenny sat a little straighter. "Do tell."

Kathryn stared at her hands. "I know you wanted to get to Forrester through me, and that's fine, but now that that's over, so it seems are we. That bothers me, because I thought we were becoming friends."

Jenny had never seen this version of Kathryn, and it caught her off guard. "Say, you are insecure."

Kathryn looked solemn and hurt by the remark. "I haven't many friends. I'd hate to lose one without knowing why."

Jenny reached out and touched her forearm. "Gosh, I'm awfully sorry. It's not like that at all. In fact, it's just the opposite."

"How so?"

Jenny hesitated and then removed her hand. Now was certainly not the time to admit her true feelings, especially since the jury was still out on the *Casablanca* test, but she could be honest about one thing.

"When you were hurt in that accident because of me."

"Jenny ..."

"It brought up some painful memories." A familiar ache surrounding her father's death gathered in her chest, and, thankfully, Kathryn didn't protest further. "It scared me. I couldn't bear it if something happened to you because of me."

Kathryn reached out and covered Jenny's hand with her own. "That's over now."

Jenny agreed with a silent nod, fighting back tears.

Kathryn squeezed her hand. "I've upset you. I'm sorry."

Jenny put her hand on Kathryn's and shook her head. "It's not you. It just happens sometimes."

Kathryn pressed her lips together in a regretful smile, and Jenny knew she understood completely.

"Some party, huh?" Jenny said, pulling her hands away to wipe tears from her lower lids before they fell. "I have to pull myself together before Bernie gets back or I'll never hear the end of it. We have a rule. No crying on my birthday."

"It's a good rule."

Jenny sniffed and raised her chin, shaking off the unwanted emotions. "I'm sorry I made you feel used. Honestly, you confuse me, Kathryn, and I'm not sure what to do about it."

"I'm not that complicated, I promise."

Jenny laughed. "You're the most complicated person I've ever met."

Kathryn stared at her for a moment and then tilted her head. "Because of Forrester?"

"Yes."

"He has nothing to do with our friendship."

"I disagree."

"Because he's married?"

"Because he's a pig, and a Nazi, and he had my father killed, and you can do much better."

"Much better like you?"

Jenny was shocked by her unexpected candor and eyed the room as if everyone knew what they were talking about. "I hardly know what you mean."

"You know exactly what I mean."

There was nothing jovial in Kathryn's voice, and if personal history was any indication, coming right up would be the usual revulsion that comes with unwanted advances toward a straight woman. "Are you disgusted?"

"Do I look disgusted?"

She looked beautiful, that's how she looked. Too beautiful, and too attached. Nothing about her made any sense. "Well, you've made it abundantly clear that Forrester is a permanent fixture, so ..."

Kathryn clasped her hands together on the table and leaned forward. "Let me tell you something about Forrester—"

"Hey!" Bernie interrupted. "Look who I found disrobing in the bathroom." He pointed to Cal, who had one sleeve of his olive drab shirt soaking wet.

"Did you fall in, soldier?" Jenny asked pleasantly, not sure she wanted to hear what Kathryn had to say about Forrester.

"Hi ya, Kathryn," Cal said. "Swell job tonight."

"Hi ya, Sergeant, thank you. Do I dare ask why you were disrobing in the bathroom?"

He tugged at the wet fabric. "Aw, some dope sloshed a drink on me. I was tryin' to wash it out."

Jenny stared at Bernie expectantly, hoping he would fill the awkward silence. Unfortunately, he misinterpreted the look as her *amscray* signal and slapped Cal on the back. "Listen, buddy, whaddaya say we play some pool."

"Uh, yeah ... okay," Cal said. He snuck Jenny a thumbs up before following Bernie to the pool tables.

Jenny inwardly cringed and then slowly turned toward Kathryn to take whatever she was about to dish out. "You were saying?"

"Marc Forrester is a very powerful man."

Jenny disliked the casual use of his first name, and if Kathryn made some flimsy excuse about his wealth and position bolstering her career or some other nonsense, she might scream, but she held her tongue and simply nodded.

"Powerful men get what they want."

"And he wants you." Big surprise.

"Yes. He can also be a very brutal man when he doesn't get what he wants."

Jenny's eyes widened. Kathryn's situation was not what she thought. "My God, has he hurt you? Did he threaten you?" She was surprised to find her fists clenched, ready to come to Kathryn's rescue.

"No," Kathryn said. "He doesn't have to, because I give him what he wants, you see?"

She did see, and it conjured up the most distasteful images. "I'm so sorry. Sleeping with that bastard because he threatens you—God." She looked away and shook her head. When she looked back, Kathryn was smiling.

"What?"

"I don't sleep with him."

"You don't?"

Kathryn shook her head.

Jenny snapped her fingers. "I knew it!" She covered her mouth. "Sorry." She leaned in and lowered her voice. She was almost giddy at the news. "I knew there was no way you were really involved with him ... romantically, sexually, I mean." Jenny basked in the revelation for a moment, and then reality set in and she wondered how Kathryn could avoid sex with him.

"It's complicated," Kathryn said, as if she could read her mind.

"But you're not complicated."

"Correct."

"Hm," Jenny said skeptically.

Kathryn smiled. "You'll see."

That sounded like a tantalizing invitation. A public bar wasn't the place to press that further. Pressing would follow in a more private setting, she hoped, and the thought of it made her warm in all the right places. For now, it was enough that Kathryn wasn't with Forrester willingly. The revelation made them allies again. As for complications, something still gave her pause.

"Is he?"

"Is he what?"

"A Nazi sympathizer."

"I thought you had proof," Kathryn said with a grin.

Jenny smirked as another lie fell at her feet.

"I'm not going to comment on that," Kathryn said.

Jenny's face darkened. "Why are you protecting him?"

"You're a reporter, Jenny. You print anything I say, and what do you think he'll do to me?"

"Give me some credit, Kathryn. I would never reveal my source."

"Jenny," Kathryn said with an admonishing tilt of her head. "You've been stalking him at every turn, and you and I had a very public display the other night. Do you think you're invisible? I know you have your reasons for chasing down Forrester, and I respect that, but I'm in a tough spot, and I'm doing the best I can to—"

"I'm not writing that story," Jenny interrupted. The longer she was in Kathryn's presence, the stronger she felt about it.

"I didn't ask you not to write the story, just that I have no comment."

"I'm not going to sacrifice your safety for some story," Jenny said.

Kathryn raised her brow slightly but didn't say anything. Jenny couldn't believe how easy it was to demote justice for her father to "some story," but gazing into Kathryn's eyes, there wasn't anything she wouldn't do to keep her safe.

Kathryn finally blinked. "I'm afraid our friendship has cost you something. I know it was important, and I'm sorry."

Jenny smiled. "It's going to be worth it."

Kathryn smiled in return and then glanced toward Bernie at the pool table. "I would prefer that my situation stay between you and me, okay?"

"Absolutely." Jenny got up and then slid into the seat next to Kathryn, to be as close as possible. "I mean, I won't say anything if you don't want me to, but wouldn't you rather he know that you're being coerced into spending time with that pig? Rather than having him think ... well ... you know ..." She considered the tables around them and then whispered, "That you're a prostitute or something?"

"I guess I am, really," Kathryn said. "Aren't I?"

"Hardly."

Kathryn stared into her beer. "Being with Forrester ..." She paused, then looked up. "Being coerced. It's humiliating. I'd rather be seen as a prostitute, slut, whore, or what have you, than a victim, weak and helpless."

Jenny thought she saw tears forming in Kathryn's eyes and laid a comforting hand on her arm.

Kathryn pressed her lips into a smile, dismissing the concern. "It's not something I'm proud of, and I'd rather keep it between you and me. I hope you understand."

Jenny held up three fingers in a Girl Scout oath. "Completely. On my honor, my lips are sealed."

"Why am I not surprised you were a Girl Scout?"

"Golden Eaglet recipient, thank you very much."

"Of course!"

They both laughed, and then Jenny turned serious.

"I'm sorry you're in such a tough spot."

Kathryn shrugged. "The curse of being beautiful instead of rich."

Jenny lifted her glass. "Poor you."

"Literally," Kathryn said, clinking her glass to Jenny's.

They both laughed again and exhaled the cloud that had gathered over their conversation.

Jenny sat back, traces of a smile still on her face. She had a new friend who trusted her with secrets and who wasn't really romantically involved with one of the most contemptible men in town.

"What?" Kathryn asked.

Jenny waved her hand dismissively, not wanting to bring up Forrester again. "It's nothing."

"Oh, no," Kathryn said. "I tell you my secrets, you tell me yours. Especially ones that make you grin like that."

"You have no idea how happy it makes me that you're not really with him," she said.

"Thank you for saying that," Kathryn said. "And thank you for your discretion. I'm happy to have someone I can confide in, and hey, anything that makes you happy on your birthday."

Happy was an understatement. Every previous encounter had Forrester's dark shadow looming over it. Jenny's view of Kathryn now was brighter, cleaner, hopeful. Every obstacle vanished, including her story. Kathryn followed her this time to retrieve something she'd lost —their friendship. Jenny felt pursued, noticed, and wanted by the most beautiful woman she'd ever met, and if that pursuit was for friendship only, she would take it, and how, but something in Kathryn's eyes hinted there was something more.

Today was her birthday, a fresh start after an *annus horribilis.* She would draw clear lines around this new relationship because there was no way to hide where she wanted it to go. She kept an eye on the pool tables because she didn't want an interruption. Not now.

"I have to tell you," she said, voice low for discretion, while she ignored the nervous cramp in her gut giving her final warning to quit while she was ahead. "I'm not very good at playing games."

"Is that what we've been doing?" Kathryn asked.

"Actually," Jenny said, "I think you've been nothing but up front with me. I was unfairly critical of you before, and I felt awful about it. And now that I know you're not what I thought you were, I feel even worse."

The cramp in her gut turned into a lump in her throat, and she swallowed it down before going on.

"When I first met you, I told myself that I wanted to get close to you because of Forrester. And when chasing Forrester through you was no longer a possibility, you were right, I tried to avoid you. I actually vowed to never see you again."

She glanced at Kathryn, who raised her brow.

"I couldn't get past Forrester and your unapologetic devotion to him. But when you told me you weren't with him, romantically, that is, the sense of relief I felt ... well, it was more than just ..." She stopped and stared straight ahead, as a sense of doom weighed her down. Her face was warm and perspiration gathered on her brow. "What I'm trying to say is that I'd be very interested in getting to know you." She could feel Kathryn's eyes boring into her, but she didn't dare look her way. "As a friend, of course, but I think you can sense that I'm open to something more."

Jenny no longer felt Kathryn's eyes on her. She looked to the side to find her gazing nonchalantly into the crowded bar as she lifted her beer to her lips and took a long swallow.

Jenny had never had a panic attack before, but the way her heart was hammering in her chest made her think she was having one now.

"I'm sorry if I've misconstrued your presence here," she said, "But I'm assuming you have some measure of interest in me or you wouldn't be here." She paused, but Kathryn still didn't answer. "Unless, of course, I'm just arrogant and conceited, which is entirely possible, and you're really here because you have a penchant for warm beer and stale pretzels."

Kathryn finally smiled and lifted her glass again. "The trick is to drink the beer *before* it gets warm. I have no words of wisdom about stale pretzels."

Jenny smiled, but Kathryn's deflection didn't bode well. Jenny was sure she'd blown it and looked away, pretending to respond to a noisy table next to them. She wished she could rewind the past few minutes.

Kathryn took another sip of her beer and returned the glass to the table, close to where Jenny's hand was resting. "You're honest to a fault, Jenny Ryan."

"It's quite often my downfall," Jenny said, then lifted her own beer and took a bracing swallow in preparation for Kathryn's rejection.

Kathryn still stared nonchalantly into the room as her hand slid slowly from her glass to Jenny's idle hand and lightly brushed it with her pinky. "I'm very interested in getting to know you. As a friend." She paused. "Or more if you'd like."

Jenny could barely contain her full-faced grin. This was going to be the best birthday ever. "I most definitely would like."

Kathryn countered with a full-faced grin of her own, and Jenny decided she didn't smile enough and would make it her mission to make sure she did it more often.

"Are you still mad I asked her out here?" Bernie asked with a smug grin, as Jenny watched Kathryn weave her way through the bar to the telephone cabinet near the front door.

"Mad?" Jenny feigned innocence. "Who was mad?"

She purposely didn't say any more, knowing it would drive Bernie insane. As she predicted, he grabbed her arm and said, "Tell me everything!"

Jenny felt an unusual sense of calm as she realized how exhausting it had been trying to deny her feelings and how good it felt to have her heart be right for a change. For the first time, she wouldn't tell Bernie everything. She had a secret, and she would keep her word.

"Uh-huh," Bernie said. "Momma owes me dinner, I think."

"I guess you two worked things out," Cal said. "You were a little prickly there for a while."

"You could say we've come to an understanding," Jenny said cryptically.

"And ..." Bernie said, prodding.

"And that's all you need to know."

"Uh-oh," Bernie said in mock alarm. "We've been cut off. This must be serious."

"Well, good for you, Jenny," Cal said. "I hope that works out for ya."

Bernie glared at Cal. "No, soldier. She does not get off the hook. You dig, and you dig until she tells you *everything*. This is how it works. Understand?" He turned to Jenny. "Now, tell me everything. Starting with hello."

She stared back blankly.

"You will tell me," he said. "I will know. You cannot stop me. I will be informed."

That was the truth, secrets or not; he did have a way of needling things out of her, so she was relieved when Kathryn returned to the table and interrupted the interrogation.

Kathryn couldn't help but mirror the bright smile on Jenny's upturned face as she arrived back at the table. There was nothing to smile about, but there was something infectious in such a welcome.

"Everything okay?" Jenny asked.

"Yes," Kathryn lied.

She called Smitty to check on the tag, but he wasn't home. The tag information was a long shot, but his unanswered phone meant he was worried out of his mind and searching the city trying to find her. She would get an earful tomorrow for not telling him where she was.

The bar was about to close, and waiting outside was a mystery tail whose intentions couldn't be good. The element of danger usually excited her, but she was worried this time because she didn't know where it was coming from or why. The only good thing so far was that Jenny confirmed her intention to drop her tell-all exposé of Forrester. That seemed to hinge on their friendship, and Kathryn decided that was the easiest part of her assignment. Jenny was ill-tempered at times, but likable and lovely, and whatever else she had to do to retrieve Daniel Ryan's files, getting close to Jenny Ryan wasn't a hardship.

As soon as she got settled in her seat, Jenny's shoe-less foot began slowly rubbing her ankle.

Kathryn smiled down through the table at the action below and raised her eyes approvingly.

Jenny smiled back and then turned to Bernie.

"All right. Where is it?"

He blinked in mock innocence. "Where's what?"

She held out her hand impatiently. "Come on, come on. Where's my present?"

"You're worse than a kid on Christmas," he said, as he dug into his jacket pocket. He pulled out a thin, palm-length brown box and gently placed it in her hand.

Jenny's face drained of color and she stared at him for a moment. "Bernie."

Kathryn watched the exchange with great interest. Bernie was more than serious; he was solemn. "Please don't cry, Bug."

Jenny seemed to know what was in the box before she opened it. With trembling hands, she opened it and removed a black Wirt fountain pen with a beautiful barrel of inlaid mother of pearl. She gently unscrewed the cap to reveal the pristine 14k gold nib. She capped the pen and wordlessly stood as Bernie did the same and took her in his arms.

"He wanted to give it to you last year," he said softly as he rocked her gently. "He asked me to pick it up from the shop on my way over to the house, and well, after what happened ... I just held on to it."

"Thank you," she said in a hoarse whisper.

Bernie squeezed his eyes shut and then loosened his embrace to look in her eyes. "No crying, right?"

Jenny forced a smile and nodded. "Right."

Kathryn saw emotion building in Jenny's eyes and knew tears were imminent. Right on cue, Jenny excused herself.

"I'll be right back," she said.

Kathryn reflexively moved to follow her to the ladies' room, but Bernie stilled her with a look. "She'll be all right. Just give her a minute."

"Just the same," Kathryn said, getting up anyway.

Bernie reached out. "While we've got a minute."

Kathryn eyed Jenny's retreating back but sat again.

"She seems like a tough kid," he said, "but she's been through hell this past year. I don't know what your intentions are, but I don't want to see her get hurt."

"Then we both want the same thing."

They stared at each other, each measuring their respective concerns until, finally, Bernie said, "Good."

Kathryn nodded and headed toward the restroom.

Jenny put her hands on each side of the sink and bowed her head. "Pull yourself together," she pleaded quietly. "It's been a year. You have to stop this." She heard the outer door of the ladies' room open and, with a glance in the mirror, quickly wiped her eyes and sniffed, in a futile attempt to look presentable. It was hopeless, so she turned on the water and splashed her face, hoping to disguise the trail of tears.

"Hey," Kathryn said as she entered the room.

"Hey," Jenny said without looking up.

Kathryn stood behind her. "What can I do?"

Jenny appreciated the absence of the usual, "Are you okay?" Kathryn's direct approach belied an understanding of her grief that made them kindred spirits, and Jenny felt comforted by her presence alone.

"I'll be okay in a minute."

Kathryn put a hand on her back. "Okay." She grabbed a towel from the counter behind her and waited patiently.

Jenny splashed her face with water again. "I'm sorry," she said, as she stared at the bottom of the sink and shook the excess water from her hands.

Kathryn handed her the towel. "For what?"

"I'm not usually like this." She buried her face in the towel and exhaled a heavy sigh.

She looked in the mirror at her blotchy red face and then at Kathryn's pained compassion reflected over her shoulder, and she knew she wasn't getting away with anything.

"Who am I kidding? I'm like this more often than I care to be, and I'm getting pretty sick of it." She sniffed again and wiped her tears with an irritated hand. "Welcome to my life. Run while you can."

Kathryn crossed her arms and didn't say anything, a stark contrast to Bernie, who would unleash a stream of uplifting banter, trying to cheer her up.

Jenny was thankful for Kathryn's silence and thankful that upset was giving way to annoyance. Annoyance she could control. Tears had a mind of their own.

She faced the mirror again. "Good grief, what a mess."

Kathryn moved close behind her and shared the mirror. "You look fine," she said, placing her hands on her shoulders. "We're all friends here. Who are you trying to impress?"

Jenny looked at Kathryn's smiling reflection. "I think that would be you."

Kathryn squeezed her shoulders. "You've already made quite an impression. Believe me."

"I'm sure."

"I mean that in a good way."

Jenny smiled.

Kathryn rubbed her arms. "Better?"

"Yeah."

Jenny cursed her lack of emotional stability, especially in front of Kathryn.

Kathryn didn't seem to care. Her eyes spoke sympathetic volumes about what she wasn't saying, and she just pursed her lips into a smile and squeezed her arms again. "It's okay. You don't have to tell me anything."

Jenny turned to face her. "No. I want to tell you." She paused. "Just not now." She looked around the room. "And certainly not here." She turned to the mirror again and made a final attempt at looking presentable.

"You tell me whenever you're ready," Kathryn said, "and until then, just let me know if there's anything I can do. Okay?"

Jenny exhaled in relief. "Thank you. Just hearing that is a big help. I appreciate your patience."

Kathryn released her hold with a final squeeze and smiled. "What are friends for?"

Jenny smiled. It felt so right for them to be friends, so natural. How could she have ever thought otherwise? Satisfaction replaced the angst of the moments before, and she lifted her chin as she regained her confidence. She concentrated on her reflection again and patted her pockets, as if she'd lost something. "My kingdom for—" Before she could finish her sentence, Kathryn produced a lipstick from her pocket.

"Ah!" Jenny beamed with delight as she took it. "A woman after my own heart." She expertly traced her lips and then pressed them together.

"Good color on you," Kathryn said.

"You think?" Jenny asked, as she plucked a tissue from the dispenser to blot her lips. "Not too bold?"

Kathryn took the lipstick from her fingers and leaned into the mirror to trace her own lips. "Bold suits you."

Jenny looked at the name of the color embossed on the cap in her hand. "Victory Red." She paused. "I can get behind that."

Kathryn retracted the color and offered back the shiny cylinder. "Here, keep it."

Jenny hesitated, not sure if she could pull off the color.

Kathryn grinned. "For when you feel bold."

Just being alone with Kathryn made Jenny feel bold, and she looked her in the eyes as she reached up and slowly closed her hand around the long fingers holding the lipstick.

Kathryn's eyes grew dark, and she held tight to the lipstick when Jenny tried to slip it from her grasp. She stepped closer and Jenny's breathing faltered. She was sure Kathryn was going to kiss her, just like the night outside the club.

Jenny eyed the door. "We probably shouldn't do this here."

A slow grin formed on Kathryn's lips and she released the lipstick. "You started it."

Jenny took the lipstick and secured the cap. She tugged at the hem of her suit jacket and cleared her throat, confident in her next step.

"May I ask you a favor?"

"I gave you the lipstick," Kathryn said. "What more do you want from me?"

Her deadpan delivery made Jenny pause, but Kathryn chuckled and put her hand on her shoulder. "Sure, ask away."

"Drive me home tonight? It's not far."

This time Kathryn paused, and Jenny felt the need to explain. "The boys were going to see me home, but they should head downtown before Cal gets in trouble with the post MPs. I live in the opposite direction.

"I'm heading downtown. Why don't I take Cal home?" Kathryn said.

Jenny stared at her. After the moment they just shared, Kathryn couldn't possibly be serious.

Kathryn finally laughed and elbowed her. "Kidding. Of course I'll take you home."

Jenny shook her head and smiled in relief. "Okay, you're going to take some getting used to. I've heard of dry humor, but you should come with a glass of water."

Kathryn put her arm around her shoulders. "Come on, let's get out of here."

"Yeah, before Bernie comes looking for us."

"And don't you think he won't."

Jenny stopped mid-stride. "What did he say to you?"

"Not much," Kathryn said, almost running into her back. "Just a few words of encouragement."

"Like fragile, handle with care, don't hurt me or he'll kick your behind?"

"Something like that."

Jenny chuckled as she headed for the exit. "Well, you're safe then. Bernie couldn't kick his own behind."

"Whew," Kathryn said, following her out the door. "I feel safer already."

The bar was closing as they got back to the table, and after assurances all around that she was okay, Jenny announced that Kathryn was driving her home, which drew a raised, but approving, brow from Bernie.

He slapped Cal on the back. "We've been dumped, my friend."

"That's okay, buddy," Cal said, "you still got me."

Jenny smiled sweetly and put a hand to Bernie's cheek. "We'll always have Paris," she said, mocking his *Casablanca* obsession.

He clutched his chest and grabbed Cal's shoulder for support. "Hail me a taxi, brother, I'm going to cry."

Everyone laughed, and Jenny gave him a sincere hug goodbye. "Thank you for tonight, Bernie. I love you so much."

"I love you too, Bug. You kids be safe, and have fun."

Kathryn's senses heightened as they shuffled out of the bar. She was on high alert and ready for possible danger from whomever waited in the tail car. She was glad that Jenny had asked her to drive her home and thankful that the kiosk blocked the stranger's view. Hopefully, he would follow Bernie's taxi, not realizing until they were long gone that his target was not among the passengers. She could only hope for the boys' sakes that malice was not the stranger's intent.

She led Jenny to her car, parked on the side street, and waited for the tail to pull out after the taxi. The taxi drove off, but no one followed. She stalled for time, fumbling in her purse for her gas ration book, which she then tucked in the sun visor so she could lean forward and check on the tail. The stranger's car was still parked out front. He didn't take the bait.

"Turn right at the stop and just follow that road," Jenny said, as Kathryn started the car.

"Check."

Not wanting to take any chances, Kathryn distracted Jenny in case the stranger happened to look their way as they turned in front of his waiting car. She reached up in the guise of adding her pencil to the ration book tucked in the sun visor and surreptitiously flicked it to the floor at Jenny's feet.

"Nuts. Could you get that for me?"

Jenny leaned down and out of sight just as they passed the tail.

While Jenny fumbled in the darkness for the pencil, Kathryn tried to get a good look at the stranger in the car. His head was resting on the back of the seat with his hat pulled over his eyes. He was sleeping. Kathryn exhaled in relief. At least Jenny was safe. For now. Whomever was doing the stakeout either wasn't very good at it, or wasn't very serious, or she was just paranoid.

Kathryn's preoccupation with the mystery tail derailed her charm offensive, and they'd gone blocks in silence until Jenny said, "So, how did you wind up with that swell job at The Grotto?" She paused and then added, "If it's not too sordid."

Kathryn hesitated, sensing disapproval. Jenny probably thought Forrester got her the job. The Grotto was the best gig she'd ever had, and that was thanks to the owner, Dominic Vignelli, who treated her like the daughter he never had. She looked sideways at her judgmental passenger. She'd have to work hard to wash off Forrester's stench.

"I got the job at The Grotto because the owner is a connoisseur of fine music, and, technically, I have perfect relative pitch and exceptional breath control, which makes me a better than average singer."

"Of course. Sorry," Jenny said. "I didn't mean ..."

Kathryn looked her way. "It's okay. No offense taken. Truth be told, the owner's son is a very dear friend of mine. His dad found himself without a singer and I filled in." It was always nice when the truth served the narrative. "I guess he liked what he heard because I've been there ever since."

"Well, obviously the man knows talent," Jenny said. "And don't kid yourself; you're more than just a better than average singer."

Kathryn grinned. "You're snowed by the long sequined gowns."

Jenny chuckled. "Your voice is amazing, and you'd look stunning with or without sequins ... or gowns."

Kathryn laughed and watched Jenny beam because of it. The smile was a welcome sight after seeing her struggle through the pain of grief. She knew that pain too well, and every reprieve from it was a gift. She hoped she could complete her assignment without triggering more painful memories for Jenny, but when the subject of her assignment was the cause of Jenny's grief, it would be a tight needle to thread.

"So," Kathryn said dramatically, "how *did* you get that swell job at the *Daily Chronicle*? Your uncle's the boss, so you just waltzed right in there and what, you're a columnist times two?"

Jenny smiled a full-faced grin. "Touché."

Kathryn returned the full-faced grin while Jenny buried her face in her hands. "I'm such a pain in the ass."

Kathryn rolled her eyes. "*Now* you tell me."

They both laughed.

"So," Kathryn said, "you're a writer, obviously."

"I didn't start there—" She paused to give directions. "Turn left up here until you hit Broadway, and then turn right. I started at the bottom, spending summers in the mailroom when I was young. Writing wasn't a plan; it was just something I did for myself. I also worked in the cataloging department of a newsreel room before I almost died of boredom."

"You got paid to watch movies? Nice work if you can get it."

"Hey, now," Jenny said. "In defense of the unheralded catalog clerks of America, once that reel goes into the vault, the only record of what's on there is on that index card. You have to catalog every single image on that reel. Every place—" She ticked the items off on her fingers. "Occasion, person of note, car, ship, plane ... if it's a P-47 Thunderbolt or a B-26 Marauder, you need to know that and indicate it on that card. I didn't just sit around drinking coffee with my feet propped up on a desk. It's very tedious and time-consuming and, yes, I'd venture to say, important." She crossed her arms.

Kathryn raised her brow and pressed her lips into a smile. Jenny's ferocious defense of the position epitomized the all or nothing passion in which she undertook everything. She loved the hand gestures punctuating every point.

"Do you miss it?"

"Cataloging? No." Jenny relaxed and slipped her hands into her coat pockets. "I do miss its importance, though."

Kathryn sensed a shift in Jenny's mood. "Is that why you were so determined to go after Forrester?"

Jenny nodded. "That, and what he did to my father, of course." She raised her hands helplessly without removing them from her pockets. "I just want to make a difference. Do something important. The paper isn't my long-term goal, much to my uncle's chagrin. I don't even know that I have a long-term goal. I just know that I need to do *something*. And now, with the war ..." She shook her head, no clarification necessary.

Kathryn recognized Jenny's frustration as that of so many longing for their place in the world. Kathryn's place in the world spiraled out of control at an early age, and life's cruel indifference carried her far from places able to nurture things like dreams and ambitions. She wanted to preserve Jenny's dreams and ambitions, even if she didn't know what they were yet. No one deserved to have them stolen.

"You'll find your way," Kathryn said.

Jenny shrugged. "I thought about joining the WAACs, but my uncle would absolutely *kill* me. The paper will have to do for now, and it's important in its way, I guess. I'm doing a story on the WAVEs over at Hunter College next week. The public is so woefully ignorant of so much of what's going on out there." She pointed at a road up ahead. "Turn left there, at the end of the station. They scan the paper for the latest headlines on the war and couldn't care less about the details as they turn to the *Lifestyle* and *Arts* sections. That's how people like Forrester slither through the system. He lulls the public into blind acceptance by giving fundraisers for widows and orphans with one hand while aiding the enemy with the other. It's maddening."

Kathryn noticed that Jenny had taken the pen from her coat pocket and had its box clenched tightly in her fist. From her reaction to the gift in the bar, she could only assume it had something to do with her father. This was her opening, a way to bring up her father without causing suspicion, but she hesitated, loathe to do it for Jenny's emotional sake. Jenny caught her looking, and Kathryn merely smiled, turning her attention back to the road.

Jenny was silent for a few moments and then turned the box over in her hands and told its story. "This belonged to my grandfather. He gave it to my father when he entered medical school at twenty-three."

"Your father was a doctor?" Kathryn asked, even though she knew the answer.

Jenny nodded. "He promised it to me when I turned twenty-three. I'm sure at the time, he thought I would be entering medical school."

"No interest?"

"Oh, no. Medical school was the plan. I took all the expected classes through high school, did my undergrad prep, but, in the end, it just wasn't for me. Writing is my passion, and words can impact so many, so I pursued journalism. I'm afraid my father was terribly disappointed."

"I'm sure he was very proud of you."

Jenny pressed her lips into a smile and stared at the box in her hand. "I broke this pen when I was fifteen. I was leaving a note on Dad's desk in the study, and when I set down the pen to fold the piece of paper, it promptly rolled off the desk and onto the parquet floor, bending the nib and chipping out some of the mother of pearl in the barrel. He wasn't happy. It went into a drawer and I thought I'd never see it again." She held it up. "It's a year late in getting to me, but he kept his promise."

Kathryn expected tears, but Jenny just stared out the window, deep in thought, until she pointed up ahead and said quietly, "Take that next right, and it's the only drive at the top of the hill." She put the pen back into her pocket.

Kathryn put a comforting hand on Jenny's knee but removed it to make the turn onto the winding street.

"I used to write," Jenny said. "For myself. Journals and such, before Dad died."

"No more?"

Jenny exhaled a humorless chuckle. "Well, at first I wasn't sober long enough to write anything, and then there's only so much self-pity a person can spew until they're sick of themselves."

"Sorry."

Jenny took in and released a deep breath. "You know what they say: what doesn't kill us ..."

Kathryn pulled into the well-kept drive and finished the sentence. "Brings us to our knees and beats us until we wish that it had." She stopped the car and applied the parking brake.

Jenny looked at her curiously. "You're very cynical."

It wasn't an accusation, merely an observation, and Kathryn cursed herself for letting her facade slip. "Sorry. I don't know where that came from."

"Experience, I think."

True, but it had no place in securing her assignment. "Sarcasm isn't particularly attractive," Kathryn said.

Jenny shifted in her seat to face her. "We're all friends here. Who are you trying to impress?"

Kathryn laughed as her own words hit her in the face. "That would be you, I suppose."

Jenny grinned. "All you've got to do is show up to impress me."

Kathryn snorted. "You're easy."

"Guilty."

They gazed into each other's eyes until the sexual tension disturbed even Kathryn. For someone who had cultivated the art of seduction into one of her finest tools, it was disconcerting to lose control of it, especially during an assignment. She broke from Jenny's gaze and squinted at the gleaming chromium bumper of an exotic-looking maroon convertible in the open garage, illuminated by the car's headlights. "Nice car," she said.

"My father's 1937 Cord 812." She paused. "Supercharged."

Kathryn had never heard the word *supercharged* sound so sexy, and she bit her lip to stifle a pleasurable moan. "Not something you see every day."

"She's a temperamental thing, but you'll never forget the ride."

Kathryn wondered if she was still talking about the car.

"Would you like a tour of the house?"

Kathryn looked up at the Tudor-style house. She was dangerously exhausted. Jenny had a way of luring her into a sense of normalcy. Like she could say anything because they were just two friends sharing their day. She'd made good progress tonight and should go home. When she opened her mouth to offer her regrets, she was met with Jenny's open and inviting gaze. She couldn't say no to it. "Sure."

CHAPTER TWENTY-FOUR

*A*s the two-story Tudor rose before her, Kathryn was reminded of Forrester's Long Island estate, not in grandeur or scale, but in the desolation and unnerving silence. Used to the disparate hum of the city, this quiet neighborhood magnified the energy between her and Jenny, and it put her on edge.

Even the thick board and batten wood front door was silent as Jenny shouldered it open. She turned on the hallway lights, and the sconce lighting filled the long hallway with a warm glow. Jenny placed her keys in a blue porcelain bowl on the foyer table next to the bouquet of yellow roses, and Kathryn followed her in.

Once inside, it felt nothing like Forrester's estate. This place was a home. Just two steps into the foyer, anxiety melted away. The unique scent that Jenny carried with her filled the air, and uncertainty turned to calm.

Kathryn smiled at the bouquet, obviously the origin of the single rose Jenny had given her, and she pointed at it. "Thanks for sharing."

Jenny smiled as she gathered their coats and hung them on the hall tree. "I'm going to make some tea. Would you like some?

"Whatever you're having is fine," Kathryn said, as she took in the new surroundings.

Jenny slipped out of her shoes and motioned in the direction of the living room. "Make yourself at home. Lights are on your left there." She pointed to the switch on the wall and then walked toward the kitchen.

Kathryn slipped out of her own shoes and slid them next to Jenny's. "Do you need any help?"

"Nope," Jenny said over her shoulder as she disappeared around the corner and the kitchen light came on.

Kathryn took the few moments she'd have alone to do some investigating. A jolt of adrenaline hit her as she effortlessly slipped into operative mode. She looked at the closed door to her right, off the foyer, and recalled from studying the floor plans that it led to the master bedroom and bath. She offered a reassuring glance toward the kitchen and then headed left into the open archway of the living room and hit the light switch. More out of habit than design, she made a quick scan of the room, knowing she would not find what she was looking for here.

A comfortable looking russet colored leather couch looked inviting, as did the lush pair of flowered chairs on each side of the fireplace. Beside one of the chairs was a box of neatly packed rolled up wool socks, obviously ready to go to the Red Cross or some other relief organization, and a knitting bag made from a fabric replica of a wartime poster that read *Remember Pearl Harbor! Purl harder!*

Kathryn smiled at Jenny's devotion to her patriotic duty.

The room contained the standard fare, but the quality of the contents and the size of the house revealed obvious family wealth. A portrait of a distinguished looking older gentleman hung over the ornate fireplace mantel. Various family photos and oil paintings decorated the pale green and blue willow bough wallpapered walls, interrupted by large casement windows that faced the front yard. Kathryn lingered on the paintings and admired the Impressionist technique. Someone liked cows and landscapes.

Her interest quickly disappeared as she remembered she had a job to do. Another quick glance around the room revealed half open double sliding pocket doors to what she knew from the plans was the study. She slipped inside and fumbled on the wall to find the light switch in the dark room. She hit the top button, which lit the right side of the room, and she instantly knew this was the room she was looking for. It was a stark contrast to the warm and inviting living room. This room was cold and imposing, with its floor-to-ceiling bookcases and dark ornate wood trim. A man's room. Daniel Ryan's office. She would wait there and easily segue into his research. By the end of the evening, she would know for sure if Jenny knew anything about it, and then this assignment would end.

She looked over her shoulder into the living room out of paranoid habit and made a beeline for the heavy mahogany desk situated under the bay window at the end of the lit side of the room.

Typical desktop items dotted the surface: a pipe caddy, desk lamp, a fountain pen in its stand with a dried-up inkwell beside it, a black telephone, and a desk calendar with last year's date circled. *J's Birthday* it said in a controlled scrawl under the circled date. She lifted the blotter carefully, hoping for some clue hidden beneath it. Nothing. She made another cautious glance at the door before she sat in the leather chair and checked the desk drawers. All locked. She looked up at the bookcases looming like sentries over the entire room. Rows and rows of books on science, nature, medical textbooks, botany books, sporting books, political commentary, and contemporary fiction lined the shelves.

There was nothing more the room could tell her without breaking into the desk, and she didn't have time for that, so while she let the adrenaline rush dissipate, she steepled her hands and relaxed into the leather chair, which acknowledged her presence with a creak. It was a nice space, Kathryn reflected as she took in the long room. With the two bay windows on each end, she imagined sunlight would lift the dour seriousness of the place and make it lovely.

She slowly whirled the chair around and caught her reflection in the bay window behind the desk. It was not a subtle image, and she thought better of it immediately. She got up and positioned the chair where she'd found it.

Stepping deeper into the unlit side of the room, she found a beautiful grand piano taking up the entire space, with various pieces of sheet music propped up on the piano's music rack. She turned on the floor lamp beside the piano and straightened with a raised brow.

"Holy smokes," she said in a restrained whisper. "An Imperial." She ran a reverent hand across the maker's gold letters. Bösendorfer.

The case lid was closed, and family photos floated on the pristine polished black surface like sailboats on a motionless midnight sea.

Work was forgotten, and her mind drifted back to a simpler time in her life. She'd heard about the magnificent instrument from her mother but never dreamed she'd have the opportunity to play one. She slid onto the padded bench and rubbed her hands together before carefully opening the fallboard, uncovering the keys. The familiar scent of wood and felt filled her nostrils, and she reflexively sat up straight, preparing to play. Her excitement over a piano was juvenile, and she laughed at herself, but inheriting her mother's worship of this particular instrument, she took in and released a calming breath anyway.

The top piece of sheet music on the music rack was one she knew, and she positioned her fingers on the keys, ready to find out if it sounded as good as its reputation.

Kathryn didn't notice Jenny standing silently in the doorway of the study. She didn't notice the stricken look on her face, or feel her heart pounding, or see her trembling hand on the doorjamb about to take the first few hesitant steps into a room filled with memories she couldn't bear to face.

Jenny wanted to kick herself for telling Kathryn to make herself at home. She should have added, "Whatever you do, don't go into the study." The intrusion was unexpected. Not only was Kathryn in the banished study, but she was about to play the piano. Her father's piano.

Don't touch it! She wanted to scream, as if Kathryn's touch would displace her father's ghost from the room and he would be gone forever. But he was gone already, and whatever was left of him lived in Jenny's heart and mind as joy and pain, in equal measure. She'd spent countless hours with her father at the piano, laughing and playing, creating some of the best memories of her life. She had also sealed his fate in the very same room, creating the worst memory of her life, and one that had kept her from entering the study for a year.

Forced now to face her guilt, the emotion sapped the strength from her limbs and left her skin cold. She clutched the doorjamb in an effort to remain standing and willed herself not to break down. Not now, not in front of Kathryn again.

The room was nothing like she remembered. This room was cold and dark and smelled of stale air and old books instead of her father's pipe tobacco and subtle aftershave. It was a tomb, and she had made it that way.

Kathryn was the antithesis of everything the study represented. She was beautiful, bright, strong, and very much alive. Jenny was drawn to her strength, and she squared her shoulders before crossing the threshold. She traveled the few steps to the piano and arrived just as Kathryn played the first few notes of her chosen song.

Kathryn looked up and immediately stopped playing. She pulled her hands back as if she were caught doing something she oughtn't. "Sorry. I hope you don't mind."

Jenny put on a fake grin. "Not at all." She tucked her skirt under her legs and slid next to her on the bench. "I didn't know you played."

"Oh, yes," Kathryn said. "Since I was a child. My mother was a piano teacher. A concert pianist, really, but she gave it up for marriage and family. I was drafted into it by default, I guess." She caressed the ivory keys.

Jenny was struck by Kathryn's childlike demeanor. Her eyes were wide and bright, despite the late hour. "I see you like the piano," she said, glad to focus on Kathryn rather than the room.

"Oh, I do. This is one of the finest instruments made. You could buy a house for what this thing costs. Well, maybe not this house, but ...." She slid her fingers across the mirrored black surface. "It's all handmade in Vienna. Look at this ..." She pointed at a hinged section at the bass end of the keyboard. "Extended keys ... and here ..." She rapped a knuckle on the side of the piano case, making the strings ring. "Solid spruce rim."

Jenny raised her brow, unsure if she was impressed with the instrument or Kathryn's knowledge of it.

Kathryn looked her way and smiled sheepishly. "I'm drooling, aren't I?"

Jenny laughed. "I guess I've just taken it for granted." She timidly ran her hand along the keys. "It's always been here, for as long as I can remember. Granddad had it sent from Europe. I had no idea it was so unusual. It was just another piece of furniture." She paused. "Until I took to it with crayons, and then, hoo, boy, did I hear it."

Kathryn's eyes went round with shock. "Oh, you didn't."

"I'm afraid I did. Yellow crayon."

"Oh, no."

"I think my name is still scribbled underneath somewhere." She made a half-hearted effort to look. "It was then that I was informed that it was special and not a slate board to be drawn upon."

"It's special, all right," Kathryn said, her fingers resting on the keys. "The Rolls Royce of pianos. Beautifully balanced tone up and down the range of keys." She motioned toward the lower keys. "More bass here." She played a few scales from the lowest to the highest keys, to prove her point about the tone, and then she played a progression of chords. "Wow. Can you hear that?" She leaned into the sound. "Perfection. Those extra bass strings?" She pointed at them. "Even unused, they vibrate in sympathy with the other notes, giving the piano a richer, fuller sound. It's quite stunning, really."

Jenny took her word for it. She couldn't recall ever hearing a *bad* piano, and she supposed this one sounded better than most, but she always attributed that to the cavernous room and the company. She avoided casting her eyes toward the empty chair behind the desk. She had an intense instinct to flee the room, but seeing Kathryn so enthralled by the piano piqued her interest and resolve just enough to hold her to her seat.

"Go ahead and play," she said.

Kathryn offered her a questioning glance. "Are you sure?"

Jenny paused and imagined she looked shell-shocked, because that's how she felt.

Kathryn put a reassuring hand on her shoulder. "Are you okay?"

Jenny nodded. "I'm sure. I want to hear you play." She looked at the piano affectionately. She wanted to hear it sing again.

Kathryn nodded and began to play.

The song turned Jenny to stone. It was the last song she'd heard her father play. The memory took her breath away, and when she lifted her eyes to the sheet music, the title, "It Isn't a Dream Anymore," blurred into a swell of tears.

Kathryn drew back her hands. "I don't think—"

Jenny's left hand captured Kathryn's right to stop her retreat. It would have been so easy to run, from the room, the piano, the song, the combined weight of them. She refused. "Please go on," she said.

When Kathryn didn't move, Jenny squeezed her hand, assuring her that it was okay to proceed. "Please go on," she repeated softly. She didn't look up; she just waited patiently for the song to begin and steeled herself against the emotional wave about to crash down on her.

As Kathryn played the introduction again and then began to sing, Jenny bowed her head and clutched the soft edge of the piano bench with both hands for strength.

Hearing a female voice carry the tune, even though anticipated, threw her. She still expected her father's baritone to drift softly to her ears. The reminder that she'd never hear that voice again swirled around her like a malicious spirit until it seized her by the throat, forcing her to swallow hard. She pressed her eyes shut, trying to hold in her tears and her grief.

Kathryn's voice was lower than she remembered but, as always, emotive and beautiful. Her smooth timbre, combined with the rich thrum of the piano, resonated deep within Jenny's core, and the extended bass strings weren't the only thing vibrating in sympathy.

As the strings and vocals filled her heart, warm remembrance and comfort overpowered the familiar stab of guilt, forcing her tears to spill over. She let them fall. They were tears of relief and love. For the past year, she had allowed her father's love to become something painful, and she, something ugly and unworthy. She had closed herself off to any comfort fond memories could offer, and it had cost her the gift of her father's unconditional love.

She sobbed and quickly found it the only sound in the room. Kathryn's arms were around her, holding her tight and rocking her gently. Jenny didn't fight the emotions or the welcome embrace.

Kathryn held her and told her it was okay. Her voice was hoarse when she whispered, "I'm so sorry," over and over again.

When Jenny's tears subsided, she wiped her face with her forearm sleeve and straightened. Kathryn's arms fell away, and Jenny saw that she had tears in her eyes.

Jenny sniffed. "Why are you apologizing? And for Pete's sake, don't you cry too."

Kathryn chuckled as she dabbed under her eye with a knuckle, catching a tear before it fell. "I think I ruined your birthday."

Jenny reached out and put her hand on Kathryn's thigh. "No. You gave me the best gift of all." She looked around the room and wiped the lingering tears from her cheeks. "This used to be my favorite room in the house." She paused and looked at a picture on the piano of her with her father. "I haven't been in here since ..." She paused again and smiled at Kathryn. "Thank you for helping me face it."

Kathryn raised her brow. "You're welcome, I guess?"

Jenny smiled and wrapped her fingers around the edge of the piano bench again. "You're supposed to face this stuff and eventually it gets better. Isn't that how it works?" She looked to Kathryn as if she had the answer.

"You're asking the wrong person."

"But obviously you've dealt with some demons. Yes?"

"Obviously?"

"Well ... you have, haven't you?"

Kathryn hesitated. "Let's just say I have my demons."

"But you're together. You don't break down at the drop of a hat, so you've dealt with that in some way."

Kathryn shook her head. "I run as fast as I can."

"You can't run forever."

"I can try."

Kathryn's answer was unapologetic, and Jenny supposed whatever happened must have been pretty awful. She put her hand on Kathryn's forearm. "I want you to know, if you ever need to talk about it, I'm here."

Kathryn smiled and patted her hand. "Oh no. One emotionally distraught person a night. That's my limit." She stood.

Jenny held fast to her arm. "I'm serious."

Kathryn sat again and covered Jenny's hand with her own. "Thank you."

They stared into each other's eyes, and Jenny marveled at the stillness she found in Kathryn's soft gaze. Her blue eyes hid her pain well, whatever it was, but everyone breaks down sometime, and Jenny vowed to comfort Kathryn in any way she could if she would let her.

Kathryn patted her hand again. "How about that tea?"

Jenny smiled in agreement and offered a parting glance at the study as they rose to move their evening into the living room. Her legs were solid beneath her, and the wave of guilt that only moments before threatened to destroy her, washed over her and deposited her safely into Kathryn's arms. She turned off the lights on the way out and began closing the doors, but then stopped and pushed them all the way open. Tonight was a new beginning. No more running.

While Jenny went to the kitchen to retrieve their tea, Kathryn made a fire in the fireplace. She sat on the edge of the hearth and basked in the fire's warm glow while the gentle popping and crackling of the burning seasoned oak lulled her into distracted contemplation.

She hadn't planned on comforting a distraught Jenny Ryan as part of her scheme to get close to her. In fact, she felt like a grade A heel because of the distress she'd caused her, but before she knew it, she'd taken Jenny into her arms, as if the action, and her words, could erase the pain. She wanted it to. Jenny's struggle with grief felt too familiar. She wanted to make it stop, not just for Jenny, but for herself —to stop the memories before they crawled out of the dark corners of her mind.

Her own grief had taken her down a path of ruination. She would never recover, but Jenny had a long, beautiful life before her, and Kathryn wanted it to stay that way. She couldn't spare Jenny the pain of losing her father, but she could spare her the truth of his work.

One good deed, one saved life, would not erase her despicable past, but saving Jenny felt like saving herself, and for the first time in a long time, she wanted to be saved.

"Honey?" Jenny said from behind her.

"Hm?" Kathryn said absentmindedly, as if it were the most natural thing for Jenny to call her. She turned to see her indicating the jar of honey on the tray she'd set on the coffee table.

Kathryn quickly recovered. "Yes, please." She moved to sit beside Jenny on the large russet colored leather couch facing the study.

"Lemon?"

"Yes, thank you."

"That's what you singers take to soothe your voice, right? Honey and lemon?"

"Entertain a lot of singers, do you?"

Jenny smiled. "No, but it works for a sore throat, and being a doctor's daughter, I've got the skinny on that."

Kathryn cleared her throat and glanced toward the study. "That bad in there, huh? I'm sorry. I didn't warm up properly before the performance tonight." More like hardly at all. When one of her band mates called to ask why she wasn't with them entertaining the troops, she took it as the perfect opportunity to take another run at Jenny Ryan. She got in as many vocal exercises as she could on the harried drive up to the armory, but it was no substitute for a proper warm up. "Serves me right. I know better."

Jenny stirred her tea. "Don't apologize. You sounded fantastic.

Different, that's all, but fantastic. Kind of sexy. All midnight and warm brandy." She smiled, but then it faded and she became serious. "I'm sorry I fell apart on you in there."

Kathryn put her hand on Jenny's thigh to show sympathy but removed it when she became self-conscious of her motives. Her desire for physicality was not inspired by her assignment but by need —her need to comfort this person, her need to save this person, her need to become a better person because of it. Jenny would not understand this. She would interpret every touch as a sign of intimacy. She would relax defensive walls, and that would make her vulnerable, malleable, and perfectly primed for exploitation. Normally, that was the intent, but not this time, not this person.

"Don't ever apologize for expressing your emotions," Kathryn said.

Jenny nodded, but Kathryn could tell she felt it a shortcoming. This time she reached out in comfort and left her hand on Jenny's thigh. "I'll happily give you a rain check on any song of your choosing."

Jenny smiled. "I'd like that."

Silence fell between them, and Kathryn fought the comfortable lull. She had a job to do, and the sooner she got her information, the sooner she would be out of Jenny's life.

After that, she would go as far as her assignment to Forrester would take her, prove she was stable and reliable, and then, hopefully, brass would assign her to the European Theater of Operations, where the war would welcome her back into its hellish realm and she would pay her debt to her dead.

Kathryn removed her hand and slowly eyed the room to find a topic of conversation that would bring Jenny back to her family and then gently to her father. "This is a beautiful house."

Jenny's eyes lingered on hers, as if she hadn't heard what she'd said, but then she glanced around the room and nodded her agreement. "It's been in the family for ages."

"Did you grow up here?"

"I did. Dad moved back here soon after I arrived. My mom died when I was born, so ..." her voice trailed off as she smoothed a nonexistent wrinkle on her skirt.

"I'm sorry."

Jenny shrugged. "You can't really miss what you never had. I guess I miss the idea of her sometimes, you know? But I had Gran, and she was amazing, and Aunt Betsy is always there for me. I was loved, so I don't feel like I missed out on anything." She set the fine china teacup carefully on its saucer and then got up and headed toward the darkened study.

Kathryn noticed that Jenny hesitated with her hand on the door jamb when she reached the threshold, but she raised her chin and entered the room without further trepidation. She returned with one of the framed photos from the piano and held it out.

"That's my mom," she said, as she reclaimed her position on the couch. "And Dad, of course, behind her, and me."

Kathryn took the photo with interest. Jenny wasn't actually in the picture, but her mother was very pregnant, wrapped safely in the loving arms of Daniel Ryan. The couple looked happy, as they enjoyed a picnic on a blanket beneath the canopy of a large oak tree.

Kathryn held up the photo at eye level. She focused on Jenny's face and then back to her mother's in the photograph. "Wow. The resemblance is uncanny." It could have been Jenny staring back at her from the black and white image.

"I know. Kind of spooky, isn't it? She's the same age there as I am now."

"What was her name?"

"Bess."

Kathryn smiled. "Pretty." She could tell Jenny didn't know if she was referring to the name or the dead-ringer in the photo. She let her wonder.

"Do you know your mother's family?"

"No, not at all. No one ever talked about her. In deference to Dad's grief, I guess."

Kathryn made another comparative glance. "Wow." She handed the photo back, and Jenny propped it up on the coffee table.

"Poor Dad," Jenny said. "Gran said he was utterly devastated after Mom died. He just couldn't pull himself together. He dropped me off here with them and disappeared for a while."

"Where did he go?"

"Europe, I guess. He spent a lot of time there before I was born."

Jenny sipped her tea as she stared into the darkened study. Kathryn thought she was going to grow serious again, but a smile graced her lips instead.

"I'm soothed suddenly by the notion that my parents are together again. I never thought of it that way before. It's not logical, of course, but it's a nice thought."

Kathryn smiled, not about to challenge anything that eased someone's pain.

"Anyway," Jenny said with a dismissive wave, "Dad eventually came back, and we were inseparable after that."

Kathryn waited for more, but Jenny's attention slowly drifted back to the study, and this time she didn't smile. She grew still, and the color drained from her face.

"Jenny?"

She didn't respond, but just as Kathryn was about to repeat herself, Jenny said, "It was my fault. His death."

Jenny didn't look at her when she spoke. She was eerily calm, as if the words were coming from outside herself. Kathryn leaned forward, trying to catch her eyes. "I thought you said Forrester was responsible for his death."

That got Jenny's attention, and she looked at her briefly, but then she returned her focus to the study.

"An anonymous caller at the paper told me that. I was desperate to believe it. I still am. It's easier than blaming myself."

Kathryn had never seen Jenny so defeated. The self-confidence and determination that straightened her spine was gone, and she slumped beside her. She'd given up her source, anonymous though it was, and admitted she'd been bluffing about Forrester's connection to her father. She wasn't playing the game anymore, which made Kathryn want to abandon it as well. The urge to embrace her surfaced again, but duty won out and she pushed on. "Why would you blame yourself?"

"I was on the phone with him when he was killed. I was sitting on the edge of his desk in the study." She lifted her chin in the direction of the dark room.

Kathryn didn't know that detail, and having witnessed death first-hand, it sickened her to know that Jenny carried such a horrific memory.

"We'd had an argument earlier in the day," Jenny went on. "He was calling to apologize and tell me he'd be late for my party." She looked at her hands. "My birthday."

Kathryn nodded silently.

"A meeting ran over, or some such thing. I was still upset from the morning and not happy that he was going to be late, so I reignited the argument, like a jackass." She clenched her jaw and shook her head. "The line went dead."

Kathryn couldn't stop herself. She took Jenny's hand. "That's awful. I'm so sorry."

"Oh, no," Jenny said, as she exhaled a humorless chuckle and pulled her hand away. "It gets better."

Kathryn remained silent as Jenny's gleeful sarcasm betrayed a nasty case of self-loathing.

"See, I thought he'd hung up on me. So, I'm furious, slamming doors, behaving like the spoiled brat I am until I wound up down at the dock cursing his name to the moon, and the whole time, he's lying dead on the pavement. Run over in a telephone booth because I kept him on the line, arguing about how his work always came first. Isn't that rich?" She drained her teacup of its contents with a single aggravated swallow.

The rise in Jenny's blood pressure caused a pattern of red splotches to appear from her neck to her cheeks.

"I don't know what to say," Kathryn said honestly.

"That's because there's nothing *to* say," Jenny said, slamming her empty teacup onto the saucer on the coffee table. Both the teacup and the saucer shattered, sending porcelain skittering in all directions across the table.

A piece of saucer headed Kathryn's way and she instinctively put out her hand to catch it. The shard sliced into her left palm, causing her to hiss and drop it. She looked at the half-inch long cut and the emerging blood and quickly put her teacup down and pressed her right thumb against the wound to stop the bleeding and the inevitable swoon because of it. After everything she'd experienced in her life, it was ridiculous that such a small cut could make her woozy, but it did, and while Jenny stood and unleashed an impressive string of curse words over the broken china, Kathryn sought to diffuse the situation while she restored her equilibrium.

"So, how does a well brought up young lady find herself with such a colorful vocabulary?" she asked.

Jenny stopped ranting and exhaled an exasperated breath as she sat down. "Sorry." She used her napkin to corral the shards into a small pile and shook her head. "Believe it or not, I'm trying to curtail that. My 'colorful vocabulary,' as you so graciously put it, got me a lot of attention during my rebellious youth. Now it's just a bad habit."

"I assure you, you have my complete attention."

Jenny blushed. It was an endearing look, one that did more to distract Kathryn from her plight than her own plan.

Unfortunately, Jenny noticed her awkward hand positioning. "Are you all right?"

"Yes, it's nothing."

Jenny's eyes widened. "You're cut!" She slid over and then took Kathryn's hand. "I'm so sorry, Kathryn. Let me see."

Kathryn tried to pull her hand back. "It's nothing, Jenny. Nothing."

"Come on, let me see."

Kathryn reluctantly surrendered her hand and lifted her thumb, uncovering the wound. Blood quickly oozed from the small gash, and Kathryn caught just enough of it to set her off. She closed her eyes and swallowed.

Jenny placed a napkin over the wound and guided her up. "Let's take *nothing* to the first aid kit in the bathroom and get you fixed up."

The cut wasn't that bad, and there wasn't that much blood, so Kathryn tried to mentally overpower the queasy feeling. Much to her dismay, she couldn't stop the first wave of lightheadedness that pounced on her as soon as she stood up. She grabbed Jenny's arm for support.

"Kat?"

"Uh ..." She sat on the couch. "How about we bring the first aid kit to nothing."

"Kat?" Jenny put her warm hand on Kathryn's cool, pale face. "Okay. Just lie down here." She eased her into a prone position on the couch and propped some pillows under her legs. "I'm so sorry, Kathryn."

Kathryn felt much better now that she was lying down. "Relax, Jenny, I'm not going to bleed out or anything, I promise."

"No, but you might pass out, and that's just as scary to me right now."

Kathryn laughed at herself and at the expression on Jenny's face. "This is so embarrassing."

"Are you kidding?" Jenny said. "I'm mortified." She ran a worried hand through her hair and sat on the cleared end of the coffee table. "Look what I've done to you."

"I hardly think you forced me to stick my hand in the direct path of a sharp projectile." She looked at her hand. "I don't know what I thought I was going to do."

Jenny was looking nervous and mortified as she clasped her hands and chewed her lower lip.

"I'm fine, Jenny. Really. Just bring the first aid kit and we can both mercifully forget this ever happened."

Jenny slowly got to her feet. "I'm so sorry, Kat," she said, as she backed out of the room.

Kathryn could hear her cursing herself as she went down the hallway. She relaxed and exhaled a weary but amused breath. "What a night."

Jenny must have apologized twenty times in the time it took to clean the wound and apply two thin medical tape strips to keep it closed. Her hands shook as she carefully stretched the final strip of tape perpendicular over the cut and then lifted her eyes to Kathryn's to make sure she was being gentle enough.

"You're doing great," Kathryn said with a smile. "My own personal nurse."

Jenny looked at her trembling hands. "I would make a terrible nurse."

"I would too, obviously," Kathryn said about her aversion to blood.

Jenny sat back. "Oh, Kathryn ... the night of the accident ... there was blood everywhere! How did you manage to stay conscious?"

"You didn't see me in the hallway with my feet propped up on the nearest bench. I seem to hold my own in a crisis. But after that's over ..." She thumbed over her shoulder. "Out for the count."

"Amazing."

"Inconvenient and embarrassing."

Jenny grinned. "But I hear it's the perfect opportunity for the look, listen, and feel."

Kathryn chuckled at the nursing manual text thrown back at her.

"Well, you did ask for a rain check."

Jenny arched a brow. "Do I have to pass out to collect?"

"Preferably not."

"Good to know."

Kathryn shook her head. "I wasn't always like this. I actually thought about being a nurse once upon a time."

"Really?"

"Briefly. I enjoyed the book work. You know, biology, anatomy, physiology ... I find it utterly fascinating."

"I loved biology," Jenny said, as she took a bandage from the first aid kit and then tore open its paper sleeve. "I know Dad wished I'd pursued it. I think he wanted me to grow up to be a mad scientist or something."

Kathryn grinned. "Back when I went to school, a woman was going to be a nurse, a teacher, or a librarian."

"You make it sound like you're an old lady, Kat. You aren't *that* much older than I am. What are you, twenty-nine, thirty?"

Kathryn raised her brow. Most people low-balled guesses on age, so Jenny must have thought her somewhere in the mid-thirties, which was disconcerting. "Twenty-seven."

Jenny cringed. "Jeez. Put my foot in that, didn't I? Sorry."

Kathryn smiled her forgiveness. "I'm tall for my age."

Jenny laughed.

"I'm sure I look like hell too," Kathryn said, smoothing over a victory roll.

Jenny leaned in and applied the bandage over the strips of tape. "Well, if you look like hell, book me a one-way ticket."

Kathryn smiled outwardly but silently thought Jenny should be careful what she wished for.

"So, did you continue with the science?" Jenny asked. "I mean, you didn't have to be a nurse. You could have chosen a specific path, been a mad scientist," she said with a wink.

"No, I decided teaching might be the way to go, but I wasn't serious about it. I was in school on a choral scholarship, and, well, being young and not particularly serious about anything, I'm afraid I wasted my opportunity for a useful education."

"How so?"

"I was two years through my three-year teaching degree when the school choir won a national championship and we embarked on a goodwill concert tour of Europe. Halfway through the tour, a few of us ditched the choir to ... well, have some fun, enjoy the sights, you know, live a little. We figured we were never going to get the chance to go to Europe again, so why not? Naturally, that got us expelled, and there went the scholarship."

"Did they send you home?"

Kathryn chuckled. "They tried. We cashed in our tickets and

managed to stay in Europe for a while, singing for our supper. I never went back to school. I'm a singer, after all. I don't need a degree for that."

Jenny concurred with a smile. "No regrets then?"

"About school? No." She matched Jenny's smile, but dark echoes from the past condemned it as a lie. In truth, she regretted everything that happened that summer and everything that came after, but those memories had no place here. Get information. Get out. Leave Jenny to her beautiful life.

"Where did you go in Europe?" Jenny asked.

"Paris mostly. A short stint in Spain, some time in England."

"Nice," Jenny said and then frowned. "Wait, Spain? During the conflict?"

Kathryn silently bristled at the relatively inane term *conflict* to describe the civil war in Spain, but she politely smiled. "Yes. It was hard to be that close and not try to do something to help."

Jenny stared at her for a beat. "It wasn't what you thought it was."

Kathryn was surprised by the statement. She'd never encountered anyone who wasn't there who had a clue about what was really going on. "No. It wasn't."

Most thought it was a fight for democracy over fascism. At least that was how it was portrayed to eager young Americans willing to fight for the cause.

Years of social and economic unrest culminated in a brutal civil war ignored by most of the outside world until Italy and Germany brought in their military might to back the fascist Nationalists, and the Soviets, in turn, provided military hardware to the Republicans. Democracy was not part of the equation, and when all was said and done, participants fighting for it left with their ideology bruised and battered.

Jenny nodded. "It was complicated."

Kathryn eyed her curiously. "You seem to know something about it."

"I wrote a paper on it once."

A paper. The answer made Kathryn bristle again. It made the

whole action seem like an exercise put on for military scholars to debate in the sterile halls of academia while they pushed toy soldiers about on topographical battlefields. A paper. She barely stopped herself from scoffing out loud. She'd had her fill of garden party critics who stood under umbrellas of apathy and isolationism while bombs fell from the sky and slaughtered thousands.

A long dormant anger began to rise to the surface until Kathryn's heartbeat throbbed in her temples. Her facial muscles began to contract into a sneer, and she fought hard against it. This was neither the time nor the place to rage against past transgressions. She silently inhaled and exhaled slowly so Jenny wouldn't notice.

"It was a prelude to this war, and no one paid any attention," Jenny said, as she picked up the discarded bandage wrapper.

Kathryn snapped her eyes to Jenny's face. She understood. In an instant, anger turned to gratitude in a heady wave of relief that Jenny wasn't one of *them*. "Yes, exactly," she said.

Jenny shook her head. "It was horrific."

"How do you—"

"I cataloged the newsreels," Jenny answered before the question was finished.

Kathryn nodded. "Sorry you had to see that."

"I'm sorry you were there."

"I wasn't there long, and I didn't see the worst of it, but what I saw I'll never forget."

Jenny placed a hand on Kathryn's shoulder. "Sorry I brought it up."

Kathryn covered Jenny's hand with her own. No apology necessary.

They sat with their eyes locked in silence for a moment as Kathryn let the past drift away. Jenny's gaze held a depth of understanding, comfort, and forgiveness that she'd never allowed herself. This simple interaction caused a new sensation to bloom in her chest. It was warm and bright and weightless. Peace made manifest. The feeling seeped deeper into her wounded soul, and she took it like a hit of morphine until it reached her center and turned into something else.

She wanted Jenny in her arms again. It wasn't sexual, she told herself. It was gratitude. It took only a second for *that's a lie* to hit her in the back of the head like a boomerang returning from her dark subconscious. She ignored it.

She blinked their connection closed before it did become a lie and let her hand fall away to trace the bandage on her other hand as a distraction.

"Excellent work, Nurse Ryan." Her voice came out a little huskier than she'd intended.

"Thank you, Miss Hammond. You're an excellent patient."

"It's not too late to start your medical career," Kathryn said with a smile.

Jenny laughed. "That's not going to happen, but if you're still interested in the science, you should read Dad's books."

"Books?" Nothing in the reports she'd read about Daniel Ryan mentioned books.

Jenny nodded as she closed the box of bandages. "A three-volume compilation of papers that he wrote early in his career. Theoretical research that did not impress his contemporaries. He couldn't even get a peer review, so they were never officially published."

"That's gotta hurt," Kathryn said.

"Dad insisted he was just ahead of his time. It's all Greek to me, but you might find it interesting."

Trying not to sound too eager, Kathryn steadied her breathing and said, "I'd be very interested."

Jenny gathered up the discarded bandage wrappers. "Remind me to let you borrow them before you go." She paused briefly with the crumpled wrappers in her hand. "Are you sure you don't need stitches?"

Kathryn smoothed the edges of the large rectangular bandage covering the strips of tape. "This'll work just fine."

"I'm really sorry about your hand."

"Stop apologizing. My pride hurts more than my hand. I'm

beyond embarrassed." She shook her head as she slowly sat upright. "I don't usually pass out until the second date."

Jenny looked up in surprise, but then smiled. "I'm glad you concede that we're dating. It saves me the trouble of chasing you."

Kathryn laughed. "Well, technically, Bernie asked me out."

"Damn him," Jenny said, "always moving in on my action."

"To be fair, you're the one who asked me to drive you home and invited me in. For a tour, was it?"

"That I did." Jenny stood and held out her hand. "Come on. I'll show you around. Are you okay to stand?"

"Sure." Kathryn took Jenny's hand and hoped her head and legs cooperated.

Jenny squeezed her hand as she stood to her full height. "Okay?"

"Fine."

Kathryn put an arm around Jenny's shoulder. Not because she needed to but because she wanted to.

Kathryn glanced up at the vaulted ceiling as Jenny led her through the elegant dining room toward the kitchen. The floor plans she'd studied at HQ didn't do the house justice.

"I love these ceilings."

Jenny turned her head and smiled broadly. "I do too."

Her pride was obvious as she moved through each room and pointed out little details that her grandfather had designed into the house. Kathryn was glad to see her so relaxed and at ease after the emotional turmoil of the evening.

"Typical kitchen," Jenny said, as she entered the room.

Kathryn raised her brow. Jenny's typical kitchen was larger than her apartment.

"Breakfast room and laundry over there," Jenny said, pointing at a doorway to the left, and then she pointed to the right. "Through the boot room over there is the terrace and backyard, and beyond that, the lake."

Kathryn leaned in to look just as Jenny stepped back, and their bodies met in a crush of apologies.

"Whoops," Kathryn said, as she grasped Jenny by the shoulders to steady her.

"Sorry," Jenny said, but she made no effort to free herself.

Kathryn didn't move either. Jenny's gentle fragrance drifted around her and filled her head. "What are you wearing?"

Jenny relaxed into Kathryn's hold and ran a hand down her skirt. "Oh, this ol' thing?"

Kathryn chuckled. "Your scent."

Jenny still didn't move, so Kathryn stepped back and removed her hands before Jenny pressed into her any further and gave her no choice but to bury her face into her soft hair and kiss her neck.

Jenny turned around with a smile. "It's a combination of calendula, citrus, and lavender. My aunt makes it for me. Soap, hand cream, sachets for my drawers and closets, scent jars." She pointed to a lidded cut-glass jar on the shelf filled with the heavenly potpourri. "I prefer it to perfume. Do you like it?"

"I do. It's lovely." *You're lovely*, she wanted to say as Jenny gazed at her. Her close proximity was pulling her off course like a magnet too close to a compass needle, and she didn't like it. She was on the verge of ending her assignment and did not need any complications. It was time to get this house tour over and accelerate her exit. She looked to the ceiling. "How about that second floor?"

"If you insist," Jenny said with a grin that dripped with innuendo.

On the way up the stairs, Kathryn noticed an extra sway to Jenny's hips, and she shook her head with a smile at the unrelenting attempts at seduction.

"You're going to love the view up here," Jenny said.

Kathryn couldn't resist. "I love the view back here just fine."

Jenny glanced back. "I'm glad you noticed."

"I'm tired. I'm not dead."

Jenny stopped at the top step and turned, leaving Kathryn one step below, with their lips inches apart. Kathryn didn't dare move.

"I'm sorry," Jenny said after a beat. "I know you're tired. Would you rather just go home?"

Jenny's low and inviting voice was the exact opposite of her words. The agent in Kathryn's head screamed, *Yes, you're exhausted. Go home. Get Daniel Ryan's books, and go home.* It was a long-lost stranger that said, "I want to see the wonderful view."

The broad grin on Jenny's face as she stepped aside and held out her hand toward the landing told Kathryn that Jenny had a plan of her own, and she was playing right into it.

Jenny started walking along the landing. "The bedrooms are this way."

Kathryn avoided laughing out loud. "Is that where I'll find the aforementioned wonderful view?"

"If you play your cards right."

Kathryn paused with her hand on the landing railing. This was her game. Seduction. Conquest. Victory. She was losing her edge. When it came to Jenny, she found her advantage dulled by genuine affection. If circumstances were different, they might be friends. Maybe more than friends. She mentally shook her head. She didn't deserve someone like Jenny as a friend, or anything else, and Jenny certainly deserved better than her. Jenny's laughter brought her back to the present.

"You look terrified. Come on. I'll make it quick."

Kathryn wasn't sure if she meant the tour or something else, but she took the offered hand and followed an arm's length behind, uncharacteristically wary.

True to her word, Jenny was making quick work of the second-floor tour. She pointed at the first closed door. "Granddad's man room. His trophy room, smoking room, drinking room, poker room—walls adorned with dead animal heads staring at you with hollow glass eyes." She shuddered as she moved on.

"Oh, dear," Kathryn said.

"You said it."

At the next door, Jenny hit the light switch. "Spare bedroom."

Boxes and antique furnishings filled the room, which included an old-fashioned canopy bed. Kathryn hesitated in the doorway, questioning the boxes strewn about the room, a stark contrast to the otherwise orderly house.

"I've yet to unpack my apartment," Jenny said, as she shut off the light and closed the door.

Kathryn sensed there was more to the story but left it alone.

"Bathroom at the end of the hall there," Jenny said, pointing as she crossed the hall and started back the way they came. She passed the next closed door without stopping. "My childhood room."

Kathryn stopped in front of the door with an undeniable urge to see inside. "May I?" she asked, before her brain remembered her mission was to get out of there quickly.

"Sure," Jenny said, but the pause before she turned around told Kathryn the room was not a space she wanted to share.

When Jenny came back to her side and reached for the doorknob, Kathryn put a hand on her shoulder. "You don't have to show me. After all, a girl's got to have her secrets."

Jenny turned and looked into her eyes. "I don't want to have any secrets from you."

The words struck Kathryn in a soft spot. She longed for that life. A life without secrets. A life of looking into someone's eyes and finding only innocence and trust. She had nothing *but* secrets from Jenny, and that would never change. One more reason on the long list of reasons to end this assignment quickly and move on.

When the lights lit up the room, Kathryn couldn't help but smile. She entered a warm palette of dated decor with Hollywood-themed wallpaper obscured by movie posters and shelves lined with stuffed animals and sports trophies. Jenny excelled in tennis and field hockey, evidently.

"A real film buff, eh?"

"Bernie says drama is in my blood."

"Uh-oh. Sounds like I'm in for it."

Jenny laughed. "I promise to keep a lid on it."

As much as Kathryn wanted to get a closer look at the young Jenny Ryan in the row of family photos on the writing desk, she took pity on her and indicated with a satisfied nod that her curiosity was sated.

The next room was the antithesis of the described man room across the hall. Delicate Queen Anne style furniture commingled with more landscape paintings, framed floral prints, a small book-case, and a comfy window seat.

"Sitting room," Jenny said. "Nice view of the lake. I used to read up here."

"No more?"

"It was a quiet place. Now the whole house is quiet."

Kathryn imagined Jenny bearing her grief and guilt all alone in a house filled with the ghosts of happier times, and she wanted to take her in her arms again. Instead, she took the safer route and placed a hand on her back. "Sorry."

Jenny shrugged off the shift in mood.

"I don't really use the second floor. It's insane that I even live here alone with all this space." She turned off the light and headed toward the next wing. "I thought about renting out some of the rooms because of the housing shortage, but the thought of strangers trudging through the house just ... I don't know." She shrugged again. "I know that's selfish of me, but I'm just not ready."

"If it would make you uncomfortable in your own home, then you shouldn't do it," Kathryn said.

Jenny nodded, but her downturned eyes betrayed the guilt of her decision.

Kathryn followed her toward the next hallway but hesitated when they passed the row of diamond grilled casement windows connecting the two wings. The moon had disappeared behind a cloud, and the dark void outside pressed up against the windows like a menacing voyeur. She was used to the darker than usual city, due to the wartime dim-out, but the absence of light and other humans nearby was eerie. It reminded her of Forrester's place again: dark and desolate, but he had a handful of servants skulking about, so the isolation was tempered. The thought of Jenny living here by herself caused a pang of panic. She was irrationally relieved when the moonlight reappeared and painted highlights on the bare tree branches and the shoreline. Peering closer, she saw a single distant light shimmering on the calm waters of the lake. "Not many neighbors up here."

Jenny stopped walking and took a step back to glance at Kathryn's view. "Yeah, that's the Hansons' house. We've only got five lots on the lake with homes on them, so it is pretty desolate. We're the only year-round residents. Most of the lake homes are summer homes."

She continued down the hallway, and Kathryn marveled at her lack of concern.

"Aren't you afraid?" she asked. "Living up here all alone in this big house?"

Jenny stopped and turned. "Afraid? Afraid of what?"

A list of things came to mind, but Kathryn kept them to herself. She would let Jenny hold on to her innocence for as long as possible. "Uh, I dunno ... I guess I'm just a city girl. All this peace and quiet makes me nervous."

Jenny smiled. "I know what you mean. It took me a while to adjust when I moved back from the city last year." She held out her hand. "Come on, this is the room I wanted to show you."

Kathryn took the offered hand, and Jenny led her down the hallway.

"Granddad was a chemist, but he dabbled in botany and authored several nature books. Gran illustrated them. All the oil paintings in the house are hers, as are the framed floral prints."

"On the level?"

"Yes. I think she was brilliant."

Kathryn agreed. She stopped when she came to one of the framed intricate flower prints on the hallway wall and leaned in to get a closer look. The line work was exquisite beneath the subtle watercolor wash of colors. "Is this acid etched or drypoint?"

"Oh, you're familiar with the process."

"A little. I studied art way back in my youth." She cut Jenny a sly grin for the liberal guess about her age earlier.

Jenny chuckled and nudged her in the ribs. "Drypoint."

Kathryn nodded and straightened. "A very talented lady."

"Yeah, I've got a lot to live up to in this family."

"Don't be so hard on yourself. You're just getting started," Kathryn said.

Jenny shook her head. "I feel like a rudderless ship, just drifting aimlessly. Even Uncle Paul, the black sheep of the family, knew what he wanted to do from an early age."

"Why is he the black sheep?"

"Granddad wanted him to be *a man of substance*, whatever that means. Uncle Paul wanted to get into the newspaper business. They had quite a row about it, and Granddad cut him off financially until he came to his senses. He made the *Daily Chronicle* a success and still didn't measure up."

"Tough crowd."

"You said it. It was pretty awful for him. He would come over to the house to see me and Gran when Granddad and Dad weren't around."

"Your uncle didn't get along with your dad either?"

"Not really. They never said a negative thing about each other in my presence, but there was a sibling rivalry that Uncle Paul just never got over. He was the oldest, but Dad was the favorite. That's how Uncle Paul saw it, anyway. After my grandparents were gone, I thought they might work things out, but as far as I know, they never saw each other again. Uncle Paul never mentions it, but I know their strained relationship upset Dad terribly. Uncle Paul came to Dad's funeral for me. He didn't want to be there. They were brothers, you know? It shouldn't have been that way." She shook her head and squeezed Kathryn's elbow. "Come on, this is the last room."

Kathryn understood now why the agency's investigation to get information about Daniel Ryan through Paul came up empty.

"Do you get along with your uncle?"

"Oh, absolutely. He and Aunt Betsy didn't have kids, so I was the daughter they never had. Whatever was going on between him and Dad, they kept me out of it."

Kathryn was glad that Paul did something right.

Jenny turned on the light in the final room. "The art studio."

"Wow," Kathryn said as she entered.

More floral prints adorned the walls, along with slotted shelves filled with canvases and engraving plates. A large artist's desk sat facing the window at one end of the room, and large flat file drawers and easels filled out the other side.

"Do you paint?"

Jenny chuckled. "I'm afraid that particular talent passed me by."

The pitched roof made for interesting wall angles, as it did in all the rooms on the second floor. In this room, the angled wall contained a floor-to-ceiling skylight that spanned half the room and was covered with a wide pleated white fabric shade.

"Wow," Kathryn said again as she eyed the skylight. "The light must be incredible in here in the daytime."

"Not only the daytime," Jenny said. She led Kathryn under the window and put a hand on her back.

"Close your eyes and stay right here. This is the view I wanted you to see."

Kathryn heard the light switch click, then another click, and then the whirring of a small motor. Soft footfalls on the large area rug came toward her, and then she felt a gentle hand on the small of her back.

"Okay. Open."

The large shade slowly descended into a collection box at the base of the skylight, revealing the moody night sky as the moon played hide-and-seek with the clouds.

"Oh," Kathryn drew out. "This must be amazing on a full moon."

"You'll have to come back and see."

Kathryn agreed without thinking. "It's a date."

The moonlight through the skylight's rectangular panels splayed a grid pattern across the floor.

"I feel like I'm in a Hitchcock film," Kathryn said, as they were bathed in shades of gray.

"*Suspicion.*"

"Yes, that's the one."

"The spider web effect," they both said simultaneously, referring to a lighting effect in the film.

"The stairwell," Jenny said, "With the ominous glowing—"

"Glass of milk," they said in unison.

While Jenny laughed, a chill skittered up Kathryn's spine. If things didn't go as expected tonight, Jenny could be caught in a web of intrigue that would ruin her life. Jenny's future was her responsibility. It was also her responsibility to make sure her assessment was unbiased.

Jenny rubbed her back. "Are you cold?"

"Mm. A little." She wasn't sure if it was the temperature in the room or the realization that Jenny was becoming more important than was prudent. Her personal detachment was the key to her success, and that was eroding quickly. Jenny continued to rub her back, which wasn't helping. She had to focus on her job.

"Sorry," Jenny said. "I guess it is a little cold up here. Bernie tells me I'm part Eskimo. I don't usually heat the upstairs. Come on, we'll go back down."

Kathryn turned to head toward the door, but Jenny stopped her and directed her to the front corner of the room. "This way." She led Kathryn through the darkness until she got to the left corner and turned on the light switch. It lit the downstairs, illuminating a small spiral staircase winding up from the room below.

They descended the stairs and wound up back in the study. "Oh," Kathryn said. This wasn't in the floor plan.

"Let me get you those books," Jenny said, striding across the room to the sliding library ladder.

She climbed halfway up the ladder and searched along the highest shelf. "There you are." She held on to the ladder with one hand and reached her full length with the other, getting up on her toes to close the final inches on the three-volume set.

Kathryn stood at the ready next to the ladder, half expecting, with their track record so far, for Jenny to fall off the ladder, or the bookcase to fall on them, or some other disaster. She purposely avoided the shapely leg flexing beside her.

Jenny passed down the small books. "Here you go."

"Thank you."

Jenny climbed off the ladder. "You'll probably be the last person to read them."

Kathryn looked at the three gray paper bound books in her hands. They were simply titled in black, Volume I, Volume II, Volume III on the covers and bindings.

"Have you read them?"

"I tried once, but my eyes glazed over after the first three pages."

Kathryn chuckled and was pleased that Jenny apparently had no interest in her father's work. "I'm sure it's fascinating."

Jenny headed toward the living room. "You'd be the only one who thinks so." She stopped at the broken china and shook her head.

Kathryn set the books down on the coffee table. "Here, let me help you."

Jenny raised her hand and then pointed at the couch. "Oh, no. Sit. My mess. I'll clean it up."

Kathryn sat as Jenny gathered the good cup and saucer and the larger broken pieces of her cup and saucer and set them on the service tray.

"Don't move. I'll be right back."

Kathryn sat on the edge of the couch and thumbed through Volume I. It was filled with medical jargon, chemical equations, and full-page biological line drawings of what she assumed were cells. The drawings looked suspiciously like the grandmother's delicate work. She offered an accusatory glance at one of the landscapes on the wall and then one to the portrait of Jenny's grandfather over the fireplace. Were they part of this? The room suddenly felt smaller and colder.

She shook off the paranoia. The volumes were created decades ago. Nothing to do with this war, Nazis, or her current assignment. She perused through the rest of the volume without trying to make sense of it. It wasn't her job to dissect Daniel Ryan's early work or question anyone else's role in it. It was her job to clear his daughter. Check that. It was her job to mine his daughter for any information that pertained to his work. The three volumes before her would help her do that, and then she was out. Jenny would live her life with the memories of her beloved father intact.

"Learn anything new?"

Kathryn looked up to see Jenny standing before her holding a dustpan and brush.

"I'm trying to wrap my head around the lingo. It's been a while."

Jenny smiled. "Fairly complicated and awfully wordy, as I recall. The drawings are pretty though."

"Your grandmother's work?"

Jenny paused and knit her brow, as if the thought had never occurred to her before. "I wouldn't think so. Dad was in Europe at the time."

Well, that answered that. Kathryn closed the book and set it atop the other volumes. Time to get back to the matter at hand. "So, your father just gave up research after he wrote these?"

Jenny nodded as she stooped down to sweep up the former cup and saucer set. "That particular avenue." She corralled shards into the dustpan. "He wrote those papers early in his career, when he was heavily into research. He got his medical training in Europe, where their industrial research laboratories provided funding for things like theoretical pathology. When he came home, he found that our labs weren't run like that. There was no funding, and we were so far behind in the science of medicine that they dismissed what he had to say as useless nonsense."

"Not very open-minded."

"Sad to say, that's how it was then."

"Surely we've caught up by now."

"Oh, we have, and then some. Dad was very happy at the institute."

Kathryn agreed with a nod, but it wasn't enough. If Jenny knew anything more about her father's work, now was the time to find out. "Did he keep any journals or anything? More recent ideas and such?"

Jenny stopped what she was doing and straightened. "Not that I know of. Why?"

"Oh, I just thought it would be interesting to see where these ideas and theories led him. Medical science changes so quickly and, soon, theories become reality. It's kind of exciting, don't you think?"

Jenny paused with a quizzical look on her face, and Kathryn worried she'd gone too far in her haste to complete her assignment.

The pause ended with a grin. "Dad would have liked you." She went back to cleaning up. "I never thought about it, but I guess you're right."

Still not enough. Kathryn picked up Volume I again and pretended to study a random page. "I just find it odd that a man passionate enough about his ideas to write these papers would just give it up and never go back to it, out of curiosity, at the very least."

Jenny slowed her sweeping movements and then stopped. "Dad never talked about his work, so I haven't any idea, really, but I can ask Dr. Stevens. He may know."

"Dr. Stevens?"

"Martin Stevens, old family friend. I turned over Dad's midtown office to him. I just couldn't face it. Equipment, text books, files, the works." She lifted a hand. "What am I going to do with that stuff, right?"

Kathryn nodded and kept her expression neutral. Inside, her heart was racing in a combination of triumph, relief, and adrenaline. *Dr. Martin Stevens.* Brass would be pleased. She'd gotten their answer and more.

Jenny swept the last of the debris into the dust pan. "I'll ask him if he came across anything like that."

Kathryn downplayed the prospect with a shrug. "Just curious."

Triumph and adrenaline were no match for the relief that sapped the last of Kathryn's energy. Her assignment was all over but the typing. Best of all, Jenny didn't suspect a thing. The final report would be filed in the morning, and they'd send someone to investigate Dr. Stevens.

She silently exhaled the long day, and her finely-tuned focus went with it. She felt Jenny staring at her and looked up. "What?"

"You look different."

"How so?"

"I don't know ... content."

Kathryn's first instinct was to sit up straighter, annoyed that she'd let her relief show, but she'd been caught, so she smiled and let the moment play out. "Lovely evening, lovely home, lovely company. I am content."

Jenny set the dustpan and brush down. "Good." She stepped around the coffee table and sat facing Kathryn on the couch. She tucked her legs up and sank into the back of the seat. She looked nervous. "I hope what I'm about to say doesn't change that."

"Uh-oh," Kathryn said.

Instead of chuckling, as Kathryn expected, Jenny clasped her hands in her lap and stared at them, her demeanor serious.

Kathryn reached out and took her hand in concern, wondering what changed the mood so quickly.

"Were you serious before? About dating?" Jenny asked.

Kathryn hesitated and then pulled her hand back. Just a week ago, the answer would have been an automatic yes. She would have bedded Jenny by the end of the night and congratulated herself on a swift conquest. Instead, she found herself in no man's land. Persona dropped, guard down, she was paralyzed by the prospect of a personal relationship that she would want to last more than the customary roll in the sack, or few curious dates, or, on the rare occasion, several what-was-I-thinking weeks.

Green eyes bored into her, waiting for an answer. A quick response was warranted, but, instead, scenarios raced through her mind. She couldn't keep her job at the OSS secret forever. The lies to cover it up would poison the best relationship, and when Jenny found out—and she would—she would find out about the investigation and the circumstances of their meeting. The fragile trust that binds a relationship would be broken. The relationship would end like all her relationships ended, for one reason or another—irrevocably broken.

It usually didn't matter, but this time was different. This time she would be the one with regrets as Jenny stormed out of her life.

She mentally shook herself out of such ridiculous scenarios. There was no future with Jenny Ryan. There was no future past the war. She would get back to the fight and die repaying her debt. The last thing she needed was one more heartbroken person in her wake. Jenny didn't know anything about her or her sins, and it would stay that way.

She had to let her down gently. No hard feelings. The typical *it's not you, it's me.*

The pause made Jenny nervous, and she fumbled for words when she realized she may have misinterpreted the entire evening. "I mean ... is that what we're doing? I mean ... would you be interested in that? With me, I mean. Dating?" She paused, mortified at her inelegant attempt to clarify the situation and vowed to ban the phase "I mean" from her vocabulary forever.

Now was not the time for a hiccup in self-confidence. She stepped on the gas before she lost her nerve.

"Don't get me wrong," she continued, "I could sit here and flirt you to death, but I'd hate to waste all my best pick-up lines if you're not interested."

She hoped for a sexually aggressive confirmation of the attraction she'd felt between them or a flirty comment from Kathryn, but all that came back was an uncomfortable grin and eyes masked by indecision.

Jenny unfolded a leg and nudged Kathryn's knee with her foot. "Someday you may find me irresistible," she said, her voice rising to a singsong quality at the end. "And poor me, fresh out of lines. However will I win you over then?"

She paused, and absent a reaction, gently nudged Kathryn's knee again. Kathryn looked at the foot and then slowly lifted her gaze. Her blue eyes were darker, her stare more intense. It was an unmistakable invitation.

Jenny's heartbeat quickened and she did not falter as she returned the stare. She let her foot slide from Kathryn's knee to her inner thigh and waited for any indication the move was unwelcome.

The subtle increase in Kathryn's breathing urged her to continue. Jenny's eyes darted from her brazen foot to Kathryn's face, as she timidly gauged how far she could go.

Her foot had just disappeared beneath Kathryn's dress when a firm grip on her ankle made her stop.

Kathryn leaned in with a smoldering look filled with equal parts provocation and promise. "Should I find you irresistible ..." She slid her hand slowly up Jenny's extended leg. "You won't need any lines to win me over."

Jenny swallowed. "Uh, okay." She wasn't sure if she saw anger staring back at her or a guarantee that this was going to be the best birthday ever. She looked hard into those half-lidded blue eyes and decided it definitely wasn't anger.

What made her think she could win the seduction war was beyond her, but she was unprepared for Kathryn in full counter-seduction mode. She had disarmed her with one sentence, one touch, and one look. When she turned it on, she was undeniable.

As Kathryn hovered close, her hand poised to continue its path up her tingling leg, Jenny shrank into the couch. This incredibly beautiful woman, surely about to pounce on her, probably had infinitely more experience in seduction and sex than she did, and it made her feel like a rank amateur in the presence of a master. She made no effort to hide her surprise or insecurity, and judging from Kathryn's triumphant smirk, that was the point.

Kathryn's plan to intimidate Jenny until she backed off worked faster than anticipated. She didn't know if it was the intense stare or the hand sliding up Jenny's leg that got the job done, but it was just in time. A few more inches and Jenny's foot would have started something that she may not have stopped. As it was, she enjoyed the shapely leg in her hand, and her sensual gaze wasn't altogether an act.

The amorous blush on Jenny's cheeks made Kathryn regret that she couldn't give her what she wanted. This was their last night together, and if it were anyone else, she would give in to lust and give them something to remember her by.

Jenny deserved much more than that, more than Kathryn could ever give her. The sooner she was out of her life, the better.

The desire in Jenny's eyes disagreed, and Kathryn wasn't surprised when she was undeterred in her seduction.

"So, I seem to find myself out of lines at the moment. Do I need to find some, or are you finding me irresistible yet?"

Kathryn laughed out loud. "Do you ever give up?"

"You haven't answered my first question yet." Jenny lowered her gaze to the hand cradling her lower thigh, just above the bend in her knee. "That does look like something people who are dating would do, though."

Kathryn leaned back from her hovering position and slowly removed her hand from Jenny's leg. She didn't want to do this the hard way. In moments of irrational hope for a future together, she didn't want to do it at all, but she knew she had to leave hope for a future and Jenny behind.

Jenny withdrew her leg and tucked it back under herself. Her eyes were downcast and her disappointment evident when she said, "You don't have to answer."

The defeated tone seeped through Kathryn's resolve and amplified her regret.

Jenny was giving her an easy out, but all she wanted to do was take her in her arms and tell her the rejection wasn't her fault. That in a different world, in a different life, they would be friends, or more, if that's where their paths led. But this was not that life.

"I've put you on the spot," Jenny said. "And I can see from your expression that you're trying to find a way to let me down easy, so I'll relieve you of that duty. You don't have to say anything." She shrugged. "Just friends it is. No hard feelings." She stuck her hand out to shake on it.

Kathryn stared at the offered hand. She loved how easy Jenny was. How she knew the right thing to say at the right time, to save her from more excuses and more lies.

She took the offered hand, which, to her surprise, had the same effect as the foot sliding up her thigh. The transition from *do whatever it takes* to *stand down and disengage* had lost all meaning.

The gentle smile in Jenny's eyes turned serious, and Kathryn knew it was in response to her hungry stare. She couldn't help it. What she *wanted* to do was beating what she *should* do into submission. Jenny's hand in hers only made her want more of her. The touch was purposeful this time, not one of comfort or contrivance. It was a seal of friendship, one that could never be, but Kathryn wanted it. And more. Just for tonight. Their last night.

"It's not like that," Kathryn finally managed to whisper, trying hard to gain control of the reasoning center of her brain.

"Not like what?" Jenny said breathlessly.

Kathryn had no answer as she got lost in desirous green eyes, causing an overwhelming urge to pull Jenny into her. Damn the debt, damn the assignment; she'd wrap her in her arms and kiss her as she'd wanted to kiss her ever since that night on the staircase behind The Grotto. The thought of it caused her heart to race and her body to react. Unfolding her legs, she tightened her grasp on Jenny's hand.

She didn't remember pulling, but she soon found Jenny hovering above her, just within focus. Jenny's eyes looked into hers, looked into *her*. Her gaze was searching, probing, as if she could see it all: all the terror, all the ugliness, all the secrets hidden in the recesses of her mind. She waited for Jenny to turn away, repulsed by what she found. She didn't. She simply waited, pleading, searching, wanting— wanting to know it all. Wanting to take it all.

Kathryn knew the next move was hers, and there would be no one to blame but herself for how the rest of the evening played out.

She slowly brought her hand up to Jenny's chest, and with her last ounce of resistance, planned to gently push her away. She was an assignment, finished or not, and there was a war to get back to, debts to pay. She knew better than to let this happen.

The right thing to do was the last thing on her mind when she felt Jenny's weight settle on her need. Jenny's heart was hammering under her hand, and it was intoxicating. She found her hand sliding mindlessly from the warm chest over the collarbone and up toward the back of Jenny's neck, where she tangled her fingers in the soft blonde hair cascading over her hand. She drew her closer, out of focus, lips hungry, but patient. She pulled her just within reach but paused, inhaling the scent of her, anticipating the taste of her.

She felt Jenny's hand slide up her abdomen and then stop to unfasten the top button of her dress's V-neckline and then another. This was happening. Kathryn's breasts ached for Jenny's touch. She hadn't wanted anyone like this in ages. Unfettered desire burned through her precious control and left her vulnerable. Too vulnerable. Panic burst through her arousal and warned, *Save Jenny Ryan; don't condemn her to your world!*

The words swam in Kathryn's head, negating the pleasure of Jenny's hand sliding inside her dress. Jenny was no reprieve, no enlightened path to happiness. This hope for the future was a mirage. She owed a debt, one she could never repay, but one that she had no right to set aside. These things she knew, all too well, but here she was, lost in a few moments of selfish pleasure.

She understood, for the first time, how great men betrayed all for the love of another or the promised salvation of their souls. She'd seen it happen, some in her own bed, as she mined for information that would give her side the edge in a world turned upside down. She thought them weak-minded fools, and now she was becoming what she so often despised.

Kathryn turned her head. "I'm sorry." She released Jenny and buttoned her dress.

Jenny thumped her head on her shoulder, and Kathryn could almost hear her unspoken *Ugh.*

Jenny exhaled her frustration as she raised her head and then sat back on her heels. "Yeah, me too. What's the matter?"

Kathryn hesitated, then released a shaky breath, as recrimination battled with an immediate sense of loss. "I can't do this."

"Would it help if I begged to differ."

"'Fraid not."

"What's the matter?" Jenny asked again, this time absent the frustrated tone.

Kathryn paused a beat. She had standard answers for these types of situations: a borrowed life, just for work. There were a hundred excuses she could choose. Assignments didn't rate the truth. She barely gave the truth a thought, other than how to bend it to get what she wanted.

It was different with Jenny. She hated lying to her. She had suffered enough with the loss of her father. This was a clean assignment, and now it was finished. Get out, go home, move on.

Kathryn blamed exhaustion for the uncharacteristic longing for Jenny Ryan. The longing wasn't real. It was a product of delayed disengagement, remnants of feelings manufactured to complete her assignment. Wasn't it?

It had been so long since she'd been honest about her feelings. Maybe it had been too long since her feelings were honest. The truth felt uncomfortable, just as the lies had been uncomfortable once. Now the lies were a way of life. Often her survival depended on it. Without so much as a whisper goodbye, genuine emotion had become foreign to her, and the fine art of betrayal had taken its place. Could she even discern the truth from playacting anymore? She closed her eyes and searched for the person who used to know. She looked up into innocent green eyes and thought she saw someone she remembered, someone she wanted to be again.

"I don't think you'd believe me if I told you," she said honestly.

"Try me."

"Because I like you too much."

Jenny raised her brow. "Okay. Could you like me a little less? Say, for an hour?" She paused and smiled. "Maybe two?"

Kathryn grinned, as the unrelenting conflict within her stopped its incessant saber rattling. Jenny had that effect on her. Lulling her into normalcy. No wonder it was so hard to let her go. She wasn't a spy, or a war criminal, or someone to be on guard against at all times. She was an innocent drawn into the ugly world of intrigue by tragedy. One more reason to set her free.

Her resolve was interrupted by Jenny's hand on her cheek.

"Seriously, Kat. What's the matter? I know you want to. I've sensed it all night."

Kathryn tensed under the warm hand on her face and got lost in Jenny's searching eyes.

"No strings, if that's what the problem is."

Oh, if it were only that simple, Kathryn lamented. She leaned into Jenny's touch, something she would never feel again, and Jenny took it as an answer.

"Yes?"

The lean became a regretful tilt of her head, with no words to soften the blow.

Jenny removed her hand and rested it on her thigh with a bewildering shake of her head. "I apologize for my forward behavior. I've been told I have a vivid imagination." She shook her head again. "I thought you wanted ... that we both wanted ..." She slumped back on her heels. "Sorry, I'm making a fool of myself."

Kathryn wouldn't let Jenny blame herself. "No, please. You're not. It's not that." She took Jenny's hand again. "I did ... I do ... it's ... it's complicated."

As her graceful exit evaporated into adolescent stammering, Kathryn could tell from Jenny's face that she was only adding to the confusion. "It's nothing personal, Jenny. I'm not good dating material, that's all."

Jenny ran her eyes up and down Kathryn's reposing form in obvious disagreement. "You're going to have to explain that one."

"What I'm trying to say is, it's not you. It's me." It was getting easier to tell the truth—maybe a little too easy. "There's a lot about me that you don't know."

"Well, isn't that what dating is for? Besides …" Jenny tugged on Kathryn's hand. "What I do know, I like."

Kathryn let go of Jenny's hand and looked away. She became still as her sins lined up to stake their claim. "There's a lot not to like."

Jenny frowned. "Maybe I should be allowed to decide that."

"And what if you decide I was right?" Kathryn stared directly into perplexed green eyes and dared her to answer.

"Are you trying to scare me off, or are you just playing hard to get?"

"Just stating facts."

Kathryn knew how it would go. If Jenny got to know her, she wouldn't want anything to do with her. She was awash in demons, secrets, and a trail of sins she could never explain. She barely had Jenny as a friend and she missed her already. She never wanted to see that horrified look in Jenny's eyes when she found out who she really was. It would hurt too much.

Jenny reached out and touched Kathryn's knee. "Hey, Kat, relax. This isn't life or death. Look …" She lifted her voice to a more pleasant tone. "Forget I said anything."

"Jenny, I don't want to forget it, and I don't want you to think …" She didn't know what she wanted to say next. She only knew she didn't want to make promises she wouldn't keep. "Things are just going on right now that—"

"What kind of things?" Jenny interrupted. "Are you talking about Forrester? Your situation with him?"

"Well, yes. Forrester, among other things." She was glad someone's brain was working.

Jenny held up a hand. "Look, Kathryn, I meant it. You don't have to explain. I can't imagine what your situation is like. I'm being incredibly selfish. I'm sorry."

Kathryn paused, wondering why the hell she was trying so hard to explain herself when Jenny had repeatedly given her a way out. She took the out this time and prepared to get out of there on a lighter note. "It's your birthday. You're supposed to be selfish."

Jenny chuckled. "Don't give me a license to be selfish. It could be dangerous."

Kathryn agreed with a grin. She stared at Jenny's smiling face and a calm washed over her. She didn't know if it was relief that her assignment was over and Jenny was still smiling or the fact that Jenny kneeling between her legs, wearing that smile, was an image she would save as a touchstone for when her world turned to chaos again.

The same dreamy expression stared back at her, but it was quickly broken by a curt, "Well," as Jenny unfolded herself and eyed the dustpan filled with broken china on the coffee table. "Let me get rid of this."

She stood and straightened her skirt and hair, as if a marvelous tryst had actually occurred. She picked up the mess. "Be right back," she said, as she strode purposefully toward the kitchen.

Kathryn held her breath until she heard the back door slam and then exhaled in exasperation as she buried her face in her hands. "Pull yourself together, Hammond."

Jenny stood in front of the garbage can beside her back steps and dumped the broken china set into it. "You're an idiot!" she said in an animated whisper as she slammed the lid down. "An absolute idiot." She leaned on the lid and shook her head.

"Forget I said anything," she mocked in a whiny voice to the dustpan in her hand. "Sure. I'll forget that I saw her desire me. I'll forget that I was one second away from caressing her breast, tasting her lips, and losing myself in what would have been the most erotic, mind-altering, life-changing sexual experience of my entire life. Yeah, that's it. I'll just forget all that."

She straightened and then collapsed onto the steps, where she exhaled her frustration. Just when she thought they'd come to a mutual understanding, Kathryn pulled the rip cord. Jenny didn't understand it. Sure, there was Forrester, but he had always been there. No, there was something else going on. With excuses like *I want to, but I can't*, and the ultimate doozy, *because I like you too much*, Jenny was left utterly confused. If Kathryn only wanted to be friends, she'd better knock off the sexy looks and flirty banter, because Jenny couldn't take much more teasing without bursting into flames.

She filled her lungs with the cold night air to calm her frustration and her raging libido and exhaled it slowly. Maybe if she sat out here long enough, Kathryn would realize what she was missing. Jenny shook her head and chuckled at her wishful thinking. She was positive she wasn't misreading the signals, but short of undignified begging, whatever was going on with Kathryn Hammond would remain a mystery for the moment.

Time—that's all she needed. A good mystery always reveals its secrets in time. She was moving too fast for Kathryn. She decided gentle, but persistent, pressure would ensure Kathryn's inevitable surrender. She smiled at the thought of it. Then her body warmed at the thought of it too.

Kathryn paced the living room with her hands on her hips. What was taking Jenny so long? She was anxious to get home, where she could clear her head and get her priorities in order. No more sitting on couches playing footsie. There was serious work to get back to.

Tensely pacing the living room would not be a good look when Jenny returned, so Kathryn shook out her arms and rolled her shoulders to relax. She found herself standing in front of a writing desk, where a letter sized notepad peeked out from under two magazines.

The agent in her found her footing, and after a quick glance toward the doorway Jenny exited, Kathryn casually pushed aside the magazines to expose the writing on the notepad. On it, Jenny had composed a letter to the editor of the *Daily News* about their constant derision of her beloved president in this time of war.

She peeked at the next page, where Jenny had begun an article on the strikers down at the machine factory. This one had the same theme as the first: in times of war, the rules were different. Kathryn couldn't disagree with the sentiment. Jenny was a good writer, concise and to the point. She fervently put country and unity before all. The second article came down hard on the strikers and their union for allowing the strike. If it were published, it could cause quite a stir.

Kathryn raised her brow at one particularly direct passage. "Good heavens."

"Is that good or bad?" She heard Jenny say from the doorway of the living room.

Kathryn quickly looked over with a start and then put everything back the way she found it, as if she hadn't been caught snooping. "Sorry. Didn't mean to pry."

"Please," Jenny said with a dismissive wave of her hand as she crossed the room to her side. "If you weren't your nosey self, I probably never would have seen the inside of the study again."

Kathryn tilted her head in confusion.

"If you hadn't opened the doors and gone in, they'd still be shut. I haven't seen the inside of that study in a year."

"But ..." Kathryn glanced at the room in question. The doors were open when she entered the living room. Her eyes instinctively darted around the room as if an intruder were there. Her body tensed as her adrenaline surged. "You mean you never open those doors?"

"Never."

"Ever?"

"Never. That's why I was so shocked to see you in there."

Kathryn tried to hide her alarm. "Gosh, Jenny, I'm awfully sorry. I didn't realize."

"No, don't apologize." Jenny briefly touched her back. "I'm thanking you." Jenny glanced down at the notebook beneath the magazines and looked back up to Kathryn's face, inviting her opinion on what she'd read.

"Volatile stuff," Kathryn said casually, but she was on edge.

Someone had been in the house. Why? Were they still in the house? She didn't have a sense of that, but her mind hadn't exactly been on work. She played back the evening and realized she'd seen every room in the house save one, the grandfather's man room upstairs.

"But is it good?" Jenny asked about the article.

"Very good. Too good, maybe," Kathryn said. "Be careful, Jenny. Unions are nothing to mess around with. It can be a nasty business, I know." It wouldn't hurt to remind Jenny of her connection to Forrester and his nefarious dealings.

It wasn't her job to protect Jenny, but this external threat had Kathryn on high alert. It was her job to uncover anything and anyone connected with Daniel Ryan and his treachery. That included someone breaking into Jenny Ryan's house. *Especially* someone breaking into Jenny Ryan's house. It appeared her assignment wasn't quite over. That gave her a sense of comfort. This she knew how to do.

"I like your protective side," Jenny said with a grin.

Kathryn forced a smile as she tried to think of a way to secure the house. "I just found you. I don't want anything to happen to you."

Jenny beamed and put her hand on the small of Kathryn's back. "You look tired."

"Throwing me out?"

"Actually, I thought I'd ask you to stay."

Kathryn paused. She had to sell her reaction.

"Jenny, I ..." Page 36, How to Be a Spy—protest a little.

"Don't worry," Jenny broke in. "I'll be a good girl and make up a room for you upstairs."

Upstairs was too far away to keep watch, and *in* her bed was too close—for many reasons. "Don't bother." Kathryn looked around the room and indicated the couch with a tilt of her head. "I'll be fine here." It was perfect, with a direct view of the master bedroom.

"Don't be ridiculous," Jenny said. "I've got two perfectly good beds upstairs." She headed in that direction. Kathryn grabbed her trailing hand and convinced her that heating the upstairs would be a waste of energy when the fire had already warmed the living room. Jenny couldn't argue with that, and, thankfully, she didn't offer her own bed.

She left the room and returned with bedding, which she laid on the couch and held up two pillows. "One or two?"

"Two."

Jenny smiled. "A hugger. Me too."

Kathryn decided that jokes about being alone in a big bed were not a good idea, so she just smiled as Jenny arranged a comfortable nest on the couch.

She needed to call Smitty. He'd be angry at the late-night call until he realized it was her, and then all would be forgiven. She was hoping that he had been the one in the house. He knew that Jenny would be out all evening. It was the perfect opportunity to sneak in and have a look around.

"May I use your telephone?"

"Sure. Right there." Jenny pointed to the end table. "Someone expecting you at home?"

Jenny's voice had a tinge of jealousy to it, and Kathryn smiled inwardly as she slipped easily back into *keep Jenny close and interested* mode. "No. A friend was going to pick me up for an early rehearsal tomorrow. I need to let him know I won't be home."

"Sorry," Jenny said. "That was none of my business."

Kathryn picked up the phone. "That's all right. I'll let you know when it's none of your business." She grinned and then asked for the exchange.

Jenny pointed vaguely at the hallway. "I'm just going to ..." She slipped out of the room without finishing her sentence.

Kathryn nodded to her retreating form. No answer at Smitty's. Still. She hoped it had been him in the house, but she knew that wasn't the case. He'd never leave the doors open.

"All set?" Jenny asked from behind.

"Yes." She turned and found Jenny holding a towel set, a robe, and a brand-new toothbrush. "Wow. Looks like you've been expecting someone."

Jenny's grin said *all my life*. "You can use my shower, through the bedroom there." She thumbed over her shoulder. "Or the tub upstairs, whichever you prefer."

"A soak sounds good tonight," Kathryn said. And she could check the man room for the intruder.

"Okay," Jenny said with her hands behind her back.

An awkward moment of parting for the evening had them both tongue-tied, and they just stared at each other for a beat.

"I have a bag in the car with some clothes for the morning," Kathryn said into the silence.

Jenny raised a brow. "Like you expected to stay?"

Kathryn paused and wondered if she was serious until they both broke their gaze and snickered. They were getting a little punchy in the early morning hours.

"Laundry day, as it happens," Kathryn lied with a grin. She had some clothes for the training range in her gear bag, and she wanted to retrieve her gun from under the dash, just in case.

"Okay ... well." Jenny rubbed her hands together. "Make yourself at home. I'll get you an extra blanket if you need it."

"Thank you, I'm sure I'll be fine."

Another awkward silence ensued until Jenny said, "Okay," and rubbed Kathryn's arm.

Kathryn smiled at the gesture and pulled her into a goodnight hug. She kissed her on the top of the head without thinking. "Thank you for sharing your birthday. I had a good time."

"So did I. I'm glad you showed up."

Kathryn enjoyed the hug a little too much and loosened her grip. Jenny took the clue and backed off.

"Good night, Kat."

"Nite."

Jenny turned quickly and strode toward her bedroom. She paused briefly at the door, but then disappeared inside and gently pressed the door shut.

At the pause, an unbidden surge of arousal stole Kathryn's breath when she thought Jenny might invite her into her bed. She wanted to think she'd flat out refuse, but for a moment, she wasn't sure she would, or could.

She shook her head and exhaled. She blamed her madness on exhaustion.

. . .

After Kathryn gathered what she needed from the car, she heard Jenny in the shower as she passed the master bedroom. She hurried to the man room upstairs and checked inside. All clear, and, as promised, nothing but dead animals with glass eyes staring at her from the walls. She quickly checked the other rooms more thoroughly, just to be sure, and was satisfied that the intruder was long gone. The mystery of the study doors made her even more uncomfortable about Jenny being all alone in the house, and she vowed to figure out a way to keep her safe.

The master bedroom was silent as Kathryn crept by on her way to the living room after her bath. She padded across the room to the fireplace and put the last log on the fire before sitting on the hearth. She mindlessly finger combed her hair as she got lost in the flickering yellow and orange of the flames. She loved fires. There was comfort there, a mind-numbing, hypnotic peace, and she let it take her away from duty, and debt, and the past.

CHAPTER TWENTY-FIVE

*J*enny tightened her grip on the club-sized piece of firewood in her hand as she stood over the beautiful woman sleeping on her couch. She'd noticed the dying fire and the empty wood basket beside the fireplace on her way to the kitchen to get a glass of water, so she grabbed a small piece of firewood from the boot room by the back door and brought it back to fuel the diminishing flames.

Kathryn looked so peaceful. She was sleeping on her back, one arm draped lazily over her head and the other hugging a pillow with her face nuzzled into it. Jenny smiled. One day she'd like to take the place of that pillow. Kathryn's unconscious state gave her eyes permission to explore. She leaned closer to soak in every detail denied by propriety when one was awake. The lingering flames from the fire threw a pleasing glow on Kathryn's relaxed form, and Jenny wanted to know everything about her. Could they just be friends, she wondered silently as her eyes traced every angle on the beautiful face so tantalizingly close to hers? Before she could contemplate an answer, a blur of movement preceded immediate pain as a strong hand grabbed her wrist.

"*Shit!*" Jenny yelped, as the pressure of the grip hit a nerve and forced her to drop the small log in her hand. The log hit the floor, and she would have fallen backward over the coffee table if the vise-like grip on her wrist hadn't pinned her to her spot.

Kathryn sat straight up, her eyes wide and wild. There was a snub-nosed revolver in her other hand pointed right at Jenny's face. As fast as it was in her face, the gun was gone, and Jenny wondered if she'd imagined it. She stood frozen, the pain in her wrist lost in the shock of the moment.

Kathryn was gasping for air in short, quick breaths, and then she blinked several times. Jenny could see disorientation fade into awareness. Kathryn let go of her wrist and immediately tried to undo what she'd done.

"God, Jenny! I'm so sorry. I ... I'm so sorry."

"It ... it's okay," Jenny managed to stutter, frightened by the crazed look in Kathryn's eyes. "I wasn't going to club you, I promise," she joked uncomfortably. Kathryn's demeanor returned to someone more familiar, and Jenny sat on the coffee table before her wobbly knees gave out.

"I'm so sorry," Kathryn said again. "That's your bad wrist too." She anxiously ran her hands across it.

"It's fine." Jenny flexed her hand and worked her wrist. It was a little tender, and her fingers were tingling with the returning feeling, but she'd live. No need to make Kathryn feel any worse than she already did. Kathryn's hands were trembling, and Jenny wondered what experiences had made her so unconsciously aggressive. She looked to the balled-up blanket, where she knew there was a gun, and questioned whether she should pursue it. As Kathryn went on with apologies and gentle massages, Jenny wondered how awful a life she really led as Forrester's mistress.

She covered Kathryn's worried hands with her own and assured her she was all right. "Payback for the cut on your hand," she said with a smile. "We're even."

Kathryn didn't smile. Jenny wasn't sure she even heard what she'd said.

. . .

After hearing numerous apologies and offering assurances in kind, Jenny suggested they try to get some sleep in the dwindling hours before first light. She didn't know about Kathryn, but she didn't get any sleep. As dawn broke, she was wide awake and listening to the muffled sound of the water running down the pipes from the upstairs bathroom. She got up, started some coffee, and returned to her room to get dressed for the workday.

Tucking her blouse into her skirt as she left the bedroom, Jenny froze when she looked into the living room and saw Kathryn wearing nothing but brown slacks and a peach colored bra. She slipped a tight black turtleneck sweater over her head and worked it down her magnificent upper body. She flipped her dark mane out of the neckline, and when Jenny tore her focus away from that incredibly sexy move, she found Kathryn staring right at her.

"Oh," Kathryn said, as she gathered her hair loosely about her neck and secured it with a large barrette. "You *are* up. I knew I smelled coffee."

Jenny swallowed to make sure her voice was steady. "Sorry. I didn't mean to stare."

"Yes you did," Kathryn said with a grin, smoothing her sweater over her hips.

Jenny crossed her arms and returned the grin. "Okay, I did, and I'm not sorry."

Kathryn walked toward her. "You shouldn't be sorry, it's your house."

"Yeah, well, I'm not used to seeing half naked women in my living room."

Kathryn arched a brow. "No?"

"No," Jenny said, knowing her forward behavior the night before might lead one to question that. "Not that I couldn't get used to it."

Kathryn chuckled and casually planted a playful kiss on the top of her head. "Morning," she said, and then she stroked the molested wrist with concern. "How is that?"

"Morning," Jenny said, a little dazed from the close contact. "Fine."

Kathryn smiled. "Good."

Jenny stood motionless as Kathryn sashayed down the hallway to the kitchen as though she'd lived there her whole life.

Kathryn didn't know why she was so damn cheerful this morning. Her finished assignment was on again, thanks to an intruder who was out there somewhere; Smitty still wasn't answering his telephone; and she'd almost blown Jenny Ryan's head off, thanks to her hair-trigger paranoia even while sleeping.

Horrified by what she'd almost done, she couldn't sleep after Jenny returned to her room. *What if* wasn't a game she played often, but a horror reel played in her head every time she shut her eyes. Jenny lay dead at her feet, her lifeless eyes staring up at her in eternal surprise. Bile rose in her throat, and she swallowed it down with urgent lungfuls of air. *It didn't happen, it didn't happen*, she kept telling herself, but soon, what didn't happen morphed into what had happened in the past, and the helpless anguish, so familiar in its taunting, opened its mouth to swallow her whole.

She couldn't lose control now. Jenny could never see this side of her.

Her heart hammered in her chest and her mind flailed for something to keep her present. *Breathe*, she told herself as she began the regime of purposeful breaths meant to stave off her descent into panic. She turned to face the fire and focused on the red-hot void between two burning logs. The undulating glow of the void drew her in, and with every controlled exhale, the disturbing images were burned from her consciousness like celluloid set to flame.

When her heartbeat settled down and her breathing returned to normal, she closed her eyes and waited for the horrific visions to reappear. Her mind was quiet.

Her shoulders slumped in exhaustion and she stared blankly at the floor. Another panic episode. Two in one very long day. She refused to believe she was getting worse. Unusual circumstances, that's all. She'd gone so long without one, and she'd pulled herself out again before she sank too deep. Ever moving forward.

Satisfied with that, she settled back into the bedding. She found the gun under her hand and, this time, placed it between the sofa cushions under her pillow. Accessible, but not unconsciously so.

Thank goodness Jenny didn't see the gun. In the morning she would shrug it off as a bad dream. Everyone has those once in a while. Perfectly reasonable explanation.

She tucked the second pillow under her chin and hugged it. It smelled of lavender and calendula. Like Jenny. She inhaled deeply and drifted off with that pleasant thought.

She was clearheaded and decisive when she woke just before dawn. Finding out who broke into the house and why was second only to protecting Jenny. Amidst the rush of possible danger, a warm calm settled in her chest because she would have Jenny in her life for just a little longer.

The sensation was a welcome change from her usual doom and gloom. Caution usually dictated direction, but at the moment, sitting at the kitchen table watching Jenny put together a simple breakfast of coffee, toast, and jam made her feel lighter than she had in years. It gave her hope. It wasn't real, of course, but like a dangling carrot, it made her look forward instead of backward. This was the ideal: a peaceful home, in a peaceful kitchen, with a peaceful morning sun that painted golden streaks through flowing blonde hair as Jenny lingered in front of the window pouring coffee. Another touchstone moment. She allowed it to fill her heart so she'd never forget it, and she smiled as Jenny settled into the chair beside her.

Mornings after were interesting, partly because they were usually awkward and partly because—unless she had to, deemed necessary by an assignment—she didn't do them very often. She preferred not to spend the night with whatever conquest happened to strike her fancy the night before. Sex was recreation, after all—no need to endure the emotional baggage that most people brought with it.

She didn't mind this morning after, however. There was no sex to feel awkward about, only a nightmare with a logical explanation.

Jenny hadn't brought it up yet, but it was coming. She was filling the air with small talk, casting furtive glances, and gleefully offering trivial information on random subjects to talk about anything but what had happened the night before.

When she ran out of material, she casually pulled the pile of morning newspapers toward her and surreptitiously eyed the headlines for fresh subjects to talk about.

Kathryn said very little, learning long ago that silence can get you everywhere when companions buckled under the weight of their own thoughts. Jenny was buckling, and it made Kathryn smile into her coffee cup.

Jenny looked over as the sound of an amused exhale echoed out of the cup. "What's so funny?"

And that's when it came: a familiar feeling, like a premonition. Not distinctive at first, but enough to send a chill across her back. Kathryn ignored the sensation. Greedy demons, jealous of her reprieve. Instincts honed by years of paranoia needed to be retrained for this new age of optimism.

She ignored the question and dismissed the wrinkle in the fabric of her lovely morning with a *never mind* smile and a *go on* shake of her head.

Jenny didn't go on. She set her jaw and stared into her coffee as if she were a fortune teller reading tea leaves.

Kathryn was quickly reminded that her instincts had never failed her.

"Why do you have a gun in my house?" Jenny asked, and then she looked up for the answer.

Kathryn stopped mid-sip of coffee. The fair morning made an abrupt exit like the empty, hollow whoosh of a wave before it collapses in on itself.

She met Jenny's gaze, unsure of what to say. Her first impulse was to say *I don't know what you're talking about*, but, clearly, Jenny had seen the gun the night before. Hard to ignore in hindsight. She tried not to show concern. Jenny already knew she had a gun because she returned the cartridges, so that would not be a shock. Casual indifference was always the best plan. Normalcy breeds acceptance. She carefully set her coffee cup on its saucer, causing the porcelain to clink as it welcomed its mate.

"It's a habit. Sorry."

Jenny raised a brow. "I hear some people sleep with teddy bears. Imagine."

Kathryn was too focused on formulating a worthy apology to find any humor in the comment, if any was intended. She couldn't tell.

"I'm really sorry. I don't even know why I brought it in," she lied. "Strange places make me ... well ... I'm just ... I don't know what to say." She looked up regretfully, knowing her feeble attempt at an apology was woefully inadequate for the magnitude of the transgression. "I know sorry doesn't cover a gun in your face. I can't—"

"Kat," Jenny interrupted with a hand on her forearm. "Relax. It's a question, not an accusation. Apology accepted. Just be careful where you point that thing."

She said it with a smile, but Kathryn knew that was not the end of it. Right on cue, the question came again. This time the tone was gentle and sympathetic.

"Why did you feel the need to have a gun in my house?"

The familiar weight of deception settled squarely on her shoulders, and Kathryn loathed its return and how it made her react. "If it made you uncomfortable, you should have said something last night when you saw it."

"I thought things were uncomfortable enough last night," Jenny said. "You hid it immediately, so obviously you didn't want me to know you had it. I thought it best to leave it that way. The only reason I bring it up now is because ... well ... I know you said Forrester doesn't hurt you because you do what he says, but, apparently, you feel threatened enough to carry a gun wherever you go."

Kathryn didn't agree or disagree. Jenny was doing a good job of explaining it for her.

"His mental abuse is just as damaging as any physical abuse," she went on, "and I just want you to know that you have someone to talk to." She took her hand. "You can talk to me about anything, Kathryn.

I want to be your friend. That means the good and the bad. You don't have to hide anything from me."

Kathryn almost laughed out loud. Hide anything? How about hide just about everything. Her idyllic daydream was looking more ludicrous by the moment.

"Thank you, Jenny. That means a lot to me." If she ever did want to unburden her soul—and she couldn't imagine ever wanting to expose that wreckage—she imagined Jenny would be a good listener. She already had the makings of a good friend just for offering.

When the expected unburdening didn't ensue, Jenny patted her hand. "Well, I'm here if you need to talk."

Kathryn nodded and watched Jenny hide her disappointment behind the mundane task of shuffling through the stack of newspapers she'd gathered from the front lawn.

Jenny picked up one of the competitor's newspapers and snapped the front page to attention a little too brusquely. She was irritated but was trying not to show it. Every time she gave Kathryn the opportunity to open up, she politely declined. How were they supposed to get closer when every time she stepped out on a limb, Kathryn had a saw in her hand? One more question without an answer to add to all the other unanswered, or deflected, questions.

"Tough business, keeping up with everyone, hm?" Kathryn asked.

Jenny gently turned the page this time, hiding any hint of her mood. "Relentless. The world just never stops going to hell in a hand-basket. Look at this ..." She pointed at a headline. "Intruder murders family while they sleep." She folded the paper down and thumbed over her shoulder. "That's less than a mile from here." She shook her head. "As if the war wasn't enough."

"I worry about you up here by yourself."

Jenny looked up from her paper and smiled, hoping it would hide the annoyance behind her eyes. "Being protective again. I feel like a tiny bird, tucked beneath your wing."

"I'm serious, Jenny. I don't think you realize how dangerous it is out there."

As much as she liked Kathryn's concern—because it showed she cared—she didn't like that it made her feel like she was some helpless kid that just fell off a turnip truck. And she didn't like that Kathryn's paranoia was contagious.

"Are you calling me naïve?"

"I'm saying that I'm worried about you."

Jenny pushed the newspapers aside. "You know, Kat, I never thought twice about being safe in my own home before, and I don't like that you're making me question its safety now."

"Maybe you should."

Jenny paused for a moment and then fell victim to Kathryn's intense stare. "Maybe I should."

Kathryn was right. She was not above naïveté, and just because she refused to see danger, it didn't mean it didn't exist. She hated growing up. Little by little, the things that you treasure, and sometimes take for granted, are peeled away, leaving a fresh wound to be covered with a tougher skin, making the world a little less able to astound.

She picked up the next newspaper with an open mind and better humor. "You've made me insecure. What are you going to do about it?"

Kathryn crossed her arms on the table and leaned in. "Well, now that you mention it, I've been thinking about that."

Jenny set the newspaper down. This should be interesting. "Do tell."

"I know guns make you uncomfortable, but ..."

"Guns don't make me uncomfortable. A gun in the face, however ..."

"Yes, of course," Kathryn said, and then she cleared her throat. "Well, at the risk of compounding that unfortunate event, I'd like to leave you my gun for protection. And I'd like to show you how to use it before I go."

"That's very nice of you, but I think you need your gun more than I do."

"I can get another."

Jenny smiled, imagining a case full of unlicensed guns for every occasion. "It's really not necessary, Kathryn." Her smile quickly faded when she saw the fear in Kathryn's eyes. It startled her, and she would do anything to make it go away. "But if it'll make you feel better."

"It will."

"Okay, then."

All tension dissipated after the gun issue was settled. They went out to the backyard, and using a hill for a bullet backstop, they set up an impromptu shooting range with cans on fence posts.

Jenny was very familiar with guns and shooting. She was a competition pistol shooter before the war came along. But Kathryn was so earnest and serious about showing her how to protect herself, she didn't have the heart to deny her a lesson. It would also give them more time together, and she was all for that.

Kathryn cautiously held out her revolver, and Jenny loved the way she gently placed a hand on her shoulder when she said, "Here we go. Are you ready?"

"Ready."

"This is a double action revolver," Kathryn said, pointing to the firing mechanism. "That means you can fire consecutively without pulling the hammer back each time, but it takes more hand strength, and accuracy may suffer. So, for starters, we're just going to cock the hammer and shoot single action, okay?"

Jenny should have at least made an effort to look at the gun as Kathryn explained how to use it, but she couldn't leave Kathryn's face, which expressed an endearing combination of concern and kindness. That, together with what she would now call Kathryn's soft teacher voice, made her brain go to a completely inappropriate place. A place where she was teaching her forbidden things. Sexual things. There was no doubt Kathryn would make a wonderful lover. She dropped her eyes to focus on Kathryn's hands, which only reinforced the unexpected sensual rush. Her eyes shut as she felt heat rise to her face.

"Jenny? Okay?"

She quickly opened her eyes. "Yes. Okay." Anything. Yes.

Kathryn nodded and then lifted the gun toward the cans. She held the gun in place but stepped aside to let Jenny get into position to shoot. "Now, there's an internal safety that will prevent an accidental discharge in case you drop it, but nothing will save you from an errant trigger pull. In general, don't touch the trigger until you're ready to shoot, and don't aim it anywhere you wouldn't want a bullet to go. Got it?"

Jenny stepped into the space Kathryn made for her. "Got it."

Kathryn settled in close behind and passed the gun to her. "Both hands on the gun. Aim at the first can. Pull back the hammer."

What Jenny would now call Kathryn's intimate voice poured into her ear like a warm liquid, and she melted into the sensation of Kathryn's warm body wrapped around her. "Mmm, I could get used to this."

Kathryn straightened, forcing Jenny to stand on her own. "This is serious, Jenny."

She was absolutely right. Gunplay was serious, but something about Kathryn essentially purring *bad girl* in her ear sent shivers down her spine and heat to her center. Sex and danger. An exciting combination, and one she'd better get over immediately.

She shook off her lust-fueled fantasy and gave the situation the weight it deserved. "Sorry, Kat."

Kathryn nodded. She stepped aside and released the full weight of the gun to Jenny's outstretched arms like a parent releasing a child to their first bike ride without training wheels.

"Just aim at the cans. If you hit one, that's fine, if you don't, that's fine too. I just want you to get comfortable with a gun, in case you ever need to protect yourself. When you're ready, look down the barrel until you're on your target, then squeeze, don't—"

Jenny pulled the trigger.

"—jerk the trigger," Kathryn finished as the shot echoed across the languid lakefront property, startling the birds in the nearby trees.

The shot grazed the edge of the can with a pathetic *tink*.

Jenny groaned and looked at the gun in her hand as if it were all its fault.

"That's okay," Kathryn said. "Just relax and try again."

Jenny considered the futility of lining up an accurate shot down a two-inch barrel with the sun gleaming off a worn crescent site and went with eye-hand coordination and instinct instead.

Quick shot was her best discipline. No time to think. Just shoot. She exhaled, raised her arms, replanted her feet, and leaned into the target.

Four shots, pulled double action, rang out in quick succession. Four cans danced into the air, and more birds scattered as the percussion rolled into the distance.

Jenny shook out her wrist. She had only used Smith & Wesson revolvers, and the Colt had more stacking in the trigger than she expected. She walked back to Kathryn's side and handed her the gun.

Kathryn stared at her for a beat before she took it. "You can shoot."

Jenny couldn't tell if she was dumbfounded, angry, or impressed. "It's a hobby. Well, was a hobby until the war came along. Sorry. You aren't sore at me, are you?"

Kathryn emptied the spent casings from the revolver. "I feel like an idiot, but, no, I'm not angry. You're very good."

"I made it to Nationals a few years ago."

"Impressive."

She flexed her weak wrist. "I'm a bit rusty."

Kathryn remained silent as she reloaded the revolver, and Jenny definitely felt something roiling off her. She reached out and cupped her elbow. "I feel like you're sore at me. Please don't be. I'm just not good at anything except this one thing. I wanted to show off. I apologize."

When Kathryn looked at her and smiled, she found only kindness and what she swore was admiration in her eyes.

"I promise you, I'm not sore."

"Okay. Good."

Kathryn planted herself in a one-handed side-arm position and, without pulling back the hammer, took aim at the final can and sent it flying with a perfectly executed shot.

Jenny raised her brow. "Whoa! Show-off." The competitor in her wanted to set up the cans again to prove anything Kathryn could do shooting, she could do better, but she knew her wrist would never stand up to a one-handed shot in its current condition.

Kathryn chuckled as she replaced the spent casing with a new round and clicked the cylinder in place. "I assure you, I am not being modest when I say that shot was pure dumb luck. I'm a terrible shot."

"Most people overthink it."

"When it comes to guns, one rarely has time to think."

Jenny searched Kathryn's grim face. She didn't know the extent of her experience with gunplay, but that seemed like a good place to leave that conversation.

She put on a bright smile and put a hand on Kathryn's lower back. "Let's go in. It's a little chilly out here."

She got a curt nod and hoped there wouldn't be any repercussions because of her little exhibition.

When they returned to the house, Jenny showed off her considerable marksmanship trophy collection. There were a few in her old bedroom, which Kathryn kicked herself for not noticing among the field hockey and tennis statuettes, and the more prestigious awards were in her grandfather's man room.

Kathryn fondled a silver plate commemorating Jenny's second place finish at the Women's Championship, and a warm tendril of pride pulled her lips into a crooked grin. "Hm. Second place. Bad day?"

Jenny took the plate. "Ugh. Between the gusting wind and nerves, it was awful. My last shot went just left, and, of course, my competitor's shot was perfect."

Kathryn pointed at the award. "Beaten by perfection is nothing to hang your head about. You should be very proud of that."

Jenny settled the plate back on its shelf. "I am, really. Disappointed, though. I know I could have won. There was just so much pressure. I let it get to me. Unfortunately, that was my last competition. The war came, and wasting bullets on targets just wasn't the thing to do anymore. So, I live with being almost good enough."

Kathryn put her arm around her shoulder and gave it a squeeze. "Second in the top contest is hardly almost good enough. Well done. That's incredible."

Jenny took the compliment this time, and Kathryn could see pride straighten her spine. The next stop was the study, where Jenny revealed her father's gun collection, hidden behind a panel beside the bookcases.

A row of shotguns, rifles, and handguns were all neatly placed on a custom rack, and boxes of rounds of the appropriate sort were shelved beneath them.

"Good heavens. It's an arsenal."

"Silly, isn't it? How many different guns do you need to kill something?"

"Do you hunt?"

Jenny turned around as if she'd been asked to grow a second head. "No. I've never killed *anything* with a gun. Bull's-eyes are my quarry. I've never understood hunting for sport."

Kathryn smiled. "It's primal. The thrill of the hunt or something."

Jenny glared at her. "Play hide and seek instead." She waved her hand dismissively. "Don't get me started."

She opened a drawer beneath the rack and pointed at two pistols resting side by side. "These are my main competition pistols. The .45 caliber Colt 1911, the .22 Hamden High Standard, and this ..." she said, removing a small black leather case from the drawer below the gun rack and placing it reverently on her father's desk, "is my baby." She opened the case with a broad grin. "A gift from my father."

Her *baby* was a Browning 1935 model High Power semiautomatic, nestled in green velvet, with a magazine, cleaning rod, and flat screwdriver by its side.

Kathryn stiffened at the sight of it and fought the urge to clutch at the tightening in her chest. She focused on Jenny's face and her pure delight as she admired the weapon in the presentation box.

She'd seen all she wanted to see of High Powers when she was in Europe, and she certainly didn't expect to see one in Jenny's possession. It reminded her of Daniel Ryan's European connections and brought her mission back into sharp focus. Fortunately, Jenny hadn't sensed her discomfort, and she managed to relax her tense jaw and answer casually.

"Automatic girl, hm?"

"Definitely."

"Because?"

Jenny beamed and tilted the case in her direction. "Just look at her."

The pride in the piece was not contagious. "I don't trust 'em."

"She's never failed me yet."

"Just have one fail you when you need it most and you'll never trust it again."

Jenny looked at her sideways, and Kathryn could tell that she wanted to hear that story, but, mercifully, she didn't push for it and merely said, "I can see how that would make one less than enthusiastic."

It was much more than a lack of enthusiasm, and Kathryn's gut twisted from the trail of tragedy set off by an automatic's failure.

"He gave this to me when I won my first regional. I love how it fits in my hand." She took it out of the case and offered it to her.

The pristine rust blue finish glinted in the light streaming in from the bay window over Jenny's shoulder, but Kathryn didn't move to take the weapon.

"Go ahead, it's not loaded." Jenny dropped the empty magazine into her waiting hand and then racked the slide to reveal the empty chamber.

Kathryn had no intention of handling it and offered an empty platitude instead. "It's beautiful."

Jenny stared at her and searched her eyes before dropping her gaze in evident disappointment at the lack of interest. She nodded and lightly caressed the gun with her fingertips.

Kathryn tried to think of a rational excuse for not taking the pistol, but, in the end, the truth would do. "Sorry. Automatics make me uncomfortable."

Jenny nodded but didn't look up. Kathryn sensed a sudden shift in mood. More than her refusal to handle the gun. "What is it?" she asked.

Jenny pursed her lips and shook her head. She didn't answer, and Kathryn thought she might cry. After a few beats, she offered a tight-lipped smile, but there was more pain than pleasure in it.

"The last time I held this gun in my hand, it was to take my life."

Kathryn's heart lurched, and she barely suppressed a gasp. She had just met Jenny, but imagining a world without her struck her like a fist to her chest. She resisted the urge to reach out to her. She wanted Jenny in her arms, not only to comfort her, but to comfort herself until the helpless feeling subsided.

"It was a few months after my father's death. I was drinking then. A lot. I was overwhelmed by grief and guilt and I just ... I couldn't take it anymore."

Kathryn let the intimate confession float between them for a beat. She admired Jenny's openness and honesty. She never talked about her own dark past, but Jenny made it seem like it would be okay. "We all have our moments."

Jenny lifted her eyes, and in them Kathryn saw surprise and then a silent acknowledgement that her struggle was hardly unique. She didn't ask any questions, which Kathryn found out of character. Or maybe she didn't know her character at all.

"Why didn't you go through with it?"

Jenny raised her brow and exhaled. "The telephone rang on my father's desk just as I raised the gun to myself. It was his private line; I don't even know why I answered it. There was no one on the line. In my drunken stupor, I took it as a sign from the great beyond. My father saying *Don't do it*." She chuckled. "I unloaded the gun, put it away, closed the study door, stopped drinking to excess, and haven't been back in here until tonight."

She glanced around the room and smiled. "One less fight to have with my aunt."

"Fight?"

"She comes over once a week to clean. I really think she's just checking up on me. We recently had a blowup about her coming in here to clean, and that led to an argument about my dad's death, and my guilt, and I told her, in no uncertain terms, I didn't want to talk about it anymore, so now she leaves this door ajar as a not-so-subtle suggestion that I make my peace with this room and what it represents."

Kathryn couldn't speak for a moment. Her aunt. Her aunt left the door open. There was no mystery intruder. That meant there was no reason to delay her departure. Jenny didn't need her protection. Her assignment was truly over, and these would be the last moments she would spend with Jenny Ryan. It caused a dull ache in her chest and a need to know that she would be all right.

"Have you? Made your peace?"

Jenny smiled. "I'm closer today than I was yesterday, and I have you to thank for it." She reached out and took her hand.

Kathryn let her. The urge to pull away was nowhere to be found. Jenny's touch eased the dull ache but only until she remembered it would be their last.

Jenny squeezed her hand. "How about you?"

"Hm?"

"You said we all have our moments. Why didn't you go through with it?"

She wanted to say *Because I had yet to meet you*. That's how she felt. But she didn't believe in destiny, only surviving moment to moment.

"Afraid, I guess."

"Well, I'm glad you lost your nerve."

Kathryn offered a closed-mouth smile, but it was perfunctory. Surviving her *moment* destroyed her life.

Jenny took her hand back and held it palm up. "Gimme."

"What?"

"Your gun. I'll clean it before you go."

"No. That's all right."

"Nonsense," Jenny said. "It's my fault you had to fire it." She wiggled her fingers. "Gimme."

Kathryn looked at her watch. Smitty would be pulling his hair out with worry, wherever he was, and she had to get out of there before the inexplicable pull of Jenny Ryan caused a lapse in good judgment.

"I've got to go, Jenny. Don't worry about it. I really don't have the ti—"

"Look," Jenny interrupted, "how about I keep the gun and clean it, you have lunch with me, and I'll return it to you then?"

Kathryn hesitated. She'd not yet put up the wall that would allow her to walk away. One more meeting couldn't hurt.

"Can you live without your gun until lunchtime?" Jenny teased. "I have a revolver in the case if you can't."

"It's not that. I have a luncheon engagement. What say we get together for an early dinner? Meet you at the paper at four thirty?"

"It's a date. Gimme."

Kathryn defied a rule she lived by—never relinquish your weapon—and handed over her gun. It was just Jenny, after all; she posed no threat.

Jenny gathered up the gun and the cleaning kit and headed toward the living room. "Are you sure I can't get you anything? Coffee to go?"

Kathryn followed and declined. Time to get back to real life and leave this pleasant distraction behind. Jenny led her into the foyer and helped her into her coat. She had just buttoned the last button when the shrill sound of the telephone bell echoed off the hardwood floors.

"Stay," Jenny said with her hands raised like a dog trainer and then dashed for the telephone just inside the living room.

Kathryn chuckled. "Woof."

Jenny had a proper phone voice, she noticed, the hello carrying the appropriate respect, as if the president himself were the caller. It dissolved quickly as she heard Bernie's name exalted, then a rude "hang on" that you could only give your best friend.

Evidently, the best friend was ignoring her. Kathryn peeked into the living room and saw Jenny doing the anxiety shuffle while she tried to get Bernie to let her call him back.

"Ber ... no ... Bernie ... just ... no, listen ..." Jenny covered the telephone receiver with her hand. "I'm sorry," she whispered, "he's very excited about something."

Kathryn made her way to her side. "Shouldn't he have a hangover or something?"

Jenny muffled Bernie's rambling voice against her shoulder and waggled her eyebrows. "Maybe he got lucky."

Kathryn smiled and put her hand on Jenny's arm. "Take your call. I've got to go."

"Wuh ..."

Wait never came out, as Kathryn cut it off with a kiss to Jenny's forehead and a playful tug on her sleeve. "See you later," she said and made her exit.

Jenny's green eyes twinkled with innocent high schoolish I-just-got-me-a-date-to-the-prom adoration, which Kathryn found endearing. She smiled as she closed the front door, but the smile quickly disappeared.

The phone call was a godsend. She didn't want to say goodbye in private. She didn't want to take Jenny in her arms for the last time with nothing to stop her from going further. Being with Jenny made her doubt her resolve. It was unsettling, and she was running away.

Their dinner will be different. Easier. Spending the afternoon with Forrester will bring her back to her senses. Back to reality. Walls will be up, the persona she'd adopted for Jenny's assignment will be gone, and letting her go will be satisfying, like any successful assignment.

Lies will be unnecessary. A few words about Forrester's possessive nature, a lament about timing and circumstances, and *Oh, if only things were different*. Jenny would understand. It would sting at first, and she might protest, but in the end, she would understand. Jenny was reasonable in that way.

CHAPTER TWENTY-SIX

*J*enny parted the drapes of the bay window to watch Kathryn walk down the sidewalk, get into her car, and quickly drive away. Only then did she recognize Bernie's voice asking if she was listening to him.

"Lips, Bernie," she said. "I've been kissed on the head three times by the sexiest woman on the planet, and I have *yet* to lay my lips on her."

"What?"

The promise of a sordid tale suddenly interested Bernie more than whatever he had been going on about, and, as expected, he begged for details. Jenny told him of her night and morning, including the gun and the lesson, but left out the Forrester bit, and thus the reason Kathryn had a gun to begin with.

Bernie was silent on the other end of the line, his enthusiasm dwindling as soon as the gun was mentioned. Bernie was never silent. It gave Jenny the feeling something was about to sneak up on her while the person in front of her stared horrified over her shoulder. She almost had the urge to turn around. "What, Bernie?"

"Like I was saying before," he said carefully. "A guy was killed outside O'Malley's last night."

"What?"

"Shot in the head, sitting in his car, right out front."

Jenny processed the information, and Bernie's tone, and her heart lurched as she slowly turned and looked at the gun resting innocently on the coffee table. She remembered Kathryn's crazed look as she wielded the weapon in the early morning hours. The ensuing thought was too horrific, unthinkable. She tried to shake it off.

"Are you thinking what I'm thinking?" he asked hesitantly.

Her silence said yes, but she wasn't ready to admit it. "Don't be ridiculous. She was with us the whole time."

"Not the *whole* time."

Kathryn arrived late, and Jenny remembered watching her shapely figure as she made her way to the front of the bar during their evening, ostensibly to make a phone call.

"She wasn't gone that long."

"How long does it take to pop a guy, especially for a woman like that? The poor SOB would never suspect. *Hi handsome ...*" He pretended to be Kathryn. "*Blink, blink, blink, smile.* Boom, you're dead."

Jenny's heart was racing. He was making sense. "I don't want to hear this, Bernie."

"And the kicker," Bernie went on, "rumor has it the guy used to be a Forrester lackey. Word is he flipped and was working for the feds to nail the filthy pig."

He paused, and the information sank in.

"I think your new *friend* is doing Forrester's dirty work. That's why she came to the bar last night. What better alibi than being seen in public at the time of the murder, and *I* invited her."

Jenny found herself sitting on the floor, with no memory of collapsing there. She was too stunned to speak. It all fit.

"Jenny? Are you okay?" He waited for a response that didn't come. "Jenny?"

She felt like she'd been kicked in the head and punched in the gut for good measure. It couldn't be true. Kathryn wasn't a murderer. She felt boneless, drained of life.

"I've got to go, Bernie," she whispered faintly into the receiver resting limply in her hand.

"Are you okay? I'm sorry, Bug. Do you want me to come over?"

"No. I'm fine. I'll see you at the office."

"Call me if you need me." He paused. "Promise?"

"Cross my heart." She hung up the phone without saying goodbye and stared at the gun pointing in her direction.

Murder at the end of that barrel. She'd been around guns her whole life. She knew guns killed—she wasn't naïve about that—but for the first time, she was afraid of one, afraid to even look at it, picturing Kathryn's face, holding it, wearing a mask of pure seductive malevolence as she triumphantly pulled the trigger on the poor, unsuspecting dope in the car.

She'd seen a hint of that darkness. She shivered, remembering the hand sliding up her leg and the wicked pleasure in Kathryn's eyes as she teased her.

"God." She buried her face in her hands. *"You can tell me anything, Kathryn,"* she mocked herself out loud. "I am so fucking gullible."

To her knowledge, she'd never had a brush with such evil. Suddenly, sleeping with a gun didn't seem like such a bad idea.

She tucked her knees under her chin and wrapped her arms tightly around her legs. Her fertile imagination was getting way ahead of the circumstantial facts, and she realized she was making herself sick.

She quoted one of her father's favorite admonitions when she got worked up. "Settle down, Jenny. Think." She lifted her eyes to the gun. "She wouldn't do it," she whispered to the empty room. "She couldn't do it."

She wanted to believe that, but everything fit so perfectly. But why? Why would she do it?

She had a thought and her eyes grew wide. Maybe Forrester forced her to do it. Threatened her—kill, or else. She wasn't a murderer, not in cold blood, not without a sick bastard like Marcus Forrester giving her no other choice.

The rationalization started, as it always does, when the truth is too painful to bear. Kathryn was a victim in her mind now, not a perpetrator. She was feeling less sick, but, still, there was the gun, heavy and looming. It filled her vision, becoming the only thing in the room at that moment. She couldn't take her eyes off it. She wanted to, but she just couldn't.

Kathryn had tried to warn her. "Not really dating material, and there's a lot not to like," she muttered aloud, as if that explained everything. "She was trying to protect me. She didn't want me to get involved." She cares that much. Jenny crawled the few feet to the coffee table and stared at the gun, trying to decide what to do.

Her first instinct was to clean it. Clean it of any incriminating evidence. But then she realized they could trace the bullet, each barrel leaving a distinctive mark on the projectile. Throw it in the lake was the next thought. Get rid of it. No one would ever look for it there. She would save Kathryn, cover up her crime, and they would be linked forever by the secret.

She unfolded herself from the floor and picked up the gun. She walked with purpose to the back door and quickly made her way to the dock on the lake. Once the gun was gone, this would all be over. She drew her arm back to throw the evidence as far as she could. What kind of *them* would there be? How would she feel the next time she saw Kathryn, knowing what she'd done? How crazy was it that now, here she was, making herself an accessory to the crime, trying to protect someone she hardly knew? She let her arm fall to her side and put her hand on her forehead. "What am I doing?"

She'd seen it a hundred times in darkened movie houses. She was in her own B movie, and she was making the same mistake as every character in every clichéd foot of celluloid she'd ever seen. They always think they can get away with it. *They'll never find out* had to be the most overestimated certainty there was. Hadn't she learned anything? Tell the truth, and eventually it will be revealed as such. But what was the truth? She looked at the gun in her hand. Did Kathryn do it? Was this a murder weapon? She knew how to find out. Rico.

Rico was their contact at the police station and a good friend of

Bernie's. She was sure that this was where he had gotten his information about the killing. They affectionately called him the Mole, because if asked, he was not beyond doing small, slightly unethical, favors for them, in an effort to help get a jump on the latest news.

She would turn the gun over to him and ask him to get it tested on the sly. If it came back clean, no one's the wiser, and if it turned out to be the murder weapon, well, she'd be the best damn character witness any defendant could have. She would testify to Forrester's criminal manipulation and mental abuse of Kathryn and help prove he was behind the murder.

The path to Forrester's destruction just opened up again.

Not surprisingly, Smitty's car was parked down the street from her apartment when Kathryn arrived home. She glanced in the car window as she passed but knew the car would be empty. He wasn't on the curb outside her building, but she knew he had been, and by the pile of cigarette stubs, for quite a while.

Her apartment was quiet when she entered, but she knew where she'd find him. He was lying on the end of her bed, coat still on, hat resting on his chest, while his legs dangled over the edge of the bed. His slow, steady breathing told her he was deep in sleep.

She enjoyed the peaceful moment while it lasted, and then she gently nudged his shoe. "Hey, you."

He awoke with a start and immediately sat up and looked at his watch.

"Damn, Kat. Where the hell have you been?"

"Just doing my job. Where the hell have you been, Goldilocks?"

I've been worried sick about you, she said in her head as he said it aloud. She laughed.

"I'm serious, Kat. Worried sick."

She knew he wasn't exaggerating, but she did make an effort. "I called last night and this morning. You weren't home."

"I went out for smokes last night, and I've been here since dawn. Where the hell were you?"

She removed her coat and then sat next to him, ready to smooth his ruffled feathers. "Last night we went to O'Malley's. We had beers, some pleasant conversation, and then I escorted my assignment to her home, where I've been ever since."

Worry quickly turned to irritation, and he rose to his feet. Kathryn braced for what had gnawed at him all night. He stared at her a moment and then threw his hands in the air. "I knew you were getting too close to that girl."

"What are you, a mind reader now?"

"Cut it out! You know this is serious."

She let him pace and mutter to himself. He was frustrated, and she couldn't blame him for an accusation that, being honest with herself, had some truth in it. She should have told him where she was when she spoke with him the night before. It was irrational not to, but at that moment, she wished he'd realize that the world wouldn't fall apart if she was out of his sight for more than an hour. She didn't know why she thought that. She knew very well the world could fall apart in a heartbeat.

It was time to admit to herself that it was because of Jenny. She wanted Jenny alone for just one night. She didn't want to sense Smitty's disapproving glare as he waited down the street in his car, counting the minutes until she walked out of Jenny's house. When she was with her, the past lost its power. She looked forward instead of back, and something akin to hope appeared on the horizon. It was fleeting, because she was a prisoner of the past, but for the short time they shared, she was tempted to believe a future was a possibility and hope would lead the way.

"I'm sorry I worried you, but you can relax. Nothing happened with the tail, and nothing happened between us."

"Last night, but what about the next time, and the next! You're thawing out, and this girl's the heater. Can't you see that?"

She paused a beat while she absorbed his concern. "You would have given anything to see me thaw out not too long ago."

"Not with an assignment."

She patted the bed. "Sit down, Smitty."

He exhaled and reluctantly complied.

Kathryn reached for her coat, pulled a small piece of paper from her pocket, and offered it to him. "She's not an assignment any longer."

Smitty took the paper from her fingers and read it. "Dr. Martin Stevens." He paused and held it up questioningly.

"That man was the recipient of Daniel Ryan's office and records. And that is the extent of Jenny Ryan's knowledge of her father's work. As a bonus, she gave me some bound books of his early papers, which, I assume, will be of some use to the science crowd. The assignment is over."

He eyed her warily. "And you're not going to see her again."

It was a statement, not a question, and she ignored the pang of regret it caused in her chest.

"She's returning something to me at dinner tonight, and then I'm out."

"Will she know that?"

"She will agree to it wholeheartedly."

He raised his brow. "Oh, to be a fly on the wall."

Kathryn grinned, but it was just for show. Selfishly, she didn't want to be out of Jenny's life. She wanted to stay in the warm glow of hope's promise for as long as she could.

Smitty was right. She was thawing out. It was the worst thing that could happen to her. She had a war to return to. Jenny had a beautiful life to live.

Smitty shook his head. "Why do you let me jump to conclusions?"

"I'm just waiting for you to stop jumping to conclusions."

He stared at the paper in his hand. "Sorry."

She put her arm through his. She knew he hated confrontation, especially with her. This time the confrontation was her fault, and she'd own up to it.

"I'm really sorry about last night."

He covered her hand with his. "I can't protect you if I can't find you, Kat."

She nodded and lay back on the bed, pulling him down with her.

He had always protected her. Even as children. She stared at the ceiling, reliving simpler days that she hadn't thought about in years.

"Remember stargazing in your dad's backyard?"

Smitty glanced her way and then back to the ceiling with a smile on his face. "Some of the best days of my life."

They were healing days for her and dreaming days for Smitty. She wanted to run as far away from home as she could, and Smitty wanted to be a baseball star and marry the girl beside him. She grinned, remembering his teenage declaration of love and subsequent proposal.

He turned his head in her direction again. "That good, huh?"

She smiled. "It had its moments."

"No, the girl."

"What?"

"You're waxing poetic about your childhood. That girl must be good."

"She's not a girl, Smitty, she's a woman, and I told you, I didn't sleep with her."

He looked at her doubtfully.

"Can't I just be content for a minute?"

"Sure."

She patted his hand. "Don't worry; I'm sure it won't last long."

"What happened to you last night?"

She paused and debated how much to tell him. Keeping secrets was her stock and trade, but not from him. Not when he could see right through her. "I saw a glimpse of the future, and in it I was happy. It was brief, and it didn't stay long, but it was there, which means I'm still capable of it, believe it or not."

He stared at her, and she knew he was considering her past and the self-destructive path she'd been on.

"I can't tell you how glad I am to hear that, Kathryn. I mean it."

She rolled to her side and straightened the lapel on his coat. "I know you do." The poor guy, sticking with her through thick and thin, and more often than not, he was her punching bag, as he fought for a normal life that she no longer recognized or cared for. "I know loving me is a thankless job sometimes, and for that I'm sorry."

"Honey, after what you've been through, I'm just glad you can string two sentences together."

She smiled and rolled onto her back again. "Sometimes."

She stared up at the ceiling, enjoying the calm between them and the momentary pause of their world.

CHAPTER TWENTY-SEVEN

"*L*ook, Rico," Jenny said, as they met at the end of a quiet hallway in the police station. "You don't need to know who it belongs to. Can't you just run it and let me know what you find?"

"Listen, Jenny. You want to drop off an anonymous tip? Fine. I can keep your name out of it. But these things have registration numbers, you know. Come on. Don't make me play Dick Tracy. Just tell me who you got it from and I can tell you if it's even their gun."

Jenny balked, not wanting to involve Kathryn if she didn't have to. "It's just a friend that may be in trouble. I need to know, and I'd rather not provide a name."

Rico opened the large mustard colored envelope in his hand and then suddenly looked up. "Not that singer?"

"What?" Jenny said a little too quickly.

"The singer down at The Grotto?"

"How do you know about her?"

"Are you kidding? Forrester's moll? Bernie." He didn't have to say any more than his name for Jenny to know that Bernie had opened his big mouth. "She was booked in here a few months ago," Rico went on, oblivious to the breach of confidence, "caught in a gambling raid.

Forrester and his group slipped through the cracks, as usual, but he left her here overnight, cooling her heels. Can you believe that? He had his fancy lawyer spring her in the morning, pretended he was shocked—shocked to find her in an unlawful gambling establishment. What a swell guy." He shook his head as he numbered the envelope and stuck the gun inside. "I'll never understand why lookers like her fall for shady characters like Forrester."

"Maybe they don't have a choice."

"Yeah, well, you don't forget a dame like that. Surly broad. But when they look like that, who cares, eh?" He nudged her arm and winked. Now Jenny remembered why she let Bernie deal with Rico.

"Four thirty, Rico," she said. She pointed a warning finger at him as she turned to leave. "It's imperative that I have that back by four thirty."

"Sure thing, doll."

"Thanks. I owe you one."

"I might just hold you to that."

As Jenny walked down the hallway, she knew Rico was watching her ass. "Bernie comes next time," she said to herself. "That is, if I don't kill him first. Blabbermouth."

Jenny found the office in upheaval when she arrived. An editor was out with the flu, which meant their workload fell to her; the pressroom moved up her column deadline; and her uncle chewed her out for being late. The hectic workday was a blessing. It took her mind off wondering whether Kathryn was a murderer, and it took her mind off becoming a murderer herself when she got a hold of Bernie.

She looked at her watch as she rushed to the production department to turn in her assignment. One thirty. Surely Rico would know something by now.

"Jenny!" Bernie yelled from behind as he bounded down the hallway.

"Can't stop for lunch now, hon." She kept walking, waving her papers. "My day has been insane."

"Jenny." He grabbed her arm and pulled her off to the side.

"Honestly, Bernie ..." She paused, remembering she was mad at him. "Say, listen." She put her hands on her hips. "What's with the gossip report to Rico? I don't—"

"Where is it?" he frantically interrupted.

"Where's what?"

He looked conspiratorially both ways down the hallway, and Jenny leaned in, giving his tone the proper respect.

"The gun," he whispered. "Where is it?"

"I gave it to Rico."

"Oh, nuts."

She leaned back. "What do you mean, oh nuts?"

He put his hands to his head. "Nuts, nuts, nuts."

"Bernie. What?"

"I think you've been set up."

"What?"

"The guy who was killed ..."

"Yeah," she drew out hesitantly.

"Vincent LaPaglia."

Instant recognition widened her eyes, as horror, then confusion, took over. Scenes from her past played in her head as, piece by piece, the trail of events leading to the man's murder pointed squarely at her. Last night was a year to the day of her father's death. Vincent LaPaglia was the small-time criminal behind the wheel of the car that took his life.

The police report said that a blown tire caused Vincent LaPaglia to lose control of his car. The vehicle careened off the road, crossed the sidewalk, and plowed directly into the telephone booth where Daniel Ryan was killed. No charges were brought. It was deemed an accident. Jenny was outraged. Someone had to pay! Without another scapegoat, her father's death fell on her shoulders for keeping him on the line with her juvenile argument. She couldn't bear that weight. She marched into the police station and argued loudly with anyone who would listen that LaPaglia was no choir boy; he had a record as long as her arm and was far from innocent. He must have been speeding, or drunk, or distracted. There must be a witness—it's New York City, for crying out loud!

Her protests fell on deaf ears, so she moved on to plan B. She contacted engineers and physicists at the university, professors and students, and tried to get them to mathematically recreate the scene to prove the driver was speeding, or that the angle was wrong for an accident—anything! It couldn't be her fault. It couldn't.

In the end, she had to accept responsibility, and she buckled under the weight of it. The anonymous phone call blaming Forrester gave her a reprieve from her guilt, but only briefly. The lack of evidence connecting Forrester to her father revealed the futility of her quest, and the danger she'd put Kathryn in pushed her to finally accept the truth. It was an accident. Her guilt was self-inflicted, a product of the very human need to find answers. Especially answers that exonerate.

It was an accident. It was an accident right up until Bernie said the name Vincent LaPaglia. The guilt came rushing back, and with it the hope of a connection to Marcus Forrester. It couldn't be a coincidence. There must be something there. She'd caused Forrester a headache, and now he was going to get rid of her by pinning LaPaglia's murder on her. No one, especially the police, would doubt her capable after the public show she put on last year. She could see the scandalous headlines now: Doctor's Daughter Exacts Revenge.

Her knees went weak, and Bernie grasped her arms to steady her.

"Jenny, you didn't do anything. They can't possibly connect you."

"I was there last night, Bernie. The whole bar saw us. You stood on the table and made them sing "Happy Birthday" to me, remember?"

"So what? You never left the bar."

"I was in the bathroom for a while. The window leads right out to the street, and I was the last one out of the bar ... my fingerprints are all over that gun. They're probably at my house right now, digging bullets out of my backyard ... powder burns on my coat sleeve ... God." She slumped against the wall.

"It's all circumstantial. That singer was with you too ... the same bar, bathroom, fingerprints, powder burns."

"Yeah, but she's had time to cover her tracks." Jenny anxiously tried to recall the details of the morning. "You know, she wouldn't touch my gun? She concocted some lame story, but now I see she didn't want to leave fingerprints."

She was on the verge of crying. She'd stumbled into the middle of a murder, and she was the prime suspect. So typical. She'd laugh if it weren't so serious.

"How could I have been so stupid? Like Kathryn Hammond is going to want *me*?"

"Cut it out," Bernie said. "Call Rico. Get that gun back."

Rico wasn't at his desk when she called, and Jenny was growing frantic. She imagined the police on the way over to arrest her; they were just getting all of the paperwork in order first. She tried to concentrate on work but wasn't very successful. She was thankful that she had gotten most of it done before Bernie made her a paranoid suspect. It was three thirty by the time she finally made her way back to her desk, and she couldn't imagine what she'd say when Kathryn walked in the door in an hour.

She still tried to hang onto the hope that she actually was going to walk into the office, everything would be fine, Rico would give her good news, Bernie's crazy, and she was crazy for listening to him. They'd have a good laugh over it, and he would owe her dinner times infinity for taking years off her life and giving her an ulcer. The thought of it made her smile briefly, but the longer Rico didn't call, the more unlikely the happy scenario seemed. Her mind was working overtime.

Every minute that ticked by proved Kathryn Hammond had set her up, with Forrester pulling the strings. She couldn't get the morning's events out of her head. Kathryn pretended she didn't want to leave the gun, that she didn't want it cleaned. Jenny played into her hands by insisting, and then her fingerprints would be gone and

Jenny's would be all over it. Jenny was starting to feel sick again. Played like a damn fiddle.

She slumped into the chair at her desk and closed her eyes as paranoia swept over her. She listened to the last sounds of freedom: the collective clatter of busy typewriters, indistinct phone calls, and shuffling paper drifting through the office.

"Message for you, hon," the gum-snapping girl from the message board said, dropping a note on her desk. "Urgent."

It was from Rico, in the code they had decided on: *Laundry's clean and will be delivered before the close of your business day.*

Jenny threw her head back and almost laughed out loud.

"Yes!" she said to the ceiling.

The gun was clean. Kathryn Hammond was clean. She had been on the verge of a nervous breakdown all day for nothing. Bernie would be off the hook for the dinners because she was definitely going to kill him. He had started the whole rollercoaster ride with his phone call in the morning. She didn't think anyone had a more vivid imagination than she did, but he outdid her today.

She put her head down on the desk and let the ridiculous day drain away.

"You okay, kiddo?" her uncle asked as he passed on his way to his office.

She lifted her head. "Heck of a day, Uncle Paul. Heck of a day."

"Makes you feel alive, doesn't it?"

"I feel alive, all right."

"Are you almost through?"

"Yeah, I've got another half hour, then I'm meeting someone here at four thirty."

"Oh? That handsome soldier?"

"Not exactly. Just a friend."

Forrester's business partners talked carefully in coded words like *product* and *expiration dates*. Kathryn feigned moderate disinterest while she nursed a cigarette and took mental notes of export dates and hit lists, the meaning of the aforementioned code words. It amused her to no end that Forrester thought her oblivious to his illegal activities. At first, she was surprised that he invited her to these business meetings at all and wondered what his partners thought of it, having to speak in tongues, as it were, to keep their dirty dealings under wraps. But it was soon apparent that she was a useful tool in his negotiations, and she was glad, because some of the most valuable information had come from such occasions. She was never invited to legitimate business meetings—he needed respectability there—and flaunting his mistress just wouldn't do, but his shady dealings had their own brand of respectability, and Kathryn definitely served a purpose.

"Cigarette me, will you, sweetheart?" Forrester said, interrupting the one potential partner who was not playing well with others today. This was her cue, the reason for her attendance. She afforded the wealthy industrialist the extra push some partners required and allowed him to gleefully exact his machismo. What I want is what I get, was his message—I will tame you as I have tamed this exotic creature, and you will succumb to me and my wishes as easily and completely as she. All of this he conveyed in a hooded sneer to the man disagreeing with him.

Kathryn would have rolled her eyes had she been able to get away with it. With these men, it was nothing more than a glorified pissing contest, not far removed from chest thumping cavemen with clubs and a woman over each shoulder.

She began her show. Her moves were deliberate, seductive, a film played at half speed. She removed a cigarette from her slim silver case. She smiled, ever so slightly, eyeing Forrester through the amused corners of her eyes as she tapped the cigarette on the case. His smirk acknowledged her routine, one he loved, as he watched it through the eyes of the men around him. It started innocently enough; she brought the cigarette to her waiting lips, while she took her time retrieving the lighter on the table. The whole time, she stared directly at the disagreeable man across from her. He was distracted by her gaze, as was the intention. There was no mistaking her message as she lit the cigarette, took a drag, and let the smoke drift slowly from her lips.

The man saw lust in her half-lidded eyes, and he nervously looked to Forrester before drifting back to the magnetic blue eyes behind the eventual exhale. Forrester just smiled, bringing the man's focus back to him. He loved that part: the indecision in the man's eyes, the hope, then the fear, then Forrester's smile that told him not a chance in hell, and Kathryn's confirmation as she smirked and removed the lipstick-stained cigarette, bringing it obediently to Forrester's lips.

As he took a drag, she caressed his face with her retreating hand. The men around the table shifted uncomfortably.

The disagreeable man lost his train of thought. All in all, a successful cigarette, according to Forrester's standards. The game went on as the sputtering conversation got back on track, and Kathryn leaned back in her chair, out of Forrester's peripheral vision. She continued to look the man slowly up and down with unmistakable desire. He was distracted again. He recognized Forrester's game but wondered if Kathryn had her own agenda. She'd seen it time and time again: just the slightest glimmer of hope, the off chance that she would be interested, that she'd, perhaps, put in a good word with Forrester, would keep men like these coming back, and in line. It occurred to her that hope must be in short supply, because it made people do the craziest things.

Kathryn once wondered what Forrester would do if someone stepped outside the game and actually made a move on her. It didn't take long to find out the answer. He'd kill them. It made the game safe for her, and Forrester got the pleasure of seeing his associates burn with frustration and envy.

She watched the beads of sweat dot her target's brow, as he finally had to ignore her in order to carry on a coherent conversation with his future partner. Kathryn looked away at last and smiled under her slightly bowed head, her job done. She ignored the glare of Forrester's lawyer, Lloyd Robeson, a man she knew despised her. She always felt it was because he secretly held a torch for his boss, and he knew she knew. Forrester's unusual sexual proclivities often made her wonder if he'd acted on the attraction at one time, something that would ruin him if exposed.

The mutual loathing between Kathryn and the lawyer was interrupted by two men entering the restaurant, and from their disheveled appearance, they were not customers. Anyone with a pair of eyes could tell they were police detectives, the way they looked around, the serious expressions, and, finally, the telltale hands on hips, seeking respect as they parted their overcoats to reveal badges clipped to their waistbands.

Kathryn exhaled. This would effectively end her lunch. Police made Forrester furious, never more so than when he was in the middle of a delicate negotiation. Bad for business, cops sniffing around with one more accusation they would never make stick. They did it on purpose, of course, and as part of Forrester's misguided sense of propriety, he would send her away at the first sight of the law. It was automatic now; Kathryn no longer waited for the customary, "Would you excuse us, darling?"

The detectives weaved their way to the table. Kathryn made her excuses and stood to go to the ladies' room.

"Ugh. Where is it?" Jenny hissed under her breath as she sat at her desk and looked at her watch. Rico had promised the gun would be returned before four thirty. It was four twenty-five and nothing yet. She wracked her brain for an excuse as to why she didn't have the weapon to return. *I forgot it*, seemed daft, since it was ostensibly the reason for the meeting.

She closed her eyes and tried to concentrate. The din of the room fell away, and she was amazed at her ability to focus until she realized it wasn't the power of her concentration; the room really had gone significantly quieter. She opened her eyes and caught sight of her uncle in his office as he rose from his chair and removed his reading glasses. He wasn't pleased.

Jenny turned to follow his gaze and found her four thirty appointment slinking down the aisle.

She smiled, wondering where Kathryn learned to walk like that, each step precisely in front of the last, forming a straight line, broken only by the sway of her gorgeous hips. Kathryn was commanding all attention in the office, with her stylish tailored powder blue suit and matching pillbox hat, perched at the perfect forward angle on her head, with the netting pulled mysteriously over her face. A runway model had nothing on her.

Jenny had an ear-to-ear grin, and she didn't care who saw it. As Kathryn approached, she swore she was sneering at her uncle, who had now made his way to his office window, hands on hips.

"Boy, are you a sight for sore eyes," Jenny said. "You wouldn't believe the day I've had."

"You wouldn't believe the day *I've* had," Kathryn countered, as she pulled a large mustard colored envelope from under her arm and threw it on the wooden desk with a resounding thud. She pointed at it. "Do you know what that is?"

Jenny had an idea, but she was afraid to look. Her eyes were involuntarily stuck on Kathryn's face, which she could now make out through the netting of her hat. She was angry. Very angry. Her angular face was even more defined, which she didn't think was possible. Her chin was down and her glare burned from under the shadow of her brow. Her lips were tight and her nostrils slightly flared—a bull seeing red.

"Do you know what that is?" Kathryn repeated impatiently.

Jenny swallowed and slowly turned her eyes to the package on her desk. She recognized the writing as Rico's, and her eyes were drawn to the huge red stamp in the middle of the envelope.

"Evidence?" she said, not trying to be a smart ass, but at a total loss to explain what happened without it sounding absurd.

"Open it."

Jenny reached for it but knew what she would find there, so she withdrew her hand. "I know what it is."

"Would you care to tell me how and why it wound up at the police station?"

The office around them had begun to shift uncomfortably back to their own business, as they realized the paper's favorite daughter had managed to get herself into trouble—again. Jenny bit her lip and tried to look anywhere but Kathryn's direction. She glanced up at her uncle, who was very interested in the whole scene.

"Well?" Kathryn said, almost a whisper. Jenny would have rather she yelled at her. Controlled anger always scared her, because you never knew when it would boil over.

"Let's take this elsewhere," Jenny said, slowly rising from her chair and sliding the envelope with her.

"Fine," Kathryn said, and then she followed her down the aisle to a vacant outer office.

They entered the office, and Jenny jumped as Kathryn slammed the door shut behind her.

Jenny raised her hand. "Before you say anything ..."

Kathryn lifted the netting from her face, placing her full anger on display. Jenny was unprepared for the fury in her stare. Eyes remembered as a soothing blue were now ice grey. This was one facet of Kathryn's personality she hoped never to see again. On further reflection, from the looks of the situation, she may never see any facet of Kathryn's personality again.

"Before *you* say anything," Kathryn countered.

"I'm sorry," Jenny quickly interjected, realizing this may be a hit-and-run scalding, with no opportunity to say anything.

"You're sorry?"

"Yes."

"Do you know where I've been all afternoon?"

"Well, I have a pretty good idea." Jenny didn't mean to make light of the situation, but if she didn't laugh, she might just cry.

"I'm glad you're so damned amused, Jenny, because Marcus Forrester sure wasn't amused when I was led away from his table by the police, in a crowded restaurant, in front of his associates, during a delicate business transaction."

Jenny hadn't thought of Forrester. She wanted to speak, but the realization that she'd put Kathryn in such a compromising position tied her stomach in knots and stole her breath.

Kathryn's voice was in full shout. "How do you think it makes Forrester look to have his mistress arrested? Do you think he's ever going to trust me again? Do you think the people he does business with are ever going to trust *him*?"

Jenny wanted to say she didn't give a hang what Forrester's dirty associates thought of him. If anything, she did Kathryn a favor. "If he no longer trusts you, then maybe he'll dump you and leave you alone."

"Oh, yes," Kathryn said. "He'll dump me all right ... right into the East River, replete with a new pair of concrete shoes! And if I'm lucky, he'll slit my throat first so that he doesn't have to listen to me screaming as I go under!"

Jenny's eyes widened, visualizing the horrific scene.

Kathryn's icy wrath glared at her down an accusing finger. "You have *no* idea what you've done!" She snatched the evidence envelope from Jenny's paralyzed hand and offered one more glare before leaving. "No idea."

"Kathryn, please. I'm sorry. What can I do?"

Kathryn didn't turn around as she opened the door with a forceful jerk. "Just stay the hell away from me."

Jenny stared at the back of the slammed door, afraid to breathe. Necessity forced an exhale, and she raised a hand to her forehead, feeling lightheaded. "What have I done?"

CHAPTER TWENTY-EIGHT

*T*hat was one way to end an assignment, Kathryn thought, as she stormed down the newspaper's hallway toward the exit. Her daydream about a relationship with Jenny was a cruel joke by the time she left the police station with the knowledge that Jenny was the one who had turned her in. She was blindsided in the restaurant when the police called her out, the shocked look on her face matched only by that of Forrester's and his associates.

"Are you Kathryn Hammond?" the tall, skinny detective had asked as Kathryn rose to leave the table.

"Who wants to know?" Forrester demanded, as a matter of course.

The police showed their badges, and with one glance of approval from Forrester, Lloyd Robeson stood and proclaimed Kathryn his client and vowed she wasn't going anywhere without an explanation.

"She's wanted for questioning in the death of Vincent LaPaglia."

The name made the men around the table shift uneasily.

"What?" Forrester and Kathryn exclaimed simultaneously.

"Don't say a word," Robeson instructed with an upheld hand. "Either of you."

Kathryn didn't look at Forrester for his reaction. She looked instead to his lawyer, who betrayed nothing behind his businesslike exterior. Despite his hatred of her, he was nothing if not professional. He had to be. More important were the reactions of Forrester's lunch guests, who were looking grey around the gills. Their eyes shifted nervously from the police, to Forrester, to her, to the lawyer.

"This is preposterous," Forrester said.

"Please, Marcus," Robeson cautioned. "Not a word."

The shorter burly officer held out his hand. "Come with us, please, ma'am."

Robeson nodded, Forrester stewed, and Kathryn left silently with the detectives. She had never heard of Vincent LaPaglia, and she certainly didn't kill him.

At the station, the police purposely kept them waiting for hours, much to the delight of the desk sergeant, who spent his break time staring at Kathryn's legs. Once in the interrogation room, a detective set a gun on the table and said it belonged to her. She stared at it blankly as his voice faded into the background. That couldn't be her gun. Jenny had her gun. Then she recognized a familiar nick in the wooden grip. Her mind flailed for an explanation, and her heart began to race. Why would Jenny turn her gun over to the police?

The interrogator slapped his hand on the table and she snapped her eyes to him. "Answer me!" he said. She had no idea what the question was.

"You're our number one suspect, Miss Hammond. We practically have an eyewitness to the crime. Now answer my question! Where were you between the hours of—"

Just then, an officer entered the room, drawing all eyes to him. He whispered something to the interrogator, looked at Kathryn, and then left. The interrogator straightened with a glare and closed the file. He slid the gun back into an evidence envelope and tied it up. "You're free to go."

Robeson demanded an explanation.

Upon closer inspection, the victim's gun had been found in the car and was identified as the weapon used to take his life. Vincent LaPaglia's death had been ruled a suicide. Kathryn's gun was returned to her, and while she waited in the hallway, Lloyd Robeson lingered briefly in the interrogation room, laying into the police about harassing his boss and those connected with him.

On his way out, he breezed past Kathryn without a word, and she dutifully followed, lamenting the groveling to come. She quickened her step to catch up. "Thank you, Lloyd."

"I didn't do a damn thing," he said, without slowing down. "Lucky for you it was a suicide, because believe me, I wouldn't lift a finger to help you if I didn't have to." He burst through the outer doors, not bothering to hold one open for her.

Forrester's black Packard limousine waited at the curb, and Kathryn could see him in the backseat, watching her from under the brim of his black hat. "Stay here," Robeson commanded tersely before crossing the few yards of sidewalk to the car.

Kathryn knew she may be in trouble. Everything they'd set up, everything they'd worked for, hinged on the recommendations of a man who loathed her. He had more influence with Forrester than anyone else she'd seen. She watched Robeson settle into the jump seat opposite his boss. Forrester listened intently, nodded occasionally, and then shook his head in disapproval.

Kathryn knew it was about her, because Robeson looked her way reflexively and then threw his hands up at Forrester's reaction. He was trying hard to suggest something, and Kathryn knew it was more serious than just "stop seeing that dame."

Forrester refused Robeson's suggestion again, solidifying what she felt was a firm position in his world. Robeson finally acquiesced, anger and frustration evident in his curt movements. Kathryn ventured a quick glance up and down the street in response to Robeson motioning her over to the car. Smitty would be somewhere close by. Watching.

They had people in the police station, and she knew news of her little visit would bring him running. She caught him out of the corner of her eye, leaning against the far end of the building, his head surreptitiously buried in a newspaper. It gave her comfort to know that should Forrester change his mind and take Robeson's advice,

Smitty would be following closely behind, and at least they'd know where to find the body.

"Jenny?" Bernie stuck his head in the door of the empty office. "Was that who I thought it was?" Seeing the coast was clear, he eased the rest of the way into the room. "Did you hear they ruled it a suicide? You must be relieved. What a mix-up, huh? Maybe LaPaglia felt guilty about what happened to your dad. Say, I thought you gals were going to dinner. I mean, now that she's no longer a murderer and all."

Jenny lifted her head, revealing her stricken face.

"Hey," Bernie said, as he quickly rushed over. "What happened? I thought everything was straightened out?"

"I think I really messed up, Bernie."

He settled next to her on the empty desktop. "Talk to me."

She explained the danger Kathryn was in and then began to cry. "What if he kills her, Bernie? I don't think I can live with that."

"Shhh." He put his arm around her. "He's not going to kill her, Bug."

She leaned into his shoulder. "You know what kind of monster he is."

Bernie regretted setting off the entire series of events by inviting the woman to the birthday party in the first place. Getting involved with a mobster's mistress was the last thing Jenny needed. What had he been thinking?

"He won't kill her, Jenny." Please God, don't let him kill her.

Smitty watched Kathryn get into the car after a cock of Forrester's head sent Robeson unhappily to the street. He watched Kathryn turn it on: her apprehensive demeanor, a shake of her head, her hand covering her eyes, then her mouth, tears of remorse. God, she was good.

Forrester bought it all, supplying a handkerchief, a shoulder to lean on, and a kiss of forgiveness planted gently on her brow.

Forrester lifted her chin as he smiled in sympathetic absolution, and she hugged him in relief. Lloyd Robeson rolled his eyes as he turned from the scene. It was one more reason Smitty hated him.

Kathryn protested something Forrester said, and then she dried her tears and smiled as he cupped her face in assurance. She leaned in and kissed his cheek, rubbing the lipstick from his face with her thumb before exiting the car, still clutching the handkerchief. Robeson sneered as he passed her on the curb and took her place in the car.

The men drove away, and Kathryn stared after the receding car until they were out of sight. She offered a half-hearted glance in Smitty's general vicinity and headed down the street in the opposite direction. Smitty folded up his paper and followed an inconspicuous length behind. They had a meeting place set up if something ever went wrong with an assignment; that's where she should have been going, but she went instead to the *Daily Chronicle* building, and Smitty could only stand by helplessly, hoping Kathryn wasn't making a mistake.

Kathryn felt foolish about her optimism of the morning, and even worse, she'd told Smitty about it. Heat rushed to her face when she remembered his lukewarm acceptance of her newfound contentment. He knew it was ridiculous. Her childish fantasy about hope and a future was just that—a fantasy. It was not for people like her. After everything she'd done, the lives she'd destroyed, what made her think the universe, in its grace, would afford her happiness?

She couldn't face Smitty to explain the gun incident. It was a failure on her part in so many ways. She sent word to their meeting place, assuring him that, so far, all was well. Forrester outwardly brushed off her little run-in with the law, but there was no telling what effect it had on his business partners, and that, coupled with his attorney's attitude, told her she might not be out of the woods yet.

Forrester expected her at the estate after her show at The Grotto. He only invited her to the estate if there was a meeting or dinner

party where he needed to impress or if he was in the mood for his strange little ritual. She knew of no dinner party or meeting, and she was apathetic toward the sexual favor she saw in her future. The favor, if that was his intent, would be the usual; he rarely deviated from the routine. He was an odd man when it came to his sexual pleasure, and for that she was grateful, because she'd endured a lot worse.

The Long Island estate was mostly dark and unnaturally quiet when she arrived after her show at The Grotto. There was usually someone milling about, if not members of Forrester's organization, then servants preparing for the next day, but not tonight, and the stillness made her uneasy. The doorman greeted her, as he always did, with a pleasant smile, a "lovely to see you," and a surprising new statement to his repertoire: "The master awaits you in his room."

Kathryn frowned. Forrester had never started an evening in his room. He was getting right to it tonight. She kept her coat; Forrester liked it that way. Part of the game. She moved purposefully to her destination, and as she ascended the ridiculously large staircase to the second floor, she noticed, for the first time, how the low light cast an eerie glow on the lush interior of the mansion. Out of the corner of her eye, she watched the doorman retrieve a coat from a chair beside the entry and slip silently out the front door. That was unusual, and it couldn't be good. There didn't seem to be anyone else in the house, and she paused in her ascent, surprised to find herself gripped with trepidation. It was a true Hitchcockian moment, and she laughed silently as she thought of Jenny and her love of the movies.

She didn't like thinking of Jenny right then. At first, she didn't like associating Jenny with this house, with this man, to the things she would do here. She felt ashamed suddenly, then angry. Jenny thought her a murderer. God, that made her angry. It felt like a betrayal, but that was ridiculous. Jenny owed her nothing, least of all loyalty.

She looked for focus in the massive tapestry draped on the back wall at the head of the stairs, some random hellfire and damnation story from the Bible. Sodom and Gomorrah, she thought. It was not helping her unease. Forrester waited for her. She felt dirty. Jenny Ryan was in her head like a moral compass, and she didn't like it.

She allowed herself the anger, and the pity, just for a moment, before pushing it all out of her head, Jenny especially. She thought of the dead, her debt. It was all the motivation she needed tonight. The uncharacteristic mixing of business and pleasure dissipated, along with the trepidation, and she was an empty shell again, feeling nothing, as was always the case when she came to him like this.

Finally, more like herself, she lifted her chin confidently as she continued to the top of the stairway and headed down the cavernous hallway to Forrester's bedchamber.

No light streamed from under the door, and she hesitated. Something had changed. This was odd, even for him. She had a deep sense of foreboding that her life was about to flash before her eyes.

She tapped gently on the slightly ajar door, and it gave with a creak under her knuckle. "Marcus?"

She imagined him sitting in the darkness, lying in wait for her entrance, legs crossed, gun on his lap, pointing at the door. It would make sense. He'd cleared the house so that he'd have complete solitude for his dastardly deed—witnesses just wouldn't do.

She had to give him credit for doing it himself. That certainly wasn't his style; clean hands were a must. It gave her a peculiar sense of importance to know that he wanted to take care of her personally. Perhaps he would make her slip from her coat before firing the fatal shot, or perhaps he would ask for pleasure first, a last hurrah before ending it. That would be typical, and that would be okay. Death was still her friend. It didn't matter how the evening ended. She would walk away or she wouldn't. Being an empty shell had its advantages. Her mind was devoid of the emotion that makes one care whether one lives or dies.

She stood motionless in the face of the partially open door, thoughts forming like a train as her eyes traced the ornamental pattern on its surface. She didn't know why she was so certain that this evening would be her last, but she was. And as that thought gained steam, her empty shell began to fill. She didn't want to die *here*, for him, for nothing, and the fact that, just moments before, she'd found her death so acceptable at the hands of Marcus Forrester, made her angry. If she didn't know better, she would swear self-worth was making itself known.

"Come," he said from the darkness of the room.

She pushed the door all the way open and was startled not by a gunshot, but by a spotlight suddenly coming to life, illuminating the bed. It was the only light in the room, leaving the bed floating in a sea of darkness. She recovered from the start, and the useless self-worth, and entered the room. Whatever was going to happen, it wasn't going to be over quickly.

"Stop," Forrester said, as she stepped into the edge of the light. She complied and waited, her eyes searching, trying to adjust to the contrast in light.

"You said you were sorry." His voice sounded strange, lower than usual, and uncharacteristically emotional.

"Yes." She focused on the only thing she could see of him: the tip of his expensive shoe, protruding from the shadows, into the light, as he sat in his favorite red leather wingback chair, a few feet from the foot of the bed.

"Look at me," he said softly.

She lifted her eyes to the spot in the darkness she imagined his face would be. A tendril of cigar smoke swirled into the light as his masonic ring tinked against the glass of scotch in his hand. This was the odd man, the insecure man, the man only she was allowed to see. Now the game would begin. She marveled at people's unique sexual inclinations, that dark facet of their personalities hidden by the mask of propriety at all times in their lives save this.

"Show me how sorry you are."

A wanton smirk grew on her lips, and she untied her trench coat. She let it slide effortlessly off her shoulders and past her black see-through negligee until it was a crumpled mass around her ankles.

She heard the leather chair creak as he took in the sight of her and shifted in the darkness.

She lowered her eyes and ducked her head. This was his favorite part. Her hands seductively traced the contours of her thighs and hips as they slowly made their way up her tall, sinewy body. They slid the length of her abdomen until she reached her breasts and caressed one, then the other. She moaned as she cupped her soft, warm flesh and gasped sensuously for effect when she teased her nipples until they were hard. She stopped and looked to him with misleading half-lidded eyes.

"Would you like me to touch you," she asked, her voice filled with desire she didn't feel.

His reply was the tip of his shoe disappearing into the shadows. She made her way to the bed alone. Same ol', same ol'.

"I thought you had a date, kiddo?" Paul asked, as he folded his jacket over his arm and stood beside Jenny's desk. He purposely hid the final mock-up of the front page, certain she wouldn't approve.

"Something came up. Plans changed," Jenny said.

Paul watched her organize papers on her desk already in perfect order and could see her puffy eyes, even though she tried to hide them with her downturned face.

"Free for dinner, then?"

"I'm sorry, Uncle Paul. It's been a rough day. I think I'm just going to go home."

"Your aunt will be disappointed."

"Give her my love, will you?"

He knew something was wrong, and whatever it was, it had to do with Kathryn Hammond's visit. He would deal with her later for upsetting his niece.

"Are you all right?"

Jenny looked up briefly and smiled, and he wondered if she would ever stop trying to fool the ones who loved her into thinking she wasn't upset.

She must have thought the same thing, because she stood and faced him full on. "I'm fine. You know me. Cry at the drop of a hat."

He wrinkled his face up sympathetically and pulled her into a hug. "Well, whatever it is, I love you, and you know you can always talk to me."

She squeezed him back. "I know. Go on, get out of here, before you're in the doghouse with Aunt Betsy again."

He grinned. "I heard that. See you tomorrow."

He'd deal with the fallout from the morning edition then.

CHAPTER TWENTY-NINE

Kathryn knew Forrester watched her sleep. He always watched. He *only* watched. She lay half covered in the black negligee he'd given her. One strap rested off her shoulder, exposing most of her left breast. She waited for him to touch it, but she knew he wouldn't.

He couldn't know that she never slept in his presence, that she had honed her deceptive sleep to perfection: the slow, even breathing, the slightly parted lips. She even added rapid eye movement for effect when she sensed he was close and hovering.

Tonight, however, he did more than hover. She felt his weight slowly and gingerly settle onto the mattress beside her. She felt his hand carefully arrange the wayward strap of her negligee, methodically covering her breast as if he were embarrassed to see it. His movement stopped, and she could feel the heat of his hand floating just over her heart. Her eyes flew open, suddenly panicked that perhaps he had a gun. If this was it, if he was going to kill her, she wanted to see death coming, to look it in the eye and laugh and say, "What took you so long?" and "Thank you."

She found no gun, only his hand, which he withdrew. He was staring into her eyes with a lost, helpless look she'd never seen before. She reached up to touch his face, and he stopped her by gently encircling her wrist with his large hand. He looked at her wrist curiously as the pounding pulse under his fingers betrayed her alarm.

"Are you afraid of me?" he whispered in an odd tone. His face was tight, concerned, searching, and she wasn't sure if it registered fear or malevolence.

"No."

He tilted his head. "No?"

She looked away, pretending to be ashamed. She instinctively decided on a course of action and committed to it.

"I'll admit that I wondered if I'd leave the estate alive tonight," she said honestly, then lifted her chin slightly as a last act of defiance, her expression hard so he would know she meant it. "But I am not afraid."

He seemed to like that answer, and his face relaxed. He let go of her wrist, and traces of a grin formed on his lips. "I won't hurt you."

Kathryn wasn't sure what was happening. Was this a new beginning or her end? If it was her end, she would not go down without a fight.

"Tonight? Or ever?"

His eyes narrowed. "That's entirely up to you." He was testing her, gauging her, and she met his search with a practiced, unflinching devotion.

"I would never betray you, Marcus. You know that."

"Because I would kill you? Or because you couldn't bear to hurt me?" The last part was unmistakably sarcastic, and Kathryn could sense a shift in their relationship. He was exposing a piece of himself, using his sarcasm as a shield to deflect the blow, should it come. She recognized the technique; hell, she thought she invented it.

She reached again to stroke his face, and this time he let her. His eyes darted in the opposite direction of the hand on his cheek, and she felt him stiffen at her touch. This was so different from the man she knew. Despite his strong, mature face and slightly graying hair, he seemed a boy now, frightened by something he didn't understand.

She brought up her other hand until she was cupping his face. His eyes had nowhere to hide but in hers, which were glistening with all the false devotion she could muster.

"You don't have to threaten me," she whispered softly.

That was all she said, and whatever that meant to him, it must have been what he wanted to hear, because he laid his head on her chest, and she swore she felt a hot tear trickle between her breasts.

He fell asleep like that, and Kathryn could only stare at the absurdly high ceiling, wishing herself out from under his oppressive weight, literally and figuratively. She wasn't sure what just happened, and she was even less sure of what the morning would bring, but, apparently, getting hauled down to the police station was the best thing that could have happened to her relationship with Marcus Forrester.

In the early hours of the morning, Kathryn could no longer hold off sleep, so she gave in to it, confident that on this night, at least, it was safe to be unconscious in Forrester's presence. She was alone in the bed when she awoke to bright sunlight streaming through the sheer white full-length drapes that hung in the master bedroom. A new set of clothes had been laid at the foot of the bed: light colored slacks with generous cuffs and a billowy white silk shirt with ample sleeves and a large collar—all taboo during the wartime rationing of material. She shook her head. It was just like Forrester to thumb his nose at the wartime restrictions.

She took her time showering and dressing, fairly certain this was going to be the most interesting morning after she'd ever had.

"Good morning, dear," Forrester said, grinning amiably as she approached the breakfast table set for two in the sunbathed breakfast room. He put his paper aside and rose to greet her, taking her hand and kissing her cheek. "Sleep well?"

"Yes," she said, as he settled a chair under her. Did he just call her dear? Apparently, they are an old married couple now.

She noticed the pile of international and local newspapers beside him, and it reminded her of her breakfast with Jenny. Was it only twenty-four hours ago? It seemed like a lifetime.

Why did everything pertaining to Jenny feel like a lifetime ago? Their time together seemed to move in large blocks, ebbs and flows, moving forward an inch, only to fall back tenfold. Unbidden thoughts of Jenny filled her head, and she was only vaguely aware of her breakfast companion as she unfolded her napkin. Forrester clanked something on the table, snapping her from her reverie, and she cursed herself for allowing the intrusion, as she pushed Jenny from her mind once more.

Forrester continued to fumble with the breakfast items on the table, making no progress in his effort to make her a plate of toast to go with whatever the servants would soon offer. She eyed him warily, wondering where the Forrester she knew had gone.

He caught her curious gaze and blushed like a flustered high schooler, causing her bewildered look to deepen.

"I'm sorry," he said, and almost giggled. "I'm afraid I don't know what you like for breakfast. Ridiculous, isn't it?"

She wasn't sure what he meant by that, as they'd never had breakfast together before. He straightened quickly as a servant entered the room, and she watched the transformation with fascination as he turned back into the self-assured and confident man she knew. It was almost amusing, and she didn't hide that look in her eyes. Forrester winked at her from behind his newspaper as if it was a private game.

"Coffee, miss?" the very proper servant asked. He made no sign that this morning was any different from any other morning. He behaved as if she had always been there, the mistress of the house.

"Yes. Black, please."

"How would you like your eggs, miss?"

"Nothing for me, thank you."

"Oh, don't be silly," Forrester said. "You've got to eat something."

"No, Marcus. Really. I'm not a breakfast person. Toast and coffee will be fine."

Forrester stared at her and looked pleased that he learned what she liked for breakfast.

"Thank you, Reggie," he said, dismissing the servant. "We don't want to be disturbed." He added a knowing look to the end of the statement, and Kathryn felt it meant disturbed by anyone.

"Very well, sir," Reggie said and bowed out of the room.

After a few moments of uncomfortable silence, Forrester spoke. "Are you sure I can't get you anything?"

"This is fine, really." She reached for a piece of toast, more to have something to do than because she was hungry, and he intercepted her hand.

"Here, let me do that. Butter? Jam? Both?"

She withdrew her hand and stared at him. "What's going on, Marc?"

"I'm making you breakfast? Is that so terrible?"

She gently crossed her arms and leaned them on the table, pinning him with her soft gaze. "What's going on?"

He settled back into his chair and delayed his answer as he carefully dotted each corner of his mouth with his napkin.

Loud voices were heard coming from the other room, and Forrester exhaled a heavy sigh. Kathryn recognized the shouting as that of his lawyer, Lloyd Robeson.

"Don't be absurd, man," Robeson said, brushing Reggie off his arm. "He doesn't mean *me*."

Reggie groveled to his boss as the lawyer burst past. "I'm sorry, sir. He—"

Forrester raised his hand. "It's all right. That'll be all."

Reggie regally bowed out of the room again. "Sir."

"Ass," Robeson muttered, as he straightened his wrinkled sleeve. He had been so busy trying to free himself from the servant's grasp that he didn't notice Kathryn sitting at the breakfast table. When he did, he paled noticeably, and his gaze quickly flashed to Forrester for an explanation. It was then that Kathryn knew—last night was supposed to be her last. As in ever.

"We're having a private breakfast, Lloyd," Forrester said calmly. "Whatever it is you have to say, it can wait until later."

Robeson's gaze shifted to Kathryn. His eyes were more hateful than ever.

"Good morning, Lloyd," she smiled innocently for Forrester's benefit and Robeson's irritation. "Coffee to go?" She reached for the pot.

"Have you seen this?" He threw the *Daily Chronicle* in Kathryn's lap, his focus never leaving Forrester's glare.

"Jesus," Kathryn said, as she saw her own face staring back at her. Nightclub Singer Suspected in Mysterious Death, the minor headline screamed from below the fold.

"I've seen it, Lloyd. Now, if that's all—"

Robeson pointed at Kathryn. "This is a disaster!"

Kathryn knew he meant more than just the article.

Forrester slammed his fist into the table as he stood, causing the china, and Kathryn, to jump.

"That's enough!"

Forrester and Robeson glared at each other. Kathryn wasn't sure where to look, so she just stared at the coffee sloshing in her cup.

"Apologize to Miss Hammond and get out."

Robeson's eyes darted from his boss to his enemy and back again. His jaw worked and his breathing became uneven. Apologizing to his boss was one thing, but, evidently, he could not swallow enough spite to apologize to what he was sure would be Forrester's downfall. He glared at Kathryn and then left without saying a word.

"Lloyd!" Forrester shouted, obviously enraged by the man's disobedience and lack of respect. "I can always get another lawyer!"

Robeson turned. "And you can always buy another whore." He slammed the door on the way out.

Kathryn kept her eyes on her coffee cup, her brow now firmly planted in her hairline at Robeson's brazen defiance. Forrester was still standing, and she could feel the waves of anger pouring off him. She turned her gaze to Forrester's fist, white with rage, ground into the tablecloth beside her.

She gently touched his hand. "It's all right, Marcus." She touched him more firmly when the tension didn't ease. "It's all right. He's just concerned about you. That's his job."

"His job is to do as he's told," Forrester said, as he sat down and snapped his napkin across his lap.

Robeson's parting words sounded like a threat to her, but she didn't think Forrester would take them that way—an insult perhaps, but nothing more. The lawyer wouldn't dare threaten. He wouldn't dare.

Kathryn would never see Lloyd Robeson again.

"Don't lie to me, Bessie!" Jenny said into the receiver as she stood in her living room strangling the morning edition of the *Daily Chronicle* in her fist. "I know he's there!"

"Honestly, honey," Bessie said, her voice pleading. "He'll have my head if I put you through."

"Did you know about this?" She lifted the paper as if Bessie could see it through the phone.

"Jenny—"

"Never mind." Jenny slammed the receiver down. Poor Bessie, having to put up with her uncle's tantrums and now hers. The secretary should get a raise.

Jenny opened the crushed paper in her hand. A gorgeous rumpled picture of Kathryn Hammond stared back at her.

It was bad enough she'd caused Kathryn to be hauled in by the cops. The only saving grace of that faux pas was that unless you were at the restaurant, you'd never have known. But now, to have her picture plastered all over the paper—the front page no less! If Kathryn wasn't in trouble before, she surely would be now.

Jenny stared at the picture. "Damn it to hell. How could he do this?"

She slumped down on the couch, trying to decide what to do first: go throttle her uncle or find Kathryn and apologize. Throttle Uncle, demand a retraction, then apologize, she decided. She wondered if

Kathryn would believe that she didn't have anything to do with the article and photo. She wondered if Kathryn would see her at all.

———

Kathryn's calming touch and cooing assurances helped Forrester's anger dissipate quickly. He gave her an exasperated, apologetic look. "I don't know what's gotten into him." He shook his head, and easy as you please, his nose was back in his newspaper.

Kathryn's eyes were drawn to her article in the *Daily Chronicle*. "Why didn't you show me this?"

"*That*," he said, motioning at the paper, "will be taken care of. I must compliment them on the choice of photograph, though. Quite lovely. You must give me a copy."

Kathryn knew it was no joking matter, and he would be getting some serious flak from his associates over the publicity.

"Have I caused you trouble, Marcus?"

He looked up in confusion, as if he had no idea what she was talking about.

"With your business associates," she clarified.

"No, my dear." He patted her hand. "I've already spoken to them. In fact, I'm afraid they were all a bit disappointed that you didn't actually kill anyone."

"Ah." She smiled an uncertain, crooked smile, acknowledging their sick measure of a man, and showed just the right amount of repulsion as she cringed into her coffee cup.

Forrester smiled, respectfully allowing her opinion.

"Would you like to tell me what happened?" he asked offhandedly, turning a page.

Kathryn paused, taking an unnaturally long time to swallow and replace her cup on its saucer. She couldn't afford to lie about where the gun came from. Forrester's tone suggested he knew the who, just not the why, and, unfortunately, after everything they'd done to prevent it, Jenny would soon be front and center, the object of his attention.

Overnight, instead of being in the clear, Jenny had become a thorn in his side, the catalyst for a public embarrassment, and Kathryn was sure that the deed would not go unpunished. She found no amount of rationalizing could save her from the guilt of being the conduit of Jenny's exposure. Relinquishing her gun was stupid. So very stupid.

"A friend was in trouble. I was just trying to help."

"How kind of you," was his reply. It was neither accusatory, nor condescending, and he let it float there as he went back to his paper.

Kathryn was unsure of his intentions. Maybe he *didn't* know who turned in the gun. Jenny could have been smart about it, sent it anonymously. She thought about it. Not likely. In the brief time she'd known the feisty columnist, she imagined her walking right through the front door while announcing her name to the whole world as she turned over the she-devil's murderous tool. How very dramatic, how very Hollywood, and how very Jenny.

Thinking of Jenny made her angry again, something she would have to curtail for the moment. She had damage control to spin, and she needed to know for sure if Jenny was in the middle of it.

"What did you mean when you said you'd take care of this?" She pointed at the article.

"*That*," he emphasized the word again, "is an example of a reporter creating her own news. Rather unethical, don't you think?"

He knew Jenny was responsible for the gun, and from his comment, responsible for the article as well, even though it carried no byline. How could Jenny have done it? Why, when she said she'd given up going after Forrester. She knew how dangerous it would be, and she did it anyway. Was it spite because she'd been rejected? Or was it the plan all along, part of some harebrained scheme to discredit Forrester no matter who got hurt? She was desperate for a story, after all, and she had the perfect in.

Kathryn bit down on her anger. She'd been a fool. Jenny played right into her ego, turning the tables of deception flawlessly. So much for the sweet, innocent act. Well, Jenny was part of this whole thing now, and despite the anger and hurt from being used, it panicked her to think Forrester may do something in retribution. No one should die for trying to get a good story.

"What did you mean, Marcus?"

He stared at her, looking confused.

Kathryn warned herself to take it easy. Protesting too much would only raise his interest level.

"I'm just saying," she began calmly, trying to backtrack, "there's nothing slanderous or untrue in this article." She scanned it briefly and found that to be true. Misleading, but no outright untruths. "There's nothing to be taken care of, really."

"It's the principal of the thing," Forrester said. "That article was uncalled for. While technically correct, it leads the casual reader to believe you actually committed a crime. That's all the public will remember: sex, murder, and a beautiful dame. They've sullied your reputation, and they did it because of your association with me. I won't stand for it."

"I can take care of myself, Marcus. And as for my reputation—"

"You can take care of yourself?" he interrupted, his eyes flashing with anger again. "Is that why you carry a gun? You think that will keep you safe? Do you?" He was on the verge of yelling. "Women like you should not be afraid." He stabbed his finger into the table with each point. "They should not carry guns, and they should not have to take care of themselves!"

Kathryn wondered what in the hell was going on as she shifted uncomfortably, pretending to find his tone unpleasant, which wasn't far from the truth. Forrester had a quick temper, a lot like Paul's, she noticed, much to her chagrin. She'd seen the results firsthand, and she knew she had to nip it in the bud before it was too late. She couldn't figure out Forrester's new angle, and it put her on edge. Time to break up this little party and get the hell out, if out was still an option.

"Let's not argue, Marc."

"No." He reeled in his temper. "Let's not."

He sat back in his chair and looked across the room at nothing in particular.

Kathryn stared at the intricate pattern that graced the edge of her coffee cup as she measured her pounding heartbeats and focused on breathing. She was about to ask what was going on again, but as she turned to speak, his words filled the expectant space.

"Now ..." He exhaled the anger as he steepled his hands in front of him. He seemed perfectly calm. "This friend." He paused, waiting for a reaction that she suppressed. "The one you gave your gun to, the one who turned you in to the police."

She looked away but couldn't mask the hurt. "Yes. My friend." The words nearly caught in her throat.

"Perhaps you should choose your friends more carefully."

She thought she had. "She was afraid, Marcus. It was a misunderstanding." If there was a logical explanation, that would be it.

He casually raised his brow. "Is she more than a friend?"

"A little less than a friend, apparently," she said honestly, allowing the sting to surface. The statement hung in the air as they both contemplated its meaning. Forrester poured himself another cup of coffee, and Kathryn nursed hers.

"Is she your lover?" he asked without warning.

She managed to avoid the cliché of choking on her sip of coffee, but just barely, as she tried her best to remain neutral but appropriately shocked. She looked him up and down as if he were from another planet.

"What?"

He smiled. It was an odd smile, not comforting, more of a warning. The smile slowly turned into a smirk. "Do you think I know nothing about you?"

Her heart started to beat faster. How well had the OSS covered her ass? How well had she covered her own ass? How long did she have to live?

"Do you think I would let you this close over all these months without knowing who I was dealing with?"

He reached out and stroked her face. Her nerves were on edge, and it was all she could do not to flinch. "A beautiful woman such as yourself needs pleasure, and far be it from me to judge one's taste in the erotic arts."

She was afraid to speak or move, unsure what was next.

"I only ask that you be discreet."

Before she met Jenny, he had never made demands on her personal life before. In fact, the only directives were for *his* personal life, the things he expected her to do for him. When on public display, his instructions were to be on time, look gorgeous, and attend to him in such a way that every man in the room ached to be in his shoes. Something was definitely changing.

"She isn't my lover, Marcus."

"Shame."

Her eyes darted in his direction. "What is that supposed to mean?"

"There's something to be said for variety, don't you think?"

She wanted to say, *how the hell would you know?* And then it dawned on her. He wanted her to bring Jenny into their sexual game —for the two of them to—my God. The thought made her ill, and angry. He had tainted that part of her life with Jenny before she even had a chance to experience the beauty of it. With one sentence, he had injected himself into her personal life, and she hated him for it. She hated herself even more for holding on to the foolish, blissful dream of a normal, loving relationship—whatever the hell that was.

"I don't have a lover, Marc."

He went back to reading the morning paper. "Well, when you do, and you should ..." He glanced her way, making his sickening sugges-tion clear. "Please be discreet." He went back to reading.

She glared at him in confusion.

He looked over briefly, seeing the need to elaborate. "I don't own you, and you're not my prisoner," he said turning the page. "You give me what I need, and I allow you what you need." He looked over again. "It's quite a fair exchange, don't you think?"

Allow? So much for freedom. She couldn't argue about the rules, so she tilted her head in disbelieving agreement and picked up her coffee cup in an absentminded toast.

"I suppose it is."

"I want a retraction, Uncle Paul!" Jenny said again, slamming her hand on the article in question.

All heads had bowed to nonexistent work as Jenny stormed through the newsroom and into the front office, flinging the morning edition onto her uncle's desk. Bessie evidently related the phone call from the hour before because everyone was on the lookout for the fireworks. They would not be disappointed.

"There's nothing to retract, Jenny!" Paul said. "That's solid news right there!"

"That's bunk and you know it! We are the only paper to run that, and it is *not* news!"

He jabbed at the article. "We are also the only paper to sell out this morning. It's news to someone!"

"Sellout being the operative word, Uncle Paul!" She slammed her hand onto the paper again. "This is someone's life! Don't you know what you've done?"

Paul walked around his desk and put his hands on her shoulders like he always did just before patronizing her. "You're taking this far too personally, Jenny. That woman can take care of herself. Don't break the law if you—"

"She didn't break the law!" Jenny interrupted. She angrily shrugged his hands from her body. Screaming at each other was not going to solve anything, but damn it! "She didn't do it, Uncle Paul, that's my point! This is *my* fault, don't you see? *I* turned in that gun! Me!"

Her uncle stepped back in shock. "How did you ... why did you ... what are you doing with her gun?" His voice raised a few decibels when he said the word gun, and he looked into the newsroom to see heads ducking and gaping mouths shutting. He lowered his voice. "You stay away from that woman, Jenny. I mean it."

"You cannot tell me who my friends are, Uncle Paul!"

"And you *will* not tell me how to run my newspaper!"

Jenny knew their anger was spiraling out of control and that they were an office sideshow, but she would fight for Kathryn and her safety.

"You must retract that story. It's a matter of life and death!"

"I've had it up to here with your hysterics, Jenny." He held his hand above his head. "If you were anyone else, you'd be fired. You are being totally unprofessional."

"I don't give a flying fig about being professional," Jenny said, still having enough inbred respect not to curse at her uncle. "We're talking about a woman's life!" She pointed at Kathryn's photo. "Her life!"

Paul waved an indifferent hand in her direction and walked behind his desk. Jenny was getting nowhere with her current tact. Her uncle wasn't taking her seriously and had effectively cut her off without further discussion. She leaned into the desk where he had returned to his paperwork.

"If you don't print that retraction," she said in a low controlled voice, pausing until his eyes lifted, "I quit."

Paul stopped just short of an amused sneer and began sifting through some papers. "Stop acting like a spoiled child, Jenny. Get back to work. You've got a deadline."

It was the most condescending tone she'd ever heard from him, and Jenny stared for a moment in disbelief at his casual dismissal. Anger, like venom, rolled around in her mouth until she could no longer stand the taste of it.

"You know what you can do with your fucking deadline." She paused. "Chief." She pushed off the desk and strode confidently to the door. She had never disrespected her uncle before. The new sensation was frightening but intoxicating.

"Jenny Ryan, if you walk out that door, you're fired!"

She opened the door so the whole office could hear. "You can't fire me!" she said, angry that she was walking out with the oldest cliché in the book. "I quit!"

She slammed the office door, shattering the window, a feat

usually reserved for her uncle's rage. She cringed, more out of amazement than regret, plucked two photos and her favorite pen from her desk as she passed it, and stormed out of the office, to the stunned silence of her coworkers.

"That's coming out of your paycheck!" she heard her uncle scream from behind his desk.

She resisted the urge to give him the finger over her shoulder. Oh, how she resisted.

"What the hell are you looking at?" she heard her uncle's receding voice bellow as she rounded the corner and headed straight for the open elevator.

"Hold," she called out with an arm in the air. Once inside, she said, "Ground floor," and waited for what seemed an eternity for the attendant to comply. It would have been perfect, Jenny imagined, if her uncle had appeared barreling around the corner for another confrontation and the doors had closed on his face as she smirked from the other side. Much better than *I quit*, slam. But it was not to be. Only the sports editor hopped on at the last minute, oblivious to her triumph, and they rode the elevator to the ground floor in silence.

Forrester continued his happy couple charade, and Kathryn let him as she tried to decide the best way to secure her objectives: protect Jenny, live another day, and, maybe in the process, crawl one stinking layer closer and one disgusting step higher in Forrester's despicable kingdom. The first thing she needed to know was where she stood.

"From the look on Lloyd's face this morning, I get the feeling I wasn't supposed to be breathing today."

She said it as a by-the-way remark and casually picked up her cup of coffee as a prop in the illusion.

Forrester made a last-ditch effort to continue his charade. "Goodness." He chuckled. "What on earth gave you—"

"I want you to know that I know that," she interrupted. She

pinned him with a serious gaze before taking a sip and reverently placing the cup down, as if it were her last drink on earth.

Forrester faltered, the honesty catching him off guard. He pushed his newspapers around on the table, and Kathryn imagined he was deciding on a course of action as well.

Kathryn waited for him to buckle. She watched him until he couldn't bear the silence of the truth and he looked up.

Now she was getting somewhere. "So, if I'm in for it, I'd appreciate knowing." She smiled bravely. "I'll ask Reggie for that full-course breakfast."

Forrester failed to find the humor in the statement, and Kathryn wondered how close to the truth she was.

"Marcus ..." She hesitated, putting just the right amount of hurt and concern in her voice and expression. "Were you going to kill me last night?"

His eyes bore into hers, and he did not falter again. "Yes."

She knew, deep down, that would be the answer, but it shocked her anyway, and that threw her. Her heart lurched, and she looked away. It was her turn to shift uncomfortably, only this time she wasn't acting. She couldn't understand where her fear was coming from, or why. When did death become an unwelcome guest? She pulled her napkin from her lap and brought it to the table; the linen cloth suddenly felt like a silly remnant of a civilized world that no longer existed.

"Are you still going to kill me?" Her voice wasn't as steady as she wished it to be. She didn't look up, and she realized she was hanging on the answer.

He reached out to turn her face, and this time she did flinch, causing him to withdraw the gesture. She cursed herself for the reflex. She had to get hold of herself.

"I told you last night I wouldn't hurt you," he said sincerely. He leaned in and under to find her eyes. "Yes?"

She didn't answer. Her body was buzzing. She felt lightheaded. She closed her eyes, trying to find her center, and her nerve. *Breathe.* She hoped the silence would let him wonder if she believed him, and she needed the extra time to pull herself together. *Breathe.*

She finally opened her eyes, having found some semblance of control, and squared her shoulders to him. "What's changed from last night to this morning?" She really wanted to know the answer. He had that lost look again, but he didn't turn away this time. He looked as if he was drowning in her vulnerability, and it made him seem almost human, almost pitiable.

"I ..." he started but faltered again. "I realized that I ..."

He was anything but human, deserved no one's pity, and if he said anything about love, Kathryn thought she might throw up. The audacity. As if this monster knew the first thing about the word. As if she would recognize it if he did.

She thought he would give in to emotion, but he gathered himself enough to straighten and clear his throat, his familiar personage back in place. "I realized that would be a foolish thing to do." He lifted his coffee cup slightly in her direction. "No harm done, and certainly not your fault." He drained the contents. "But I do admire your straightforward nature. Very admirable."

Damn. Back to square one. Outside looking in. She was going to have to dig a little deeper. "I *am* talking about my life, Marcus. I just want to know your designs on it. That's something to be straightforward about. Don't you think?"

She purposely didn't meet his gaze, as if she were being braver than she actually felt. She was, in fact, feeling annoyed at that moment for her momentary loss of self-control, but she had a scene to play, a man to melt, so, with a perfectly overacted trembling hand, she reached out to pick up her cup and clumsily spilled the contents on the table. She paused, offered a curse under her breath, and waited, as if flustered, for Forrester to begin mopping up the mess. When he did, she turned her head away and dissolved into crocodile tears over the silly accident.

Sometimes she amazed herself. The tears and emotions she so rarely used in real life came so easily in this false world of deception and device.

Her little act had its desired effect, as the mess on the table was forgotten, and Forrester was on his knee, comforting a very distraught lady. On his knee!

He gave in to her emotional breakdown, swearing he would never harm her, that he had no intention of harming her, or letting anyone else harm her. He gently stroked her face, wiping her tears away with his knuckle.

"Shhh. No one's ever going to hurt you again," he whispered softly. "Never again." He brushed the scar over her eye with some authority, and a thought chilled her as she felt the touch through to her spine. Was Smitty right? Did he have something to do with the accident? Looking at him now, she thought no. But Robeson, perhaps.

"If it will make you feel better, you will have a driver from now on, and a bodyguard. Nothing is going to happen to you."

That wouldn't do. She needed her independence.

"Marcus, no. Really," she said, as she pulled her manipulative self together, adding a sniff here and a wipe there for good measure. His sudden submission was only making her stronger, thankfully, and she looked him straight in the eye with her lying, bloodshot baby blues and said sincerely, "I only need you." She lifted her hand to his cheek, which he gladly accepted and covered with his own. "I only need to trust *you*. If you tell me I'm safe, I know you'll keep your word. You are, above all, an honorable man." She almost choked on the words, even as he beamed at the notion. "Anyone who would have cause to harm me would know I have your protection. I would be safe."

He showed surprise at her comprehension of his influence, then appreciation for her trust, then acceptance when he realized she knew all about the kind of *business* he facilitated.

She sealed the deal with a final pitiful, desperate look. "Isn't that so?" She paused, using the silence to give his impending name weight, to make her plea undeniable. "Marcus?"

He melted under her hand and perceived distress. "Yes." He smothered her in an embrace, nearly pulling her from her chair. "Yes, it's so."

She felt like she couldn't breathe, his body surrounding her, the house, his smell, the tension, and lack of sleep for the past two nights closing in on her. First the fear, then the annoyance, and now both had been replaced by disgust, but at least that was understandable and easy to disguise. She backed herself away, still projecting uncertainty, her body tense, anticipating his answer. "I have your word then?"

"You have my word."

She closed her eyes and slumped in her chair, exhaling a relieved breath for his benefit. She opened her eyes to find his concerned face staring back at her. He hesitantly reached for her face, and this time she held fast, letting him touch it. She leaned into it and turned slightly to kiss his palm.

He finally smiled. "That's better."

Kathryn returned a shy smile, pretending her relief had made her giddy. "Good heavens, Marc, get off the floor. You'll crease your pants."

She looked around as if someone might be watching. She knew no one was, having gained enough of Forrester's trust months ago to have him ditch his bodyguards when they were alone. She pulled him up by his hands, which still clung to hers, and she smiled, as if the whole murderous plot had been a huge misunderstanding. She freed her hands and made a big deal of brushing off his knees as he rose with her.

"Never mind that." He stilled her busy hands and held them again. "Are we ... are you all right now?"

"I'm fine." She pretended to be embarrassed. "I'm so foolish, making a scene like that."

"Only a fool is not afraid of his own death," he said. "You are obviously no fool."

She continued her self-conscious routine, taking her hands back and wiping her manufactured tears. "Please don't make a fuss. I'm fine. Really."

"I'm sorry I frightened you," he said. "Forgive me?"

She wasn't sure what their new arrangement was going to be, but if he wanted some absurd Norman Rockwell cum gangster version of Americana with a touch of sex kitten on the side, she'd do her best to comply.

She made forgiveness a production number, hesitantly finding his eyes but not quite holding his gaze until the third try. "I'm still breathing." She smiled triumphantly and threw her head back, as if to shed the memory of his contemplated betrayal. "There's nothing to forgive. Let's forget it. I have your word now. Hm?" She patted his face lightly, trying to move on to more important matters, now that it seemed she would live another day.

She sat in her chair, Forrester's hand automatically reaching out to push it under, though not necessary. She was seated and settled before he managed to process that she had actually forgiven him and that they were going to go on like nothing had happened. She put her napkin back in her lap, the illusion of civility restored, and as Forrester settled himself into his chair, she absentmindedly reached out to test the temperature of the coffee pot—and their relationship. Let the show begin.

"Now I've done it," she said, "the coffee's gone—"

Before she could say "cold," Reggie was at her side, pouring Forrester a fresh hot cup. Someone was watching. She smiled at the servant, a compliment for his efficiency, and he did his best to acknowledge it with a slight duck of his chin, the proper servant's equivalent of the wink, she supposed. He reached for the creamer, but she stopped him.

"Thank you, Reggie, I can take it from here."

She noticed Forrester's supreme satisfaction as she took command of his coffee routine, sending Reggie from the room with just a smile.

"Cream, two sugars. Yes?" she asked, even as she did it, well aware of his habits.

He looked like a proud peacock, and Kathryn wished she could laugh out loud at his conceit. She felt at ease now, the familiar game back on. Forrester seemed amazed at her ability to get past his sin of her premeditated murder.

"Brave you," he said, as he watched her stir his coffee.

"Usually." She smiled, acknowledging her breakdown, and tapped the spoon once on the rim of his cup before placing it on the saucer.

He occupied himself with his fresh cup of coffee, the contents still swirling as he raised it to his lips. "I'm glad to see you back to yourself."

Something in his eyes, a familiar coldness seeping back in, gave Kathryn the distinct impression that suspicion lurked behind his words. She still had work to do.

"I ..." She looked away and shrank into her chair, showing him that she was swallowing her pride and not nearly as brave as she pretended to be. "I always felt ..." She stopped and worked her jaw slightly, pretending her feelings were raw, then she straightened a bit, as if she'd found some courage. "There are hundreds of women in this city. You could have had any one of them, yet you always came back to me."

She could see the coldness of his stare melting. He was searching, wanting to hear more.

"I was special in your eyes," she said with no humility. She sensed it was all Forrester could do not to reach out and agree with her assessment; he had that consoling look in his eyes, but he sat in interested silence and let her go on. She smiled inwardly that she had taken the right tack.

"That's what I thought, anyway." She shrugged slightly, as if it were a ridiculous notion. "Then, to hear you admit that you were actually going to kill me ... well ..." She pretended to be upset enough at the memory not to have to go on, but she knew weak, subservient women were a dime a dozen in Forrester's world, and he wanted a challenge. He seemed to love her courage, so she toughened up, once again donning her confident mask. "Fine blow to my conceit, as you can imagine." She smiled and raised a fearless brow.

He looked remorseful but pleased at her attempt to overcome the incident.

"But ..." she said cheerfully. "I am still here, so I guess I was right about being special." She put on a devilish grin. "And I so enjoy being right."

Forrester laughed and shook his head. "And you enjoy being special, don't you?"

"What girl doesn't?"

"Rest assured, you are special." He grinned as he smoothed his perfect hair back, a new gesture that seemed to indicate discomfort. "I'm afraid you've bewitched me, my dear," he said on an exasperated exhale. "I think I'd do anything for you, and that makes you just as dangerous to me as I am to you."

She smiled seductively. "Sounds exciting."

A low murmur of agreement escaped Forrester's throat, and Kathryn could see him settling into his chair, and their new dynamic, quite content that his mistress was indeed back to normal, and then some.

She was surprised at his admission of devotion and pleased that she'd inspired it. His few emotional releases were welcome displays as well. It meant she was getting into that unreasonable center of the brain that makes you do things you know are against your better judgment. After that happens—well—ripe for the picking was a phrase that came to mind. Now was as good a time as any to test his newfound devotion.

"What would you do for me, Marc?" she asked conversationally.

He seemed to enjoy the prospect of pleasing her. "What did you have in mind?"

"Would you ... kill for me?"

He got an evil glint in his eye and a sickening smile to go with it. "What do you have in mind?"

She paused, her eyes drifting toward the *Daily Chronicle*. "Would you *not* kill for me?"

"Ah," he drew out, following her gaze. "Your friend."

"Yes."

He pondered a moment, amusement behind his decision. "I suppose you'd never forgive me if something happened to her."

"I suppose I wouldn't."

"That's settled then."

"I want you to say it." She pinned him with a serious flash of blue. This was not something she would leave to interpretation.

"For as long as you wish it, I will afford her the same protection I have offered you."

She continued to stare, her eyes telling him that she needed more.

He smiled. "The *Daily Chronicle* and those connected to it will not be held responsible for *this* article in any way," he said officially, with a patronizing grin.

His emphasis on the word *this* told her that his patience was not limitless, and it was a warning against further provocation. Noted.

"Thank you."

He smiled, almost a smirk, and she could tell something was coming. Something she wouldn't like. He picked up a newspaper and began lazily scanning the front page.

"When the friend you just saved becomes your lover, will you bring her 'round?"

It was so casual, like a perverted joke, and it struck a nerve. She thought to suppress the rage it triggered, but he needed to understand this was not negotiable.

"That is the second time you have suggested that to me," she said a little too harshly, causing him to collapse the upper section of his paper for a better view. "Now, either you think it's funny and you enjoy watching me get upset, or you are subtly making a suggestion. You said we have an arrangement. I give you what you want, you allow me what I need. If that has strings attached, like bringing my personal life to your bedroom, then I'm here to tell you, that's not going to happen."

Words were flying out of her mouth of their own volition, and she liked what they were saying, so she made no attempt to censure herself. Kowtowing to Forrester was the furthest thing from her mind suddenly, and she found herself fighting for a personal life that wouldn't have been a consideration just a few short weeks ago. The realization was not lost on her, but she had no time to dissect that; she had a rant to finish up.

"I will continue to give you whatever you ask, whenever you ask. But what I do in *my* bedroom, for *my* pleasure, is *my* business."

He stared at her, disbelief playing across his face.

In the deafening silence after her tirade, she wondered if she had just stretched her leash to the limit.

"Have you been taking lessons from my wife?" he asked.

"I mean it, Marcus."

He smiled to show she was still in bounds. "As do I. I stand by our agreement. No strings. You scratch my back ..." He grinned the rest of the tired phrase and turned back to his paper.

Sensing the heat of her glare, he peeked over the corner and chuckled. "It's so very simple. I don't know why you're so serious."

"It's never that simple. Maybe you should spell it out for me, just so there are no misunderstandings."

Forrester put down his paper with a condescending smile, and Kathryn lifted her hand, cutting off what she could tell was going to be another casual remark.

"I'm being straightforward with you, Marc. I only ask the same of you. Up until this point, we had a business arrangement." She was glaring again, she realized, and being, perhaps, a little too demanding on her new relationship. She knew he loved the danger of losing himself in her, but she also knew he needed to be able to wrest a reasonable amount of control back for his own peace of mind. She would open up and leave him to exact his will. He needed to feel helpless but not powerless.

"Last night," she said, as if moved by the memory of his openness, "I thought something had changed. That you ... we ... had changed. That there's something more."

He stilled beside her and looked away. She waited for a response that was too long in coming. He needed a little shove. "My mistake." She tilted her head in disbelief, feigning hurt before succumbing to anger. She made a few brusque movements as she rearranged her silverware. "Fine." She reached for her newspaper. "Status quo, if you like." She picked up the paper and snapped it open. She almost laughed out loud at her horrendous overacting.

Forrester, on the other hand, ate it up, as she knew he would. He reached out with a hesitant hand and laid it on her forearm, hoping the gesture would cause her to lower the paper, along with her guard and anger. She wasn't going to make it that easy for him, though, and she waited until he asked nicely.

"Please?" he asked.

She resisted for a few more seconds—her turn to turn the screw —before lowering her paper and eyeing him with guarded interest.

He smiled his appreciation. "I'm not used to letting people in. It's dangerous in my business."

"You don't trust me?"

"Let me finish, please." He waited, giving her time to pull back her anger and become receptive.

"I do trust you, or you wouldn't be here. The moment I no longer trust you, you will know. In fact, you will be the first to know, and it will be the last thing you know."

"Don't threaten me, Marc; I don't like it."

"Oh, it's not a threat." He waited, making sure his intentions were clear, then he softened. "I apologize. I did not mean to threaten, only inform. Just so there are no misunderstandings, you see."

She smiled. "I asked for that."

He smiled in return, basking in his power and her subservience to it.

"You and I are unique," he said, as he straightened in his chair. "Kindred spirits."

Kathryn nearly physically balked at the comparison.

"We understand each other. You have no need of love from me any more than I do from you."

"I should say not," she said quickly.

"Exactly. See? You are well aware that you are not the only woman, yet you are satisfied to be my favorite, and you are my favorite. You have your playthings, I have mine. Sharing might be fun, but you have made yourself clear, and I respect that. We have had a very successful working relationship. No one reads me like you do or makes me look better." He smiled to her concurring nod. "But you are right. Something has changed." He tried to maintain his businesslike decorum, but Kathryn could see his murderous plan for her had taken its toll. He collected himself and folded his hands across his lap. "I like you, Kathryn. I would miss you. You understand me like no other, and you accept me for who I am. I don't know how you know about my business—"

"I'm not a naïve child," she interrupted. "Do you think I would let you this close to me and not know who I'm dealing with?" She smiled as she said it, hoping he recognized his own words and found the humor in them. He did smile.

"See?" He raised his hand. "Like that. You want to know what's changed? What's changed is that I now consider you a friend. You are not afraid to tell me what you think, and I am not afraid to let you. So that is what is going on, *spelled out,* as you put it."

"So," she said with a smile, "nothing has changed and everything has changed."

He grinned. "No one understands me like you do."

"Thank you, Marc. I will be glad to consider you a friend as well, and I apologize for raising my voice to you."

He nodded, accepting her words as proof that he'd made the right decision. "I'm glad you are no longer afraid of me."

There was just the slightest hint of the lost boy in his eyes again. She tilted her head, pretending that that was the furthest thing from her mind. "I have your word. Why would I be afraid?"

He swallowed, visibly moved. "Thank you for your trust."

"No ..." She took his hand and kissed it, a gesture she knew he would love. "Thank you for yours."

She smiled. Marc Forrester had just sealed his fate.

CHAPTER THIRTY

*J*enny didn't make it five feet into the club before Bobby appeared out of nowhere, blocking her view of Kathryn on stage with the band. It had been a rough morning, and she decided she may as well get it all over with in one day. She wasn't sure Kathryn would see her. "Stay the hell away from me" was a pretty straightforward request, without a lot of room for creative interpretation, but she had to give it a shot, if for no other reason than Kathryn would know she at least made the effort to apologize properly.

"Hi, Bobby. I'm here to see Kat," she said casually, as she attempted to politely brush by the man.

He quickly backpedaled, positioning himself between her and the stage. "I'm sorry, miss," he said, as if he'd never seen her before. "Rehearsals are private."

Jenny stood motionless, her brow furrowed, as she looked up to the stage, where Kathryn pretended not to notice what was going on.

"Please, Bobby."

He looked over his shoulder for direction. Kathryn looked up from some sheet music and tersely shook her head before joining the band around the piano. The band members were unfazed by the whole scene, and Jenny imagined she wasn't the first person to be barred from the club for harassing Kathryn.

"I'm sorry, miss," Bobby said. His tone told her she may have an ally, and she came prepared for the rejection. If Kathryn wouldn't listen to an apology, maybe she would read one. She reached into her coat and pulled out an envelope.

"Would you give this to her? Please?"

Bobby didn't look to the stage; instead, he looked to the side, where a copy of the *Daily Chronicle* was spread out on a table, a hole in the front page where Kathryn's article used to be. "I don't think I can, miss."

"Please, Bobby," Jenny said, seeing the clipped article under a pair of scissors. "There's been a terrible misunderstanding."

Jenny could tell he was struggling with what to do, and after a few indecisive moments, he took the envelope and headed to the stage.

She could see that Kathryn was annoyed when he offered her the note. Instead of taking it, she put her hands on her hips and glared in her direction. Jenny was glad she was so far away, not anxious to see that icy stare up close again. Bobby, to his credit, was doing his best to get her to take the envelope, countering Kathryn's agitated hand motions with reasonable ones of his own. Kathryn finally stopped resisting, with exasperation written on her face.

Jenny pleaded with her eyes as she tilted her head, wearing a pitiful look. Kathryn reacted to the look without hesitation. She snatched the envelope from Bobby's hand and tore it in two before thrusting it back into his midriff.

She had a few harsh words for Bobby to deliver that were barely audible as she pointed angrily toward the door and turned her back without another glance.

Jenny didn't wait for Bobby's return. She slipped silently from the club, feeling worse than when she entered. She was without her new friend, without her job, and at a loss as to what she would do next.

· · ·

Kathryn looked up with feigned disinterest toward the lobby of the club. The entrance doors were still swinging with Jenny's departure, sending blinding flashes of light into the dark interior of the club. She watched Bobby make his way down the aisle, scooping up the discarded front page of the *Daily Chronicle* as he passed it and then depositing it and the halved envelope into the trash bin behind the bar.

Kathryn exhaled a heavy sigh and called a break. She'd had a bad day already. Smitty had given her an earful about the missed meeting and then the third degree for spending the night at Forrester's before admitting that she didn't have a choice. She didn't trust Forrester past his next mood swing, so until she was better able to gauge his new emerging character—the friend—she didn't know how safe anyone was, including herself. *Friend,* she scoffed. Just the thought of it was ludicrous. *Friend.* The intonation softened as she watched the doors slowly wink for the last time.

Jenny had gotten to her and, even worse, poisoned her working persona. It didn't take her long to analyze her outburst about her personal life. Somewhere inside, she still held on to that lovely daydream: a relationship with the plucky young reporter who had used her so cleverly to get herself a story on the front page. It made her furious—furious that she held on to the hope, furious that she had been used, and having let the fury run its course, thoroughly amazed at the audacity of the woman to show up at the club.

She made her way to the bar, popped the top off a bottle of root beer, and flipped it toward the metal collection bucket, only to have it bounce off the side and into the trash bin. It landed on top of Jenny's torn apology. Kathryn sneered at the sight.

She stared into the club's interior, but her eyes were drawn to the trash bin. She fished out the letter, a smirk giving her permission, and pieced it together on the bar so she could read it.

Dearest Kathryn (and I mean that),

If you are reading this note, it's because you have refused to see me. I can't blame you. Sorry cannot convey the pain in my heart at causing you

—I don't even know what I've caused you, but I will say I'm sorry, because it is a place to start.

Why I turned in your gun is just too absurd to explain. To show you how absurd, I did it for you, for us. Never mind. I am a silly girl (didn't you know?).

Please, please, know that I had nothing to do with the article. God—I could strangle Uncle Paul (I almost did!). I tried to get him to retract, but I'm afraid my temper got the better of me (surprised?). I have quit the paper. I think it was a rash decision, but it feels right somehow.

I pray you are safe and no harm will come to you because of this, because of me. I couldn't bear it. I couldn't.

I don't know what else to say. Sorry? Forgive me? (Call me?)

With overflowing regret,

Jenny

Kathryn considered the apology. "She's good," she said, as she let the letter fall from her fingertips back into the garbage can. She looked around the club. "Too good." She fished it back out and put it in her pocket.

She found Bobby taping her article to Dominic's office door as a joke. She smiled, but the jury was still out as to whether Dominic would find it funny.

She held out her hand. "Done with that tape?"

Bobby's eyes dropped to the letter peeking innocently from her pocket and he smiled. "Sure thing, Kat."

She grinned as he passed the dispenser to her.

The next few weeks were uneventful for Kathryn. Forrester was out of town for an extended period, her assignment to Jenny Ryan wrapped up without the need for further contact, thankfully, and even her anger with Jenny had dissipated. She didn't want to admit how many times she'd read the apology note and smiled. She had shifted the blame for the article to Paul, because it was easier than blaming Jenny and easier than blaming herself for letting her gun out of her hands to begin with.

Fortunately, Smitty had handled Paul, ending their working relationship without a confrontation, so she was pleased to just get back to the old routine of OSS duties by day and club duties by night.

Today was Friday, which meant a trip to the city offices of the OSS. Her meetings with brass there always coincided with payday, ensuring that anyone following her would see her go into the bank housed in that same building and assume she was doing business. They wouldn't see her passing through the back of the bank offices to a pair of unattended service elevators that would take her to the floors occupied by the OSS. The red herring had always seemed clichéd to her, but she soon appreciated the ruse when she began to keep Forrester's company and it was assured that he would have someone watching her every move. In retrospect, it was simple compared to what she had to do to slip away unseen to the Long Island training center, but both precautions had become the norm, and she rarely thought about either.

Today's meeting would officially end the Jenny Ryan case. They would review the final report, address any notes, air any comments, and then consign the file to obscurity in a warehouse somewhere. She would never find out what Daniel Ryan was working on or why his files were so important. That information was irrelevant to her and her work, but a lingering affection for her former assignment left her with a reflexive need to know. That had never happened before: the lingering affection or the need to know. One caused the other, she supposed, and she didn't mind the lingering affection. It was foolish and unprofessional, but Jenny sparked something in her that she didn't want extinguished just yet. Forrester would return soon, and his presence would smother wistful thoughts of Jenny and the empathetic need to know, but until then, she would cradle the glowing ember of hope like a child cupping a firefly in awe.

She exited the elevator at the tenth floor and traveled the hallway until she stopped in front of the solid gray door with the number seventy-two painted on it. She entered and smiled at the secretary, who returned the gesture like the proper little travel agent she was pretending to be. More red herrings.

"They're expecting you, Miss Hammond. Go right in." She motioned past the travel posters on the wall to the plain looking door at the back of the small room.

"Thanks, Sal."

Sally looked unusually cheerful, she noticed. Maybe she celebrated the closing of assignments too.

Kathryn made a cursory knock on the door before entering. The room was filled with the usual suspects—the three members of the British Special Operations Executive—Colonel Archibald Holmes, his two aides, Ronald and Brian, and her handler within the OSS, Colonel Walter Forsythe, and his aide, Dennis. Conspicuously absent was Smitty, and conspicuously present was someone new. Sitting at the end of the long table, smiling like the cat that ate the canary, was Jenny Ryan.

CHAPTER THIRTY-ONE

*J*enny couldn't wait. She couldn't wait to see Kathryn Hammond's face when she walked through that door. She wished she had Bernie's camera to capture the moment. It was sure to be priceless—and it was priceless, for all of three seconds.

Kathryn seemed appropriately shocked, but that soon turned into a slow burning stare that reminded Jenny of the day at the paper when her eyes seared with anger and betrayal. Kathryn's lips parted in surprise, but in a split second, it was gone, it was all gone. She looked vaguely to her right and froze, just for a moment, somewhere else. Gathering herself? Deciding how to react? Jenny didn't know. It didn't matter.

With the barest of exhales, followed by a short intake of breath and a cock of her head, Kathryn blinked all the outward negative emotion away, returning to the room with a softer gaze, almost amusement, Jenny noticed, as if surrendering to a force greater than herself.

The British group found her reaction amusing, as did Forsythe's aide, Dennis. Colonel Forsythe was not amused and glared at his aide, who quickly composed himself. Jenny could now see that

Kathryn's expression, while passing for amusement, was anything but. Anger and betrayal danced in her eyes behind the well-practiced veil of her closed lipped smile.

Jenny was no longer pleased with herself. It should have been one of the best days of her life. Sitting at a table with two colonels and their aides was the last thing she expected when she applied to the Office of War Information. The OWI routinely sent guides to the *Daily Chronicle* about how to approach war topics in the media, so it was a job she was already doing, but now she would do it on a larger scale, for her country, instead of a local newspaper. She was shocked when her application was directed to the Office of Strategic Services, an agency she'd never heard of, and she was accepted.

Her second shock came when she found out Kathryn worked there. They said it so casually when she arrived early for the meeting. "Miss Hammond will join us today," they said, as if she should expect such a thing. She was delighted and excited. They would be working together, and she would be able to apologize properly for everything.

Despite how they parted, she hoped Kathryn would be proud of her. She wanted Kathryn to be proud of her, but she looked anything but proud when she walked into the meeting.

The sting of betrayal in her eyes, so quickly replaced with resignation, caused an ache in Jenny's chest. What could have happened to her that she swallowed perceived deception so easily. Ho hum, stabbed in the back again. Another day at the office.

Colonel Holmes made a half-hearted effort to stand while holding one hand out in presentation, like a scarecrow. "Ah, Miss Hammond. Glad you could join us. I believe you know Miss Ryan."

Jenny didn't like the smirk directed at Kathryn when he made the introduction. She sensed some animosity there, and Kathryn did nothing to dispel it when she said, "Yes. Good to see you again, Miss Ryan," without a hint of emotion.

Jenny smiled politely in return. "Miss Hammond."

Kathryn's neutral demeanor was making Jenny nervous. She'd known her only a short time, but she'd seen her angry, and she knew it was under there, just dying to get out. She wondered if anyone else in the room felt it.

"Would you excuse us for a moment please, Miss Ryan?" Colonel Holmes offered sweetly. "Just wait in the outer office. Miss Hammond will show you about when we're finished here. Won't be long."

"Certainly."

"Thank you."

Jenny gathered the papers in front of her and tucked them neatly into her folder as she stood to leave. Kathryn waited for her to choose a path around the table to the door and then purposely went in the other direction. In fact, Jenny noticed, except for the initial introduction, she was pretending she wasn't there at all. Terrific.

Jenny left the office and leaned against the outer door with an exhale.

"You all right?" Sally asked, as she finished installing a new wire spool in her stapler.

"I think my first day has made a bad impression on our tall friend."

Sally's amused snort was lost in the clattering of gathered papers as she tapped them on the desk.

Jenny eyed the secretary curiously. "This is the part where you say, 'Don't worry about it, Miss Ryan. We all have first days.'"

The secretary raised an eyebrow, and like the parrot in the poster advertising the unspoiled beauty of Rio de Janeiro behind her, she said, "Don't worry about it, Miss Ryan. We all have first days."

Jenny smirked a *thanks for nothing* and headed for a seat against the wall.

Sally gave her a smile as she prepared to staple the stack of papers in her hand. "Honestly, you'll be fine. She doesn't bite." Staple. "Hard."

Jenny rolled her eyes with a groan and sank into her seat. Really terrific.

.   .   .

Kathryn made her way to the only empty chair available, Jenny's former seat at the head of the table. Her unique scent still hung in the air, a welcome break from the smells of testosterone, floor wax, and cigarettes that usually pervaded these meetings. Even as notions of betrayal swirled in her head, Jenny's scent propelled her momentarily away from her anger to a quiet breakfast, bathed in sunlight, and that precious spark of hope.

"Thank you for joining us, Miss Hammond," Colonel Holmes said again. He was no longer smiling. In fact, as soon as Jenny left the room, the atmosphere shifted dramatically.

His tone wasn't sarcastic, nor was it welcoming, and Kathryn eyed him warily. It was the first meeting with the British group since the near disastrous run-in with the police in the weeks before. She tried to judge the mood by the only person in the room she could read consistently, but Colonel Forsythe had his game face on today, and she was forced to sit in castigated silence, as the uniformed men did final once-overs through the papers in front of them.

Her animus toward the British contingent continued when they tapped her to show Jenny Ryan around. She never could seem to find a happy medium with them. Maybe it was the way Colonel Holmes never quite looked her in the eye. Maybe it was the way his aides never stopped looking. Maybe it was just her imagination that they didn't trust her, or maybe they were simply reacting to the fact that she didn't trust them. Whatever it was, she could only wonder when her infamous apathy had morphed into perpetual anger. She was in a bad mood all the time now, and she worried that she was finally losing her grip and that her renewed loss of control was just the beginning of the fall.

"We have gone over your reports regarding the Ryan case and the Forrester incident," Holmes began, "and despite possible disaster, it seems you have landed on your feet." He scanned a piece of paper in his hand before proclaiming what seemed to her an accusation. "Again."

She wondered what particular incident in her long line of incidents he was referring to as he perused her file.

"We are pleased to inform you that your assignment to Jenny Ryan has officially been put to rest. Your assignment to Forrester is status quo."

At least brass still had some faith in her. She would take her victories where she could find them.

"We are very satisfied with the results of your efforts in the Ryan case, Miss Hammond. Well done." Colonel Holmes seemed sincere for one brief second, as he and his aides began gathering their papers. "However," he said, about to undue his good deed, "one day, you will run out of luck, and your poor judgment will cost those around you dearly."

He glared at her, and if he said *again* one more time, Kathryn thought she might leap across the table and ring his thick neck. He needn't say the word; his implication was clear.

"I believe we're finished here for today."

"Colonel Holmes," Kathryn began in a deceptively sweet tone that rightly signaled confrontation to her supervisor. Colonel Forsythe clasped his hands on the table and nudged her with his elbow in an unmistakable warning. He had never done that before, just as she had never come so close to telling a superior to kiss her ass, but she understood his meaning, and her response was immediate compliance. She dragged her lips across her gritted teeth in a cordial grin. "Have a great day."

Colonel Holmes nodded as he stood up. "Miss Hammond, always a pleasure." His tone confirmed that it had been anything but pleasurable for either of them. As the British group shuffled out, Holmes's aide, Brian, offered a sympathetic smile as an apology for his boss's attitude.

Kathryn watched them until the last back disappeared from view and the door shut. She only had one thing on her mind. "What is Jenny Ryan doing here, Colonel?"

Colonel Forsythe dismissed his aide. "That'll be all, Dennis."

"Sir," he said, as he obediently packed his briefcase and then quietly left the room.

Colonel Forsythe waited until the door clicked closed again. "You weren't going to antagonize our British friends, were you?" he asked with a scolding grin as he sifted through some papers before him.

Kathryn sat back, releasing the tension in her shoulders. "They don't think much of me."

"Actually, they requested you specifically for this case."

That was a surprise. "Why would they do that?"

"Because you get the job done, Kathryn. Always."

"I hardly did anything. This was a cakewalk. The files were right there for the asking. Anyone could have done that."

"But they didn't. You did."

She wasn't sure whether his remark meant that others had tried and failed or hers was the first and only attempt.

"Holmes's remark was uncalled for," he said, as he gathered papers. "I'm sure you're aware of that."

"Why didn't you tell me they requested me?"

He smiled into his paperwork without looking up. That told her she was entering the ubiquitous "classified information" zone.

She couldn't shake the uneasy feeling about Holmes. It could just be prior history clouding her impression, but the acrimony between them was palpable. "Do you trust Holmes?"

"You don't like him."

"No, I don't. Do you?"

"His credentials are impeccable. Holmes is as arrogant as they come, but that's not the same as not trusting him, and I don't have to like him, just work with him."

"So you trust him."

"He wouldn't be two steps into this building if he weren't trusted."

"Of course." It was silly to think otherwise. She rubbed her forehead, trying to put Holmes and his attitude out of her mind.

"Are you all right, Kathryn? You seem ... stressed lately."

She waved him off. "I'm fine."

"Maybe it was too much, having you juggle assignments."

Her eyes snapped to his. The suggestion that she was not up to her job was a precursor to dismissal, and the thought of that, of being unable to pay her debt, was absolutely unacceptable.

"I'm not falling apart," she said before he did.

He reacted by lifting his hands. "I didn't say you were." He waited a beat before continuing. "Sometimes things get out of hand, more than we bargained for."

"Don't do that to me," she said. "Not you. Don't patronize me."

"And don't try to tell me you're fine when, obviously, you're not."

She exhaled and studied a worn spot on the corner of his leather briefcase before turning to face him. "I'm fine. Really."

"Then?"

"Just ..." She paused, not sure whether revealing her paranoia was a good idea. There was only one way to alleviate it though. Colonel Forsythe would tell her the truth and understand her concern. "Please tell me this wasn't a test."

"Jenny Ryan?"

His tone made her sound like a crazy person for asking, and Kathryn regretted the question.

"I wouldn't do that to you, Kathryn. I'm sorry you don't know that by now. If I've got a problem with your performance, I'll address it with you face to face, just like I'm doing now."

She nodded. He could have only one complaint about her performance. "The gun. The arrest."

Colonel Forsythe hadn't questioned the arrest. He merely asked for an explanation and seemed satisfied with her answer. The mistake nearly cost her everything, including her life. The agency would have lost months of undercover work. A reprimand was the least she deserved.

"The gun?" he asked. "No. A brilliant gamble, that. You know how much you mean to Forrester. You just brought us closer to the inside."

He said it as if she'd done it on purpose. Before she could protest, he went on. "I'm talking about your relationship with Forrester. Your report indicated significant movement in your personal relationship. He comes back next week. How far are you willing to go with him?"

She didn't know why he was asking. "I'll do whatever it takes. You know that."

"That's not what I asked."

"I don't have a problem with any aspect of my assignment to Forrester."

He stared at her for a beat. "You're an extraordinary woman, Kathryn."

She stopped short of shaking her head. Acting like a whore was old hat and nothing that should garner admiration.

"We all do what we have to do, sir. I'm no different."

"I think I speak for everyone here when I say your efforts do not go unnoticed, or unappreciated."

Out of respect she said, "Thank you."

"Now then ..." He motioned vaguely at her uncharacteristic attitude. "What's all this about?"

You did not play coy with Col. Walter Forsythe. He treated her like a daughter, but when push came to shove, the security of the country came first, and to that end, it was his job to know his agents. Any sense of deliberate deception or roundabout fudging of details would find you busted to desk jockey or out altogether. She had never lied to him, and she wasn't going to start now.

"There was nothing brilliant about turning over my gun to Jenny Ryan. It was stupid."

"You were worried about the safety of your assignment."

Kathryn wasn't about to admit she was worried about the woman, not the assignment. "Which landed me in the police station under suspicion of murder."

"Which brought you closer to Forrester and possibly the break we need." He paused. "Brilliant."

He didn't understand. It caused Jenny to quit her job, and, somehow, by some cruel twist of fate, it brought her straight to the very life she was trying to shield her from.

"I'm more concerned with results than intent right now," Colonel Forsythe said. "It worked out." He began putting files into his briefcase.

"Don't you want to say, *this time*?" Kathryn asked, wondering if he shared Colonel Holmes's skepticism about her suitability.

She didn't expect him to be insulted, but he raised his eyes to hers and pointed to a thick folder bearing her name. "You've got a folder full of *this times*. It's called instinct, and like it or not, you've got it, and it hasn't let us down yet, has it?"

She liked the way he said *us*. It made her feel like part of something, like she belonged. It felt good.

"Anything else on your mind?"

Just one thing. "Explain to me why Jenny Ryan is here. I got your files, I got her away from Forrester, I got Forrester away from her—she was free to live a normal life. What is she doing here?"

"She came to us."

"How?" She paused. "Never mind." She paused again, about to step way out of line. She couldn't stop herself. "I don't want her here, sir."

"Care to elaborate?"

"I don't want her in the organization. She's too ... young," she said instead of innocent, "and too hotheaded," she said instead of determined.

"I see," Colonel Forsythe said. "I remember another young lady that was too young and too hotheaded."

"And look where that got me."

Kathryn watched Colonel Forsythe absorb the memories and swallow the regret, even as he recognized something behind her concern.

"How long has this been going on?"

"There's nothing going on. She's just a bad choice."

"On the contrary." He lifted her folder. "She's an exceptional candidate. We're lucky to have her."

Kathryn knew she was going from out of line to out of bounds, but this was Jenny's future. Her beautiful life was in jeopardy. "I don't want her out there. It's too dangerous."

Colonel Forsythe nodded slowly, and Kathryn was afraid she'd gone too far.

"I understand how you feel," he said. "I don't want anyone out there. I don't want you out there, but this is the world we live in. For now, she's behind a desk, producing false news stories, that's it. She's not going in the field."

"For now."

"I'm not going to promise you something I can't deliver, Kathryn." He flipped through a few pages in the folder. "You're right, though; she appears to lack the discipline for the field, but her creative mind will serve us well in MO."

He was right. Morale Operations was perfect for Jenny's vivid imagination, but it was no guarantee she would stay there. Guilt gnawed at her. Her mistake brought Jenny here. Colonel Forsythe could call it instinct if it made him feel better, but she knew the truth. She could only claim temporary insanity for letting her gun out of her hands. That's what she told herself. She didn't want to remember how Jenny muted the darkness in her soul and brought a glimmer of hope to her life, or how she would do anything to protect her, including pushing boundaries with her superiors. Seeing Jenny at headquarters was a shock, and she was angry, but now she was scared.

"I can appreciate that you're worried for Miss Ryan. It's only natural. But you don't have to protect her anymore. That's our job now."

That didn't put her mind at ease, which didn't go unnoticed.

"Tell you what," Colonel Forsythe said, "I'll oversee her performance myself."

Kathryn raised her eyes. That wasn't enough, but it was all she would get, and it was better than nothing.

He held up a hand. "That's not a blanket of protection. Only a promise that she won't be doing anything she's not ready for."

Colonel Forsythe had looked out for her when she first started working for the OSS and defended her when no one else would. She knew he would look out for Jenny too.

"I couldn't ask for anything more, sir. Thank you."

She exhaled a silent sigh of relief. Jenny no longer needed her protection. She would leave her behind after today, in the hands of good men and women who would soon become like a family to her.

The notion should have given her comfort but, instead, it made her feel empty—she'd lost something. A connection was severed and she felt it physically as a hollow ache in her chest.

Jenny's case was closed. Kathryn would get her checked in and oriented today, and then her new life as an employee of the OSS would start.

With their meeting wrapped for the day, Colonel Forsythe packed his briefcase while Kathryn made her way to the door.

"Hammond," Colonel Forsythe said as she reached for the doorknob.

She immediately stiffened and turned. "Sir?"

"If I thought for one second that you were falling apart ... you wouldn't be here."

She raised her chin with pride. She didn't realize how much his approval meant to her. He still had faith in her. He always had faith in her. If it weren't so inappropriate, she would have hugged him.

In the meantime, a heartfelt "Thank you," would have to do.

He smiled. "G'wan, get out of here. Stop worrying. We're going to turn that kid into something special."

Kathryn nodded. Jenny was already something special to her. The thought brought a wistful smile as she opened the door, but she quickly remembered it was that kind of thinking that made her lose her mind in the first place. The dull ache of loss hit her again and was accompanied by the vision of her charge for the day, as Jenny jumped out of her chair and straightened her skirt. She looked every bit the professional in her tweed suit with the broad shoulder pads and pale green shirt. She belonged at the *Daily Chronicle*. Kathryn wanted to tell Jenny she was sorry her beautiful life was on hold, but Jenny looked so proud and happy to be there that she decided strictly business was the best, and safest, approach for their final hours together.

"Ready?" she asked.

"More than," Jenny said with a smile. "Good talking with you, Sally."

Kathryn held the door open and addressed the secretary as Jenny passed by.

"Thanks for that warning, Sal," she said sarcastically.

"Gotta keep you on your toes, Hammond."

"Hmph," Kathryn grunted with a smirk.

The elevator glided past the twentieth floor on the way to the twenty-sixth, and Jenny didn't dare say anything to Kathryn. Her jaw was set in irritation, and she'd exhaled impatiently twice already since they'd entered the elevator. She obviously didn't want to speak to her unless it was absolutely necessary, so Jenny hugged her folder and stared at the wood paneling on the side wall, suppressing an impatient exhale of her own.

As they approached the twenty-sixth floor, Kathryn shifted and straightened. "Were you issued a badge?"

Jenny fished it out of her suit pocket. "Right here."

"Put it on. They won't let you on the floor without it." She hung her own around her neck. "OSS regulation: Your badge is to be worn at all times when you're in this section of the building, understand?"

Jenny wanted to roll her eyes at Kathryn's stern instructions, but she resisted. "Yes."

The doors opened and they approached the guard on duty. Kathryn offered her badge to a nod of recognition, but Jenny's badge was hidden by the folder clutched to her chest. "Do you have your badge, ma'am?"

She moved the folder. "Sorry, yes, Corporal Davis."

He seemed startled that she'd noticed his rank and name tag and smiled before checking the badge and making sure everything was in order.

"Thank you, Miss Ryan. Welcome."

She smiled as she passed, which he returned.

"Thanks, Davis," she heard Kathryn say, and he responded with a terse, "Ma'am," that had no pleasantry attached to it.

Kathryn began the tour in textbook monotone. "You'll find various offices on this floor, none of which you need to concern yourself about. You'll be working here temporarily while a ruptured pipe is repaired in the Morale Operations offices a few blocks away, off Times Square. It will be referred to as MO from this point on. We love initials up here."

That should have been funny, Jenny noted, but Kathryn said it in such a serious, bored manner that you'd think she had no personality whatsoever, and she knew that wasn't true. Or maybe it was. Jenny had no idea who this woman truly was.

Colonel Forsythe didn't mention any details, but Kathryn's connection to Forrester made perfect sense now. Her admonition of *there's a lot you don't know about me* seemed like the understatement of the century. Or did she say *there's a lot not to like?* Looking at her tense back as she made purposeful strides down the hallway, Jenny was pretty sure it was the latter.

Kathryn rambled off a litany of departments, names, and descriptions that she would interact with while doing her work in MO, and Jenny's brain was having as hard a time as her legs were keeping up with her impatient tour guide.

"There's the Counterintelligence Branch ..."

Jenny wrote it down in her notebook.

"Also referred to as X-2. Don't ask me why it's not CB." She vaguely motioned to the right. "This is a small satellite of Research and Analysis. Through those doors you'll find the R&A library, a fascinating collection of ..." Jenny was scribbling furiously in her notebook and didn't realize Kathryn had stopped walking and talking until she was standing over her with an amused grin on her face.

"Are you getting all this?" she asked.

Jenny did a double take. Finally, a smile. "Yes, I think so." She relaxed and finished scribbling *Research and Analysis,* though it was fairly illegible.

Kathryn held out a hand. "May I?"

Jenny handed her the notebook.

Kathryn flipped back a few pages and ripped out the last two with a violent flick of her wrist before crumpling the notes in her fist.

"Remember it in your head or don't remember it all." She thrust the neutered notebook into Jenny's hands. "Understand?"

Jenny was speechless.

Kathryn turned on her heel and continued her whirlwind tour, slowing briefly to toss the balled-up notebook pages into an incinerator chute in the wall.

Jenny caught up. "Are you still angry with me?" she asked, though the answer was obvious.

"Why on earth would I be angry with you?"

"That's what I'm wondering." Jenny tried to get ahead so that she could see Kathryn's face. "I apologized about the gun." She quickened her step, cursing the skirt that prevented her from keeping up with Kathryn's long slacks-encased strides. "Forrester seems to have gotten over it. Why haven't you?"

"Oh, yes," Kathryn said over her shoulder, as Jenny fell behind again. "He got over it. In fact, I think it brought us closer together, so thank you for that; it's just what I've always dreamed of." She picked up her already harried pace. "So, I've no reason whatever to be mad at you, have I?" She stopped and extended her hand. "And here we are, the temporary offices of Morale Operations."

Jenny came to a halt at the doorway. "Then stop being a first-rate bitch to me. At least pretend to be a professional. I *know* you can do *that*."

Kathryn stopped in her tracks, stunned, as Jenny pushed past her and into the office. *Pretend* to be a professional? Who the hell did Jenny Ryan think she was? She shook her head and followed her into the office.

"Hi," Jenny said, sticking her hand out to the secretary on duty. "I'm Jenny Ryan." She handed her folder over. "I think I live here now."

The secretary smiled. "Ah, you understand the requirements already. It's been crazy around here today. I'm afraid we haven't had time to set you up a desk." She stuck her head up, trying to see above the sea of busy heads. "I don't know whether I can spare the personnel to show you the ropes today." She looked to Kathryn. "But

I see you're in capable hands already." She folded her hands across the newly acquired file. "Welcome."

Jenny smiled. "Thank you, but I'm afraid Miss Hammond was just my escort up here. I'm sure she's just too horribly busy and important to babysit me all day."

The secretary raised a brow at Jenny's comment and then lifted her eyes to Kathryn with a grin. "Well, Miss Hammond, your reputation precedes you."

Kathryn sneered affectionately. "Nonsense. Come on, Jenny." She laid her hand on Jenny's shoulder, but it disappeared from under her hand, and Jenny was a dozen steps into the busy office before Kathryn made another move.

The secretary smiled. "Got a live one there, Hammond."

"You have no idea."

Kathryn stayed back and watched Jenny blend seamlessly into the buzzing office with a natural grace it took her years to cultivate. She marveled at her ability to befriend a perfect stranger.

The contrast in styles made Kathryn feel more closed off than ever. Sex as a weapon, seduction her charm; that's how she made "friends." She shook her head. She didn't make friends, she made acquaintances. People like Jenny made friends.

Kathryn could count on one hand the number of people she considered friends, but even they only knew what she showed them, and she wouldn't wish her true self on any of them, which made her think of Smitty. He knew her best of all, the length of their relationship assuring him of every ugly detail of her existence. That he loved her anyway was one of the great mysteries of her life.

She looked around the room at the busy workers, her colleagues. They all had a piteous smile and a nod or a wave when they saw her. "Oh, there's the one who screwed up and lived to tell about it," she imagined them saying. She'd raise her chin in acknowledgment, her fake smile easing their compassionate minds before they quickly turned away. It was times like this that she longed for Smitty's company. He didn't treat her with kid gloves. He told her exactly what he thought and didn't flinch doing it. He was a welcome change to these people, who politely listened and nodded in agreement with a look in their eyes like they dare not disagree for fear she'd fall off the deep end at any moment.

She was sick of that look, and she was glad the bulk of her agency time was spent out at the training center, where fresh-faced recruits were too busy trying to learn to survive to think much of anything about who was training them.

"Looks like Jenny Ryan has a friend," the secretary said to her back. "Jason's an ex-reporter from the *Daily Chronicle*."

Kathryn turned to see the secretary tossing her head in the direction of a loud whoop, as Jenny was picked up off her feet by an exuberant young man.

"Jason!" She heard Jenny say as she slapped his arm.

The man put her down. "Wow, kiddo! I can't believe it! What are you doing here? Don't tell me your uncle let you go?"

"Nope. I quit."

"You didn't!"

She held up her hand in an oath. "Swear to Howard."

The two women watched the boisterous reunion, as did most of the office, before getting back to the business of winning a war.

"Who's Howard?" the secretary asked Kathryn, who responded with a disinterested shrug.

"Wooo," Jason said, lowering his voice. "Good for us." He looked over to where Kathryn had crossed her arms and settled onto the edge of the secretary's desk. "Hey!" He waved and was met with the customary raised chin and close-lipped smile. "I see you've met Kat."

"Yeah," Jenny drew out as she scratched her cheek. "You might say that." She shook her head and thumbed in her direction. "I'm afraid she's annoyed with me at the moment."

He laughed and shook his head. "Here five minutes and in trouble already."

Jenny raised her hand in defeat. "Some things never change."

Jason put his arm around her shoulder and briefly glanced at

Kathryn, silently asking permission to take over the tour. He got another raised chin and the briefest of smiles.

"You pick her brain if you ever get back into her good graces," he said. "She's one of the best we've got around here."

Kathryn watched the two of them disappear into the crowded office, just knowing what that exchange was about. *God, that Kathryn is a bitch,* Jenny probably said. *Yeah, well,* Jason would agree, *she's got issues. Steer clear of that one.* Good advice, Kathryn decided. Smart man.

"Holy smokes," the secretary said, as she flipped through Jenny's file. "Did you see her security level? Right out of the gate." She held up the file, pointing to the appropriate line. "Do you know how long it took me to get to that level?"

Kathryn glanced at the file, noted the level, and then scanned the room to find the blonde head to connect it to. She was gone, lost in the controlled chaos. She looked at the level again. It was high, but not unheard of. She supposed the investigation had gotten Jenny a more thorough background check than most, earning her more than just the basic entry-level clearance.

The secretary wasn't done nosing through the file. "Did you see this pedigree? Private schools, summers abroad ..." She shook her head. "No wonder they call this place Oh So Snobby. Jiminy. Arms training, foreign languages, HAM radio experience ..." She flipped a page. "Did you know she can differentiate the different types of aircraft just by the sound?" She looked up in disbelief, trying to find the prodigy in the crowd. "This kid is Director Donovan's dream!"

"Isn't that file supposed to be private?" Kathryn complained, not wanting to hear how well Jenny fit into the OSS profile.

"I've got clearance." The secretary held up her ID tag with a smile. "Do you?"

Kathryn smirked, as curiosity and a slight tinge of panic got the better of her. "Give me that."

The secretary turned the file over gladly, knowing Kathryn had far more clearance than she ever would.

"Do you know her well?" Jenny asked Jason between introductions, as they walked through the office.

"Who?"

Jenny smiled at herself for thinking that everyone had Kathryn on their mind. "Kathryn Hammond."

"Oh, Hammond. Does anyone really know Hammond?"

"I thought I did." Jenny paused. "Well, I thought I was starting to, anyway."

"Well, you're one up on the rest of us then."

"That bad, eh?"

"No, just ... well ..."

Jenny leaned in. "Just?"

"She kind of keeps to herself, which is understandable. She's had it rough, that's all. She's a great gal, really. I'm sure."

"What do you mean by *rough*?"

His eyes drifted to the ID badge around her neck, and she followed them. He smiled. "Nice picture," he said, but she knew he was checking her clearance level.

"You know, I don't know any details, just that the Gerrys had her for a while, and she managed to come home in one piece." He paused. "More or less."

His statement felt like a physical blow. Held by the Germans. "God."

"Yeah," he said. "She's not up here much anymore, and she was never in MO; she spent some time in R&A, but when you're a legend ...word gets around."

Legend. That didn't sound good.

"And that Forrester business, cripes." He rolled his eyes and turned. "Did you leave the *Chronicle* before or after *the article*?"

"I left because of that article."

He raised an impressed brow. "Good girl. Their loss. How friggin' irresponsible."

Jenny resisted the urge to defend her uncle even though she knew he was wrong.

"She could have been killed for less," Jason said. "Woman's got more lives than a cat." He nudged Jenny in the arm. "Cat ... Kat. Get it?"

Jenny smiled, but the humor was wasted on her. She couldn't get past the knowledge that Kathryn had been in Nazi hands. The thought sickened her. She didn't even want to imagine what they'd done to her. Her empathy threatened to overwhelm her, and she scanned the room to focus on something else.

"How the hell her gun wound up in the hands of the police, I'll never know," Jason went on. "She's famous for her paranoia." He paused and smiled sheepishly. "I mean attention to detail. But I guess stuff happens."

Jenny cringed silently.

"All I know is that brass thinks she walks on water, and she's done some great work here, and that's good enough for me. This is Sparky ..." The introductions went on, and Jenny found she was distracted by the newfound respect for her friend, if she could still call her that, and she hoped she could. The first thing she would do is apologize and try to start over. Again.

Kathryn read Jenny's file with interest. No details followed the ticked boxes on the form that listed skills and experience. Jenny certainly was the perfect candidate for the organization, no doubt about it. She shook her head. With those skills, she wouldn't stay in MO long. It was only a matter of time before she would be stationed overseas, doing God knows what, and all of it dangerous. She closed her eyes and tried to clear her head of the possibilities. There was no sense dwelling on how she got here, and there was no reason to take out her frustration on the woman.

She couldn't believe how uncomfortable it was to be in her presence when they stepped into the elevator. She didn't know what to say. Oh, I'm sorry. Didn't I mention that I'm a spy? Welcome to the great big world of deception, Jenny Ryan. Soon, you'll be deceiving your family, your friends, even yourself, in order to do what you need to do. She hated the thought of Jenny in that position. At this point, all she could do was exhale in disbelief at her failure to keep Jenny away from it all.

And poor Jenny, standing uncharacteristically silent beside her while she clutched her folder to her chest like a shield against the unwarranted hostility.

It was time to deal with the here and now, and the here and now would include securing her selfish behavior and fashioning a well-deserved apology. She looked up to see the object of her contrition saying her goodbyes to several of the workers in the office. She'd made a bevy of friends already, and Kathryn felt a strange sense of pride because of it.

She smiled as she approached. "Ready?"

"Yeah," Jenny said softly.

Kathryn noticed something had changed, and her casual smile and resolve faded. Jenny had that piteous look in her eyes, and she scanned the room for Jason, knowing he put it there. In that moment, she realized it was one of the things that she liked about Jenny—she had been absent that look and the walking on eggshells attitude that went with it. Any respite from her anger evaporated as she exhaled and walked out of the office. "Come on."

For a moment, Jenny thought Kathryn was going to be civil to her, but no. Her terse comment and stiff body language continued their adversarial relationship. She was starting to feel less empathetic and more annoyed.

She followed Kathryn silently down the busy hallway, smiling and nodding to all she passed as her ID badge danced gleefully from around her neck with each stride. She was an official member of the OSS, and she was damn well going to savor her first day, despite

Kathryn's grumpy ass. Her eyes drifted to the body part in question. Perfection.

As they exited the main door, Jenny smiled at the guard stationed there. "Have a great day, Corporal Davis."

"Thank you, ma'am. You do the same." He looked at Kathryn, who had punched the down button on the elevator call panel. "Ma'am," he nodded.

Kathryn punched the button again. "Davis."

The elevator finally arrived and the doors opened. Jenny dutifully followed Kathryn inside and faced forward. Kathryn chose the ground floor on the control panel and stared straight ahead, as if she were alone in the elevator. The motor and ropes began their work, and Jenny was glad for the whirring hum, because the silence in the small space was crushing.

Kathryn spent the short walk to the elevator kicking herself for taking out her frustrations on Jenny again. None of this was her fault. This was a proud day for Jenny, as it would be for anyone joining the fight to save the world. Jenny was right to chastise her, and she wasn't sure how to get herself out of the corner she'd painted herself into. She wasn't good at apologies, but she wouldn't see Jenny Ryan again, and she didn't want today to be the last impression she had of her. She gathered her nerve, swallowed her pride, and released a calming exhale before attempting her apology.

Jenny snapped her head in the direction of the exhale, and Kathryn realized it was one exhale too many.

"All right," Jenny said, as she reached in front of her and mashed the stop button on the elevator.

"Hey!" Kathryn said, as she reflexively reached for the start button.

Jenny positioned herself in front of the panel, causing Kathryn's hand to wind up on her hip. Her hand stayed there for a shocked moment, but then she withdrew it.

Kathryn regained her composure. "What are you doing?"

"I'd like to ask you the same question, Kathryn."

Kathryn was shocked to hear her name used with such venom. She missed the casual ease they'd had before what was quickly becoming known as "The Gun Incident."

She crossed her arms. "I'm just trying to do my job, Jenny."

"That's BS, Kathryn, and you know it. You don't have to be so ugly to me. I made a mistake. I admit it. Okay? I apologized, even though you didn't have the grace to read it. You are being an absolute bitch to me, and I don't think I deserve it."

Kathryn agreed, but that was not what came out of her mouth. "Fine."

"Fine?" Jenny said. "Fine? That's it?"

"Fine," Kathryn repeated, recognizing that her apology skills were even worse than she thought.

Jenny pursed her lips in a disgusted scowl, and Kathryn lamented that this last impression was only getting worse. Obviously, she didn't possess the gift required to restore civility, and the sooner this elevator ride was over, the better. She began tapping her forefinger on her crossed arms and alternated glares from Jenny's face to the start button, hidden behind her hip. She narrowed her eyes, and that finally did it.

"Fine," Jenny said, as she moved and slapped the start button. She took her place at Kathryn's side with an exhale, crossing her arms in frustration.

Kathryn wanted to grin at the mirrored postures, but there was nothing funny about it. Jenny shifted in quirky movements, and Kathryn knew she wasn't done letting off steam. She finally exploded in a blur of movement, slapping the stop button again.

"Ugh," Kathryn said with an eye roll, dramatically shifting her weight to one leg. "What now?"

"Look," Jenny said, turning but making no effort this time to block the control panel with her body. "If we're going to be working together, then we can at least—"

"Oh, we're not working together," Kathryn interrupted matter-of-factly. "I showed you around *today*. That's it. From now on, you're someone else's—"

"Problem? Headache?"

"Responsibility."

"I'm not a child, Kathryn. No one has to—"

"Reel it in, Jenny," Kathryn said, as she uncrossed her arms and turned. "I meant that you will be under *someone* here, but that someone is not going to be *me*."

Jenny blinked at her in surprise. Kathryn realized the visual she'd supplied and cringed internally. Jenny got over it quickly.

"This is juvenile. I don't know where we went off the rails, but—"

"I think it was when you thought I was a murderer and turned my gun over to the police."

Jenny was silent, and Kathryn made sure her intense stare was enough to get the car moving again.

"May I?" She pointed at the start button.

"Fine," Jenny said, as she put her hands on her hips and found something interesting on her shoe.

"Fine," Kathryn said, as she started the elevator on its decent.

They passed the fourth floor, and Kathryn could almost taste the relief of the opening doors. Once swallowed into the flow of the city, thousands would absorb her discomfort, rendering it moot. Jenny, however, had more to say. She pressed the stop button again.

"I want to say, for the record—"

Their world suddenly felt like gravity times two for a brief second, as the elevator came to a screeching, jarring halt. Kathryn swore it sounded like a rope snapped. They were stopped, but who knew for how long, as she imagined the car hanging by a few thin frayed wires.

She braced herself against the walls for balance, waiting for the strength in her legs to return, and noticed Jenny doing the same. They both instinctively looked up, and then at each other, with the same apprehensive stare. Neither moved as they listened for any clue as to their fates. It was silent, and the car felt sturdy, so they both straightened and relaxed, confident they weren't going to freefall to their deaths from somewhere between the third and fourth floors. They both eyed the control panel, and Kathryn wondered if she dare try the start button. She looked to Jenny, who responded with a *what else is there to do* shrug. She swallowed and pressed it. Nothing. She pressed it again. Nothing. Stop. Start. Floor number. Nothing.

"No, no, no," Kathryn said to the ceiling. She slammed her palm against the wall. "Dammit. We're stuck."

"What do you mean *stuck?*"

Kathryn turned impatiently. "What part of *stuck* is confusing you?"

It was a mistake. Jenny had reached her limit. "I suppose you're going to blame me for this too!"

"Have I blamed you for *anything?*" Kathryn said with a glare. "Honestly, with that chip on your shoulder, it's a wonder there's any room for your head."

"Good," Jenny said with an outstretched hand. "Go ahead, yell. At least you're speaking, and while you're at it, maybe you can save your self-righteous attitude for someone who's intimidated by it."

Kathryn turned, ready for a fight. *Self ...* she stopped just short of voicing the repetitive indignation and wound up saying, "I'll try to remember that." She inwardly rolled her eyes at her lame response. She wished she'd gone with the repetitive indignation.

"You know," Jenny said, "*you're* the one who misled *me!*" She pointed to herself. "*I* should be the one who's angry."

Kathryn looked at the wall and let out another one of those ominous exhales. Shouting at each other—this was getting out of hand. She cursed her obstinate nature, pushed off the wall, and stood against the rear of the elevator before slowly sliding down the dark oak paneling and settling at the bottom, where she casually stretched her long legs before her.

Jenny stared at her, and when she didn't respond, their situation became clear. "We're going to be here a while." It wasn't a question.

"Yep."

Jenny looked at the ceiling. "This has happened before?"

"Yep."

"You?"

"No, but a group was trapped in here a few weeks ago. For what they paid for these newfangled marvels, this shouldn't happen."

"How long?"

"Three days."

Jenny's eyes went round. "You're not serious."

Kathryn smiled as she leaned her head against the back wall. "No. Three hours. But if you've ever been trapped in close quarters with Anne Greer, it'll seem like days instead of hours. Pure torture." She put her hands over her ears to block out the imaginary incessant talking.

Jenny settled next to Kathryn on the floor, where she stretched out her legs and crossed them at her ankles. "You scared me for a minute."

They were silent for a few moments. Kathryn stared at the useless control panel and took advantage of her last chance to square things with Jenny before they set on their separate paths in life.

"I don't want to yell at you, and I'm not angry with you," she said. "I'm sorry I misled you. I didn't like it, but, obviously, I had no choice."

"I know," Jenny said. "I'm sorry for what I said, and I'm sorry about the gun. I ..."

Kathryn waited for the explanation, but in the end, Jenny merely said, "I have a vivid imagination?"

Kathryn grinned. She had let go of her anger and disappointment over the gun incident long ago. "Yes, you do." Jenny's grace in contrition made it easy to let go of her cantankerous mood, too, and even made way for some well-deserved encouragement. "You'll do well here."

Jenny picked at the seam of her skirt and looked up shyly from under her brow. "Thank you. Your opinion means a lot to me. I'll try not to let you down."

"Just worry about letting yourself down," Kathryn said. "My opinion means jack."

"Not to me."

Kathryn didn't know what to say. She felt that warm feeling in her heart and gut again, the one that made her feel that taking Jenny in her arms was a perfectly natural response while in her proximity. She let the comment slide.

After a few more silent moments, Jenny said, "Should I push the alarm button?"

Kathryn looked at the red button in question. "Not unless you want the alarm ringing continually until they get us out of here."

"No thanks."

"Don't worry. They know we're here."

Almost on cue, they heard voices assuring them that they'd have them out in a jiffy.

"Exactly how long is a jiffy anyway?" Jenny asked.

"Faster than two shakes of a lamb's tail, I hope," Kathryn said. She was relieved that the tension was easing, but she knew amends were never that easy, and she hadn't even started hers. She wasn't sure where to begin, but she supposed an admonition would start things off nicely.

"Listen, Jenny ..." She spoke softly, hoping she'd recognize it for the white flag that it was. "About the gun ..."

Jenny shifted toward her, about to speak in earnest. Kathryn held up her hand to silence her. "My turn."

Jenny relaxed into the wall again.

"I'll admit to being angry—"

"That's an understatement," Jenny said and then looked up at the sudden silence. "Sorry."

Kathryn responded with a self-effacing grin before beginning again. "I was angry, and I'll also admit to thinking briefly that you used me to get a story."

"Kathryn! How could you think that?"

"How could you think me a murderer?"

Jenny slumped down against the wall. "Okay, I'll shut up now."

Kathryn smiled a thanks. "Obviously, we've had a misunderstanding. I know there was no malice in what you did. Needless to say, I was shocked, and, honestly, disappointed to find out that you'd gone to the police."

"Kathryn—"

"Let me finish."

Jenny dutifully sat back in silence.

"But, like I said, I know you didn't do it to hurt me; in fact, you said you did it *for* me, which, frankly, is an explanation I think I will find very interesting."

"Wait a minute," Jenny said. "You read my letter?"

Only fifty times. "Yes."

Jenny's face brightened. She turned to face Kathryn full on, earnestly tucking her legs under her. "Gosh, Kat," she said, laying a hand on her forearm. It felt natural, but she quickly removed it, and Kathryn regretted its absence.

"I didn't really think you were a murderer, Kathryn. Honest."

Kathryn eyed her skeptically.

"Well, okay, it crossed my mind ... briefly. But I thought Forrester made you do it. Like, do it or else, you know?" Jenny's shoulders relaxed, and with that her hands began their dance, always in motion. She put a hand momentarily on her forehead. "I tell you, Kat, I didn't know what to do." The hand moved to her cheek, then to her chin as she went on, obviously trying to remember the order in which everything happened. "Bernie told me about the shooting outside the bar, the gun was on my table—" Like a conductor, her arms went this way and that with the explanation. "I wanted to protect you. That's what I was thinking. I almost threw the gun in the lake, but that never works, and then I decided I just had to know. Then it was LaPaglia, and then I thought I was set up, and, well ... Rico. No one was supposed to know whose gun it was, and I was assured I'd get it back before you showed up. Then I'd know, and I'd know what to do. How to cover."

Kathryn stared back blankly, a little lost.

"You know?" Jenny said, as if that connected the dots.

"Not really," Kathryn said. "But obviously, as I said, it was all a big misunderstanding."

Jenny exhaled in relief. "Exactly. And then you showed up, and you were so angry, and then I thought Forrester was going to kill you,

358 | J. E. LEAK

and then the article—God." The hand was back on her forehead, with the other hand begging the air to make sense of it all.

Kathryn grinned. Jenny was so damn animated and alive, but she didn't appreciate the admiration.

"Oh, *now* you think it's funny."

"No, but thank you for doing ... whatever it was you were trying to do." She was still confused but was assured it was done with the best of intentions.

Jenny sat back on her heels with a relieved exhale.

Kathryn found Jenny's honesty endearing and refreshing, and she was glad that her suspicions were unfounded. It was a misunderstanding, and while Jenny had executed her apology, Kathryn had a long way to go. She straightened the ID tag still hanging from her neck and got ready to eat some crow.

"Today you were the recipient of some pretty selfish behavior on my part, and I want to apologize for that." She turned her head and made sure Jenny knew she meant it. "It's not about you, I promise."

Jenny put her hand on Kathryn's arm and left it there this time. "I think it is about me."

Their gazes locked and Kathryn's faltered. It couldn't be about her. She was saying goodbye. "This is serious business here."

"I know that."

"Dangerous business."

"I know that too."

"Okay," she said, as if that explained everything.

Jenny waited a moment, and Kathryn knew she was waiting for a better explanation. She didn't have one.

"So, are we on the square now?" Jenny asked.

Kathryn grinned. "Five by five."

Jenny slumped in relief against the wall again. "Whew. Having you mad at me was pretty awful, Kat, I swear."

"To Howard?"

"To Howard and anyone else who will listen."

"Jenny?"

"Yeah?"

"Who is Howard?"

"You know ... Our Father, who art in heaven, Howard be thy name?"

Kathryn laughed. "Oh, *that* Howard."

Jenny grinned. "For years, as a child, I thought God's name was Howard."

Kathryn smiled. "For years, I thought L-M-N-O-P was one letter in the alphabet."

They both chuckled as they simultaneously rested their heads on the back wall of the elevator and exhaled cleansing breaths.

"Let's not do that again, okay?" Jenny asked.

"You're right. That was pretty awful. I can be a very disagreeable person."

"Run while I can, right?"

"Probably for the best."

Jenny gazed around the small elevator space. "I don't think I'd get very far." She smiled but then turned serious. "You didn't run from me, Kat. I'm not going to run from you."

Kathryn found a tentative hand on her thigh. She stared at it for a moment but made no effort to move toward it. Her time with Jenny was over. The war was waiting. This was a clean break. It was better for both of them. She covered the hand with her own and gave it a squeeze.

"I'm sorry about today," she said, patting the hand under hers before breaking contact for good. "Luckily, you won't have to put up with me around here."

Jenny slowly removed her abandoned hand. "Are we really not going to work together? I mean, don't you work here too?"

"No. I spend more time at the training center these days." She noticed that Jenny slumped in disappointment. "Don't worry, I have to show up on the tenth floor every so often. While you're working in the building, I'll come up and see how you're doing. We'll have lunch sometime." A lie.

"That'd be great," Jenny said, although Kathryn sensed she didn't believe her.

"You'll make lots of friends here, Jenny."

That didn't seem to appease her.

"You said you read my letter, so you know I never meant to hurt you. Why were you so angry with me today?"

That was an admonition Kathryn didn't want to make to herself let alone to Jenny, who was reaching for any connection. Would she leave her floundering with a lie, or would she tell her the truth and walk away, letting the chips fall where they may?

Her decision was cut off as the elevator slowly descended with a groan.

"Hallelujah. Put away your ID now," Kathryn said, as she slipped hers from her neck and tucked it into her pocket. Jenny did the same as the car crawled the few feet to the next floor and the doors opened.

"Welcome back to civilization, ladies," the cheerful mechanic said to the applause of the few people gathered around him. He held out both hands, one for each woman. They gladly took his help and he hauled them up.

"Thank you, Jim," Kathryn said, noting his name patch—a newly acquired skill.

"You're welcome, Miss Hammond," he said, as some craned their heads at the mention of her name.

She pretended not to notice as she exited the elevator and brushed off her slacks.

"Yes, thank you, Jim," Jenny said curtly, obviously not pleased with his timing.

"My pleasure, ma'am. You were never in any danger, I assure you. Just a little rope slippage. It's all fixed up. Nothing to worry about. We'll run 'er through her paces and she'll be good as new."

The crowd quickly dispersed, and Jim stuck an Out of Order sign in front of the untested car before picking up his toolbox and disappearing himself.

An uneasy silence fell between them, and Kathryn pushed the elevator down button for the only other working car at their location.

Jenny looked at her like she was crazy. "Are you nuts?"

Kathryn grinned mischievously. "Going down?"

Jenny pointed an accusing finger. "Not in that thing. I'm taking the stairs."

Upon hearing the doors slide open behind her, Kathryn held out her hand to say goodbye.

"Well, I guess I'll see you around."

"Yes." Jenny took the offered hand with little enthusiasm. She held on tight when Kathryn tried to pull away. "Why were you so angry with me today?"

Kathryn paused, caught again between the truth and a lie. Without a word, she loosened her grip and stepped into the waiting elevator. She pushed the ground floor button and tried not to burn Jenny's furrowed brow into her memory.

When the outer door began to close, the truth forced its way past her good judgment. "Because you got to me, and I didn't like it."

Jenny stared at the closed doors and admired the perfectly executed escape before bursting into action. "Hey! Wait a minute." She began pushing the down call button, but it was futile; the elevator was gone. She looked briefly to the untested elevator and seriously considered giving it a go, but with her propensity for disaster, she thought better of it. She glanced at the stairwell down the hall, but knew Kathryn would be long gone before she got to the ground floor. She put her hands on her hips. "I got to her. That means I have a chance, right?"

Kathryn and Jenny's story continues with *In the Shadow of Love* (Shadow Series Book 2), available for preorder now at your retailer of choice. Projected release date is early 2022.

Please visit jeleak.com and sign up for my newsletter to receive updates on new book releases.

AUTHOR NOTES

My characters are not based on any particular real-life individuals; however, the Office of Strategic Services (OSS), for whom Kat and Jenny work, was a real wartime organization established in July 1942 by President Franklin D. Roosevelt, based on the British intelligence Special Operations Executive (SOE).

The New York City offices of the OSS were headquartered in the International Building at Rockefeller Center. For expediency in my story, I housed several divisions there, but, in reality, the OSS had offices scattered throughout the city, in various buildings. Morale Operations, where Jenny works, was indeed housed in a building off Times Square. The British Security Coordination (BSC), part of the British Secret Intelligence Service, was also housed in the International Building at Rockefeller Center.

OSS Director William Donovan called his recruits "Glorious Amateurs," but the contributions of these brave men and women of the intelligence services are immeasurable, and without them, the war could have had a very different outcome.

Historical fiction propels the reader into a story set in the past. Today, that time period's values and morals might be considered old-fashioned or uptight, but this was the reality for our characters. In some ways, the core of their struggle is still our struggle today. Science progresses, attitudes change, even maps and boundaries change, but the human heart still loves who it loves. Some things are timeless.

ACKNOWLEDGMENTS

Writing may be a solitary exercise, but support, encouragement, and sometimes a loving kick in the ass are all integral parts of what eventually becomes a book in your hands.

I would like to thank my wife for her patience and unfailing belief in my story. Her love and support is the reason that this series has become a reality. To the moon and back, baby. You mean everything to me.

To Pam Greer, my editor and bestie, I love you dearly. I am forever grateful for your friendship and your willingness to pour over my words ad infinitum with the same enthusiasm as the first day you read them. Your love, input, encouragement, and tolerance as I whined about "my vision" made me better at my craft. I've learned so much from you, and I would look like an idiot without you. You're aces, doll.

To my dearest friends—my TRIBE—you are all magnificent. You've been with me since the beginning, listened to me blather on about the never-ending "writing project" with nary a complaint, and cheered with relief when it was finally done (amen). You've helped me in so many ways and never failed to lift me up when I doubted myself. Thank you from the bottom of my heart. I love you all.

To my Beta readers, your honesty makes me a better writer, and I am grateful for your input.

To my ARC readers, thank you for reading, and thank you for your reviews. It means the world to this indie author.

ABOUT THE AUTHOR

J.E. Leak was born in Washington, DC, and grew up on the beautiful South Jersey shores of Long Beach Island. An antiques conservator by trade, she has always been fascinated by history and the stories objects could tell if they could speak. When she isn't bingeing 1940s noir films, she's writing or photographing nature on the spring-fed azure rivers of Central Florida. She has an Associate of Science degree in graphic design and is a devoted night owl.

In the Shadow of the Past is the first novel in the Shadow series.

facebook.com/JELeakAuthor
twitter.com/J_E_Leak
instagram.com/j.e.leak

ALSO BY J. E. LEAK

Coming Soon:

In the Shadow of Love (Shadow Series Book 2)

In the Shadow of Truth (Shadow Series Book 3)

In the Shadow of Victory (Shadow Series Book 4)

Visit jeleak.com to sign up for my newsletter and receive updates on new releases, works in progress, blog posts, giveaways, and more!

This author is part of iReadIndies, a collective of self-published independent authors of women loving women (WLW) literature. Please visit our website at iReadIndies.com for more information and to find links to the books published by our authors.